ONI PRESS
PRESENTS...

JUNIOR BRAVES

OF THE

APOCALYPSE

BOOK 2: **OUT OF THE WOODS**

WRITTEN BY
Greg Smith &
Michael Tanner

ILLUSTRATED BY
Zach Lehner

LETTERED BY
Crank!

EDITED BY
Desiree Wilson
with Charlie Chu

DESIGNED BY
Hilary Thompson

ONI PRESS

AN ONI PRESS PUBLICATION

PUBLISHED BY ONI PRESS, INC.

JOE NOZEMACK • FOUNDER & CHIEF FINANCIAL OFFICER

JAMES LUCAS JONES • PUBLISHER

CHARLIE CHU • V.P. OF CREATIVE & BUSINESS DEVELOPMENT

BRAD ROOKS • DIRECTOR OF OPERATIONS

MELISSA MESZAROS • DIRECTOR OF PUBLICITY

MARGOT WOOD • DIRECTOR OF SALES

RACHEL REED • MARKETING MANAGER

AMBER O'NEILL • SPECIAL PROJECTS MANAGER

TROY LOOK • DIRECTOR OF DESIGN & PRODUCTION

HILARY THOMPSON • SENIOR GRAPHIC DESIGNER

KATE Z. STONE • GRAPHIC DESIGNER

SONJA SYNAK • JUNIOR GRAPHIC DESIGNER

ANGIE KNOWLES • DIGITAL PREPRESS LEAD

ARI YARWOOD • EXECUTIVE EDITOR

ROBIN HERRERA • SENIOR EDITOR

DESIREE WILSON • ASSOCIATE EDITOR

ALISSA SALLAH • ADMINISTRATIVE ASSISTANT

JUNG LEE • LOGISTICS ASSOCIATE

SCOTT SHARKEY • WAREHOUSE ASSISTANT

ONI PRESS, INC
1319 SE MARTIN LUTHER KING, JR. BLVD
SUITE 240
PORTLAND, OR 97214

ONIPRESS.COM
FACEBOOK.COM/ONIPRESS
TWITTER.COM/ONIPRESS
ONIPRESS.TUMBLR.COM
INSTAGRAM.COM/ONIPRESS

THATAMAZINGTWIT.TUMBLR.COM / @THATAMAZINGTWIT
DINERWOOD.BLOGSPOT.COM / @MIKEISERNIE
@2AMAZINGWRITERS
ZLEHNER.COM / @ZLEHNER

First Edition: August 2018

Hardcover ISBN 978-1-62010-519-1
Softcover ISBN 978-1-62010-527-6
eISBN 978-1-62010-520-7

Library of Congress Control Number: 2015900806

1 3 5 7 9 10 8 6 4 2

To Linda Smith,
Thanks for reminding me even in
the "Apocalypse" to smile.

—*123 Your Son*

To Richard, Grace, and Adele,
who are exactly the kind of people you would
want with you at the end of the world.

—*Zach*

To Antoinette,
For a writer I'm not that great at expressing
my feelings toward you, so let me just say "beep boop"
which you'll understand, but everyone else reading
this will just have to guess what it means.

—*Mike*

ANIMAL PRINT IDENTIFICATION

Tracking an animal is a skill any worthy Junior Brave should master. Tracks can inform a Junior Brave as to what animals are roaming around his camp or even his own backyard.

Tracking is learned best with early preparation and study before heading out into the wild. Learn these basic animal tracks and you will be well on your way to earning your "Animal Tracking" patch.

BRAVE TIP:

Tracks are easiest to spot when in the mud and snow and when ground is soft in the early morning.

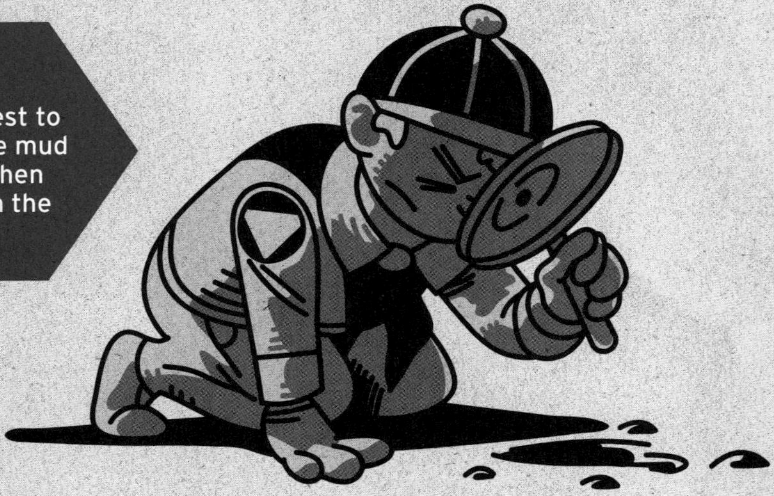

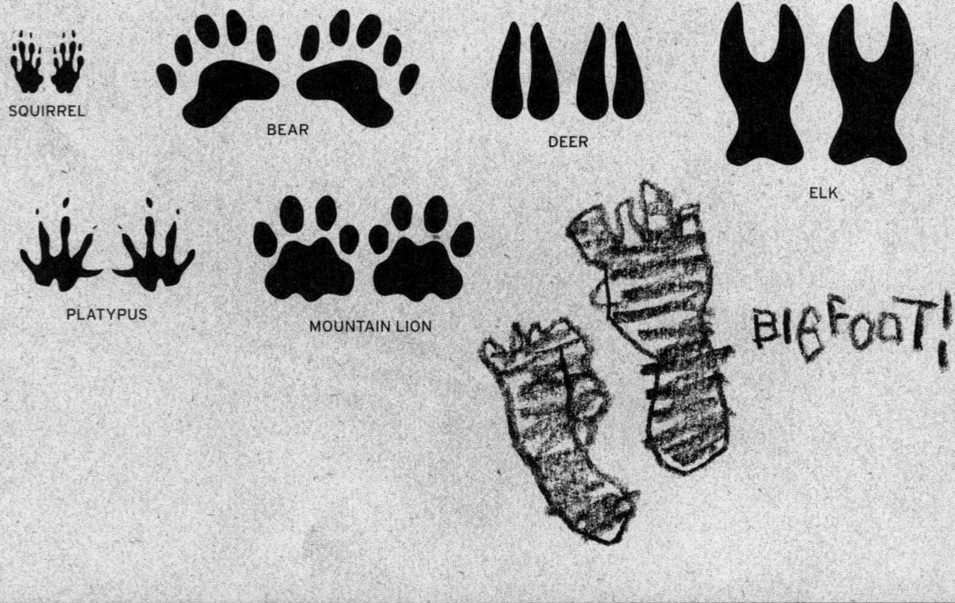
SQUIRREL
BEAR
DEER
ELK
PLATYPUS
MOUNTAIN LION
BIGFOOT!

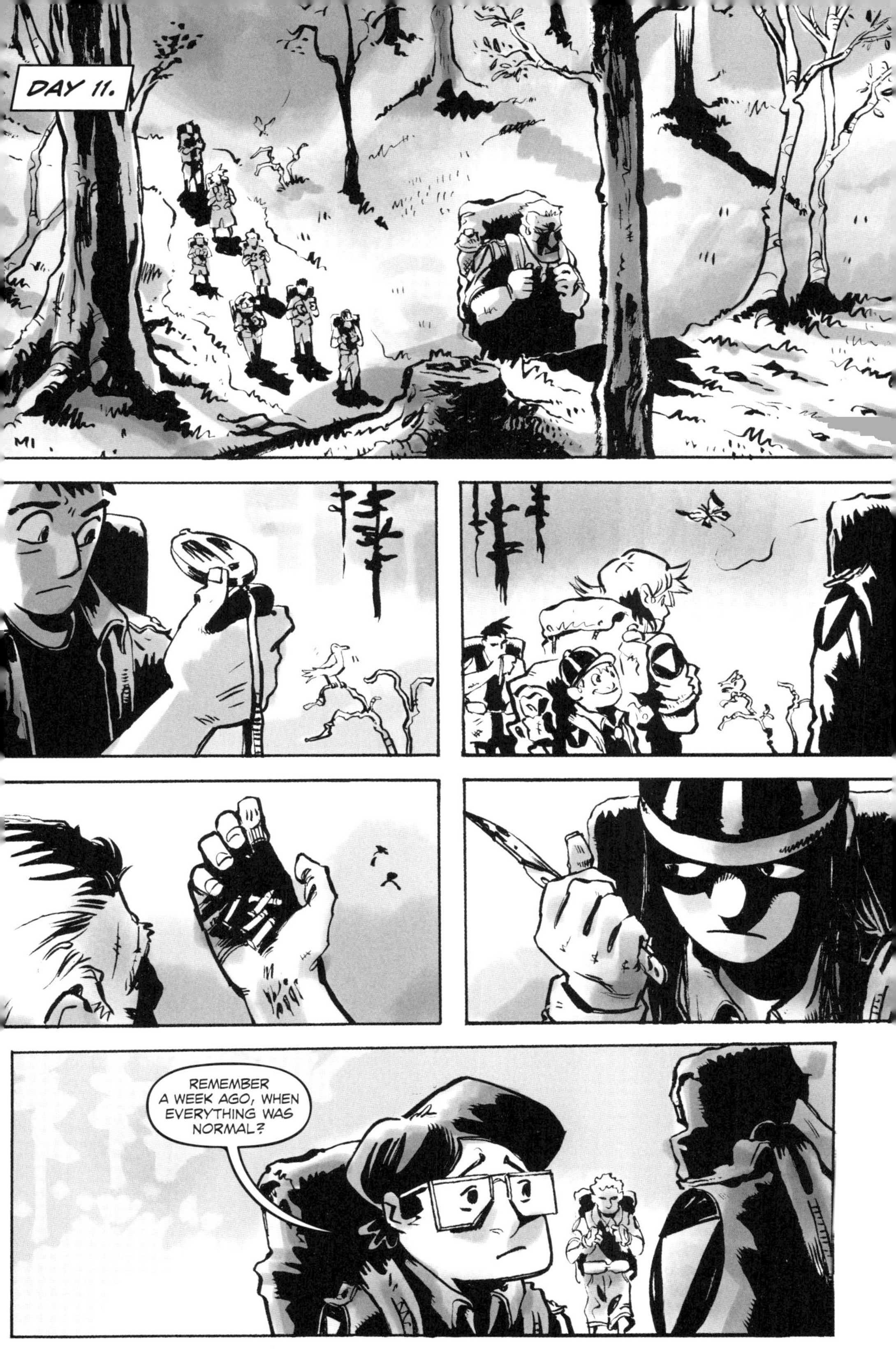
DAY 11.
REMEMBER A WEEK AGO, WHEN EVERYTHING WAS NORMAL?

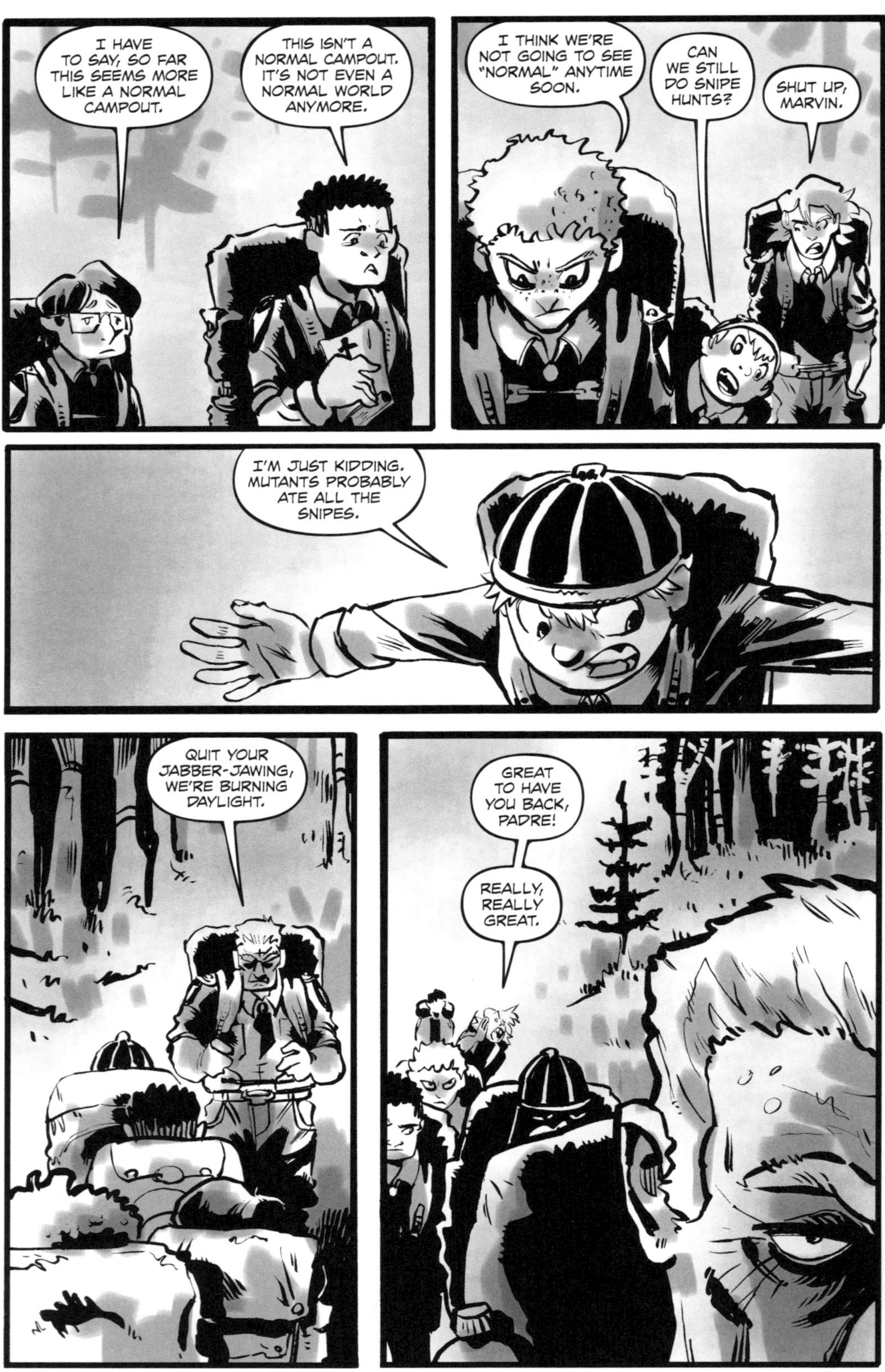
I HAVE TO SAY, SO FAR THIS SEEMS MORE LIKE A NORMAL CAMPOUT.
THIS ISN'T A NORMAL CAMPOUT. IT'S NOT EVEN A NORMAL WORLD ANYMORE.
I THINK WE'RE NOT GOING TO SEE "NORMAL" ANYTIME SOON.
CAN WE STILL DO SNIPE HUNTS?
SHUT UP, MARVIN.
I'M JUST KIDDING. MUTANTS PROBABLY ATE ALL THE SNIPES.
QUIT YOUR JABBER-JAWING, WE'RE BURNING DAYLIGHT.
GREAT TO HAVE YOU BACK, PADRE!
REALLY, REALLY GREAT.

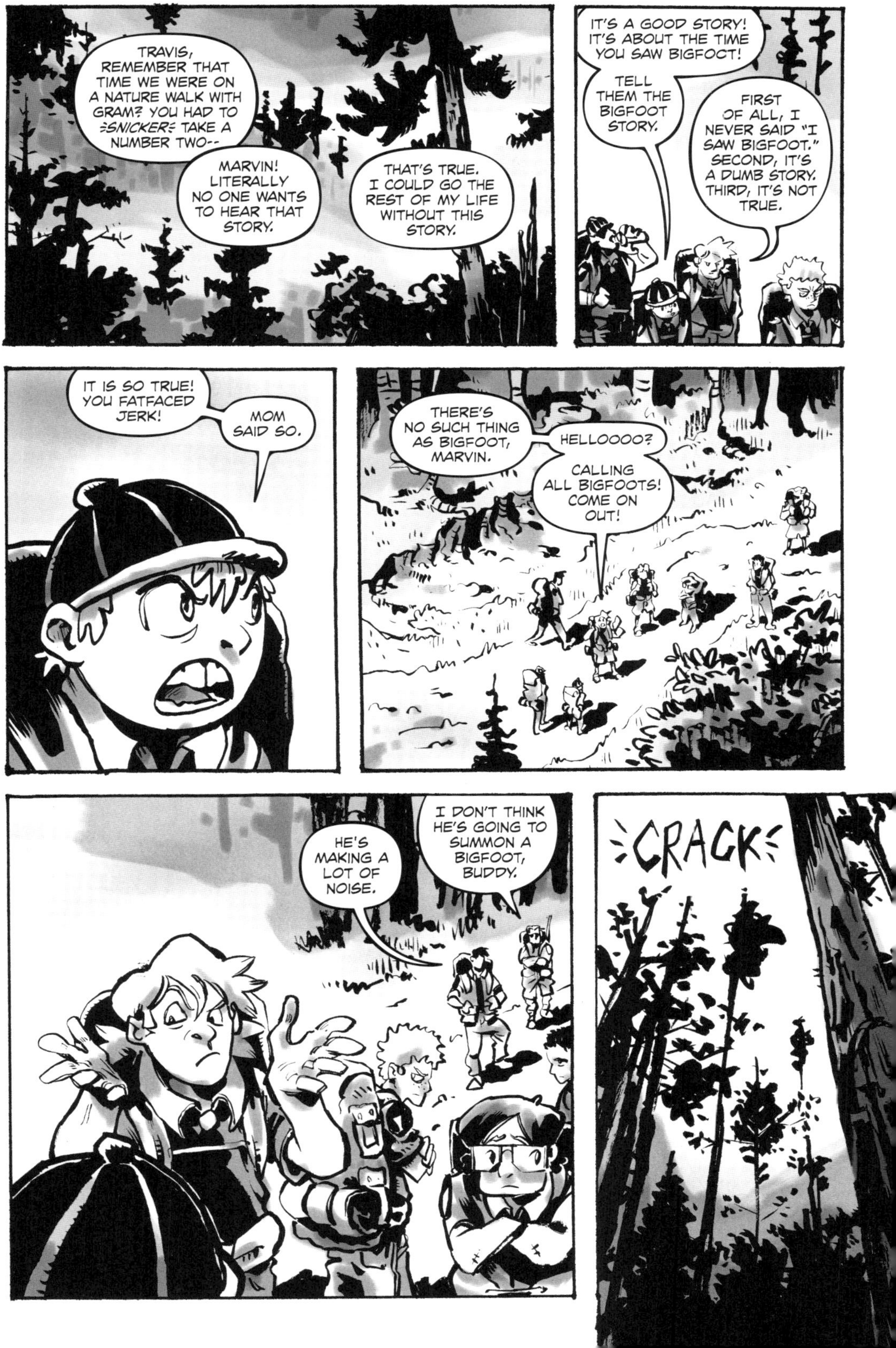
TRAVIS, REMEMBER THAT TIME WE WERE ON A NATURE WALK WITH GRAM? YOU HAD TO =SNICKER= TAKE A NUMBER TWO--
MARVIN! LITERALLY NO ONE WANTS TO HEAR THAT STORY.
THAT'S TRUE. I COULD GO THE REST OF MY LIFE WITHOUT THIS STORY.
IT'S A GOOD STORY! IT'S ABOUT THE TIME YOU SAW BIGFOOT!
TELL THEM THE BIGFOOT STORY.
FIRST OF ALL, I NEVER SAID "I SAW BIGFOOT." SECOND, IT'S A DUMB STORY. THIRD, IT'S NOT TRUE.
IT IS SO TRUE! YOU FATFACED JERK!
MOM SAID SO.
THERE'S NO SUCH THING AS BIGFOOT, MARVIN.
HELLOOOO?
CALLING ALL BIGFOOTS! COME ON OUT!
HE'S MAKING A LOT OF NOISE.
I DON'T THINK HE'S GOING TO SUMMON A BIGFOOT, BUDDY.
CRACK

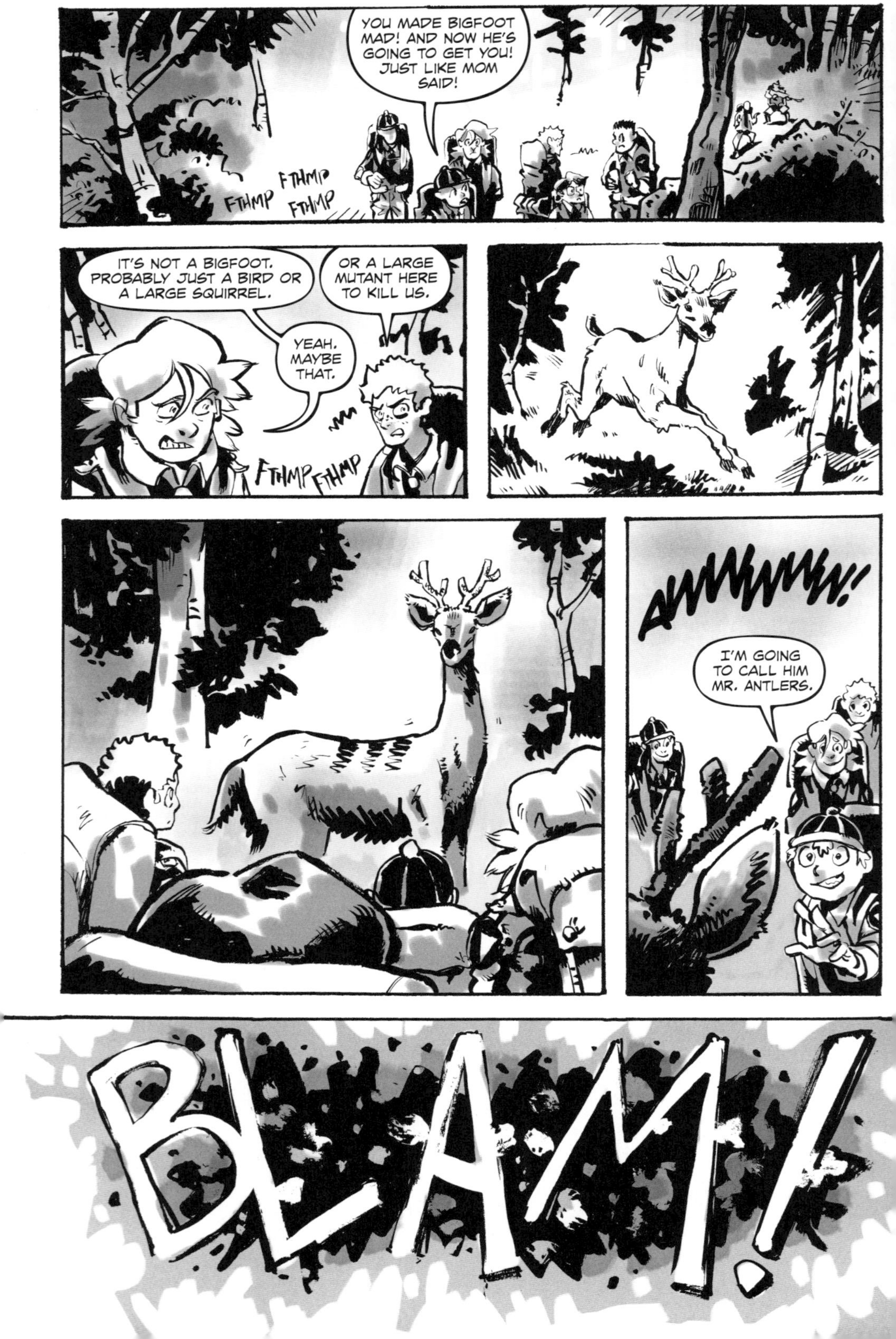
YOU MADE BIGFOOT MAD! AND NOW HE'S GOING TO GET YOU! JUST LIKE MOM SAID!
FTHMP
FTHMP
FTHMP
IT'S NOT A BIGFOOT. PROBABLY JUST A BIRD OR A LARGE SQUIRREL.
OR A LARGE MUTANT HERE TO KILL US.
YEAH. MAYBE THAT.
FTHMP FTHMP
AWWWWW!
I'M GOING TO CALL HIM MR. ANTLERS.
BLAM!

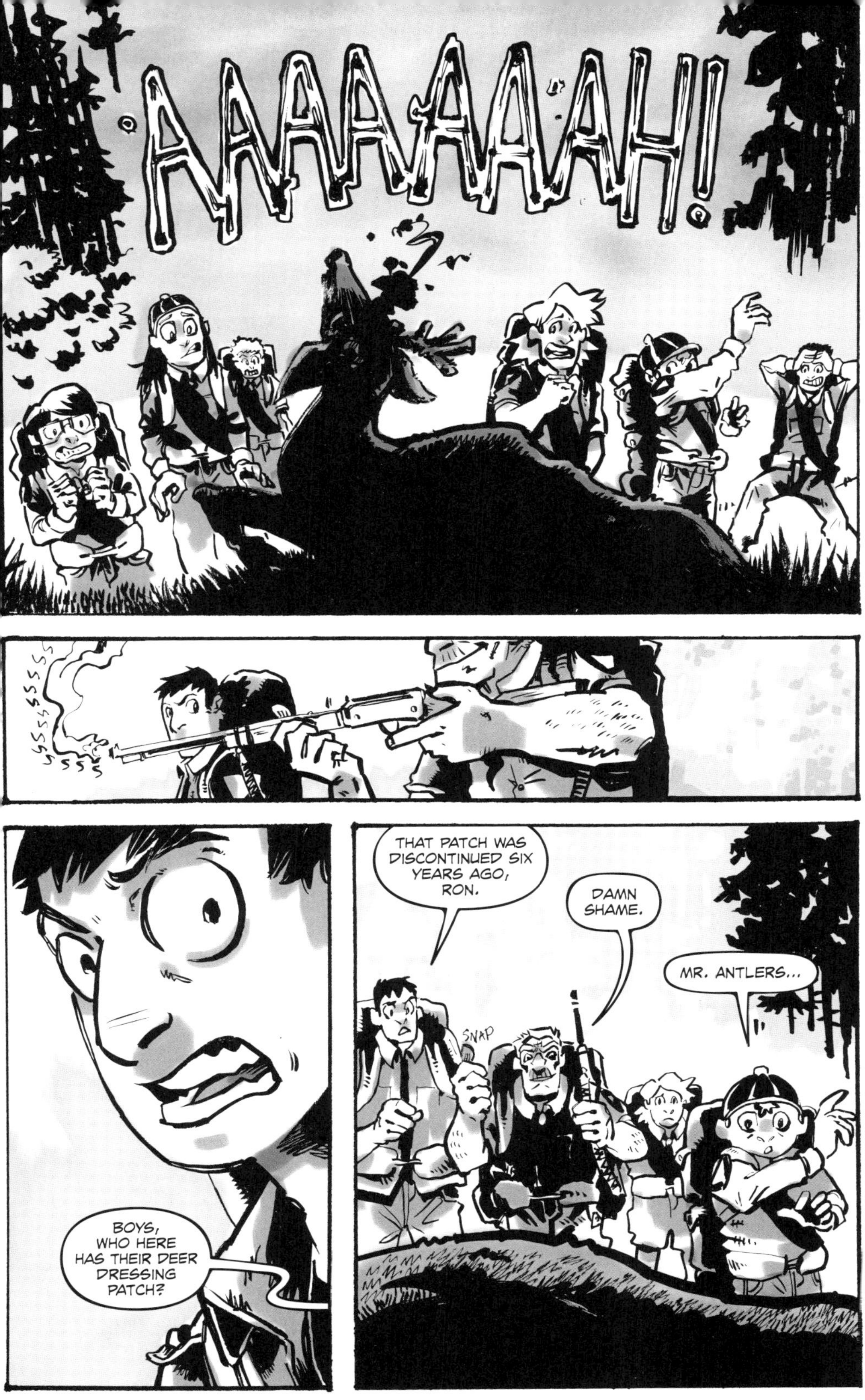
AAAAAAAH!
SSSSSSSSS
BOYS, WHO HERE HAS THEIR DEER DRESSING PATCH?
THAT PATCH WAS DISCONTINUED SIX YEARS AGO, RON.
DAMN SHAME.
SNAP
MR. ANTLERS...

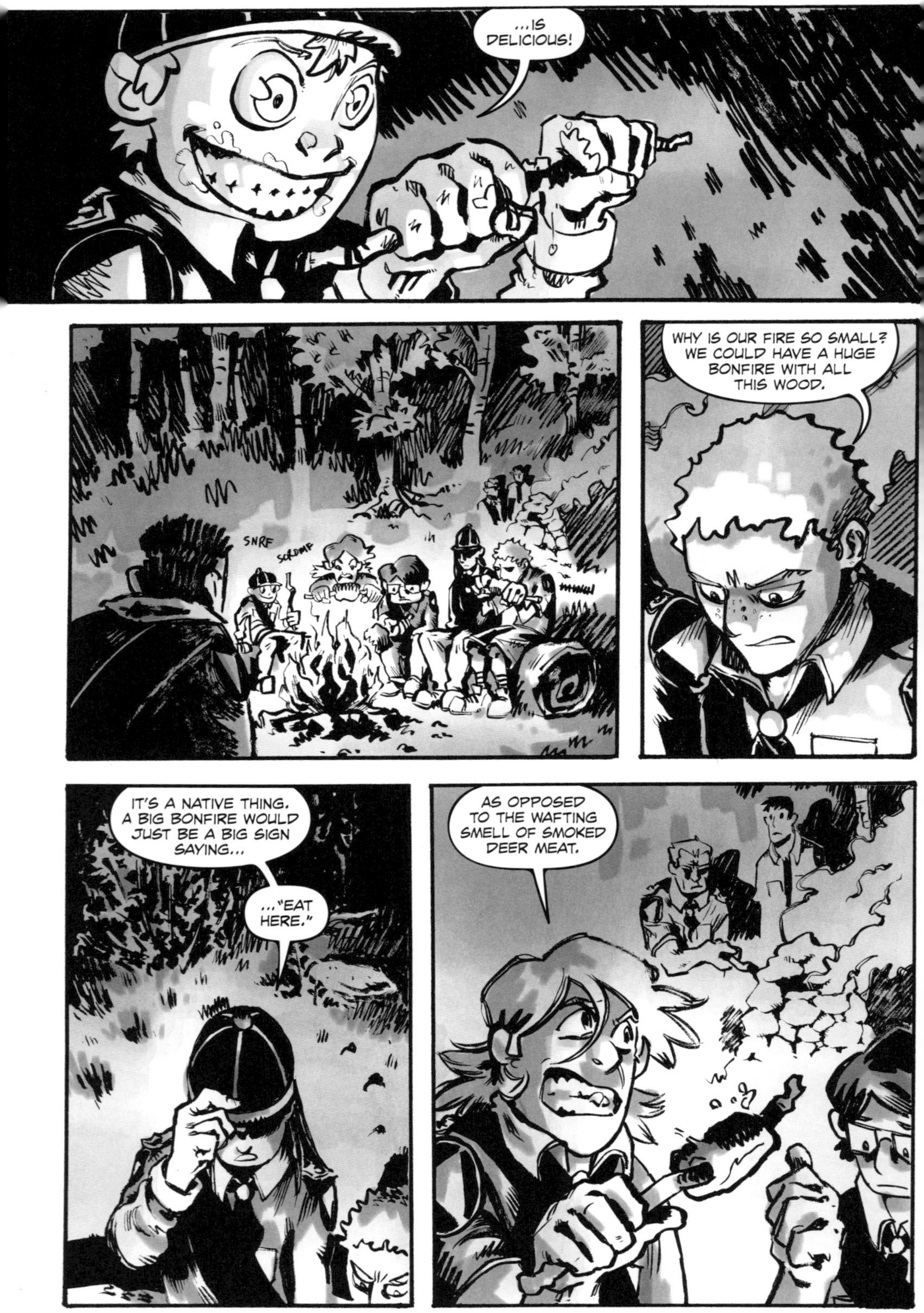
...IS DELICIOUS!
SNRF
SCRDMF
WHY IS OUR FIRE SO SMALL? WE COULD HAVE A HUGE BONFIRE WITH ALL THIS WOOD.
IT'S A NATIVE THING. A BIG BONFIRE WOULD JUST BE A BIG SIGN SAYING...
..."EAT HERE."
AS OPPOSED TO THE WAFTING SMELL OF SMOKED DEER MEAT.

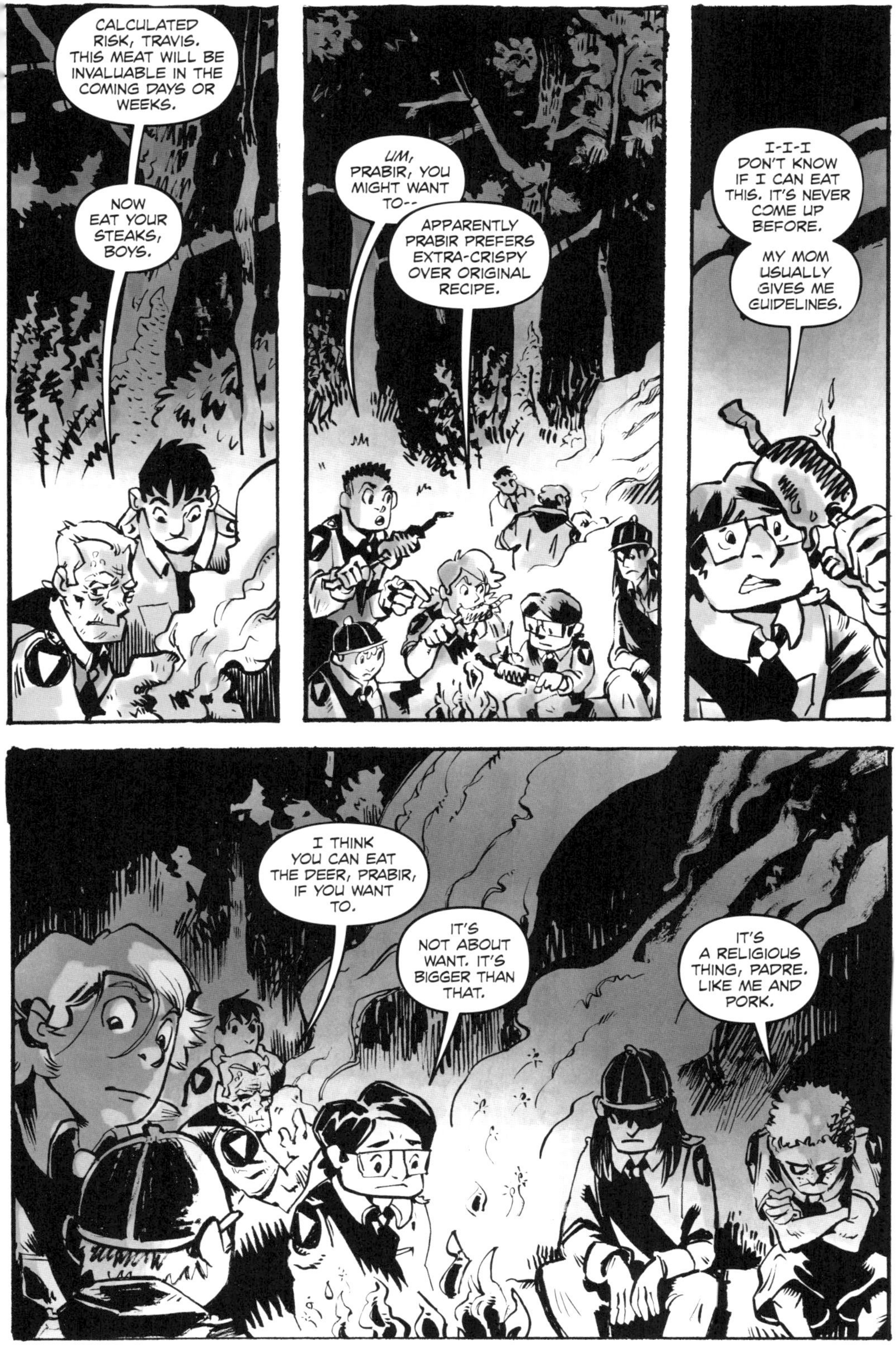
CALCULATED RISK, TRAVIS. THIS MEAT WILL BE INVALUABLE IN THE COMING DAYS OR WEEKS.
NOW EAT YOUR STEAKS, BOYS.
UM, PRABIR, YOU MIGHT WANT TO--
APPARENTLY PRABIR PREFERS EXTRA-CRISPY OVER ORIGINAL RECIPE.
I-I-I DON'T KNOW IF I CAN EAT THIS. IT'S NEVER COME UP BEFORE.
MY MOM USUALLY GIVES ME GUIDELINES.
I THINK YOU CAN EAT THE DEER, PRABIR, IF YOU WANT TO.
IT'S NOT ABOUT WANT. IT'S BIGGER THAN THAT.
IT'S A RELIGIOUS THING, PADRE. LIKE ME AND PORK.

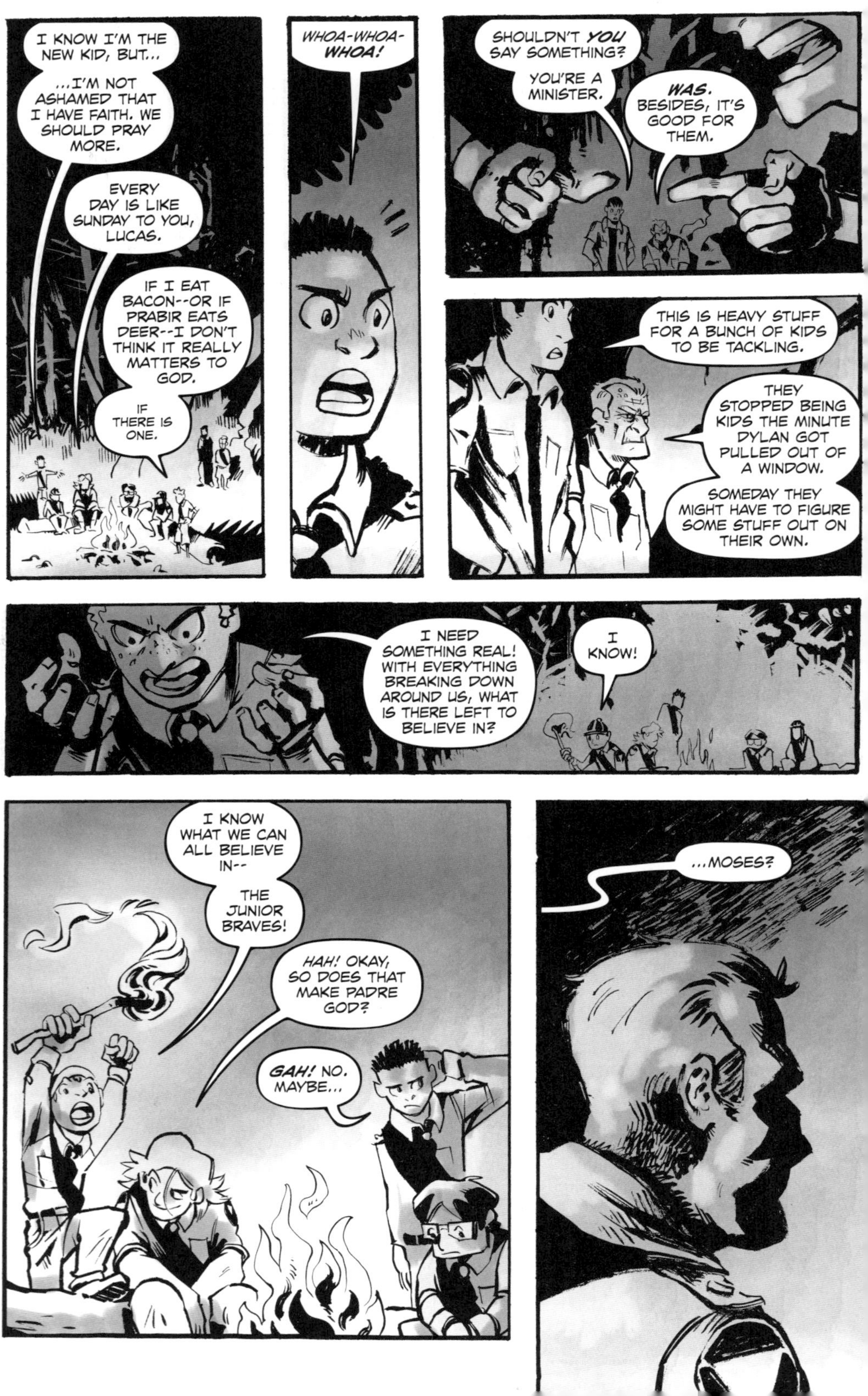
I KNOW I'M THE NEW KID, BUT...
...I'M NOT ASHAMED THAT I HAVE FAITH. WE SHOULD PRAY MORE.
EVERY DAY IS LIKE SUNDAY TO YOU, LUCAS.
IF I EAT BACON--OR IF PRABIR EATS DEER--I DON'T THINK IT REALLY MATTERS TO GOD.
IF THERE IS ONE.
WHOA-WHOA-WHOA!
SHOULDN'T YOU SAY SOMETHING?
YOU'RE A MINISTER.
WAS. BESIDES, IT'S GOOD FOR THEM.
THIS IS HEAVY STUFF FOR A BUNCH OF KIDS TO BE TACKLING.
THEY STOPPED BEING KIDS THE MINUTE DYLAN GOT PULLED OUT OF A WINDOW.
SOMEDAY THEY MIGHT HAVE TO FIGURE SOME STUFF OUT ON THEIR OWN.
I NEED SOMETHING REAL! WITH EVERYTHING BREAKING DOWN AROUND US, WHAT IS THERE LEFT TO BELIEVE IN?
I KNOW!
I KNOW WHAT WE CAN ALL BELIEVE IN--
THE JUNIOR BRAVES!
HAH! OKAY, SO DOES THAT MAKE PADRE GOD?
GAH! NO. MAYBE...
...MOSES?

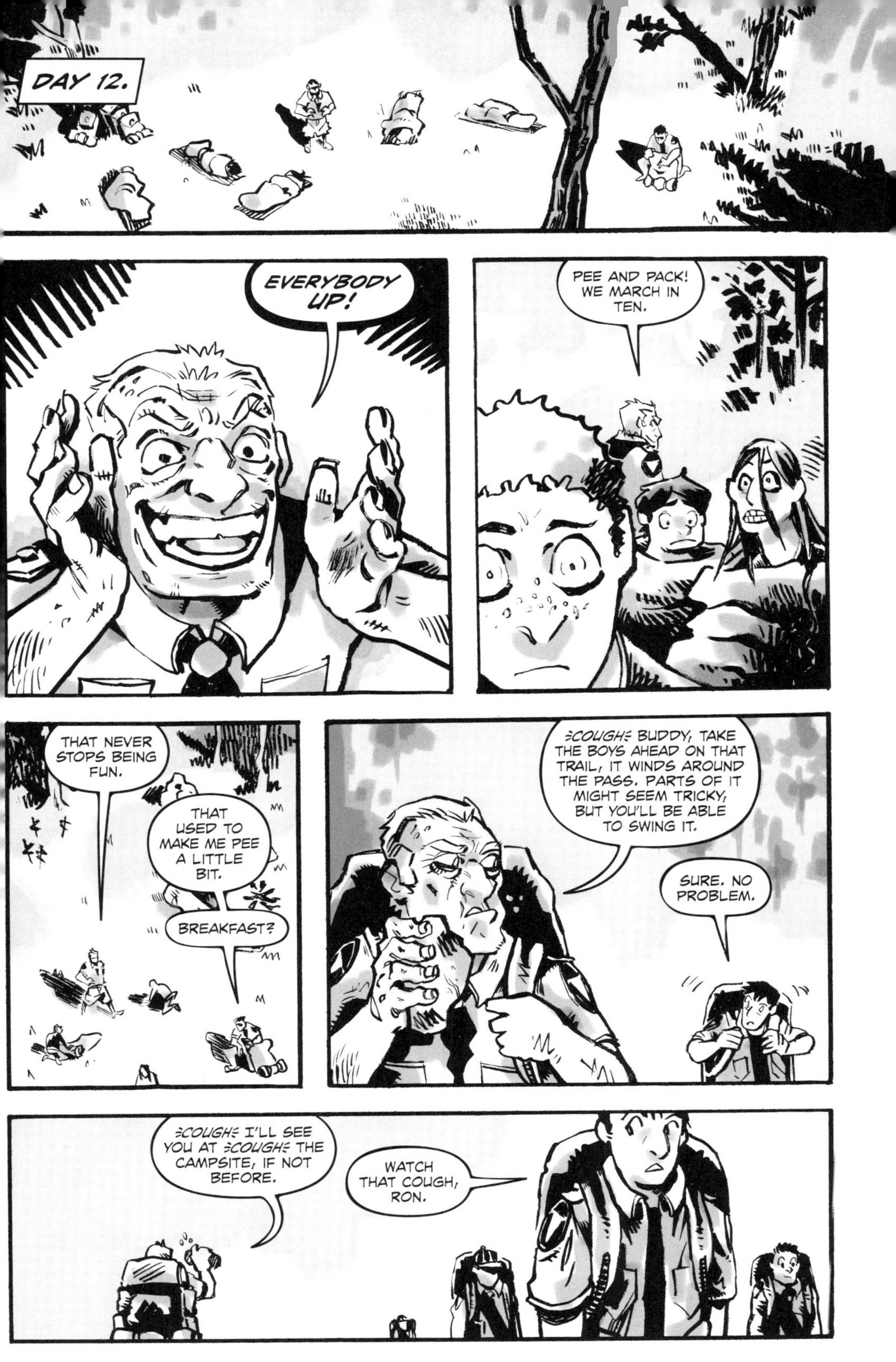
DAY 12.
EVERYBODY UP!
PEE AND PACK! WE MARCH IN TEN.
THAT NEVER STOPS BEING FUN.
THAT USED TO MAKE ME PEE A LITTLE BIT.
BREAKFAST?
COUGH BUDDY, TAKE THE BOYS AHEAD ON THAT TRAIL, IT WINDS AROUND THE PASS. PARTS OF IT MIGHT SEEM TRICKY, BUT YOU'LL BE ABLE TO SWING IT.
SURE. NO PROBLEM.
COUGH I'LL SEE YOU AT COUGH THE CAMPSITE, IF NOT BEFORE.
WATCH THAT COUGH, RON.

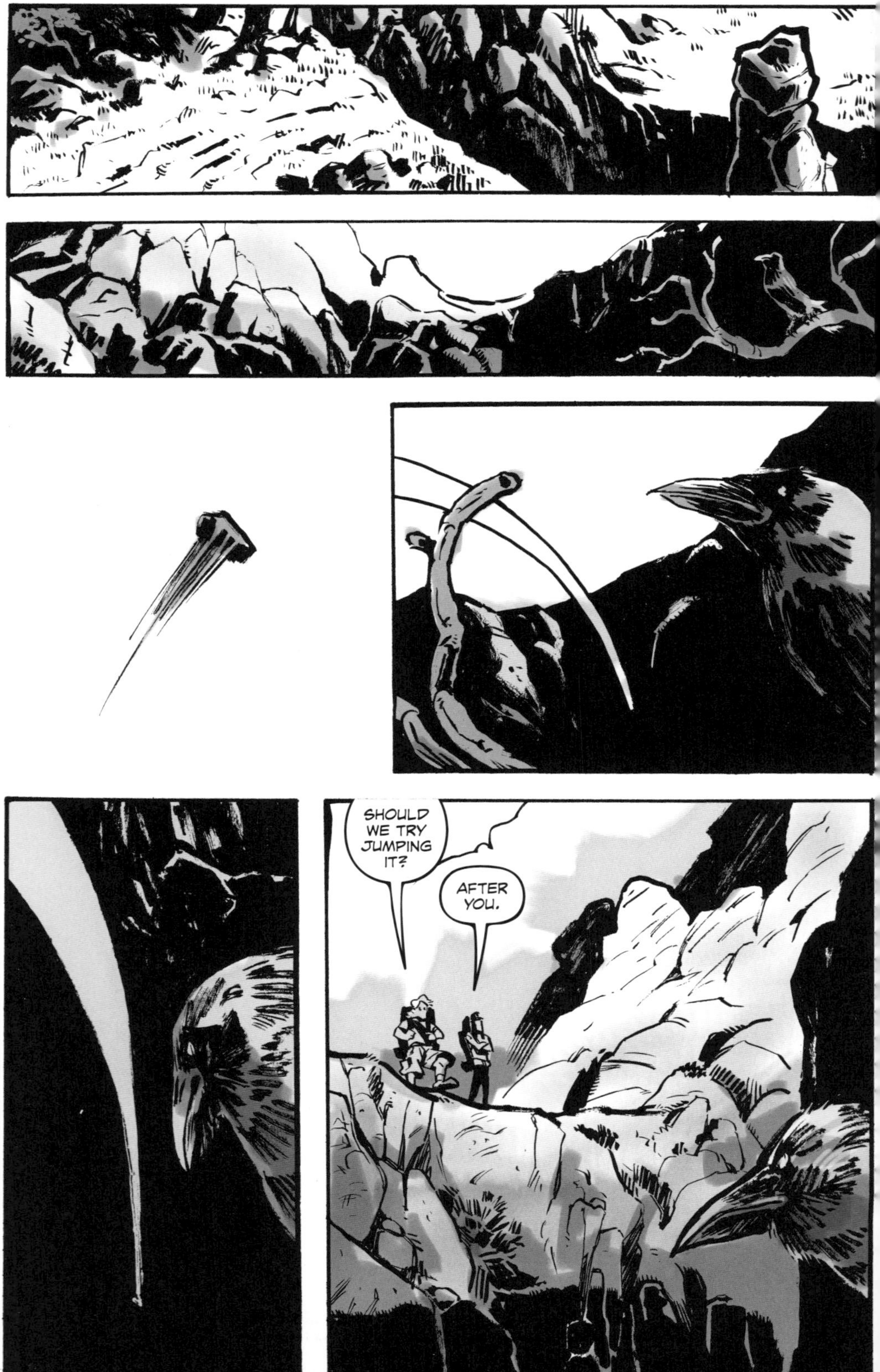
SHOULD WE TRY JUMPING IT?
AFTER YOU.

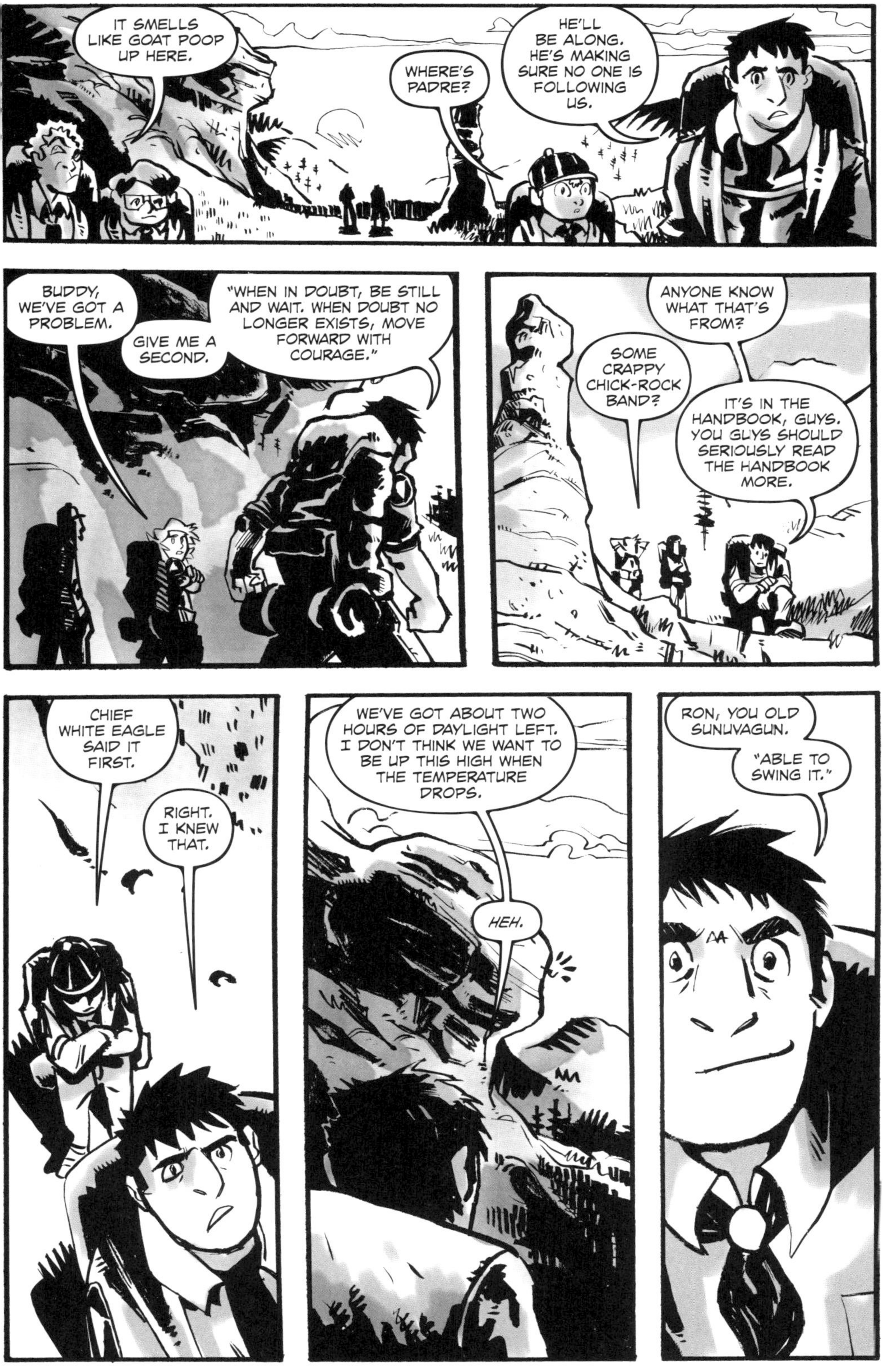
IT SMELLS LIKE GOAT POOP UP HERE.
WHERE'S PADRE?
HE'LL BE ALONG. HE'S MAKING SURE NO ONE IS FOLLOWING US.
BUDDY, WE'VE GOT A PROBLEM.
GIVE ME A SECOND.
"WHEN IN DOUBT, BE STILL AND WAIT. WHEN DOUBT NO LONGER EXISTS, MOVE FORWARD WITH COURAGE."
ANYONE KNOW WHAT THAT'S FROM?
SOME CRAPPY CHICK-ROCK BAND?
IT'S IN THE HANDBOOK, GUYS. YOU GUYS SHOULD SERIOUSLY READ THE HANDBOOK MORE.
CHIEF WHITE EAGLE SAID IT FIRST.
RIGHT. I KNEW THAT.
WE'VE GOT ABOUT TWO HOURS OF DAYLIGHT LEFT. I DON'T THINK WE WANT TO BE UP THIS HIGH WHEN THE TEMPERATURE DROPS.
HEH.
RON, YOU OLD SUNUVAGUN.
"ABLE TO SWING IT."

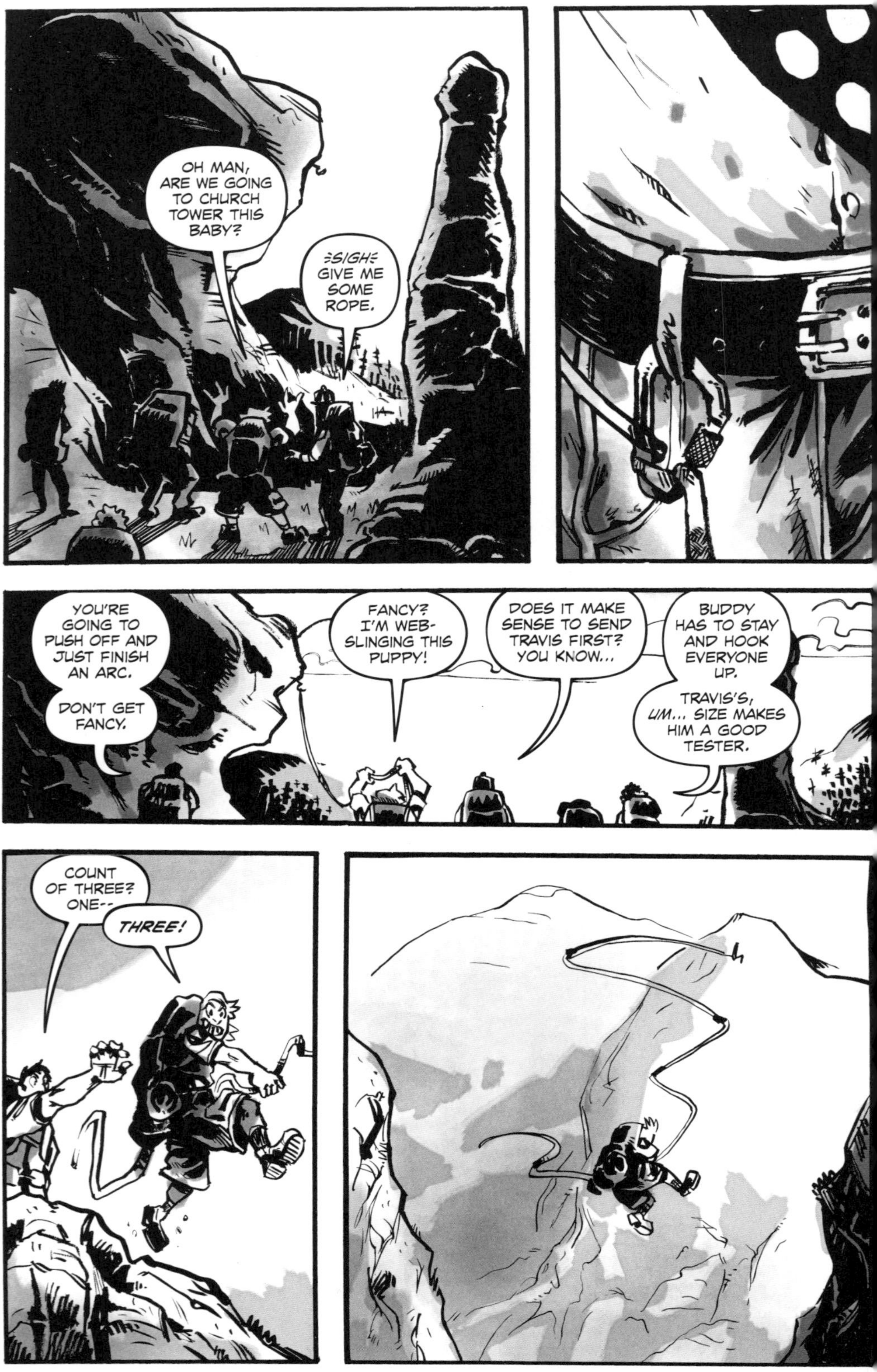
OH MAN, ARE WE GOING TO CHURCH TOWER THIS BABY?
SIGH GIVE ME SOME ROPE.
YOU'RE GOING TO PUSH OFF AND JUST FINISH AN ARC.
DON'T GET FANCY.
FANCY? I'M WEB-SLINGING THIS PUPPY!
DOES IT MAKE SENSE TO SEND TRAVIS FIRST? YOU KNOW...
BUDDY HAS TO STAY AND HOOK EVERYONE UP.
TRAVIS'S, UM... SIZE MAKES HIM A GOOD TESTER.
COUNT OF THREE? ONE--
THREE!

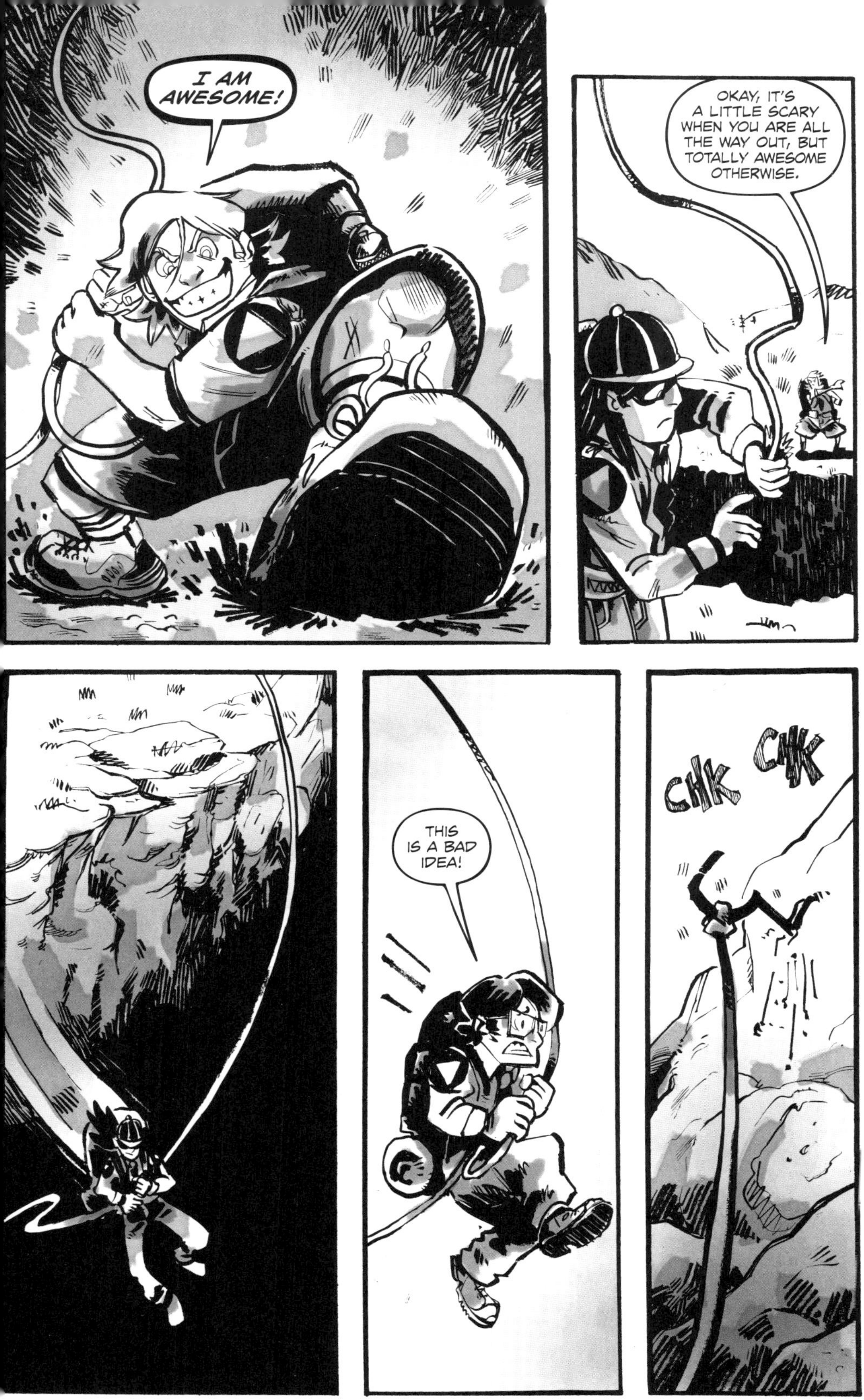
I AM AWESOME!
OKAY, IT'S A LITTLE SCARY WHEN YOU ARE ALL THE WAY OUT, BUT TOTALLY AWESOME OTHERWISE.
THIS IS A BAD IDEA!
CHK CHK

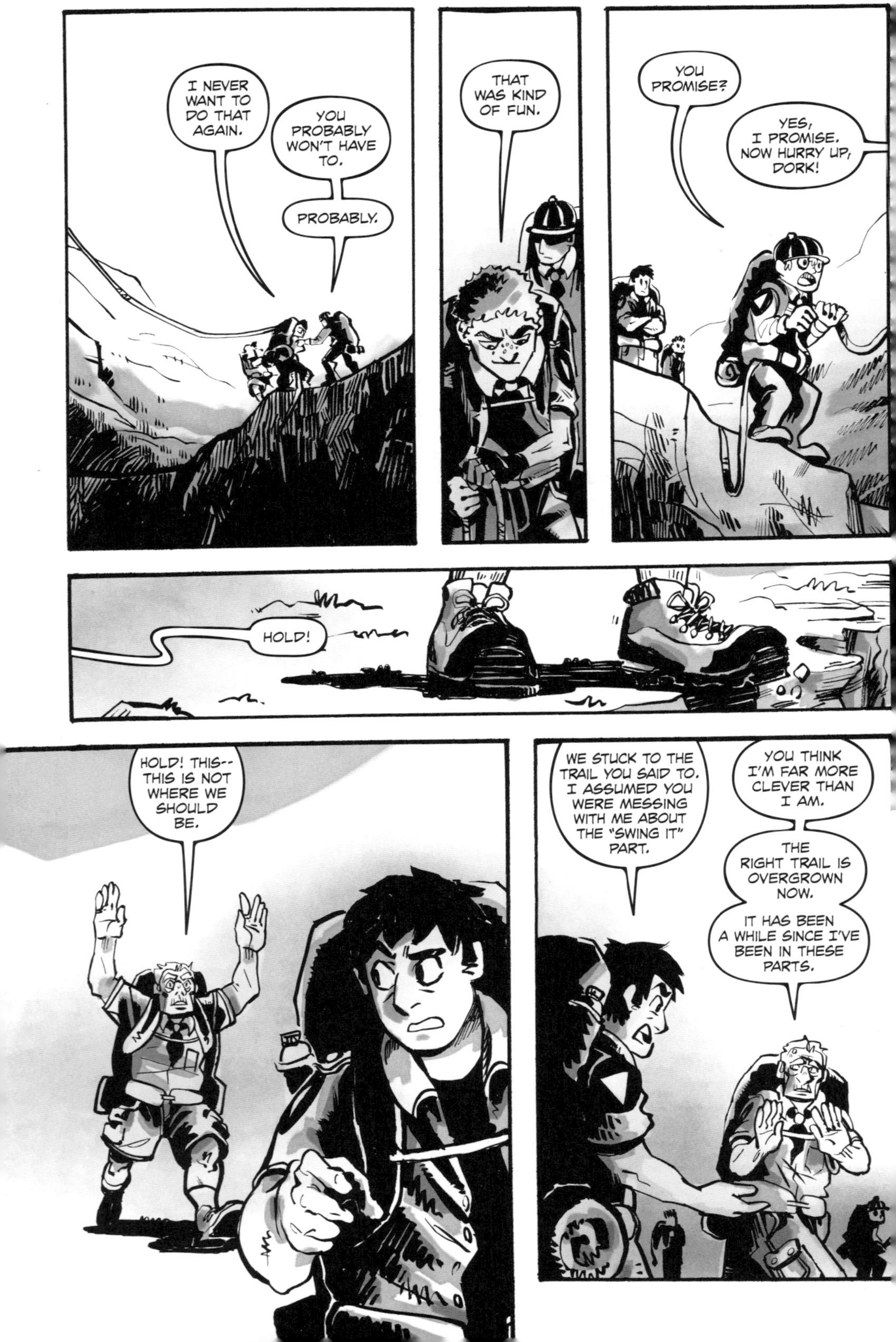
I NEVER WANT TO DO THAT AGAIN.
YOU PROBABLY WON'T HAVE TO.
PROBABLY.
THAT WAS KIND OF FUN.
YOU PROMISE?
YES, I PROMISE. NOW HURRY UP, DORK!
HOLD!
HOLD! THIS-- THIS IS NOT WHERE WE SHOULD BE.
WE STUCK TO THE TRAIL YOU SAID TO. I ASSUMED YOU WERE MESSING WITH ME ABOUT THE "SWING IT" PART.
YOU THINK I'M FAR MORE CLEVER THAN I AM.
THE RIGHT TRAIL IS OVERGROWN NOW.
IT HAS BEEN A WHILE SINCE I'VE BEEN IN THESE PARTS.

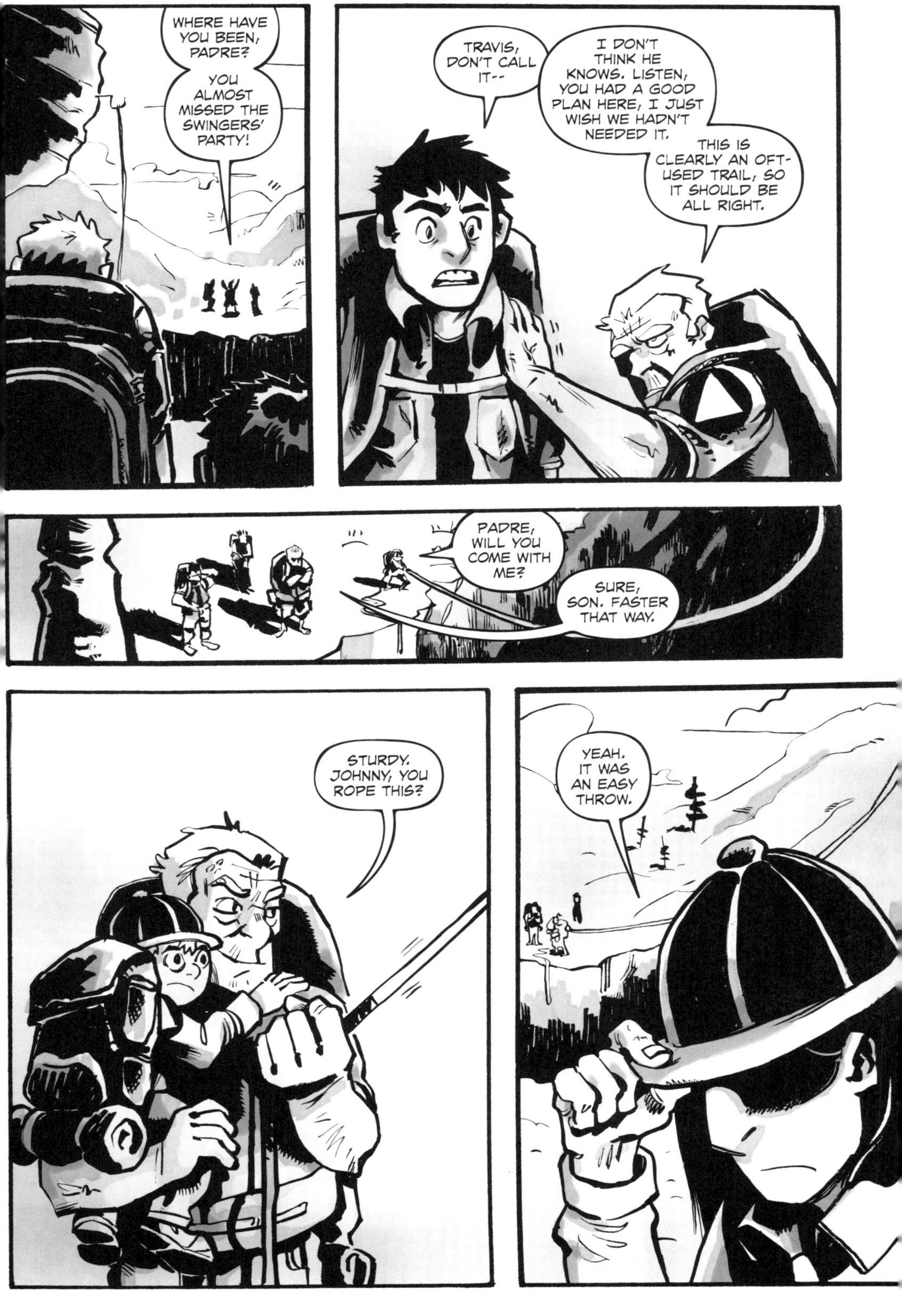
WHERE HAVE YOU BEEN, PADRE?
YOU ALMOST MISSED THE SWINGERS' PARTY!
TRAVIS, DON'T CALL IT--
I DON'T THINK HE KNOWS. LISTEN, YOU HAD A GOOD PLAN HERE, I JUST WISH WE HADN'T NEEDED IT.
THIS IS CLEARLY AN OFT-USED TRAIL, SO IT SHOULD BE ALL RIGHT.
PADRE, WILL YOU COME WITH ME?
SURE, SON. FASTER THAT WAY.
STURDY. JOHNNY, YOU ROPE THIS?
YEAH. IT WAS AN EASY THROW.

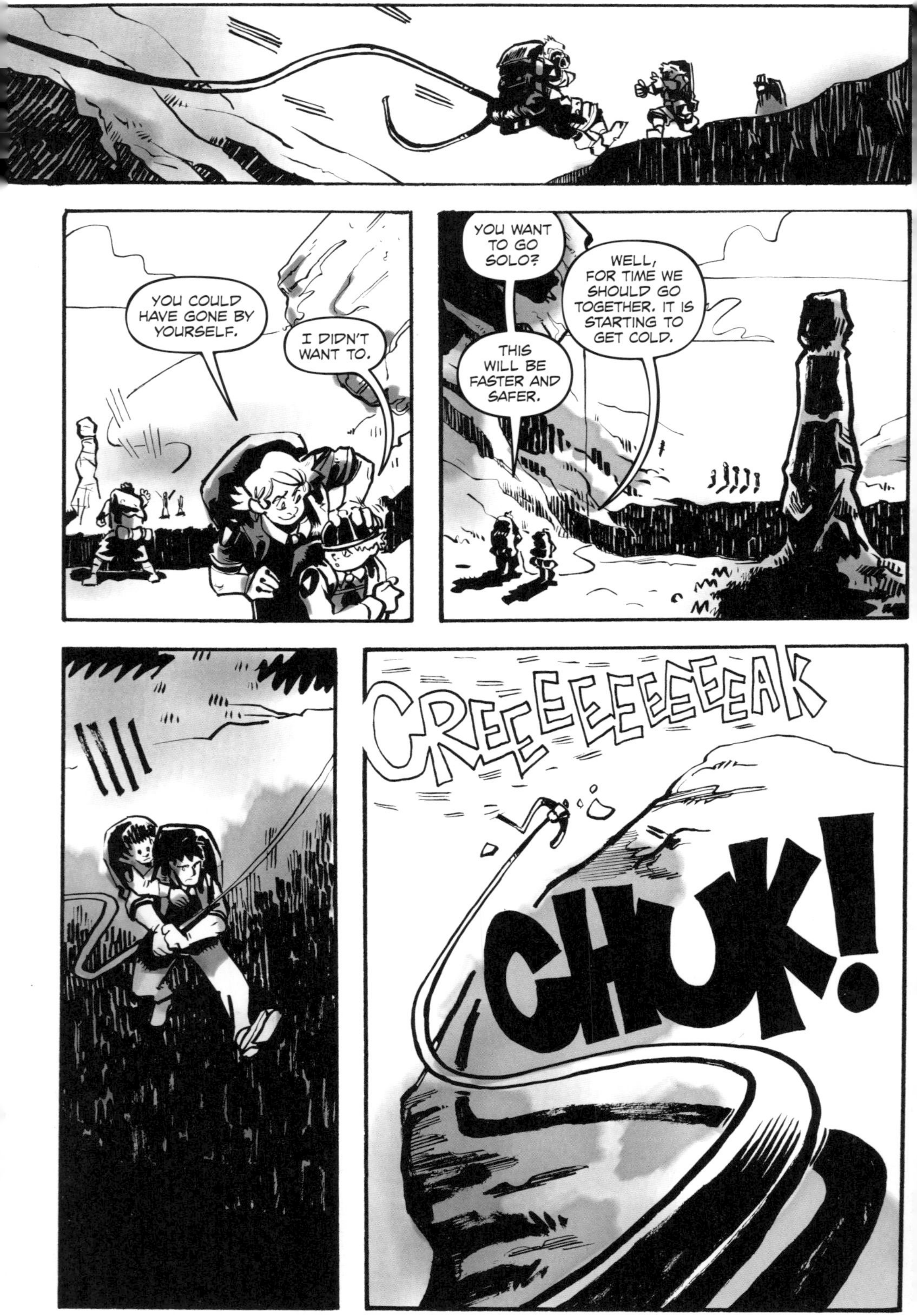

YOU COULD HAVE GONE BY YOURSELF.
I DIDN'T WANT TO.
YOU WANT TO GO SOLO?
THIS WILL BE FASTER AND SAFER.
WELL, FOR TIME WE SHOULD GO TOGETHER. IT IS STARTING TO GET COLD.
CREEEEEEEEEAK
CHUK!

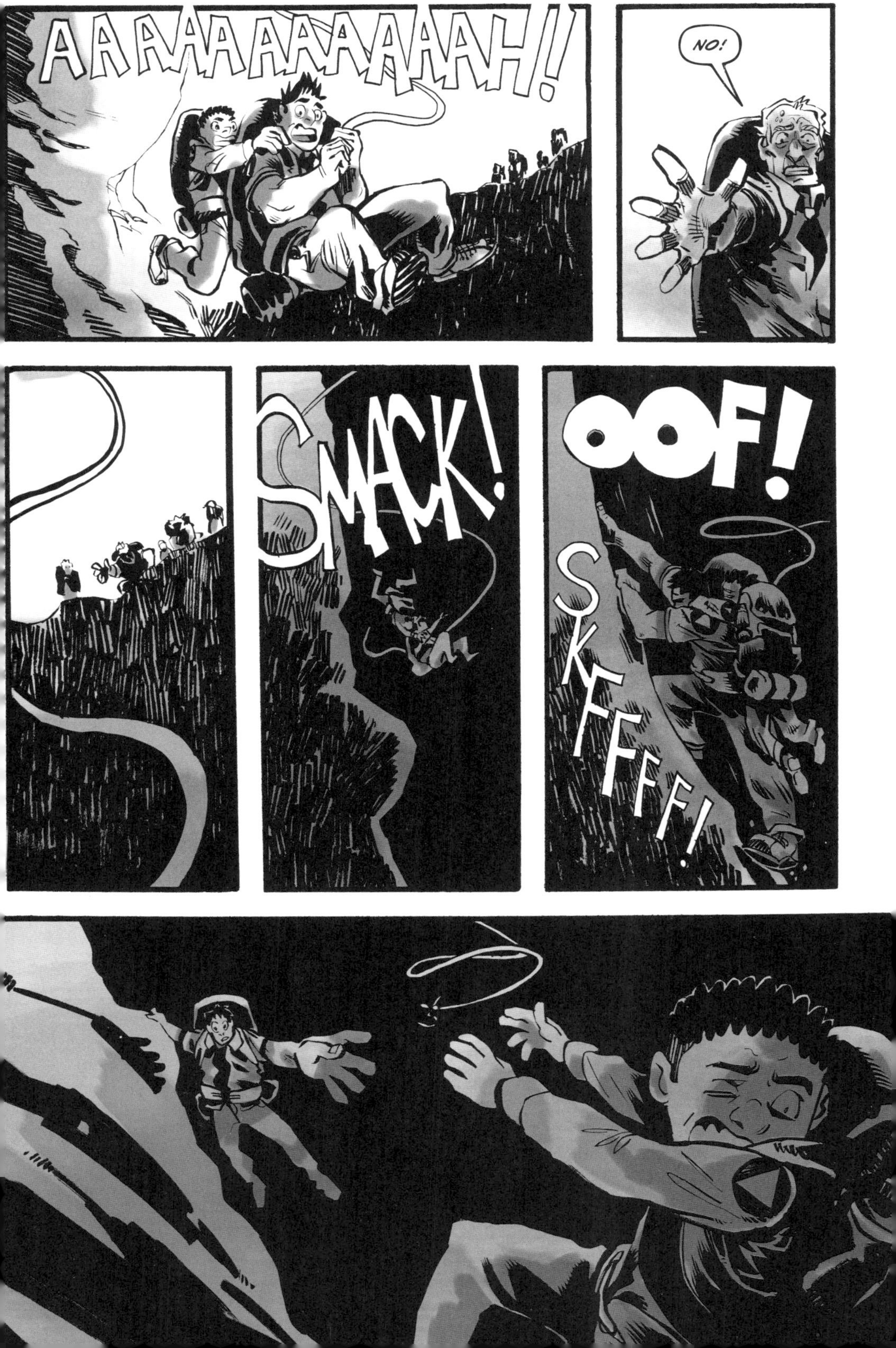
AAAAAAAAAAAH!!
NO!
SMACK!
OOF!
SKFFFFF!

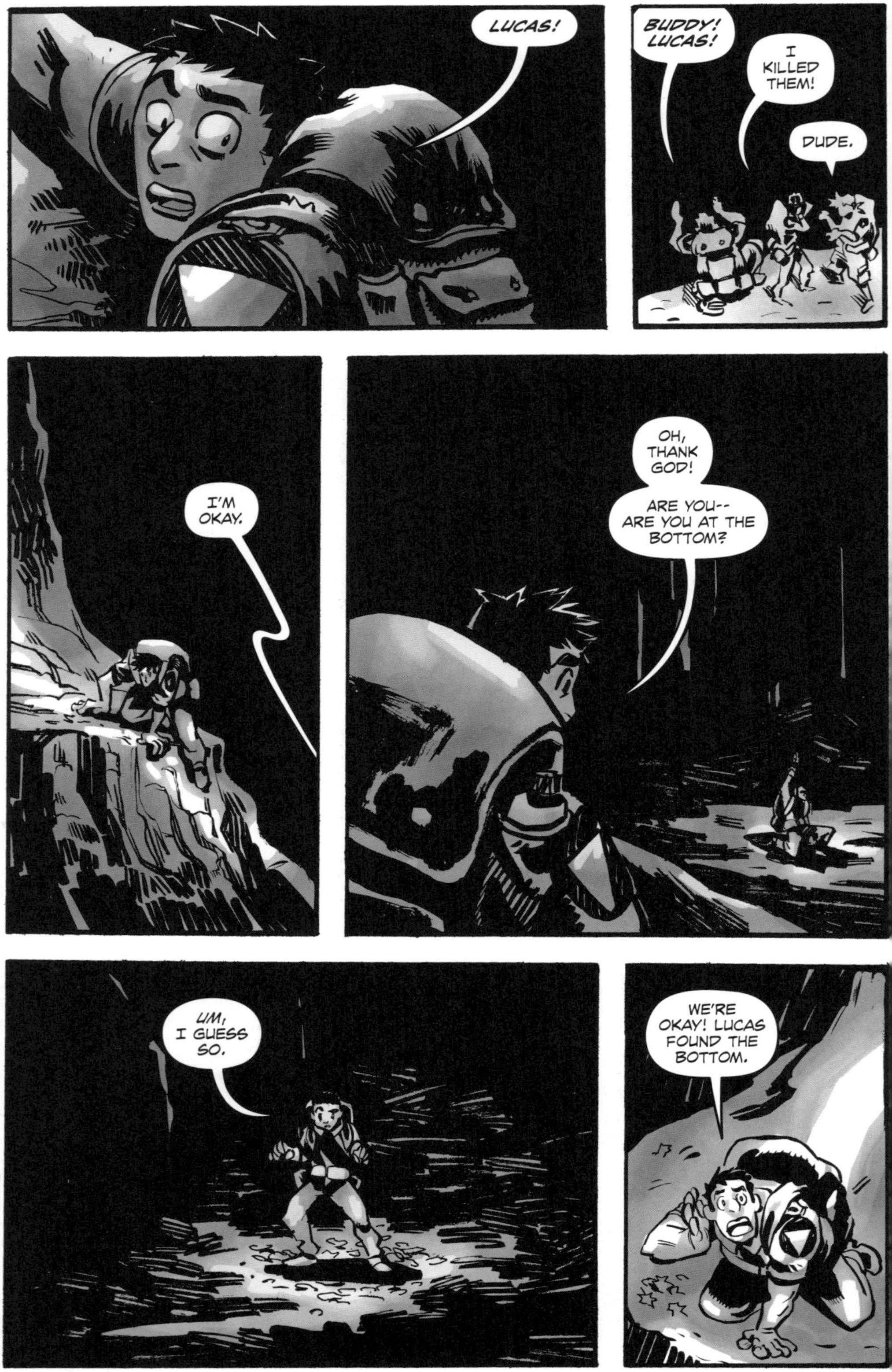
LUCAS!
BUDDY! LUCAS!
I KILLED THEM!
DUDE.
I'M OKAY.
OH, THANK GOD!
ARE YOU-- ARE YOU AT THE BOTTOM?
UM, I GUESS SO.
WE'RE OKAY! LUCAS FOUND THE BOTTOM.

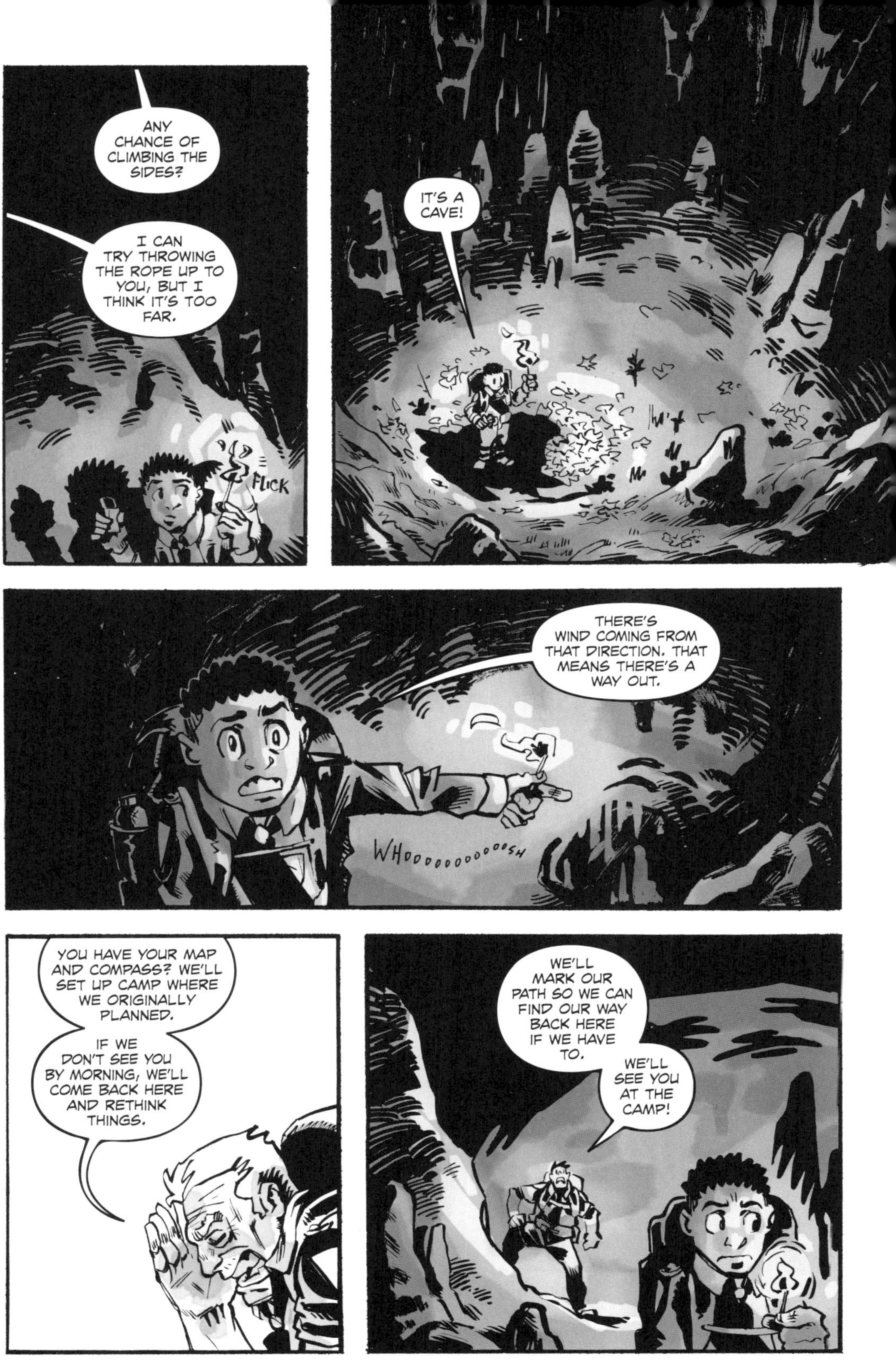
ANY CHANCE OF CLIMBING THE SIDES?
I CAN TRY THROWING THE ROPE UP TO YOU, BUT I THINK IT'S TOO FAR.
FLICK
IT'S A CAVE!
THERE'S WIND COMING FROM THAT DIRECTION. THAT MEANS THERE'S A WAY OUT.
WHOOOOOOOOOOOOSH
YOU HAVE YOUR MAP AND COMPASS? WE'LL SET UP CAMP WHERE WE ORIGINALLY PLANNED.
IF WE DON'T SEE YOU BY MORNING, WE'LL COME BACK HERE AND RETHINK THINGS.
WE'LL MARK OUR PATH SO WE CAN FIND OUR WAY BACK HERE IF WE HAVE TO.
WE'LL SEE YOU AT THE CAMP!

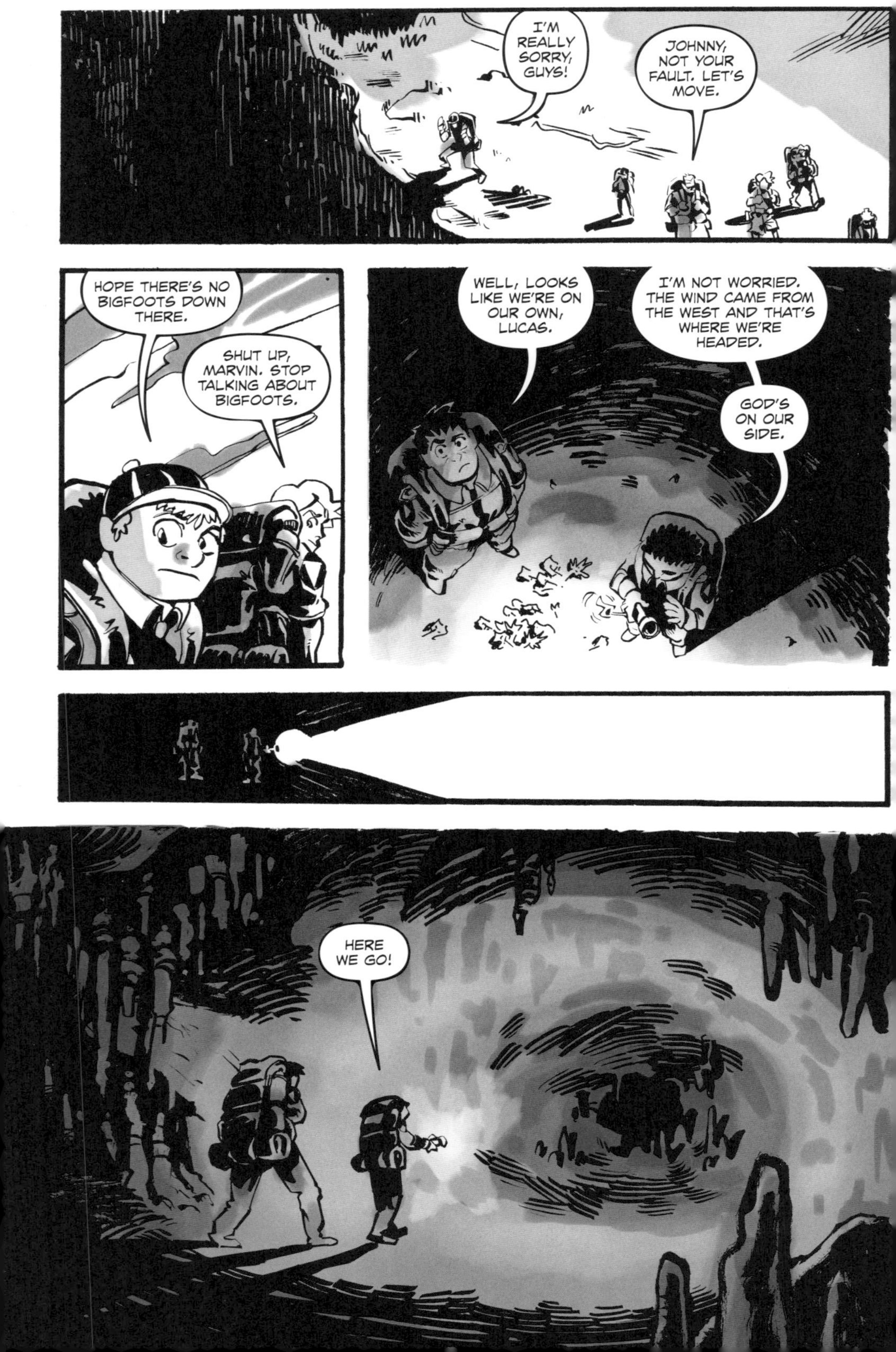
I'M REALLY SORRY, GUYS!
JOHNNY, NOT YOUR FAULT. LET'S MOVE.
HOPE THERE'S NO BIGFOOTS DOWN THERE.
SHUT UP, MARVIN. STOP TALKING ABOUT BIGFOOTS.
WELL, LOOKS LIKE WE'RE ON OUR OWN, LUCAS.
I'M NOT WORRIED. THE WIND CAME FROM THE WEST AND THAT'S WHERE WE'RE HEADED.
GOD'S ON OUR SIDE.
HERE WE GO!

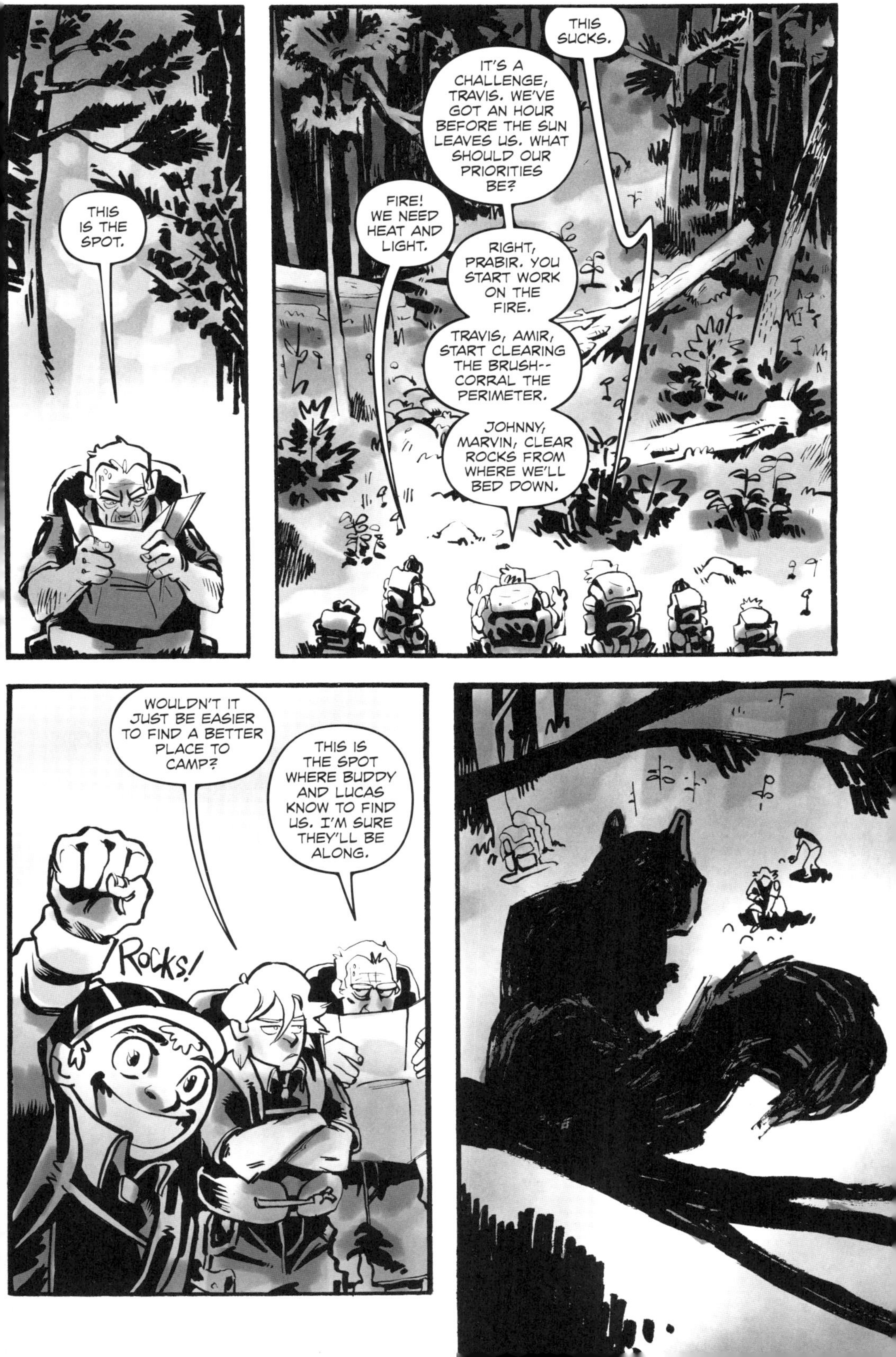
THIS IS THE SPOT.
THIS SUCKS.
IT'S A CHALLENGE, TRAVIS. WE'VE GOT AN HOUR BEFORE THE SUN LEAVES US. WHAT SHOULD OUR PRIORITIES BE?
FIRE! WE NEED HEAT AND LIGHT.
RIGHT, PRABIR. YOU START WORK ON THE FIRE.
TRAVIS, AMIR, START CLEARING THE BRUSH--CORRAL THE PERIMETER.
JOHNNY, MARVIN, CLEAR ROCKS FROM WHERE WE'LL BED DOWN.
WOULDN'T IT JUST BE EASIER TO FIND A BETTER PLACE TO CAMP?
THIS IS THE SPOT WHERE BUDDY AND LUCAS KNOW TO FIND US. I'M SURE THEY'LL BE ALONG.
ROCKS!

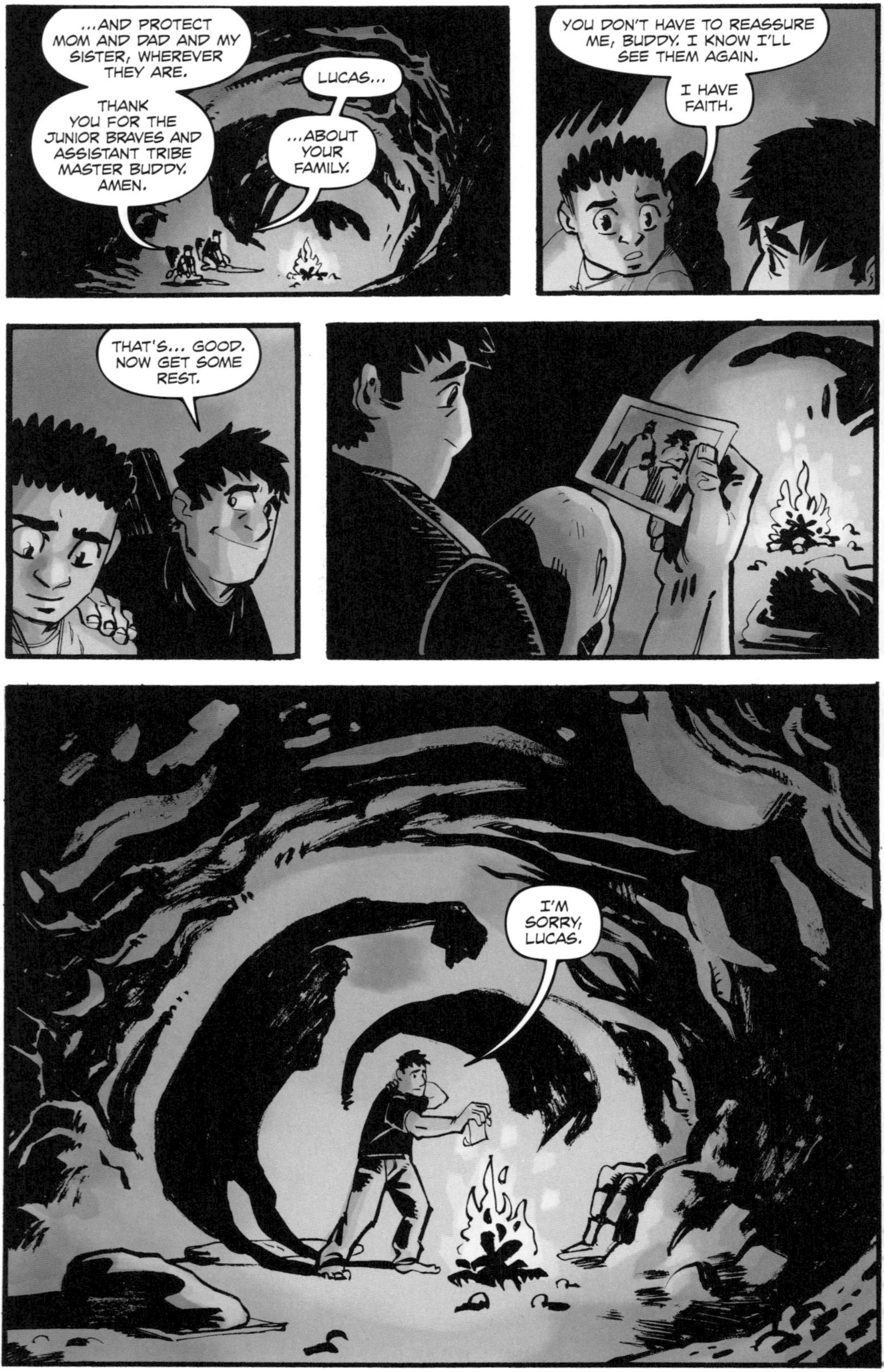
...AND PROTECT MOM AND DAD AND MY SISTER, WHEREVER THEY ARE.
THANK YOU FOR THE JUNIOR BRAVES AND ASSISTANT TRIBE MASTER BUDDY. AMEN.
LUCAS...
...ABOUT YOUR FAMILY.
YOU DON'T HAVE TO REASSURE ME, BUDDY. I KNOW I'LL SEE THEM AGAIN.
I HAVE FAITH.
THAT'S... GOOD. NOW GET SOME REST.
I'M SORRY, LUCAS.

OH MY GOD!

DAY 13.

REMEMBER, THESE TOOK THOUSANDS OF YEARS TO FORM. BE CAREFUL.

I GET IT.

TAKE ONLY MEMORIES, LEAVE ONLY--

SQUISH!

GROSS! *GROSS!* I STEPPED IN A PILE OF NASTY.

LOOKS LIKE THIS CAVE IS SOMETHING'S HOME.

MORE LIKE BATHROOM.

MWHWEEEYAAAAAAAAAAAAAAAAA

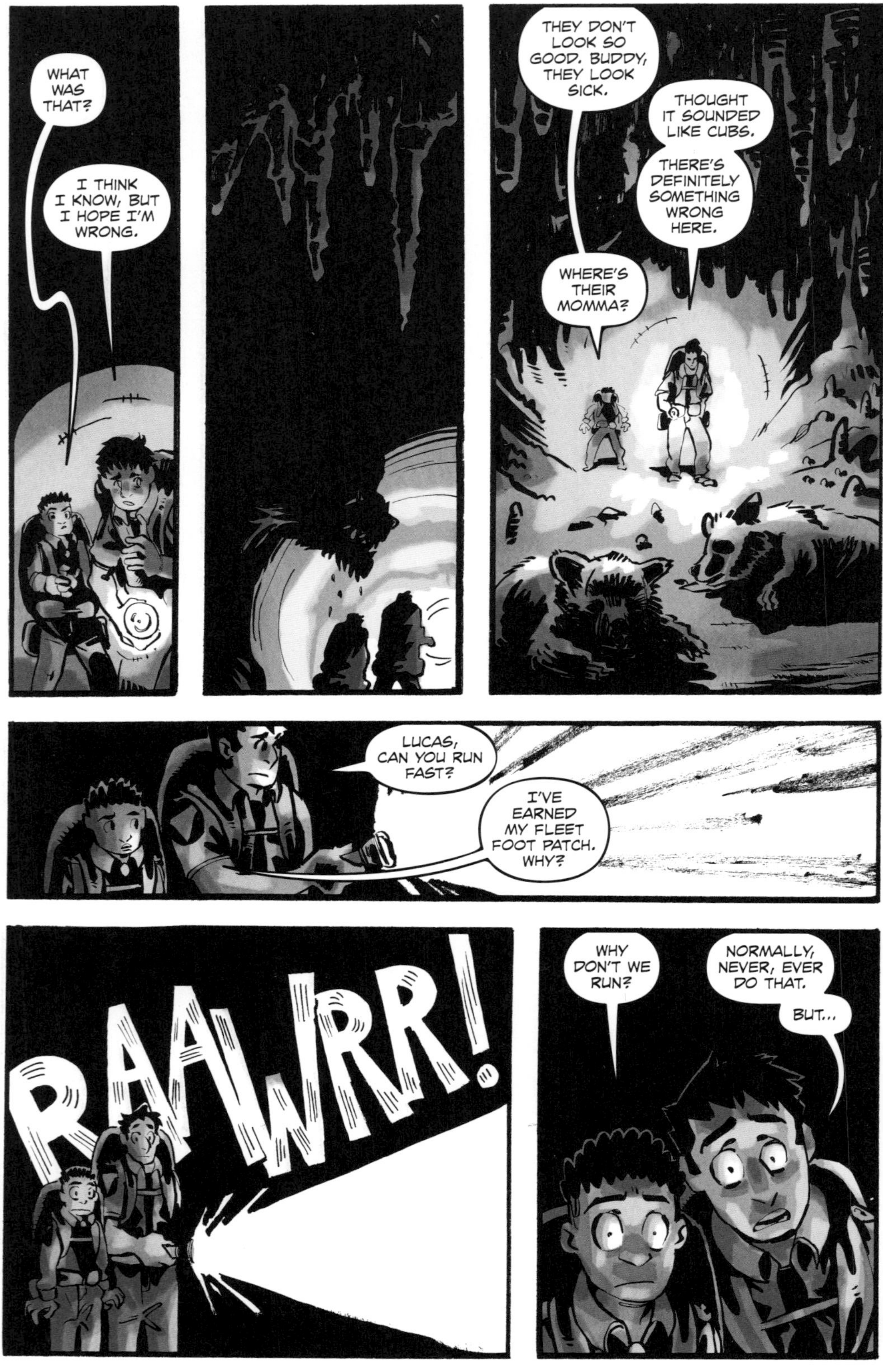
WHAT WAS THAT?
I THINK I KNOW, BUT I HOPE I'M WRONG.
THEY DON'T LOOK SO GOOD. BUDDY, THEY LOOK SICK.
THOUGHT IT SOUNDED LIKE CUBS.
THERE'S DEFINITELY SOMETHING WRONG HERE.
WHERE'S THEIR MOMMA?
LUCAS, CAN YOU RUN FAST?
I'VE EARNED MY FLEET FOOT PATCH. WHY?
RAAWRR!
WHY DON'T WE RUN?
NORMALLY, NEVER, EVER DO THAT.
BUT...

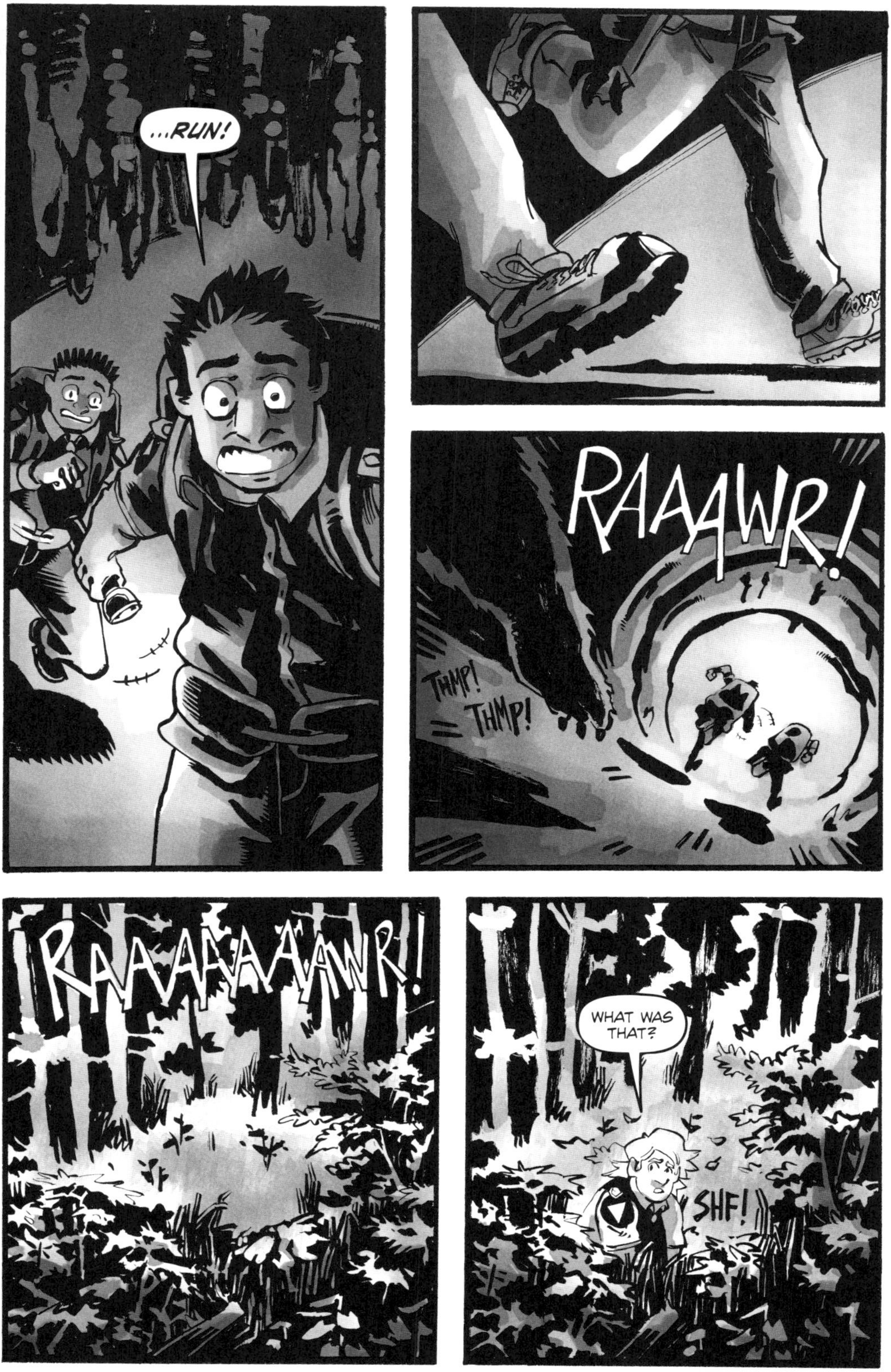
...RUN!
RAAAWR!
THMP! THMP!
RAAAAAAAWR!
WHAT WAS THAT?
SHF!

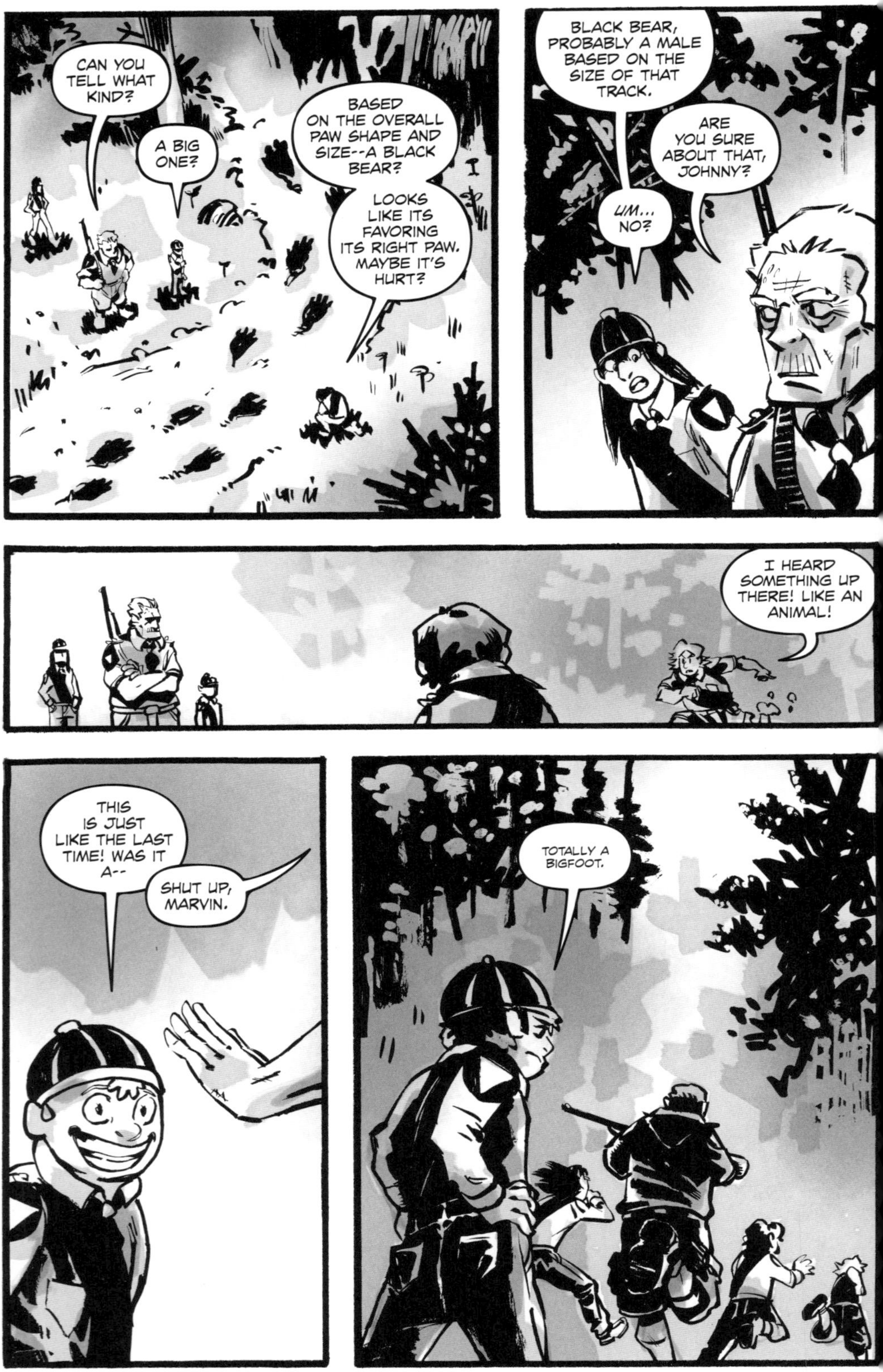
CAN YOU TELL WHAT KIND?
A BIG ONE?
BASED ON THE OVERALL PAW SHAPE AND SIZE--A BLACK BEAR?
LOOKS LIKE ITS FAVORING ITS RIGHT PAW. MAYBE IT'S HURT?
BLACK BEAR, PROBABLY A MALE BASED ON THE SIZE OF THAT TRACK.
ARE YOU SURE ABOUT THAT, JOHNNY?
UM... NO?
I HEARD SOMETHING UP THERE! LIKE AN ANIMAL!
THIS IS JUST LIKE THE LAST TIME! WAS IT A--
SHUT UP, MARVIN.
TOTALLY A BIGFOOT.

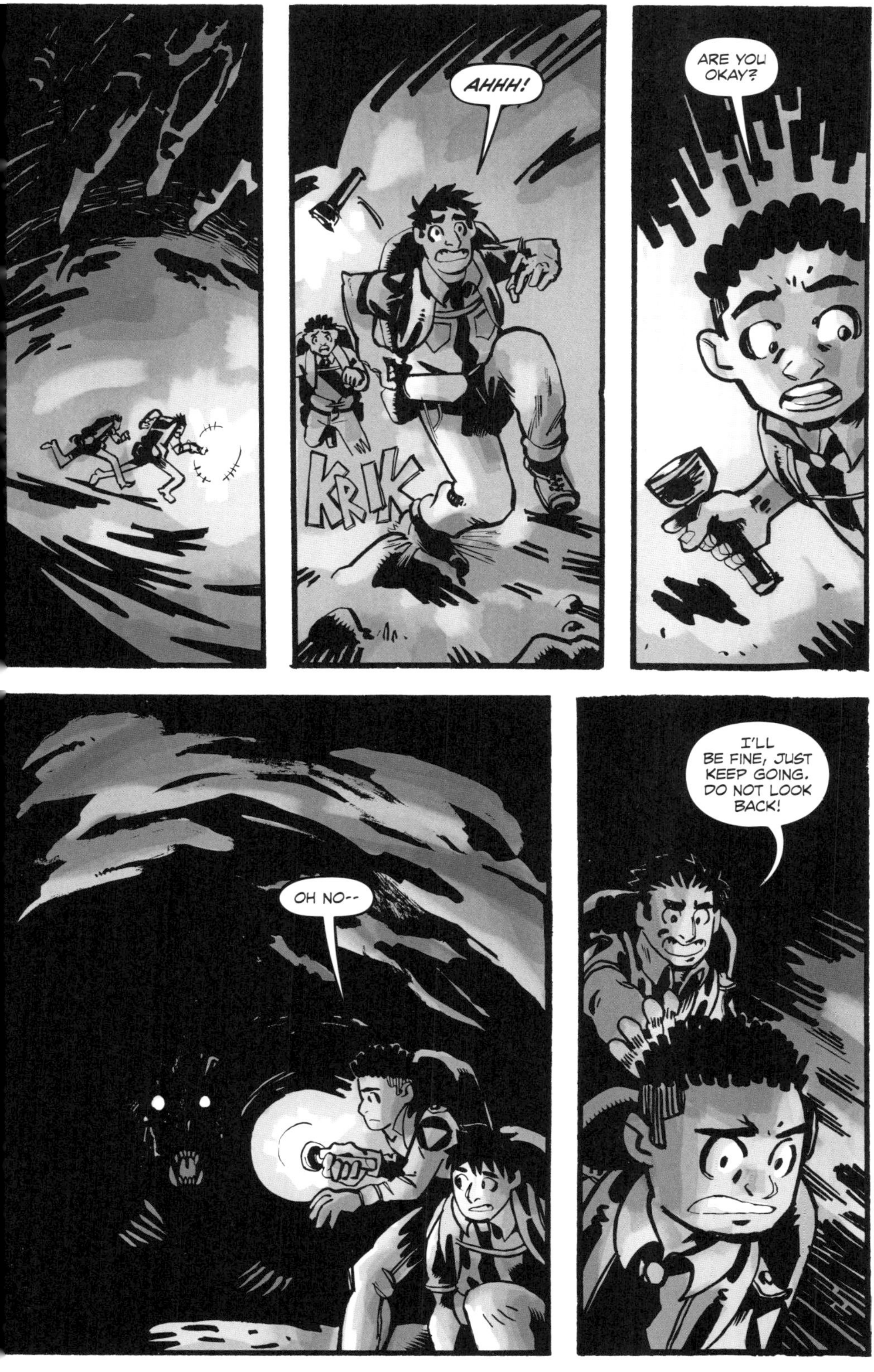
AHHH!
KRIK
ARE YOU OKAY?
OH NO--
I'LL BE FINE, JUST KEEP GOING. DO NOT LOOK BACK!

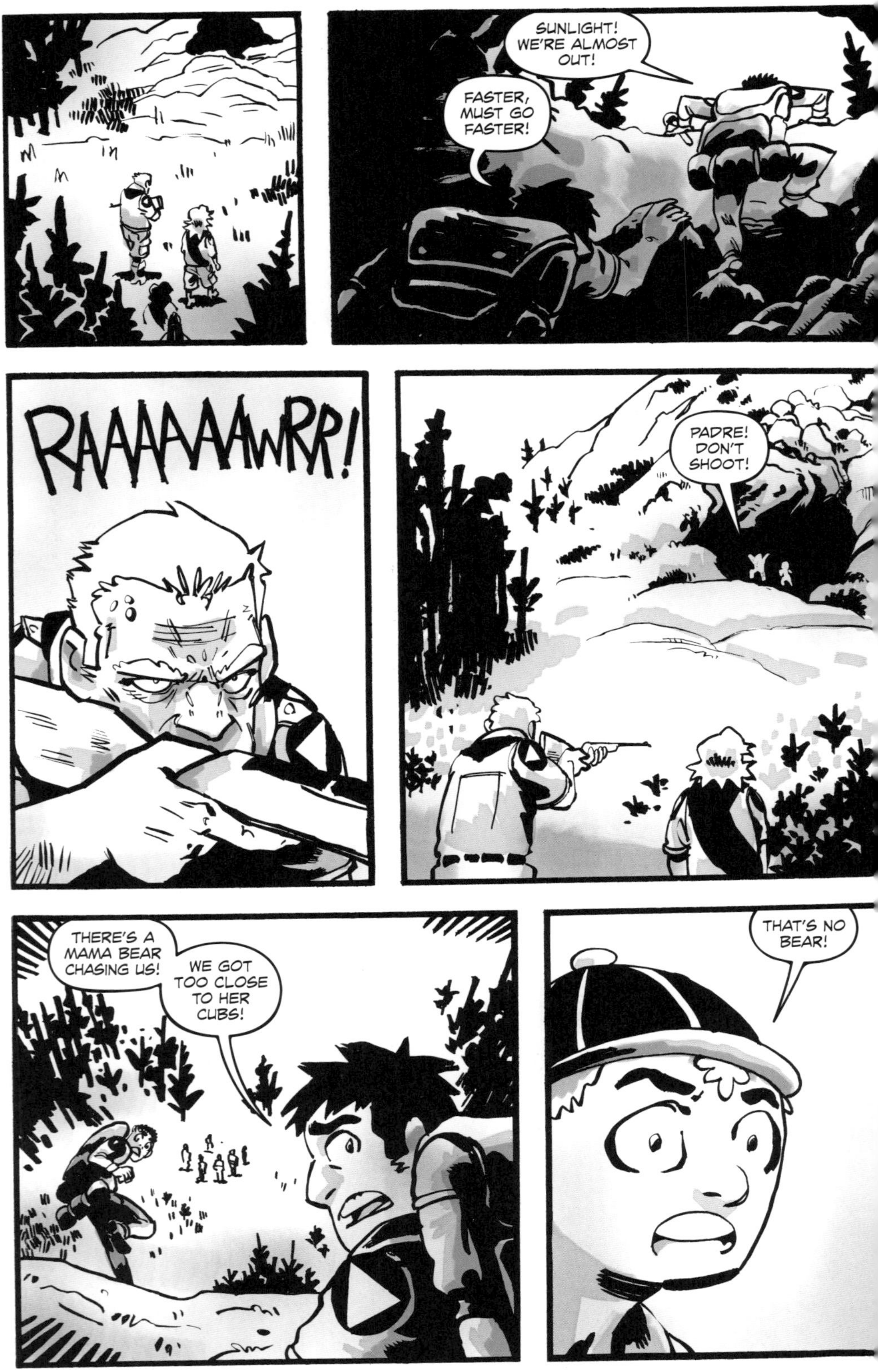
SUNLIGHT! WE'RE ALMOST OUT!
FASTER, MUST GO FASTER!
RAAAAAAAWRR!
PADRE! DON'T SHOOT!
THERE'S A MAMA BEAR CHASING US!
WE GOT TOO CLOSE TO HER CUBS!
THAT'S NO BEAR!

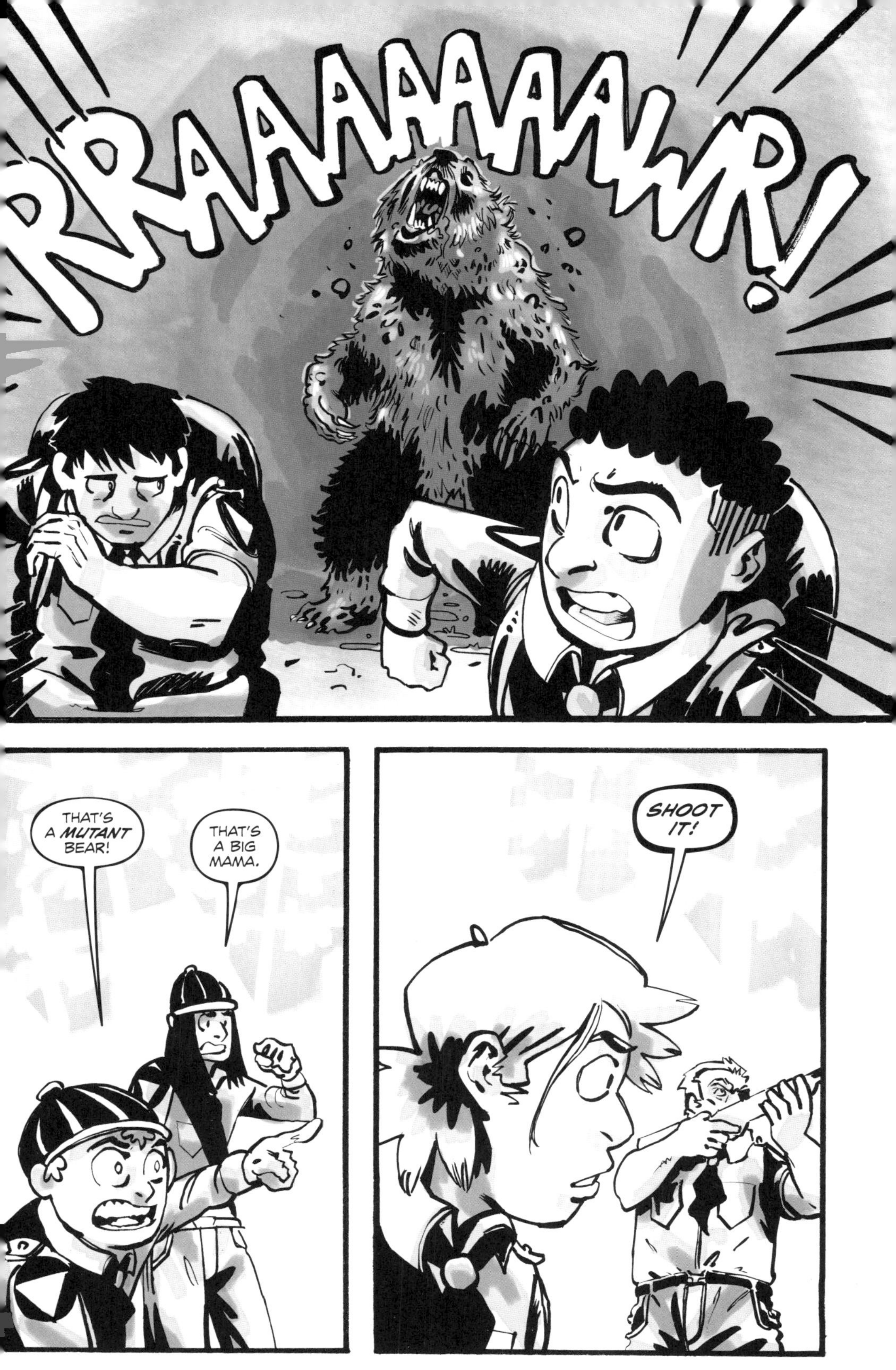
RRAAAAAAAWR!
THAT'S A *MUTANT* BEAR!
THAT'S A BIG MAMA.
SHOOT IT!

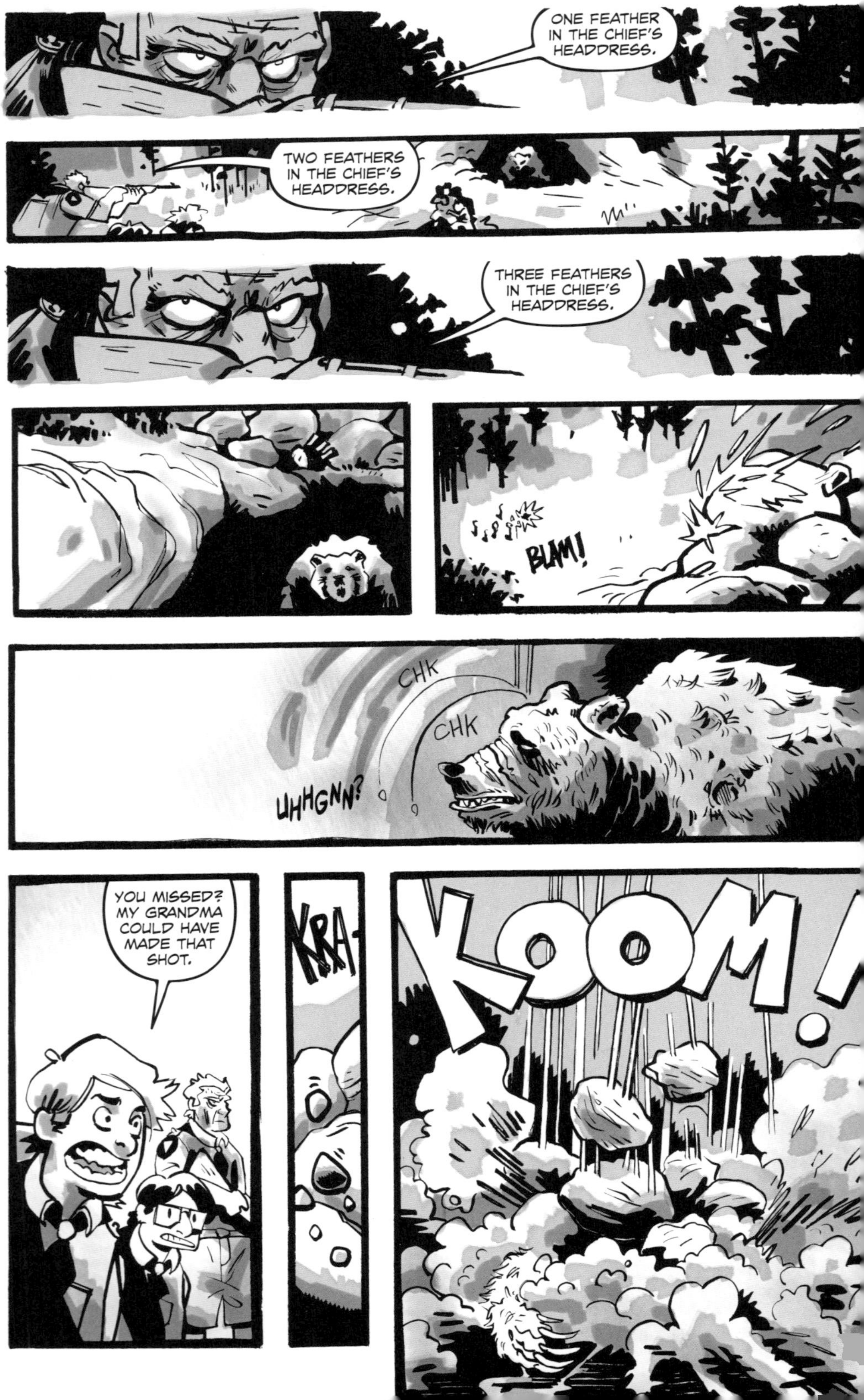

ONE FEATHER IN THE CHIEF'S HEADDRESS.
TWO FEATHERS IN THE CHIEF'S HEADDRESS.
THREE FEATHERS IN THE CHIEF'S HEADDRESS.
BLAM!
CHK
CHK
UHHGNN?
YOU MISSED? MY GRANDMA COULD HAVE MADE THAT SHOT.
KRA-
KOOM!

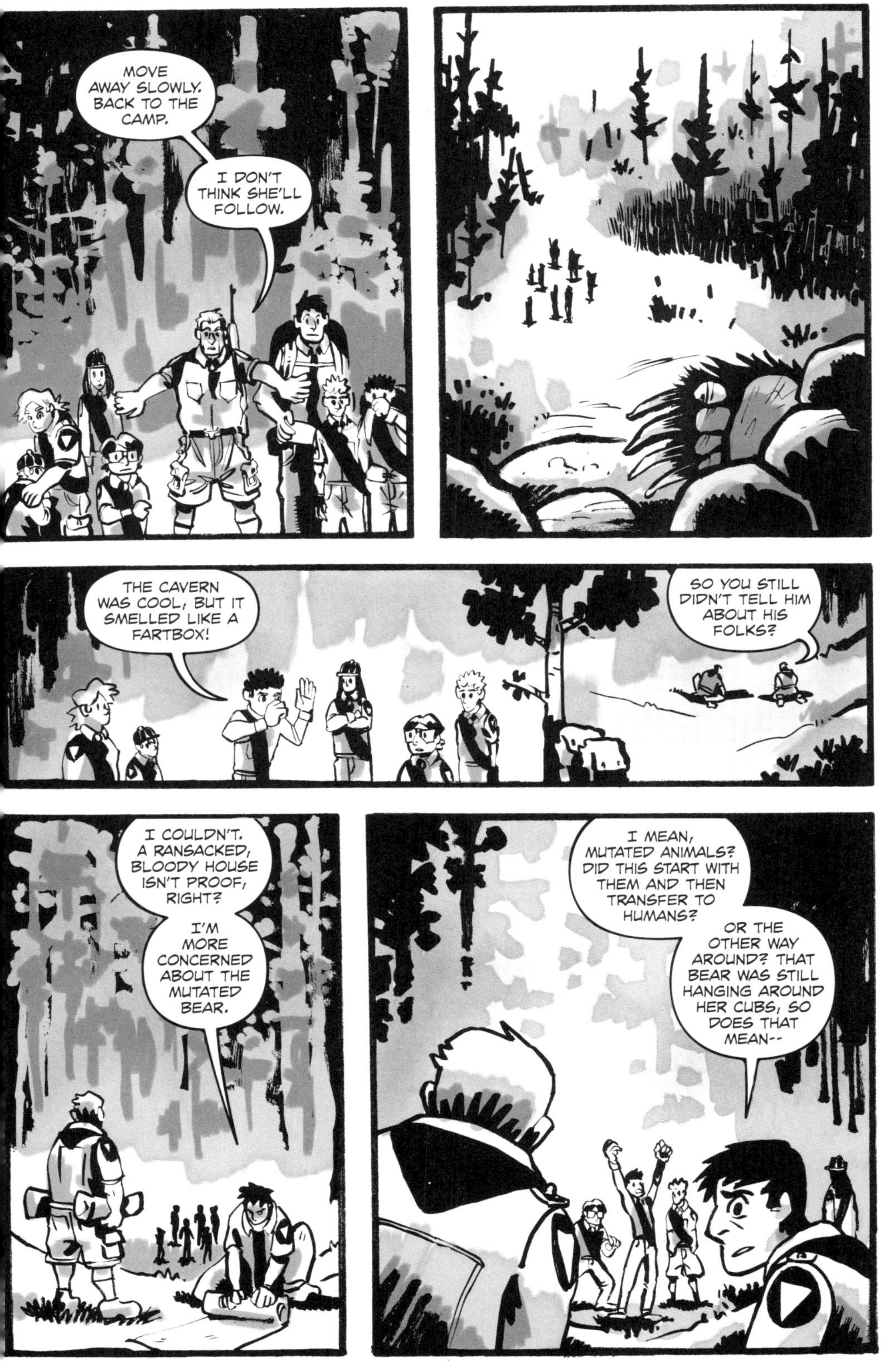
MOVE AWAY SLOWLY. BACK TO THE CAMP.
I DON'T THINK SHE'LL FOLLOW.
THE CAVERN WAS COOL, BUT IT SMELLED LIKE A FARTBOX!
SO YOU STILL DIDN'T TELL HIM ABOUT HIS FOLKS?
I COULDN'T. A RANSACKED, BLOODY HOUSE ISN'T PROOF, RIGHT?
I'M MORE CONCERNED ABOUT THE MUTATED BEAR.
I MEAN, MUTATED ANIMALS? DID THIS START WITH THEM AND THEN TRANSFER TO HUMANS?
OR THE OTHER WAY AROUND? THAT BEAR WAS STILL HANGING AROUND HER CUBS, SO DOES THAT MEAN--

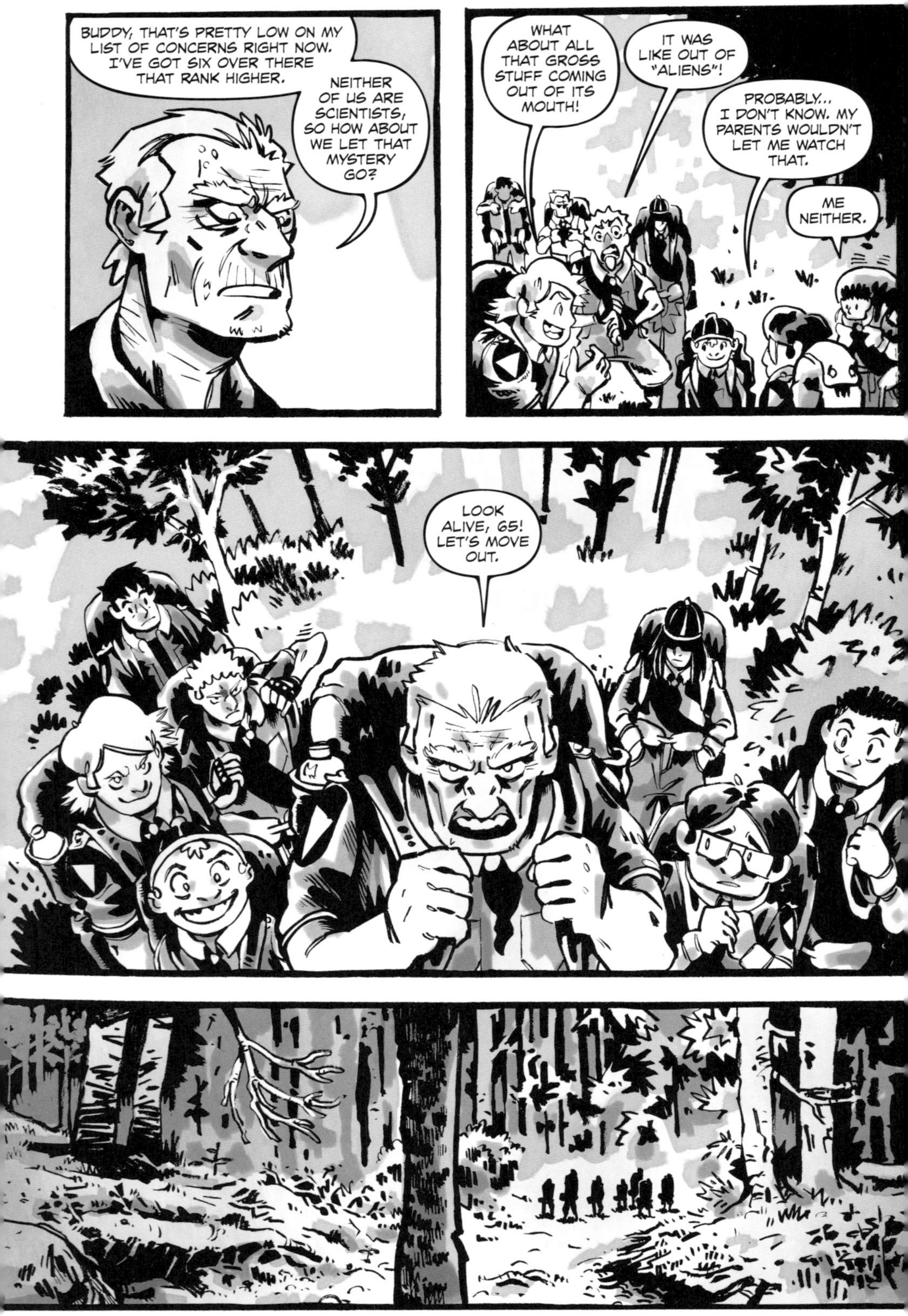
BUDDY, THAT'S PRETTY LOW ON MY LIST OF CONCERNS RIGHT NOW. I'VE GOT SIX OVER THERE THAT RANK HIGHER.
NEITHER OF US ARE SCIENTISTS, SO HOW ABOUT WE LET THAT MYSTERY GO?
WHAT ABOUT ALL THAT GROSS STUFF COMING OUT OF ITS MOUTH!
IT WAS LIKE OUT OF "ALIENS"!
PROBABLY... I DON'T KNOW. MY PARENTS WOULDN'T LET ME WATCH THAT.
ME NEITHER.
LOOK ALIVE, 65! LET'S MOVE OUT.

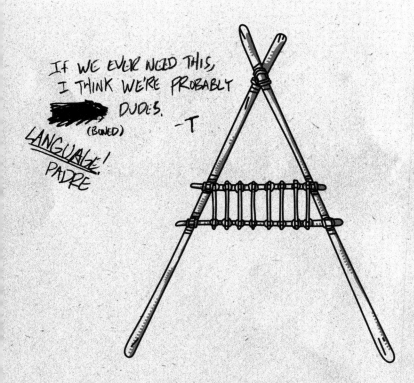

IF WE EVER NEED THIS, I THINK WE'RE PROBABLY ~~DEAD~~ (BONED) DUDES. —T

LANGUAGE! PADRE

BUILDING A TRAVOIS

The travois, also called a "drag sled," was a vehicle used by Native Americans to carry heavy objects over land.

A Junior Brave should add the construction of such a helpful item to his skill set—one never knows what the wild world could have in store for him and his Tribe.

The construction of a Travois is relatively easy given the correct tools and access to sturdy timber.

Take two long, sturdy, straight poles or de-branched sapling limbs and bind them together at their thickest ends. Spread the poles so they form a "V" from the bindings. Tie a cross beam that spans between the two poles, turning the "V" into an "A." This will complete the basic Travois frame.

At this step, a tarp or basket or even an additional crossbeam could be laid and bound to form the space which will carry the load.

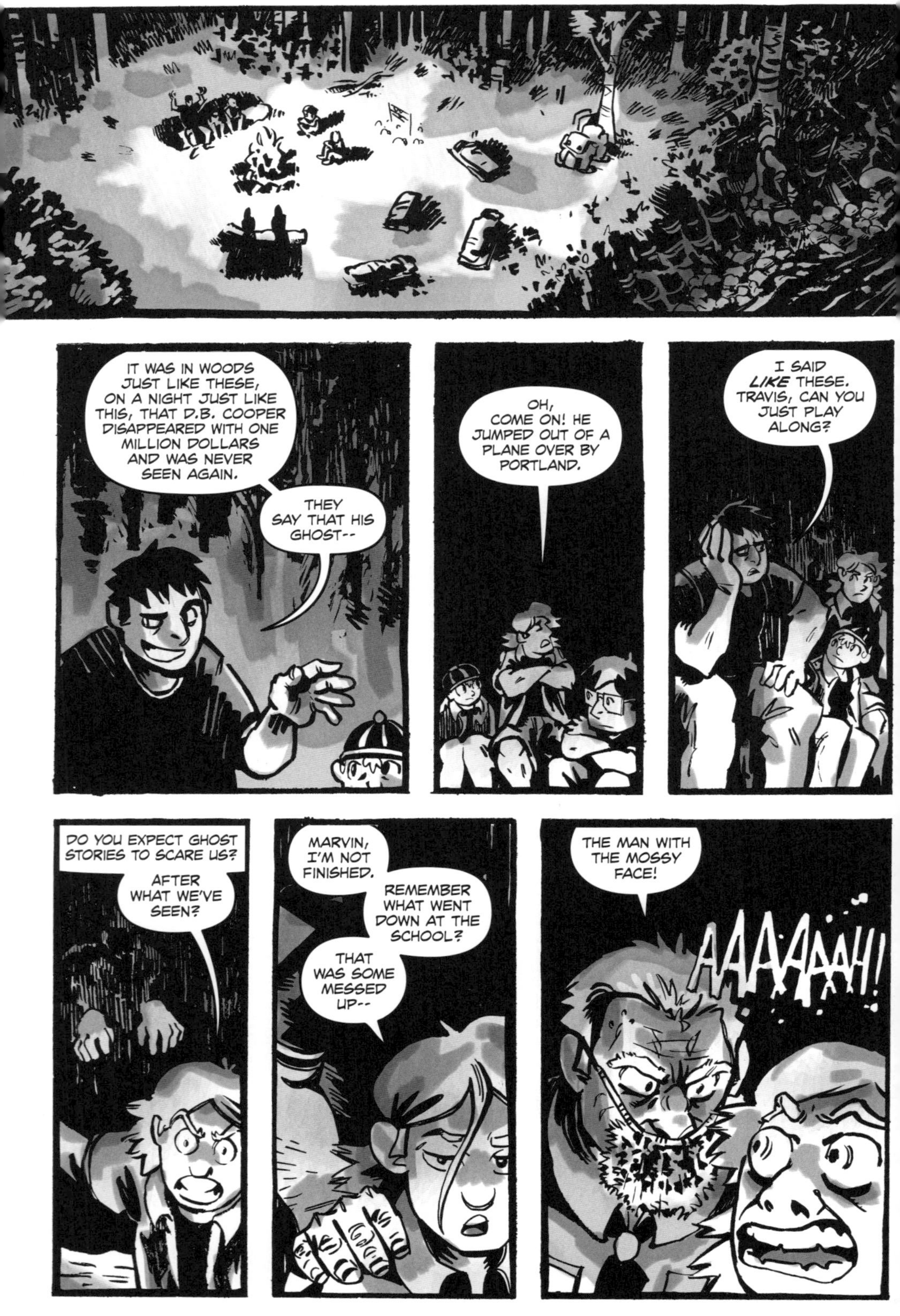
IT WAS IN WOODS JUST LIKE THESE, ON A NIGHT JUST LIKE THIS, THAT D.B. COOPER DISAPPEARED WITH ONE MILLION DOLLARS AND WAS NEVER SEEN AGAIN.
THEY SAY THAT HIS GHOST--
OH, COME ON! HE JUMPED OUT OF A PLANE OVER BY PORTLAND.
I SAID *LIKE* THESE. TRAVIS, CAN YOU JUST PLAY ALONG?
DO YOU EXPECT GHOST STORIES TO SCARE US?
AFTER WHAT WE'VE SEEN?
MARVIN, I'M NOT FINISHED.
REMEMBER WHAT WENT DOWN AT THE SCHOOL?
THAT WAS SOME MESSED UP--
THE MAN WITH THE MOSSY FACE!
AAAAAAH!

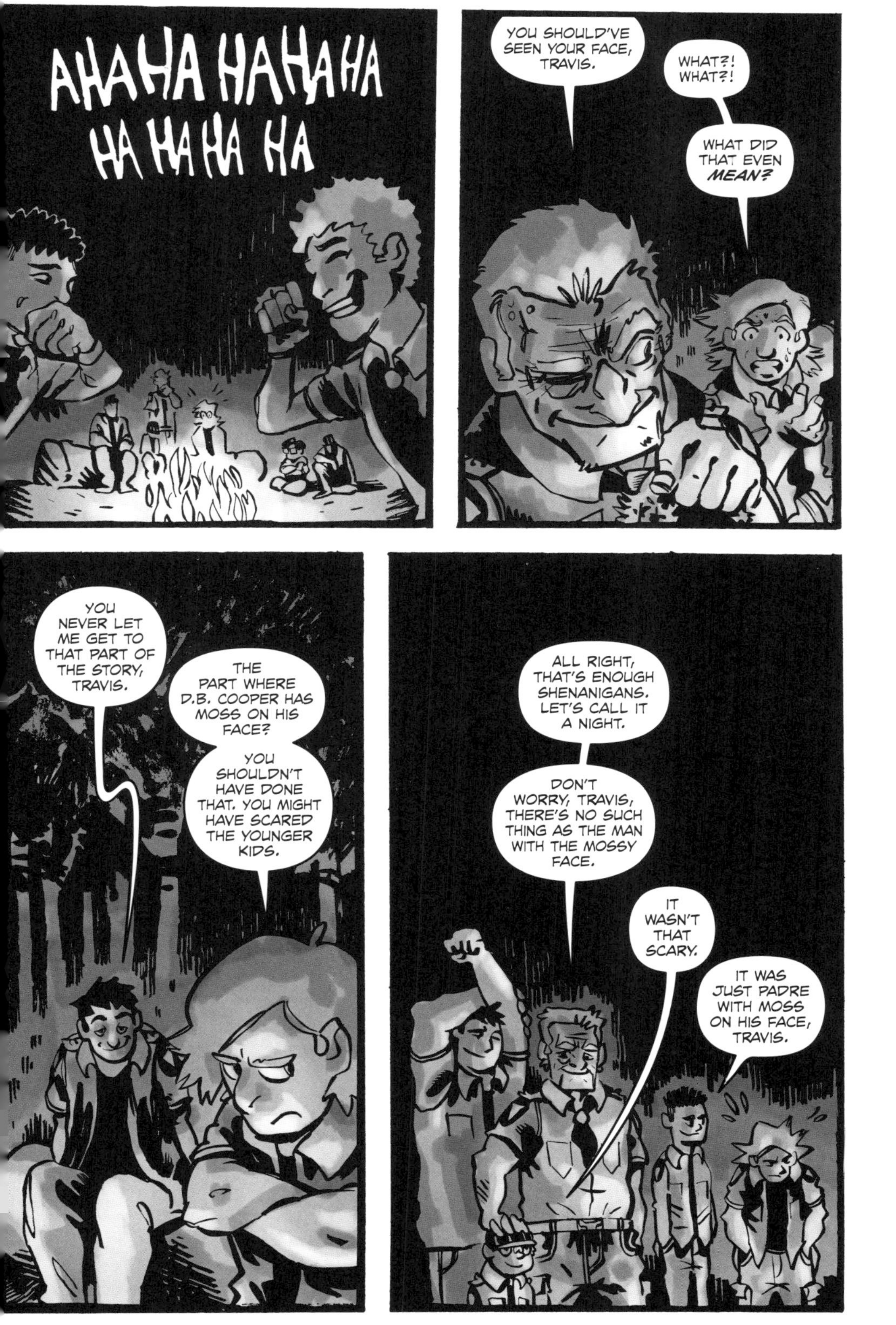

AHAHA HAHAHA HAHAHAHA HA
YOU SHOULD'VE SEEN YOUR FACE, TRAVIS.
WHAT?! WHAT?!
WHAT DID THAT EVEN *MEAN?*
YOU NEVER LET ME GET TO THAT PART OF THE STORY, TRAVIS.
THE PART WHERE D.B. COOPER HAS MOSS ON HIS FACE?
YOU SHOULDN'T HAVE DONE THAT. YOU MIGHT HAVE SCARED THE YOUNGER KIDS.
ALL RIGHT, THAT'S ENOUGH SHENANIGANS. LET'S CALL IT A NIGHT.
DON'T WORRY, TRAVIS, THERE'S NO SUCH THING AS THE MAN WITH THE MOSSY FACE.
IT WASN'T THAT SCARY.
IT WAS JUST PADRE WITH MOSS ON HIS FACE, TRAVIS.

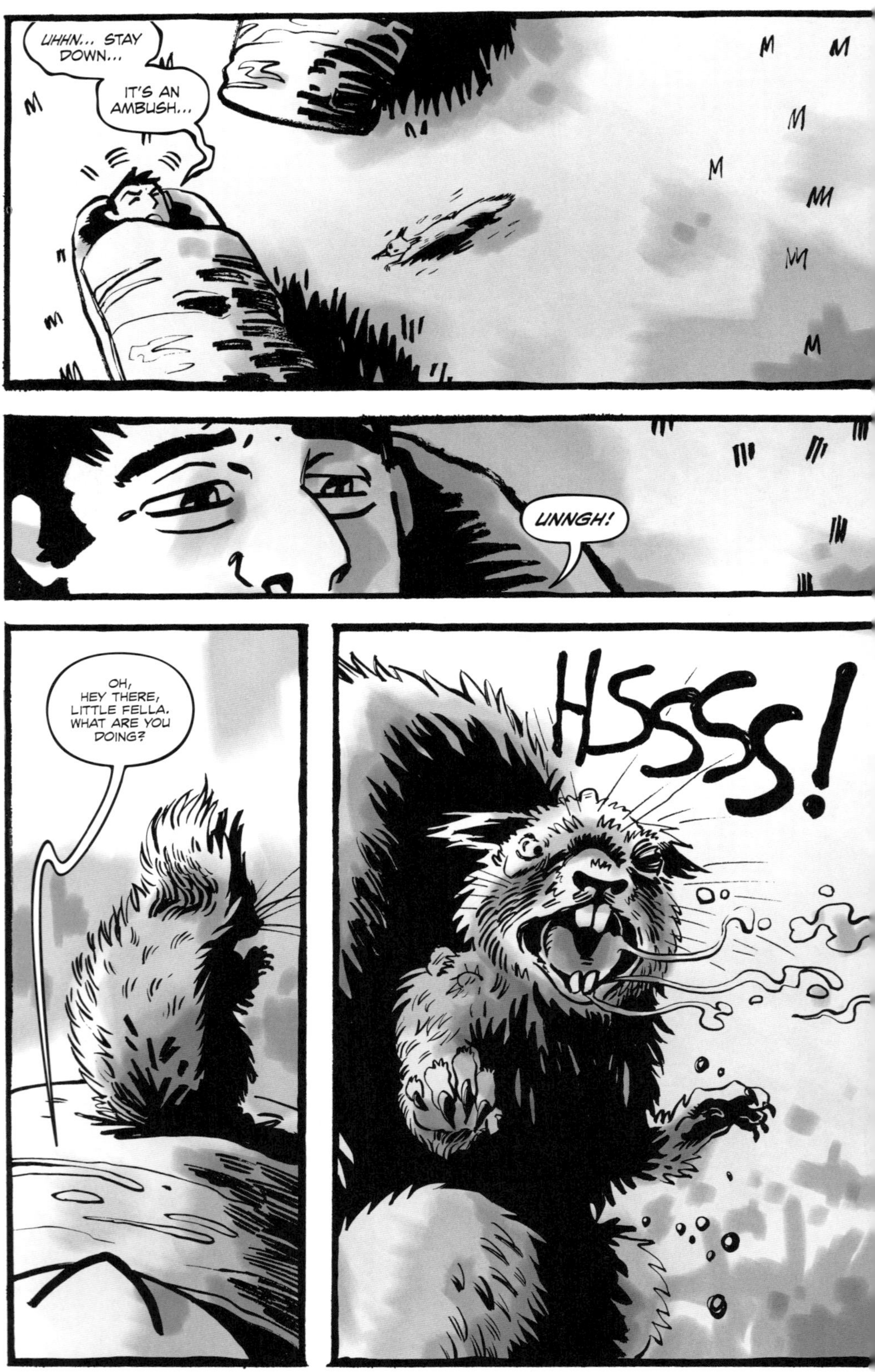
UHHN... STAY DOWN...
IT'S AN AMBUSH...
UNNGH!
OH, HEY THERE, LITTLE FELLA. WHAT ARE YOU DOING?
HSSSS!

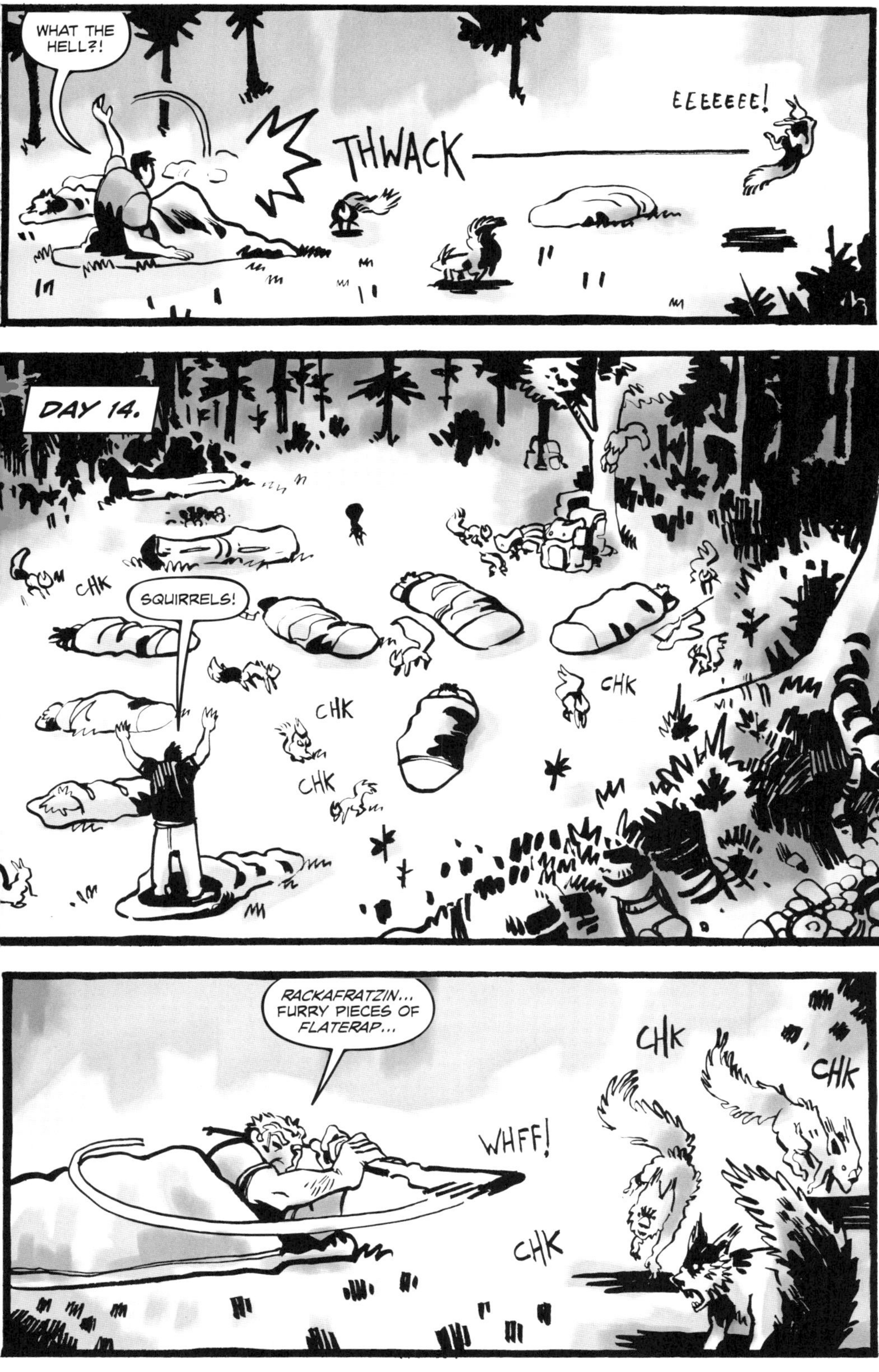
WHAT THE HELL?!
THWACK
EEEEEEE!
DAY 14.
CHK
SQUIRRELS!
CHK
CHK
CHK
RACKAFRATZIN... FURRY PIECES OF FLATERAP...
CHK
CHK
WHFF!
CHK

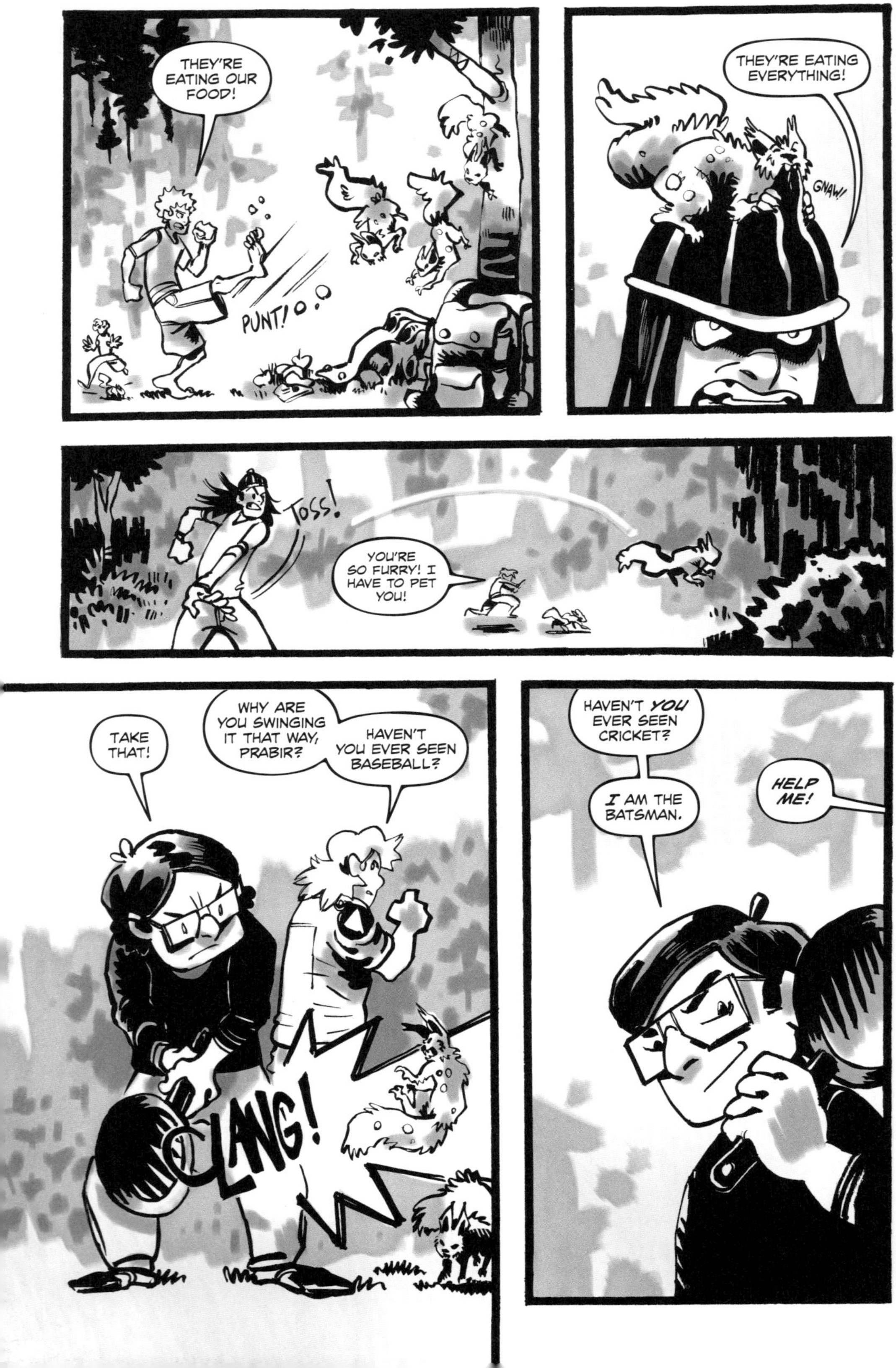

THEY'RE EATING OUR FOOD!
PUNT!
THEY'RE EATING EVERYTHING!
GNAW!
TOSS!
YOU'RE SO FURRY! I HAVE TO PET YOU!
TAKE THAT!
WHY ARE YOU SWINGING IT THAT WAY, PRABIR?
HAVEN'T YOU EVER SEEN BASEBALL?
CLANG!
HAVEN'T *YOU* EVER SEEN CRICKET?
I AM THE BATSMAN.
HELP ME!

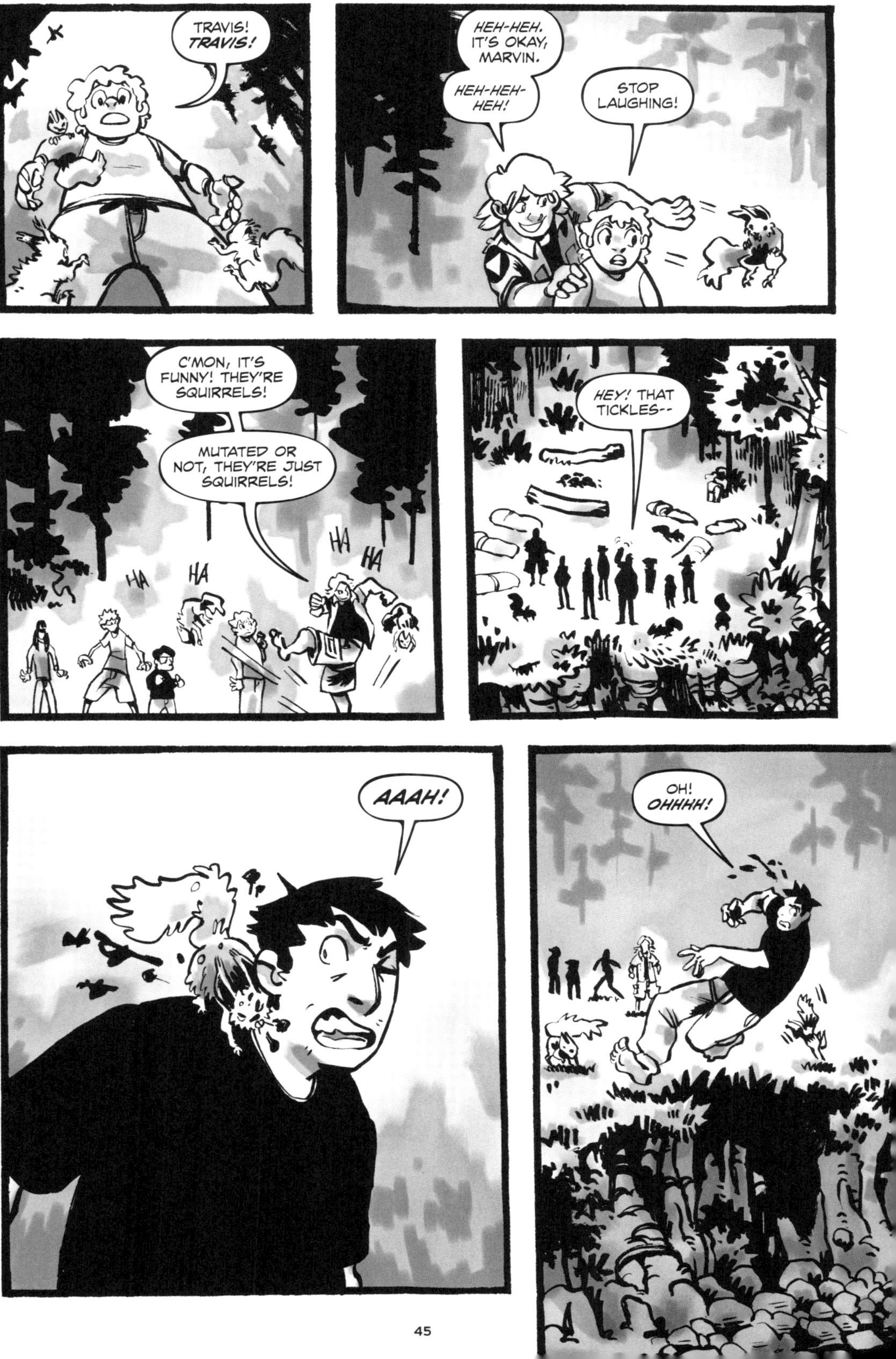
TRAVIS! TRAVIS!
HEH-HEH. IT'S OKAY, MARVIN.
HEH-HEH-HEH!
STOP LAUGHING!
C'MON, IT'S FUNNY! THEY'RE SQUIRRELS!
MUTATED OR NOT, THEY'RE JUST SQUIRRELS!
HA
HA
HA
HA
HEY! THAT TICKLES--
AAAH!
OH! OHHHH!

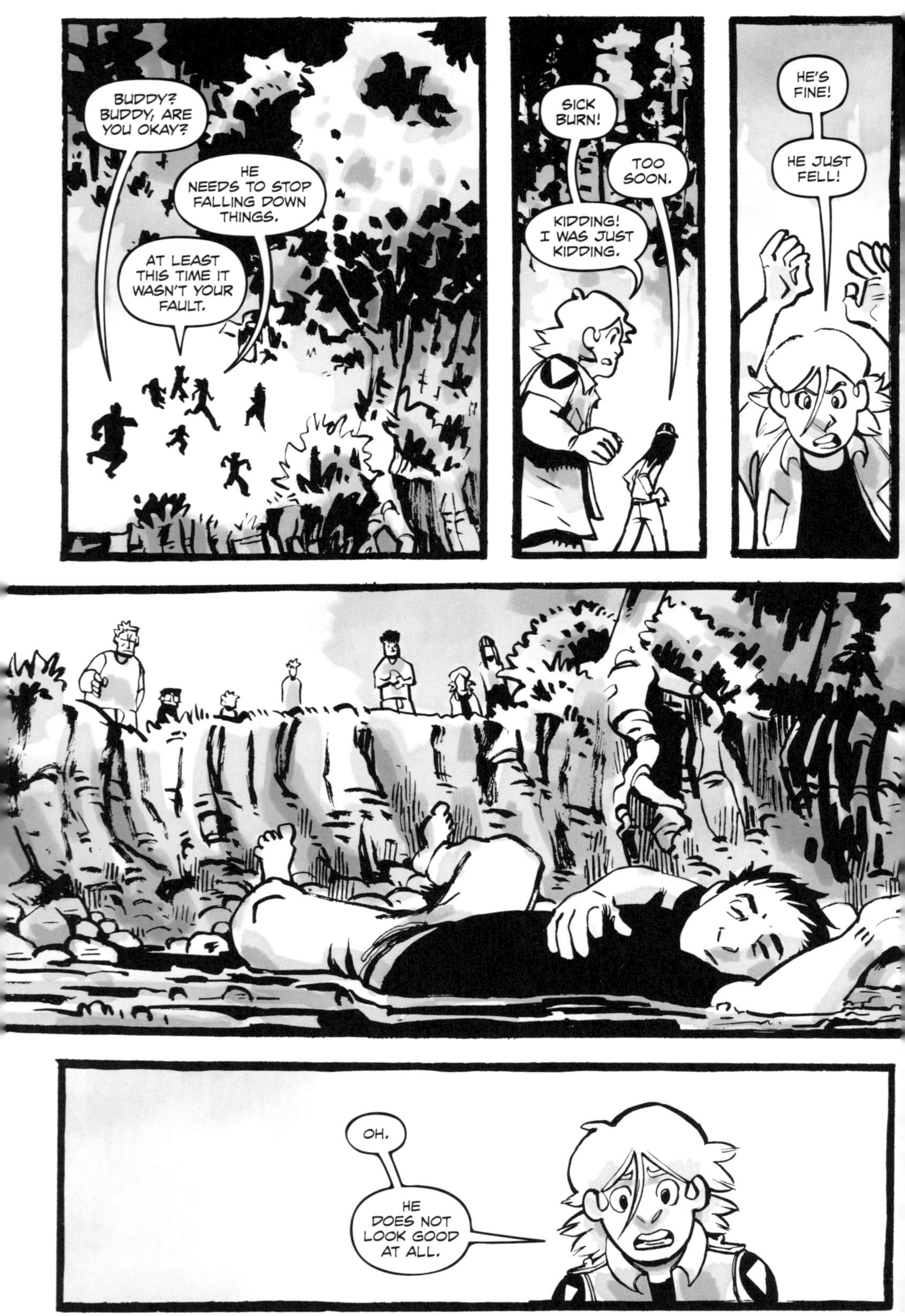
BUDDY? BUDDY, ARE YOU OKAY?
HE NEEDS TO STOP FALLING DOWN THINGS.
AT LEAST THIS TIME IT WASN'T YOUR FAULT.
SICK BURN!
TOO SOON.
KIDDING! I WAS JUST KIDDING.
HE'S FINE!
HE JUST FELL!
OH.
HE DOES NOT LOOK GOOD AT ALL.

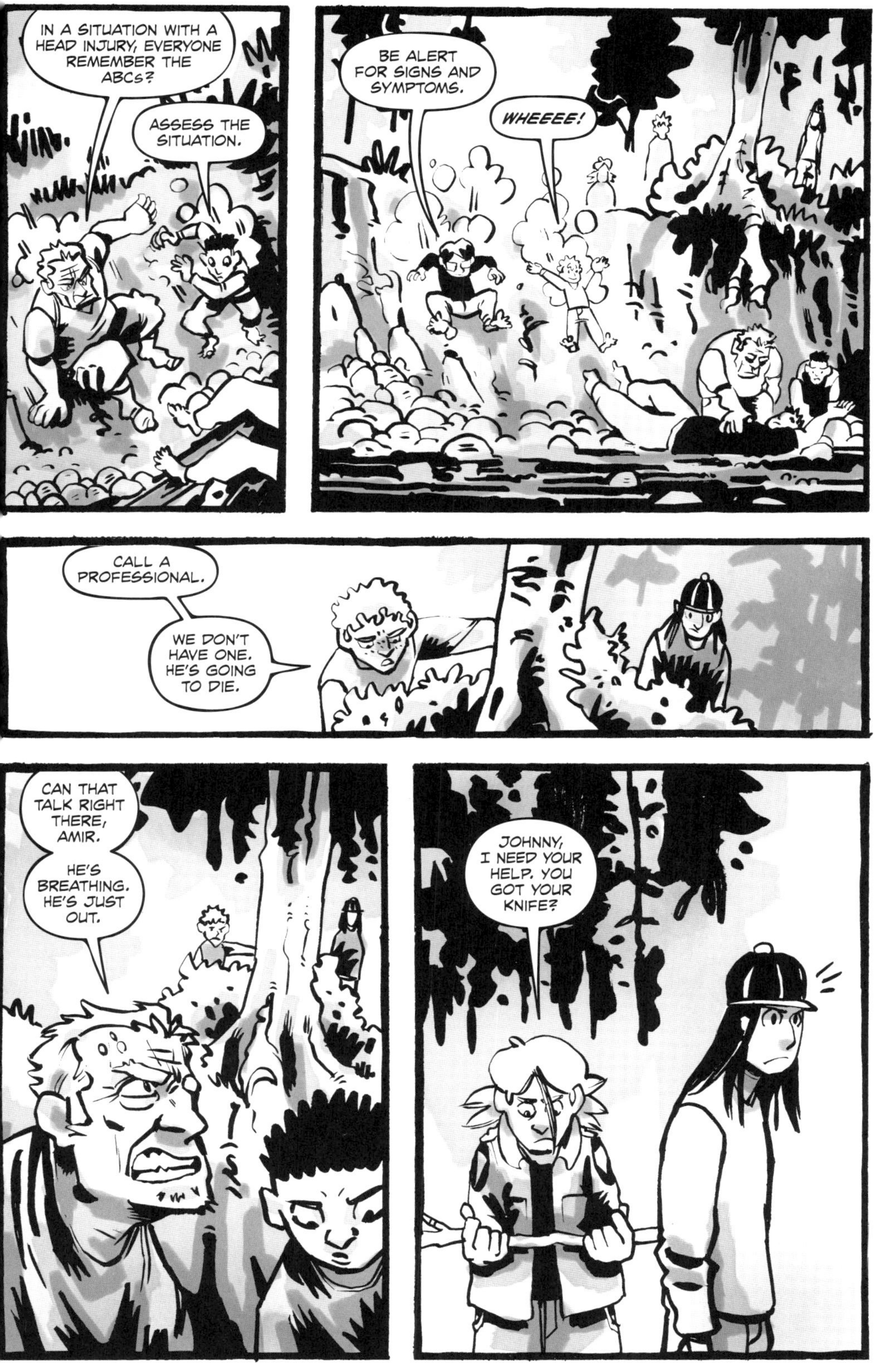
IN A SITUATION WITH A HEAD INJURY, EVERYONE REMEMBER THE ABCs?
ASSESS THE SITUATION.
BE ALERT FOR SIGNS AND SYMPTOMS.
WHEEEEE!
CALL A PROFESSIONAL.
WE DON'T HAVE ONE. HE'S GOING TO DIE.
CAN THAT TALK RIGHT THERE, AMIR.
HE'S BREATHING. HE'S JUST OUT.
JOHNNY, I NEED YOUR HELP. YOU GOT YOUR KNIFE?

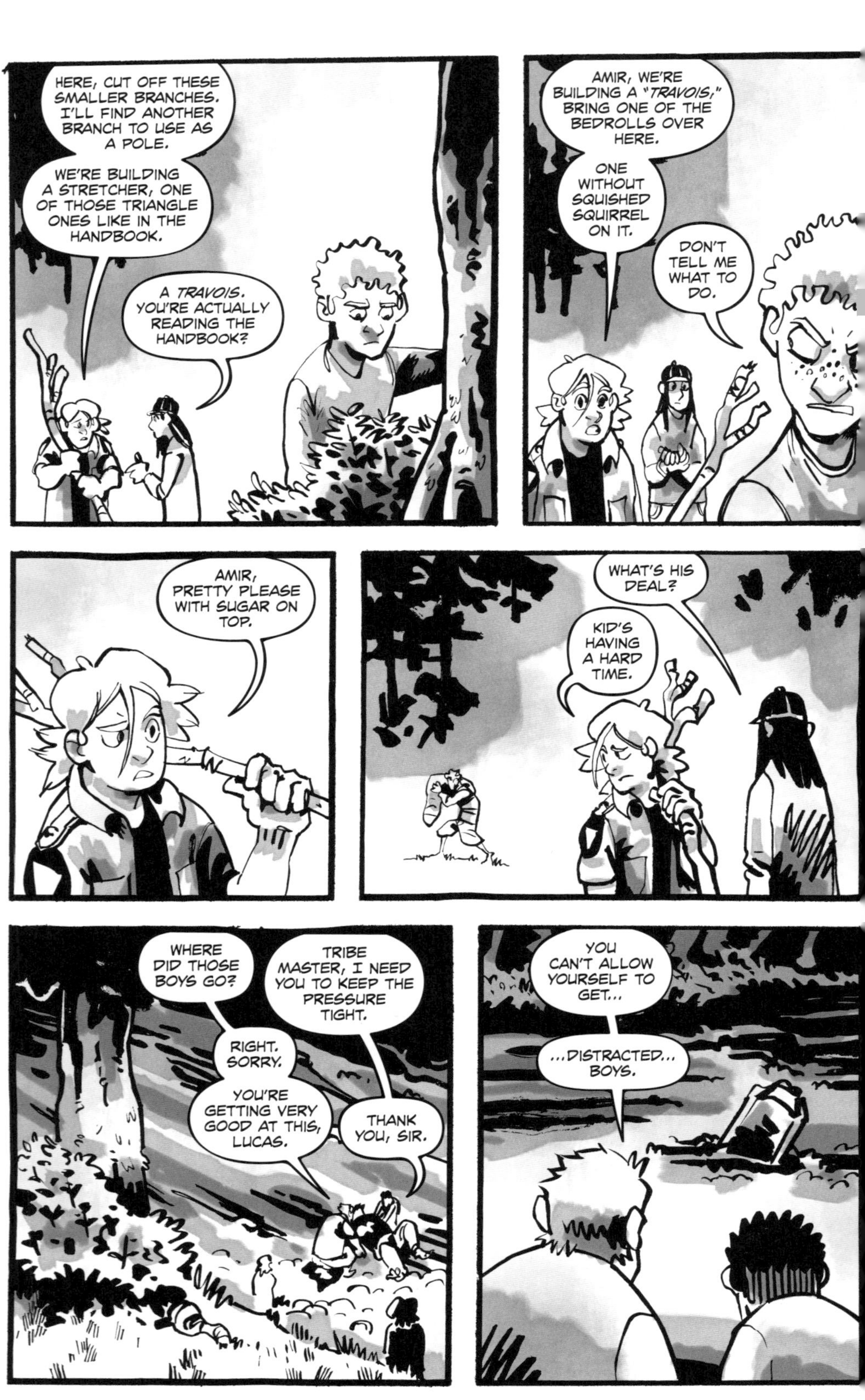
HERE, CUT OFF THESE SMALLER BRANCHES. I'LL FIND ANOTHER BRANCH TO USE AS A POLE.
WE'RE BUILDING A STRETCHER, ONE OF THOSE TRIANGLE ONES LIKE IN THE HANDBOOK.
A *TRAVOIS*. YOU'RE ACTUALLY READING THE HANDBOOK?
AMIR, WE'RE BUILDING A "*TRAVOIS*," BRING ONE OF THE BEDROLLS OVER HERE.
ONE WITHOUT SQUISHED SQUIRREL ON IT.
DON'T TELL ME WHAT TO DO.
AMIR, PRETTY PLEASE WITH SUGAR ON TOP.
WHAT'S HIS DEAL?
KID'S HAVING A HARD TIME.
WHERE DID THOSE BOYS GO?
TRIBE MASTER, I NEED YOU TO KEEP THE PRESSURE TIGHT.
RIGHT. SORRY.
YOU'RE GETTING VERY GOOD AT THIS, LUCAS.
THANK YOU, SIR.
YOU CAN'T ALLOW YOURSELF TO GET...
...DISTRACTED... BOYS.

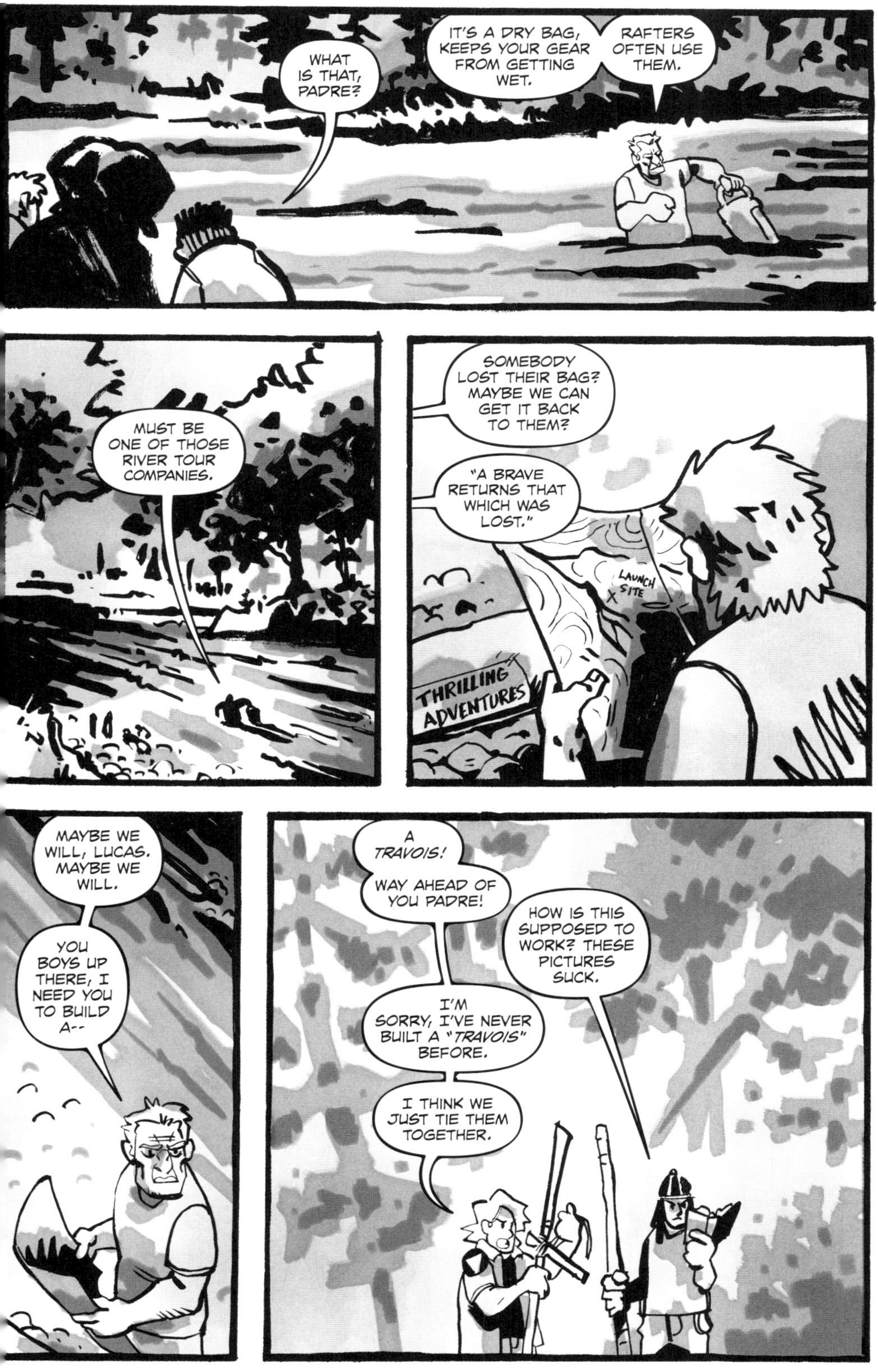
WHAT IS THAT, PADRE?
IT'S A DRY BAG, KEEPS YOUR GEAR FROM GETTING WET.
RAFTERS OFTEN USE THEM.
MUST BE ONE OF THOSE RIVER TOUR COMPANIES.
SOMEBODY LOST THEIR BAG? MAYBE WE CAN GET IT BACK TO THEM?
"A BRAVE RETURNS THAT WHICH WAS LOST."
LAUNCH SITE
X
THRILLING ADVENTURES
MAYBE WE WILL, LUCAS. MAYBE WE WILL.
YOU BOYS UP THERE, I NEED YOU TO BUILD A--
A *TRAVOIS!*
WAY AHEAD OF YOU PADRE!
HOW IS THIS SUPPOSED TO WORK? THESE PICTURES SUCK.
I'M SORRY, I'VE NEVER BUILT A "*TRAVOIS*" BEFORE.
I THINK WE JUST TIE THEM TOGETHER.

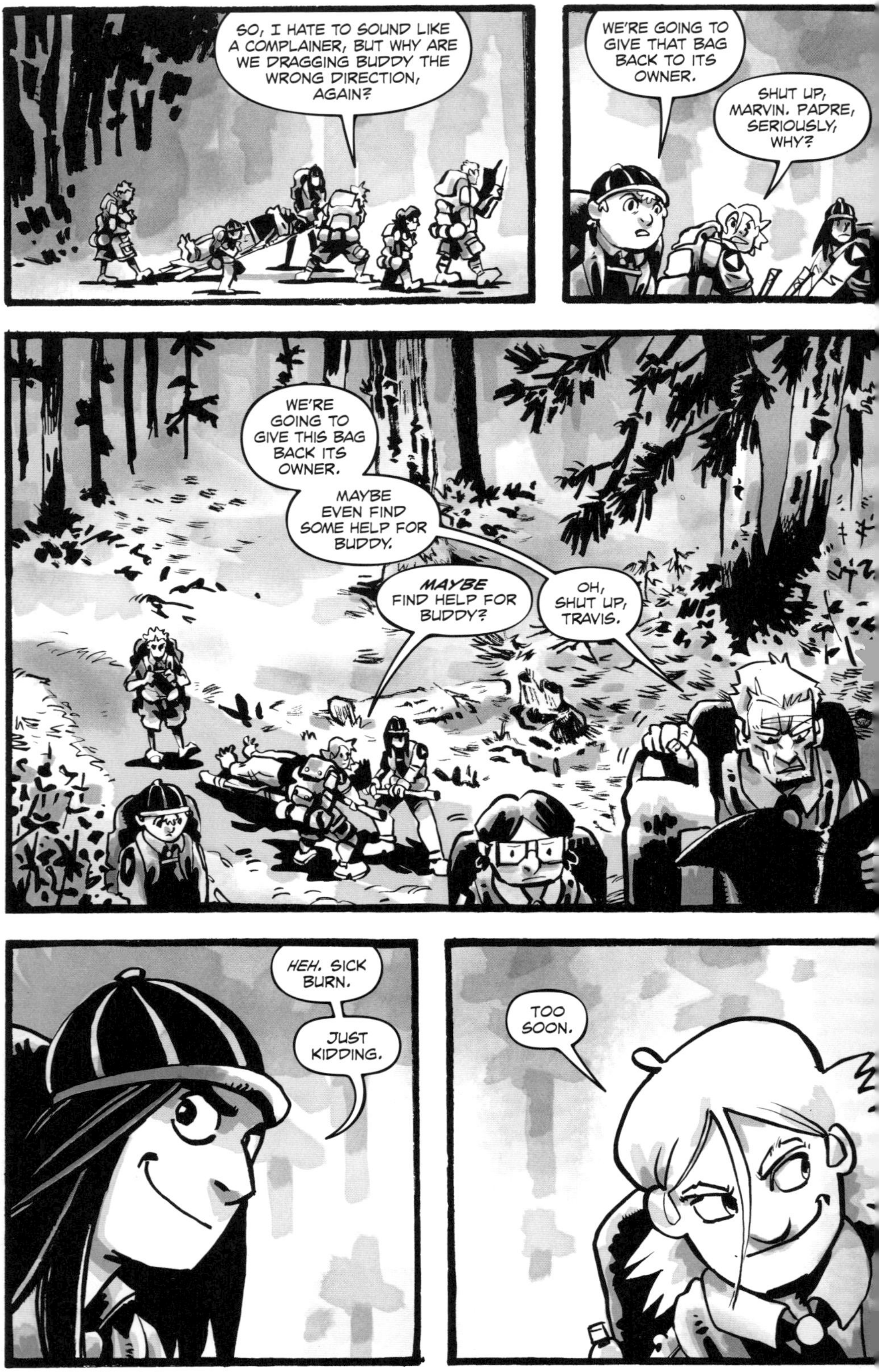

SO, I HATE TO SOUND LIKE A COMPLAINER, BUT WHY ARE WE DRAGGING BUDDY THE WRONG DIRECTION, AGAIN?
WE'RE GOING TO GIVE THAT BAG BACK TO ITS OWNER.
SHUT UP, MARVIN. PADRE, SERIOUSLY, WHY?
WE'RE GOING TO GIVE THIS BAG BACK ITS OWNER.
MAYBE EVEN FIND SOME HELP FOR BUDDY.
MAYBE FIND HELP FOR BUDDY?
OH, SHUT UP, TRAVIS.
HEH. SICK BURN.
JUST KIDDING.
TOO SOON.

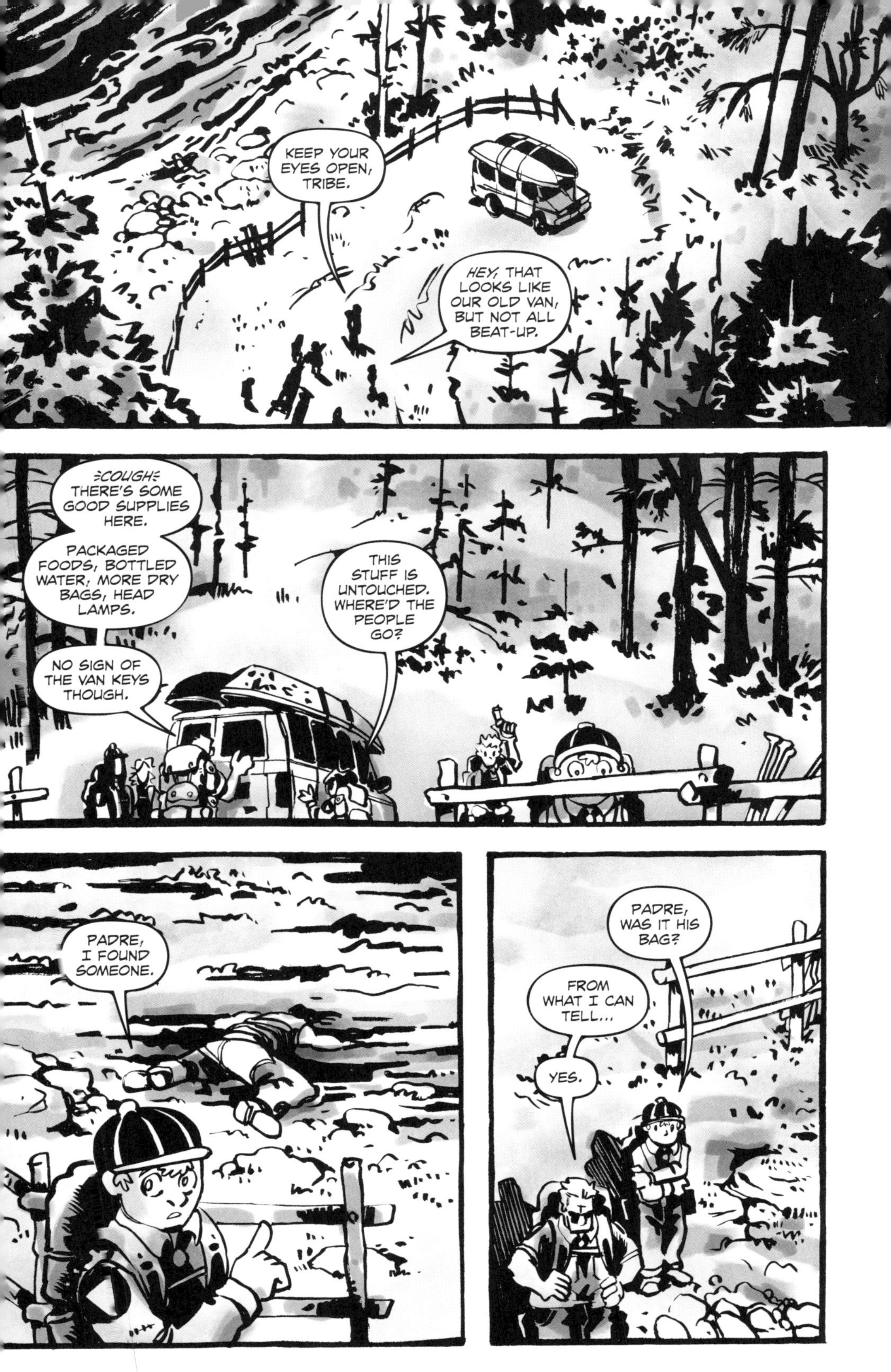
KEEP YOUR EYES OPEN, TRIBE.
HEY, THAT LOOKS LIKE OUR OLD VAN, BUT NOT ALL BEAT-UP.
=COUGH= THERE'S SOME GOOD SUPPLIES HERE.
PACKAGED FOODS, BOTTLED WATER, MORE DRY BAGS, HEAD LAMPS.
NO SIGN OF THE VAN KEYS THOUGH.
THIS STUFF IS UNTOUCHED. WHERE'D THE PEOPLE GO?
PADRE, I FOUND SOMEONE.
PADRE, WAS IT HIS BAG?
FROM WHAT I CAN TELL...
YES.

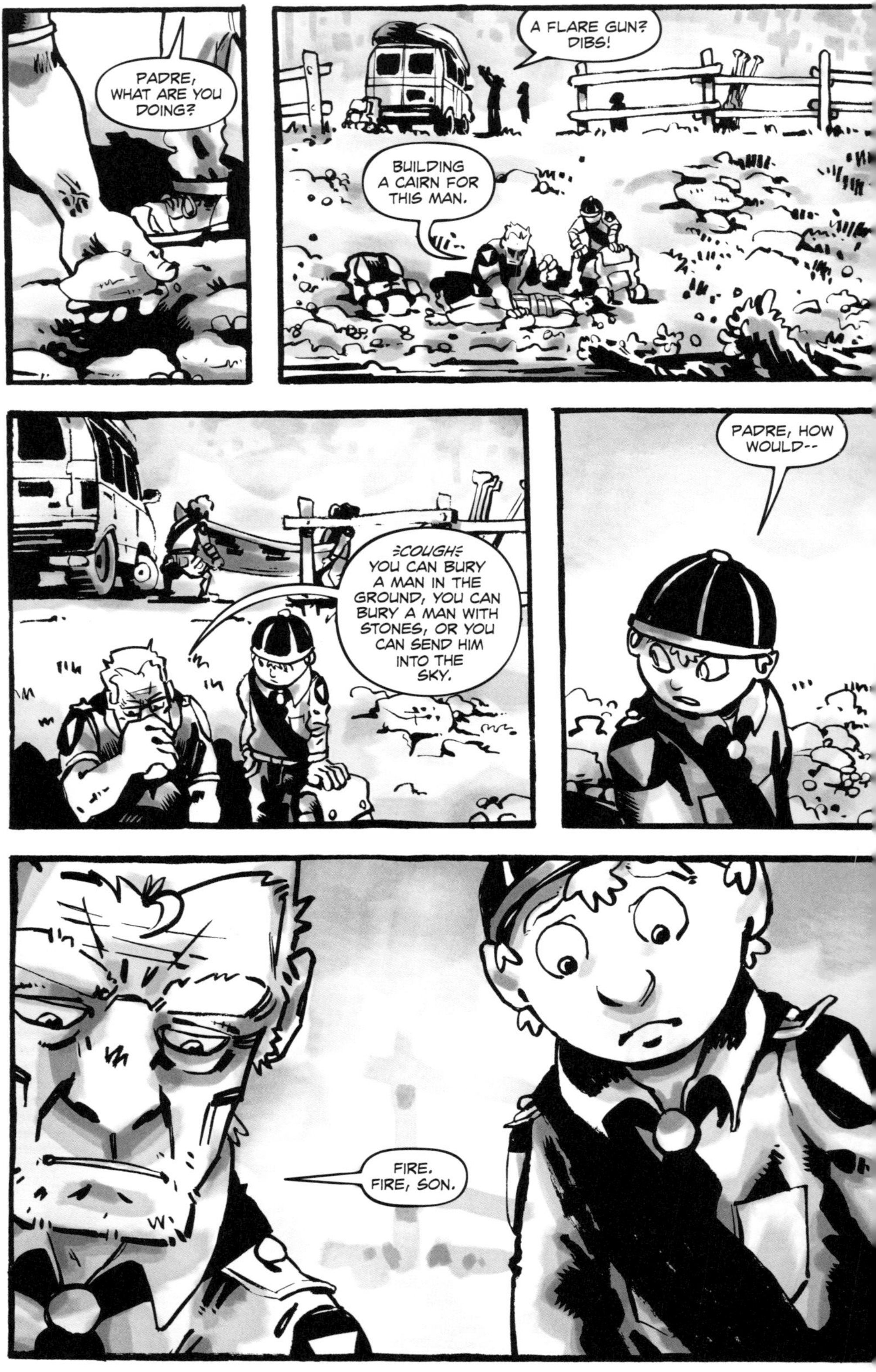
PADRE, WHAT ARE YOU DOING?
A FLARE GUN? DIBS!
BUILDING A CAIRN FOR THIS MAN.
=COUGH= YOU CAN BURY A MAN IN THE GROUND, YOU CAN BURY A MAN WITH STONES, OR YOU CAN SEND HIM INTO THE SKY.
PADRE, HOW WOULD--
FIRE. FIRE, SON.

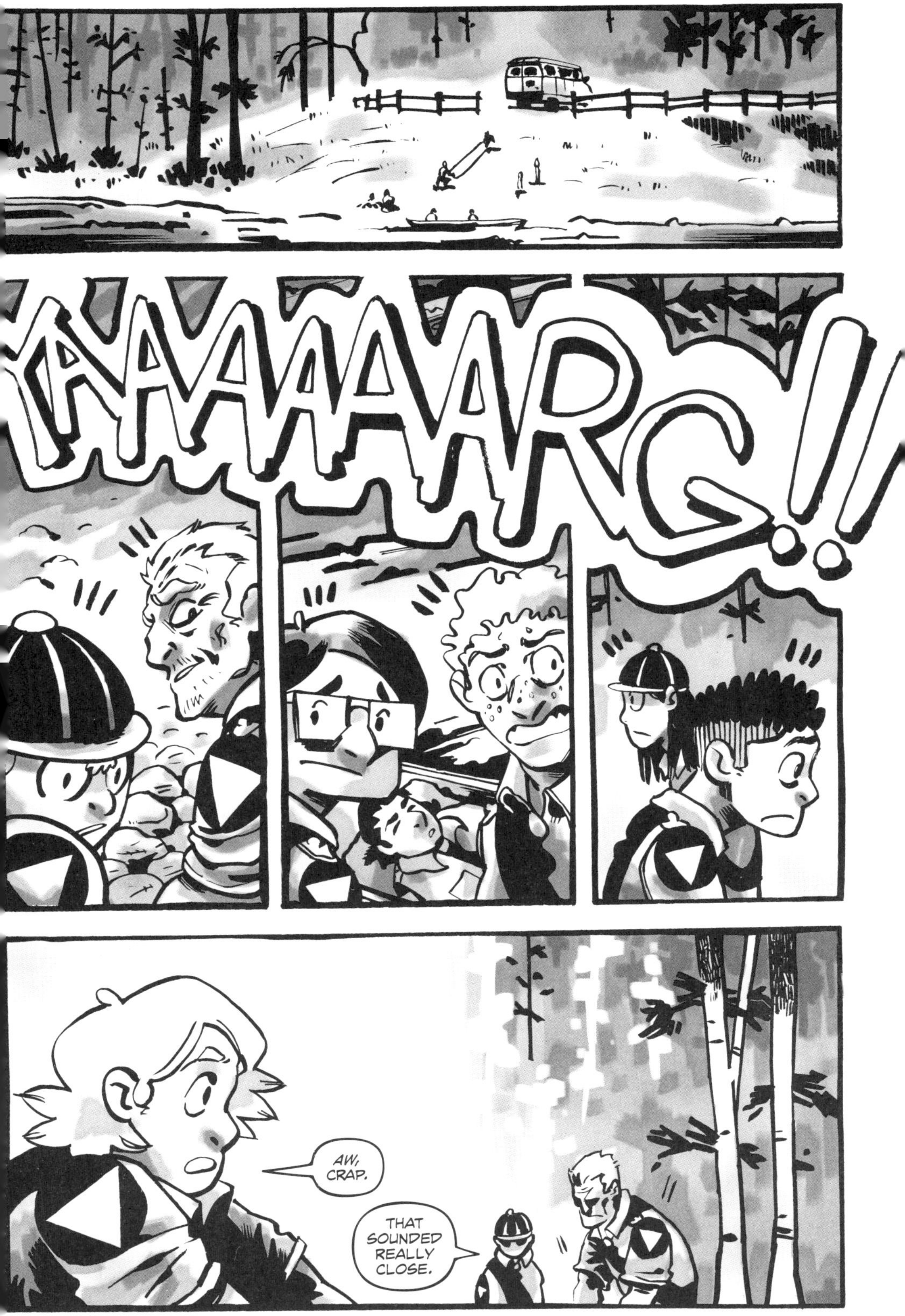
YAAAAARG!!
AW, CRAP.
THAT SOUNDED REALLY CLOSE.

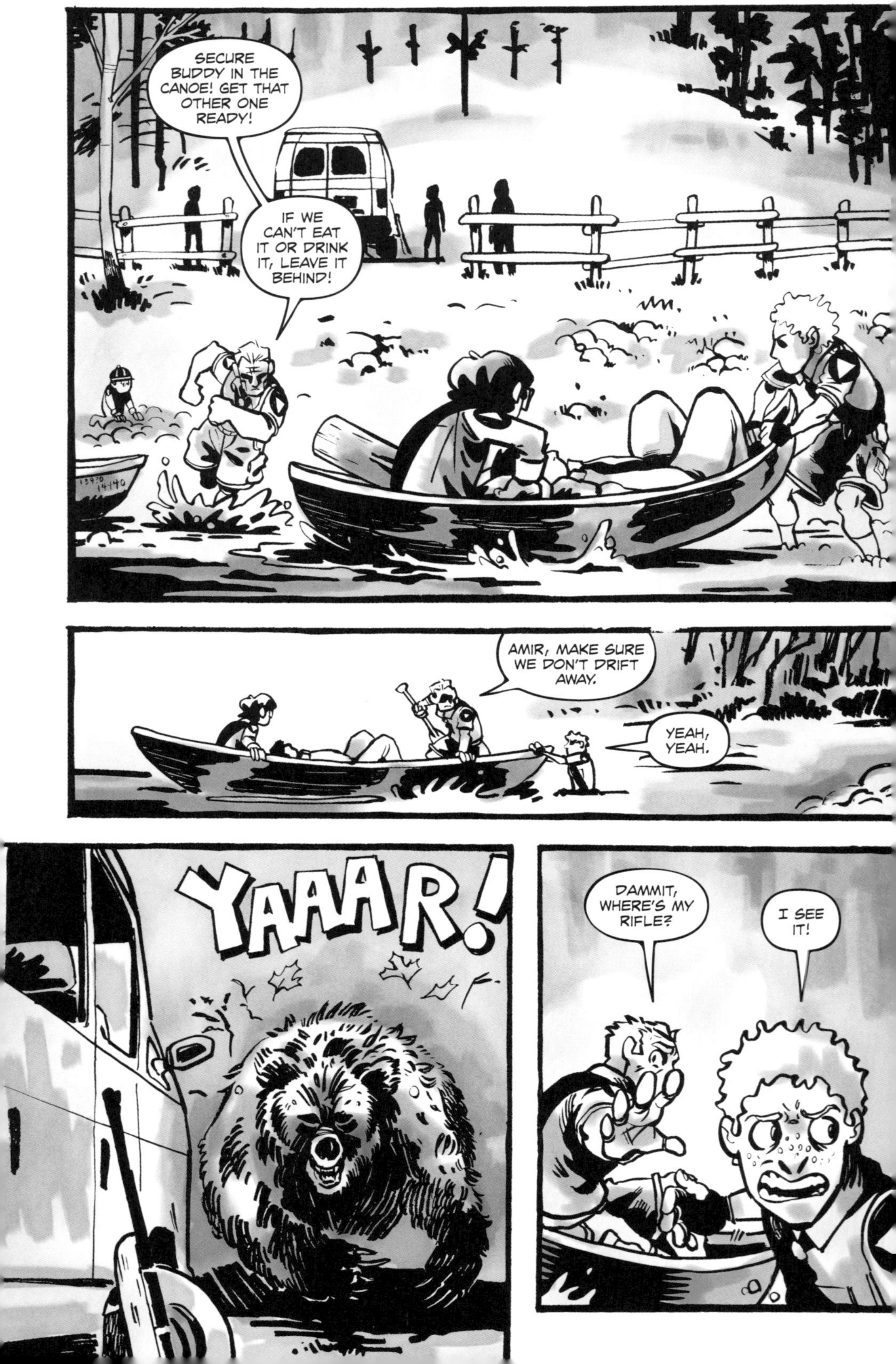
SECURE BUDDY IN THE CANOE! GET THAT OTHER ONE READY!
IF WE CAN'T EAT IT OR DRINK IT, LEAVE IT BEHIND!
AMIR, MAKE SURE WE DON'T DRIFT AWAY.
YEAH, YEAH.
YAAAR!
DAMMIT, WHERE'S MY RIFLE?
I SEE IT!

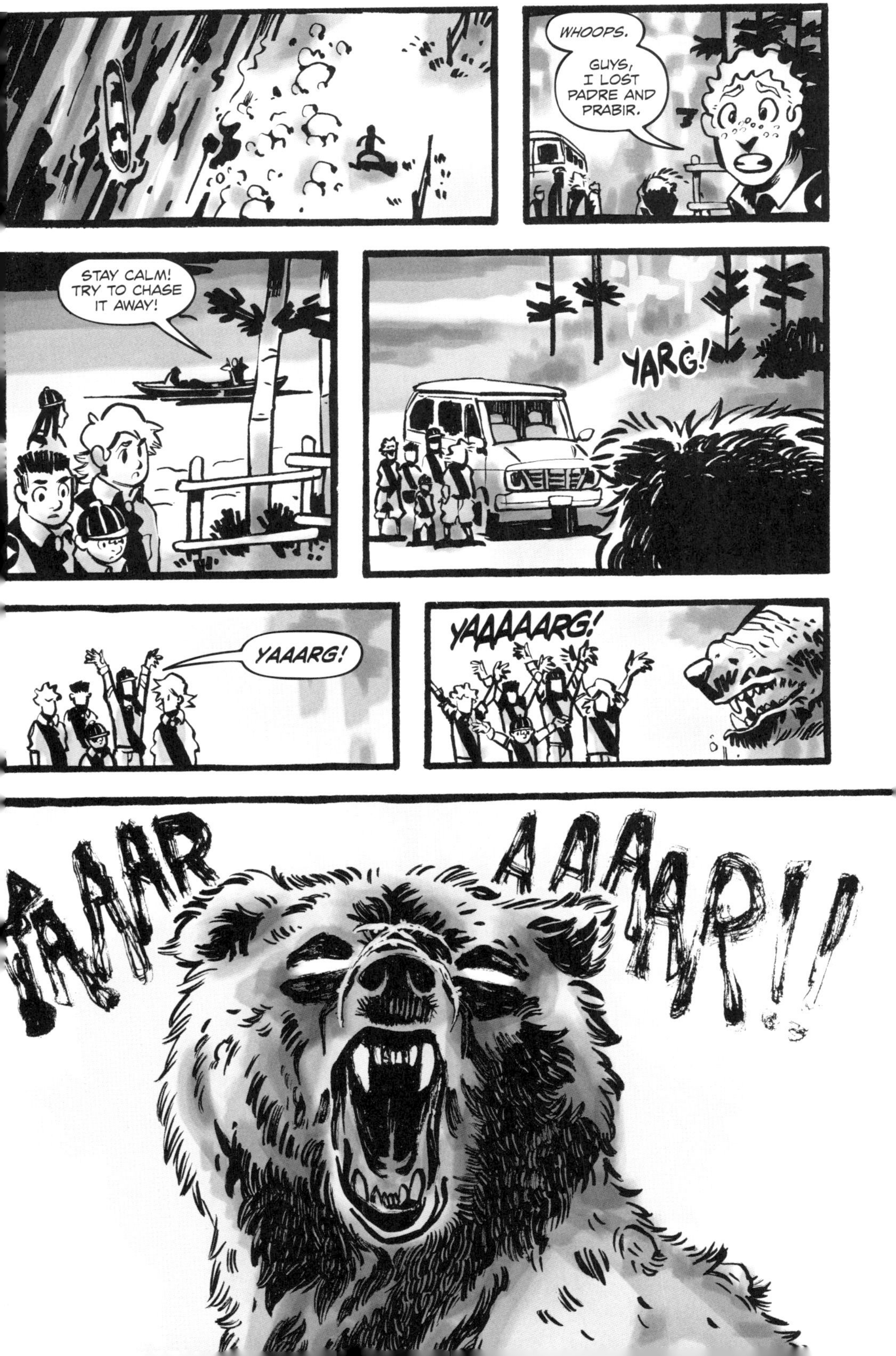
WHOOPS.
GUYS, I LOST PADRE AND PRABIR.
STAY CALM! TRY TO CHASE IT AWAY!
YARG!
YAAARG!
YAAAAARG!
AAAR AAAAR!!

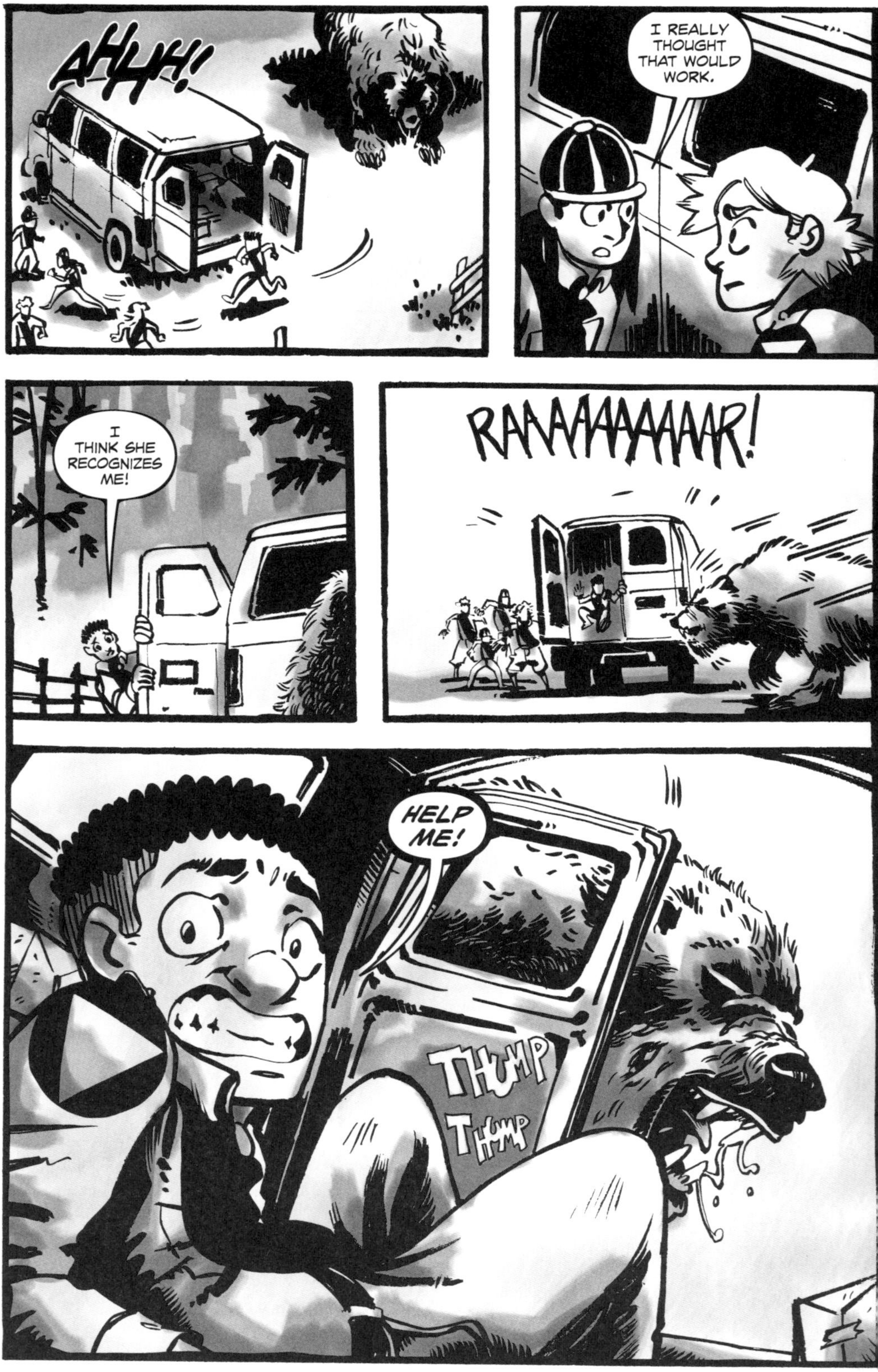
AHHH!
I REALLY THOUGHT THAT WOULD WORK.
I THINK SHE RECOGNIZES ME!
RAAAAAAAAAAR!
HELP ME!
THUMP
THUMP

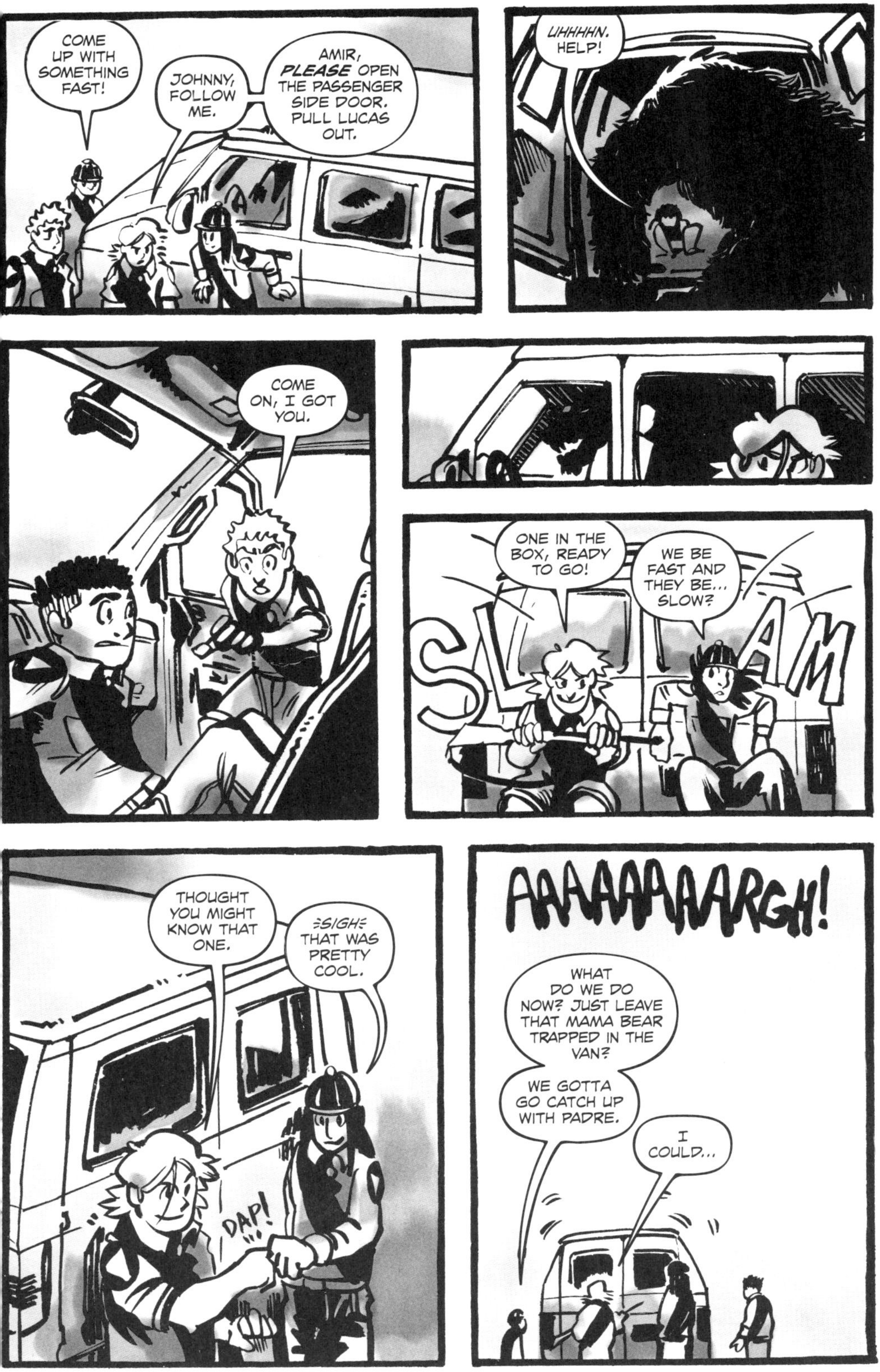
COME UP WITH SOMETHING FAST!
JOHNNY, FOLLOW ME.
AMIR, PLEASE OPEN THE PASSENGER SIDE DOOR. PULL LUCAS OUT.
UHHHHN. HELP!
COME ON, I GOT YOU.
SLAM
ONE IN THE BOX, READY TO GO!
WE BE FAST AND THEY BE... SLOW?
THOUGHT YOU MIGHT KNOW THAT ONE.
SIGH THAT WAS PRETTY COOL.
DAP!
AAAAAAAARGH!
WHAT DO WE DO NOW? JUST LEAVE THAT MAMA BEAR TRAPPED IN THE VAN?
WE GOTTA GO CATCH UP WITH PADRE.
I COULD...

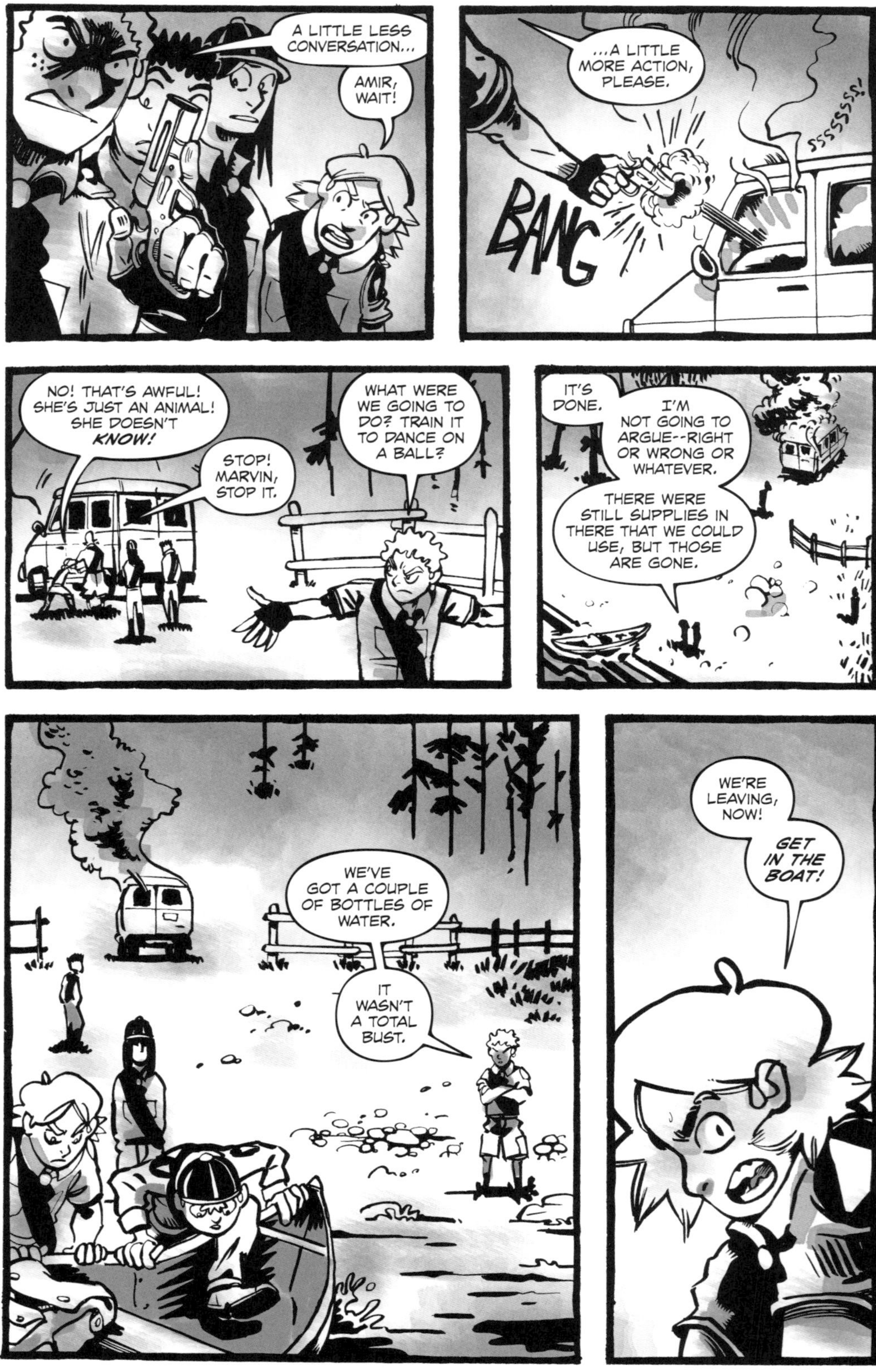
A LITTLE LESS CONVERSATION...
AMIR, WAIT!
...A LITTLE MORE ACTION, PLEASE.
BANG
SSSSSSSS!
NO! THAT'S AWFUL! SHE'S JUST AN ANIMAL! SHE DOESN'T *KNOW!*
STOP! MARVIN, STOP IT.
WHAT WERE WE GOING TO DO? TRAIN IT TO DANCE ON A BALL?
IT'S DONE.
I'M NOT GOING TO ARGUE--RIGHT OR WRONG OR WHATEVER.
THERE WERE STILL SUPPLIES IN THERE THAT WE COULD USE, BUT THOSE ARE GONE.
WE'VE GOT A COUPLE OF BOTTLES OF WATER.
IT WASN'T A TOTAL BUST.
WE'RE LEAVING, NOW!
GET IN THE BOAT!

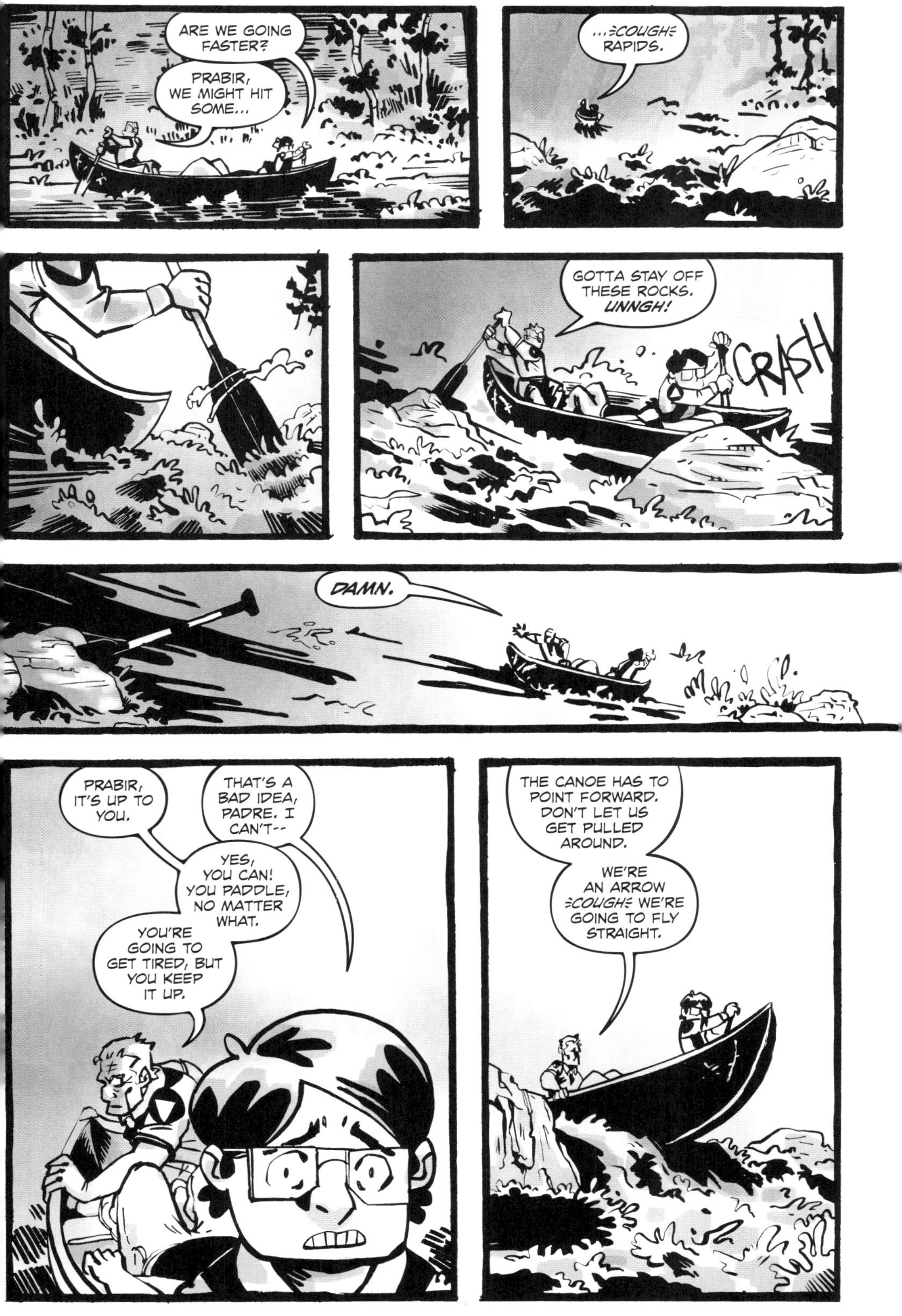
ARE WE GOING FASTER?
PRABIR, WE MIGHT HIT SOME...
...COUGH RAPIDS.
GOTTA STAY OFF THESE ROCKS. UNNGH!
CRASH
DAMN.
PRABIR, IT'S UP TO YOU.
THAT'S A BAD IDEA, PADRE. I CAN'T--
YES, YOU CAN! YOU PADDLE, NO MATTER WHAT.
YOU'RE GOING TO GET TIRED, BUT YOU KEEP IT UP.
THE CANOE HAS TO POINT FORWARD. DON'T LET US GET PULLED AROUND.
WE'RE AN ARROW COUGH WE'RE GOING TO FLY STRAIGHT.

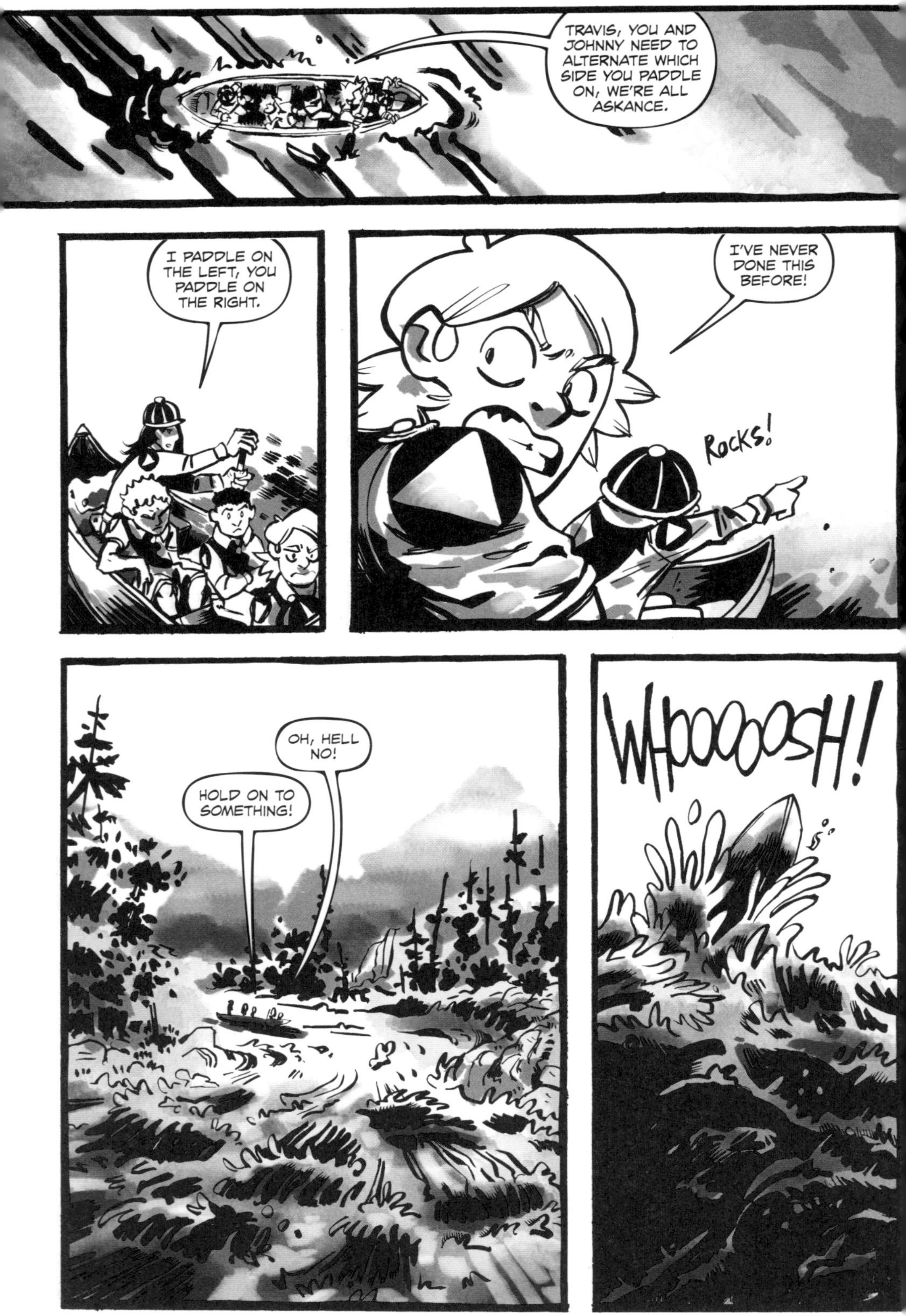
TRAVIS, YOU AND JOHNNY NEED TO ALTERNATE WHICH SIDE YOU PADDLE ON, WE'RE ALL ASKANCE.
I PADDLE ON THE LEFT, YOU PADDLE ON THE RIGHT.
I'VE NEVER DONE THIS BEFORE!
ROCKS!
OH, HELL NO!
HOLD ON TO SOMETHING!
WHOOOOOSH!

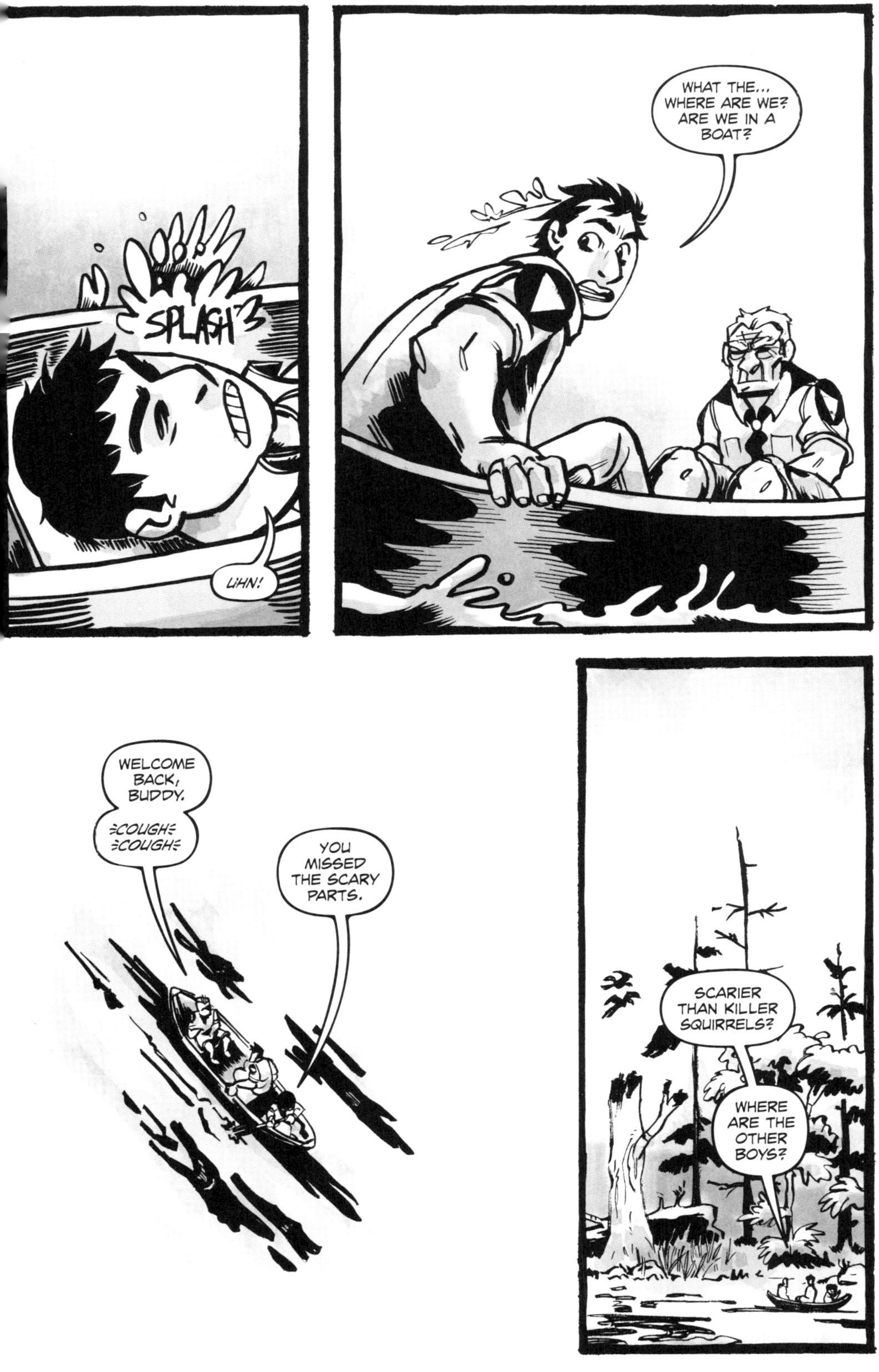
SPLASH
UHN!
WHAT THE... WHERE ARE WE? ARE WE IN A BOAT?
WELCOME BACK, BUDDY.
COUGH COUGH
YOU MISSED THE SCARY PARTS.
SCARIER THAN KILLER SQUIRRELS?
WHERE ARE THE OTHER BOYS?

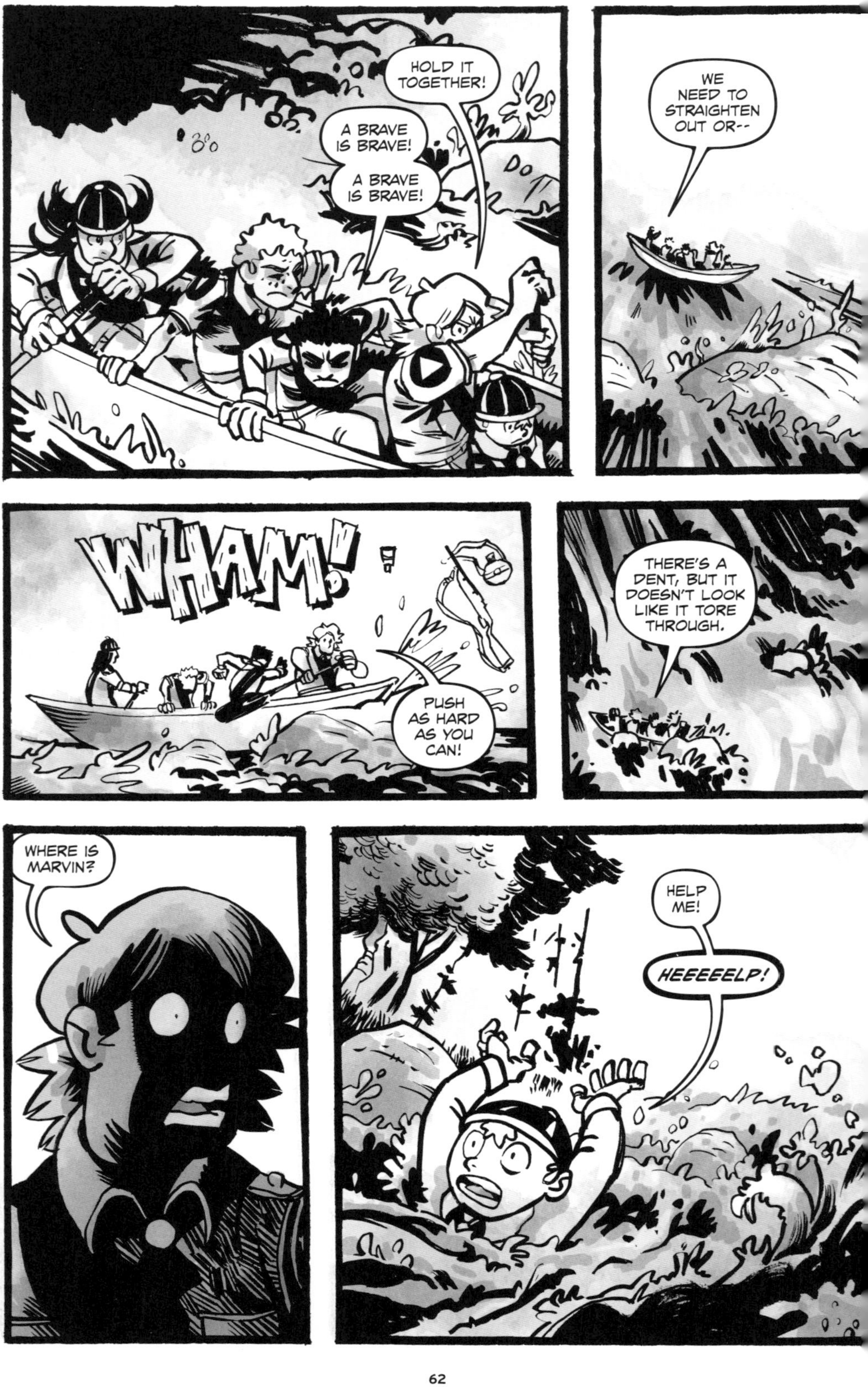
HOLD IT TOGETHER!
A BRAVE IS BRAVE!
A BRAVE IS BRAVE!
WE NEED TO STRAIGHTEN OUT OR--
WHAM!
PUSH AS HARD AS YOU CAN!
THERE'S A DENT, BUT IT DOESN'T LOOK LIKE IT TORE THROUGH.
WHERE IS MARVIN?
HELP ME!
HEEEEELP!

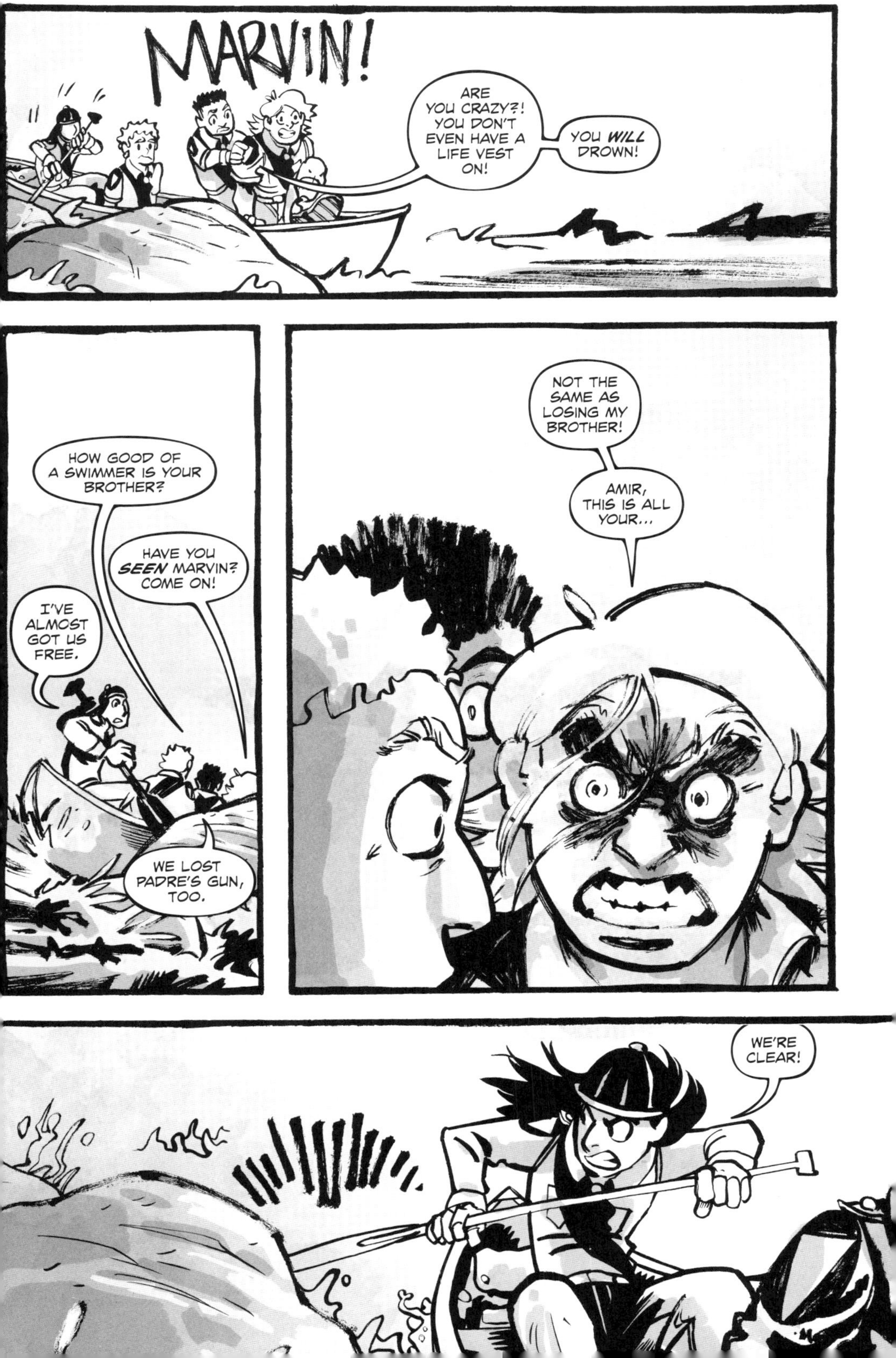
MARVIN!
ARE YOU CRAZY?! YOU DON'T EVEN HAVE A LIFE VEST ON!
YOU WILL DROWN!
HOW GOOD OF A SWIMMER IS YOUR BROTHER?
HAVE YOU SEEN MARVIN? COME ON!
I'VE ALMOST GOT US FREE.
WE LOST PADRE'S GUN, TOO.
NOT THE SAME AS LOSING MY BROTHER!
AMIR, THIS IS ALL YOUR...
WE'RE CLEAR!

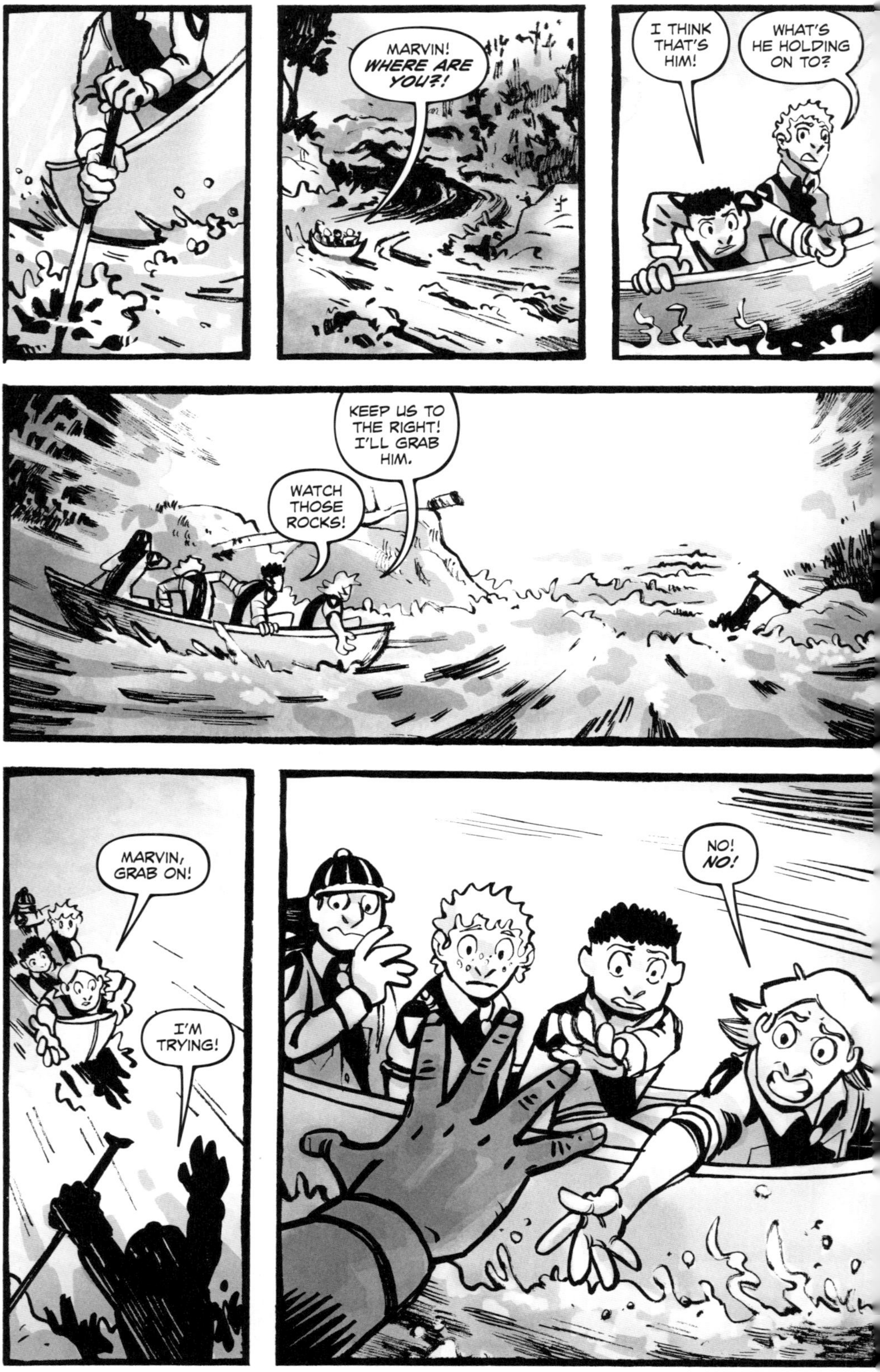
MARVIN! WHERE ARE YOU?!
I THINK THAT'S HIM!
WHAT'S HE HOLDING ON TO?
WATCH THOSE ROCKS!
KEEP US TO THE RIGHT! I'LL GRAB HIM.
MARVIN, GRAB ON!
I'M TRYING!
NO! NO!

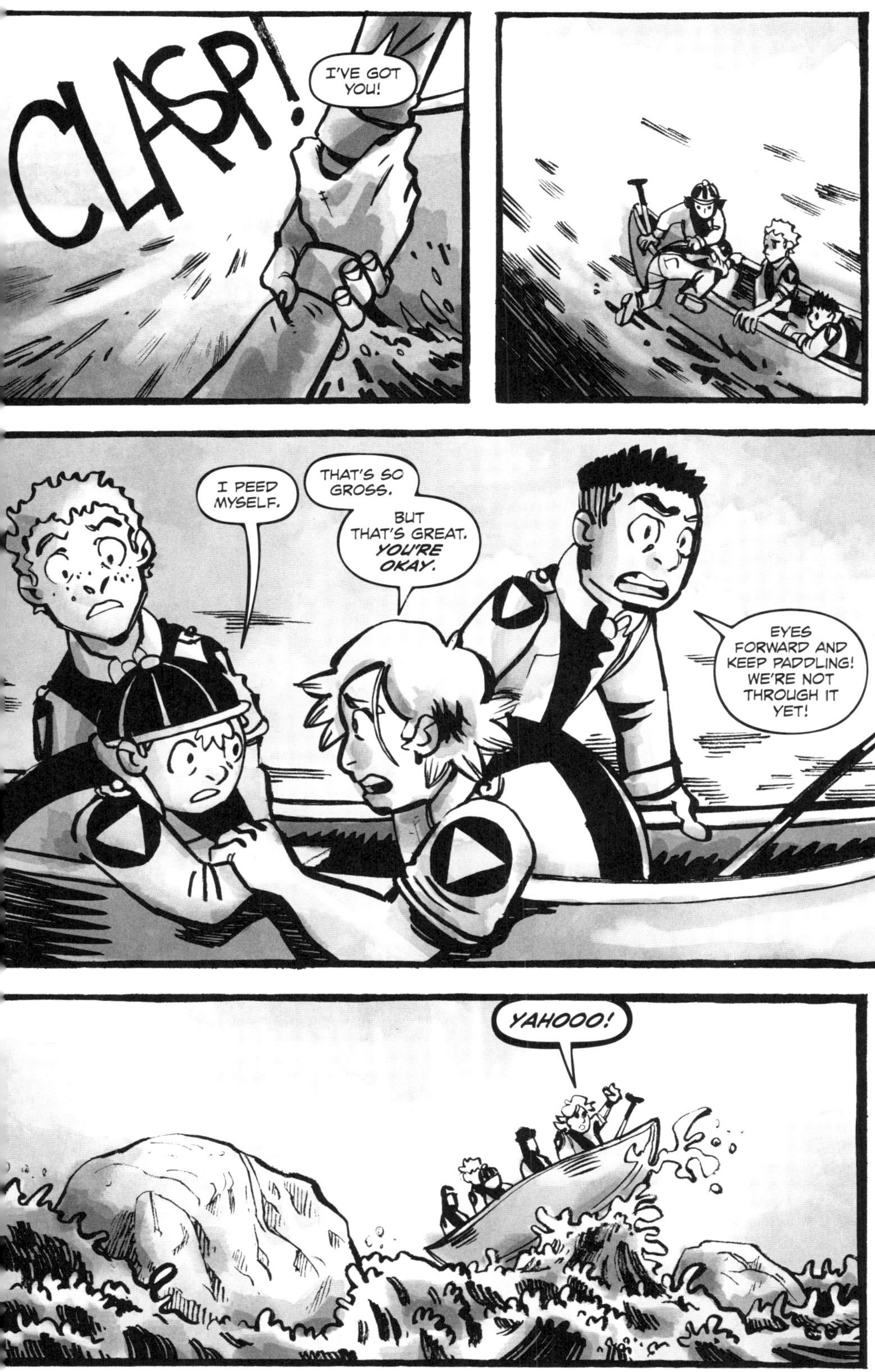
CLASP!
I'VE GOT YOU!
I PEED MYSELF.
THAT'S SO GROSS.
BUT THAT'S GREAT. *YOU'RE OKAY.*
EYES FORWARD AND KEEP PADDLING! WE'RE NOT THROUGH IT YET!
YAHOOO!

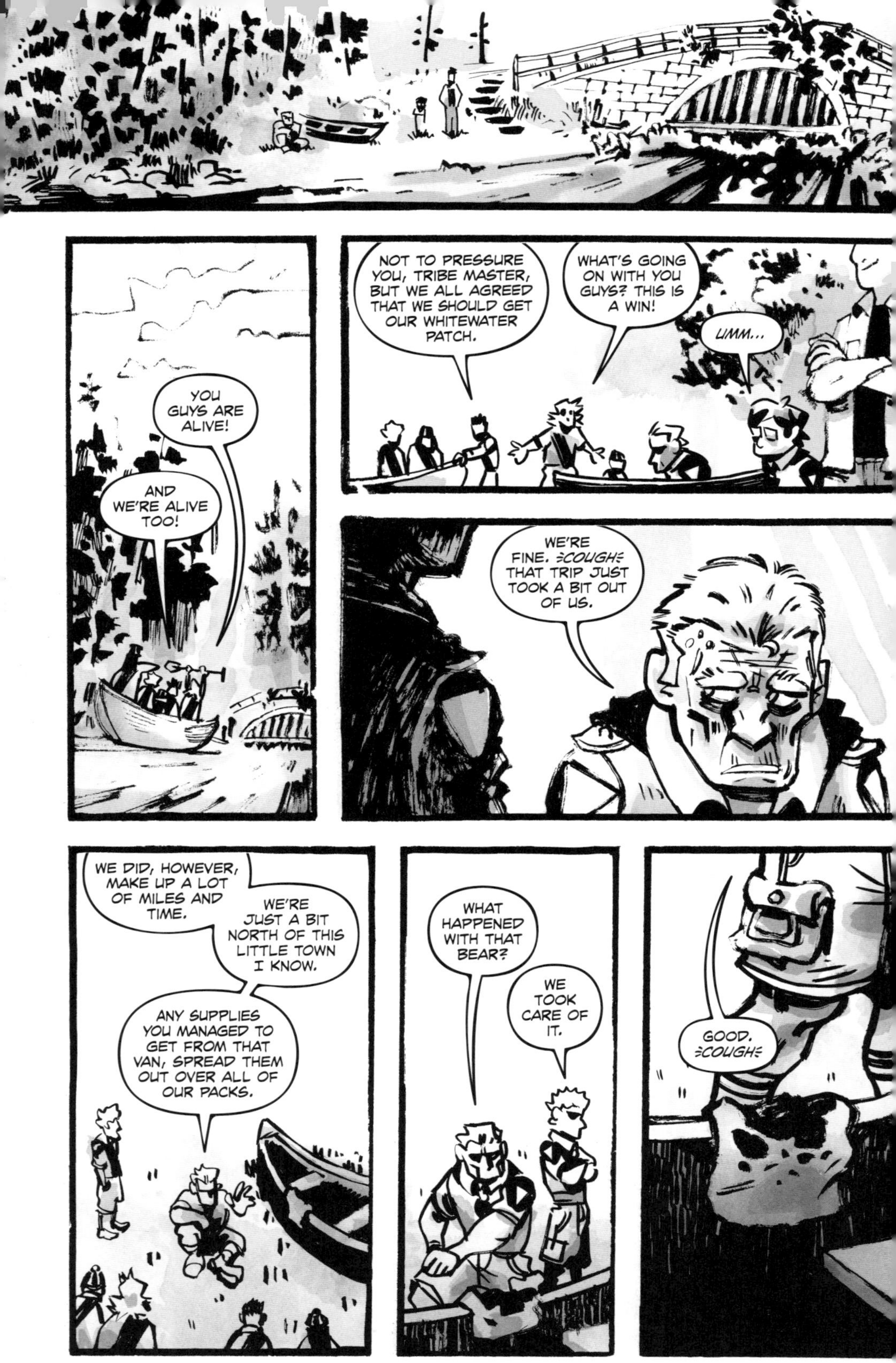
YOU GUYS ARE ALIVE!
AND WE'RE ALIVE TOO!
NOT TO PRESSURE YOU, TRIBE MASTER, BUT WE ALL AGREED THAT WE SHOULD GET OUR WHITEWATER PATCH.
WHAT'S GOING ON WITH YOU GUYS? THIS IS A WIN!
UMM...
WE'RE FINE. =COUGH= THAT TRIP JUST TOOK A BIT OUT OF US.
WE DID, HOWEVER, MAKE UP A LOT OF MILES AND TIME.
WE'RE JUST A BIT NORTH OF THIS LITTLE TOWN I KNOW.
ANY SUPPLIES YOU MANAGED TO GET FROM THAT VAN, SPREAD THEM OUT OVER ALL OF OUR PACKS.
WHAT HAPPENED WITH THAT BEAR?
WE TOOK CARE OF IT.
GOOD. =COUGH=

WATER & RAFTING SAFETY

Being out on the water can be exciting, relaxing, or even a practical means of travel, but a Junior Brave must know and follow these basic water and rafting safety rules

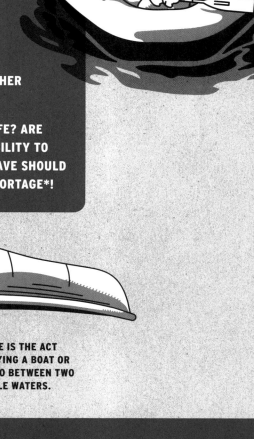

X   GO RAFTING ONLY WITH AN ADULT.

X   OUR TRIBE MASTER SHOULD BE PRESENT FOR ANY OFFICIAL JUNIOR BRAVES AQUATIC ADVENTURE.

X   DON'T OVERLOAD THE RAFT.

X   ALWAYS WEAR A LIFE-JACKET.

X   BALANCE YOUR LOAD.

X   DISTRIBUTE WEIGHT EVENLY FROM BOW TO STERN AND SIDE TO SIDE.

X   STAY IN THE RAFT, EVEN IF IT LEAKS. IT WILL STILL KEEP YOU AFLOAT.

X   FOLLOW THE PROPER CATCH-PULL-FEATHER OARING TECHNIQUE.

X   DOES THE WATER AHEAD APPEAR UNSAFE? ARE YOU NO LONGER CONFIDENT IN YOUR ABILITY TO TRAVEL SAFELY? WHEN IN DOUBT, A BRAVE SHOULD STOP AND SCOUT. IF DOUBT REMAINS, PORTAGE*!

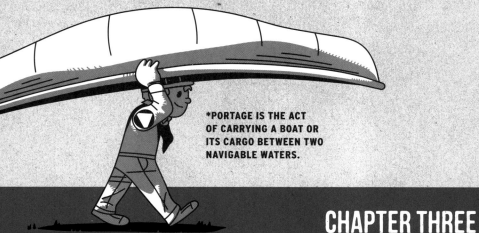

*PORTAGE IS THE ACT OF CARRYING A BOAT OR ITS CARGO BETWEEN TWO NAVIGABLE WATERS.

CHAPTER THREE

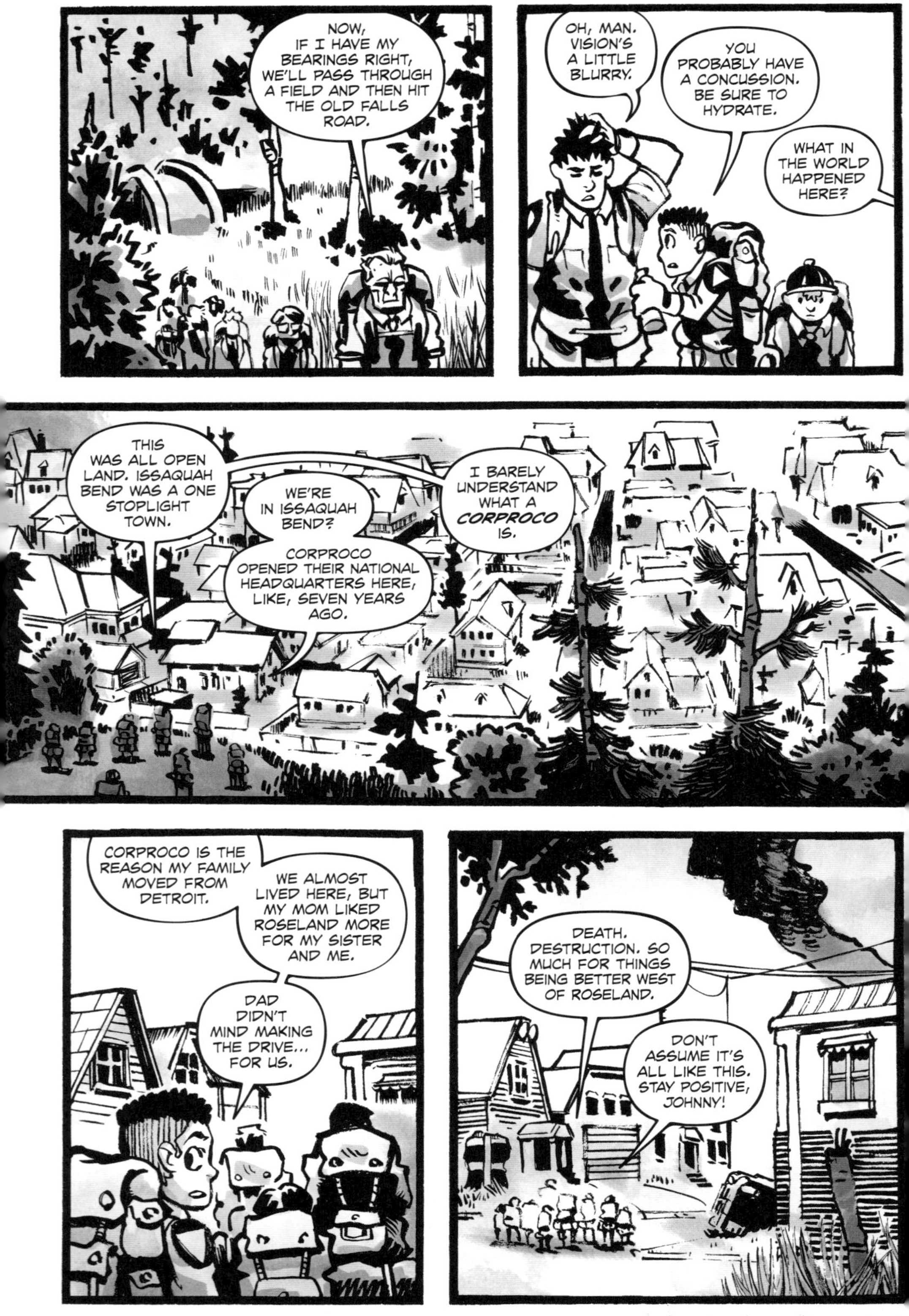
NOW, IF I HAVE MY BEARINGS RIGHT, WE'LL PASS THROUGH A FIELD AND THEN HIT THE OLD FALLS ROAD.
OH, MAN. VISION'S A LITTLE BLURRY.
YOU PROBABLY HAVE A CONCUSSION. BE SURE TO HYDRATE.
WHAT IN THE WORLD HAPPENED HERE?
THIS WAS ALL OPEN LAND. ISSAQUAH BEND WAS A ONE STOPLIGHT TOWN.
I BARELY UNDERSTAND WHAT A *CORPROCO* IS.
WE'RE IN ISSAQUAH BEND?
CORPROCO OPENED THEIR NATIONAL HEADQUARTERS HERE, LIKE, SEVEN YEARS AGO.
CORPROCO IS THE REASON MY FAMILY MOVED FROM DETROIT.
WE ALMOST LIVED HERE, BUT MY MOM LIKED ROSELAND MORE FOR MY SISTER AND ME.
DAD DIDN'T MIND MAKING THE DRIVE... FOR US.
DEATH. DESTRUCTION. SO MUCH FOR THINGS BEING BETTER WEST OF ROSELAND.
DON'T ASSUME IT'S ALL LIKE THIS. STAY POSITIVE, JOHNNY!

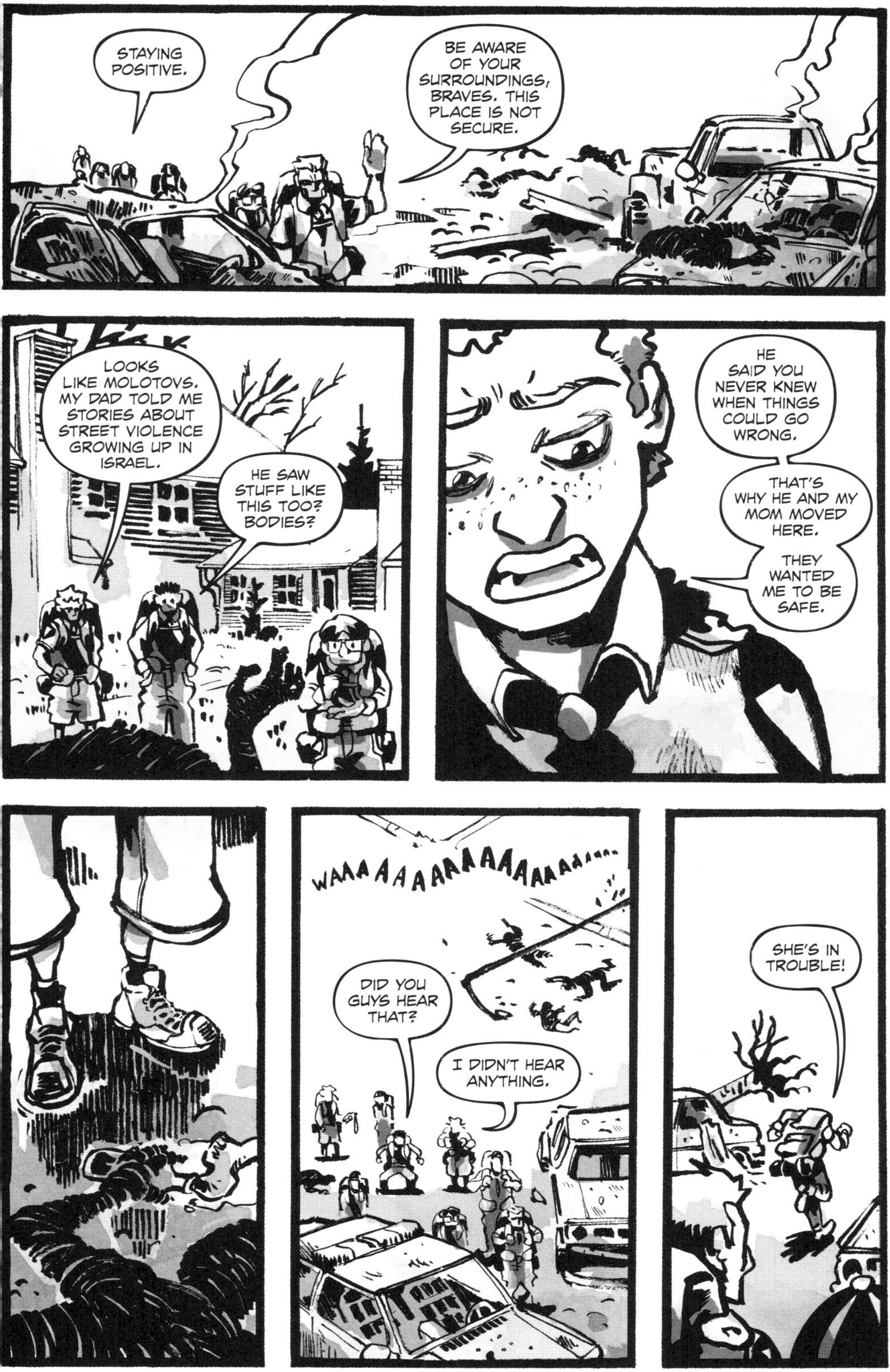
STAYING POSITIVE.
BE AWARE OF YOUR SURROUNDINGS, BRAVES. THIS PLACE IS NOT SECURE.
LOOKS LIKE MOLOTOVS. MY DAD TOLD ME STORIES ABOUT STREET VIOLENCE GROWING UP IN ISRAEL.
HE SAW STUFF LIKE THIS TOO? BODIES?
HE SAID YOU NEVER KNEW WHEN THINGS COULD GO WRONG.
THAT'S WHY HE AND MY MOM MOVED HERE.
THEY WANTED ME TO BE SAFE.
WAAAAAAAAAAAAAAAaaa...
DID YOU GUYS HEAR THAT?
I DIDN'T HEAR ANYTHING.
SHE'S IN TROUBLE!

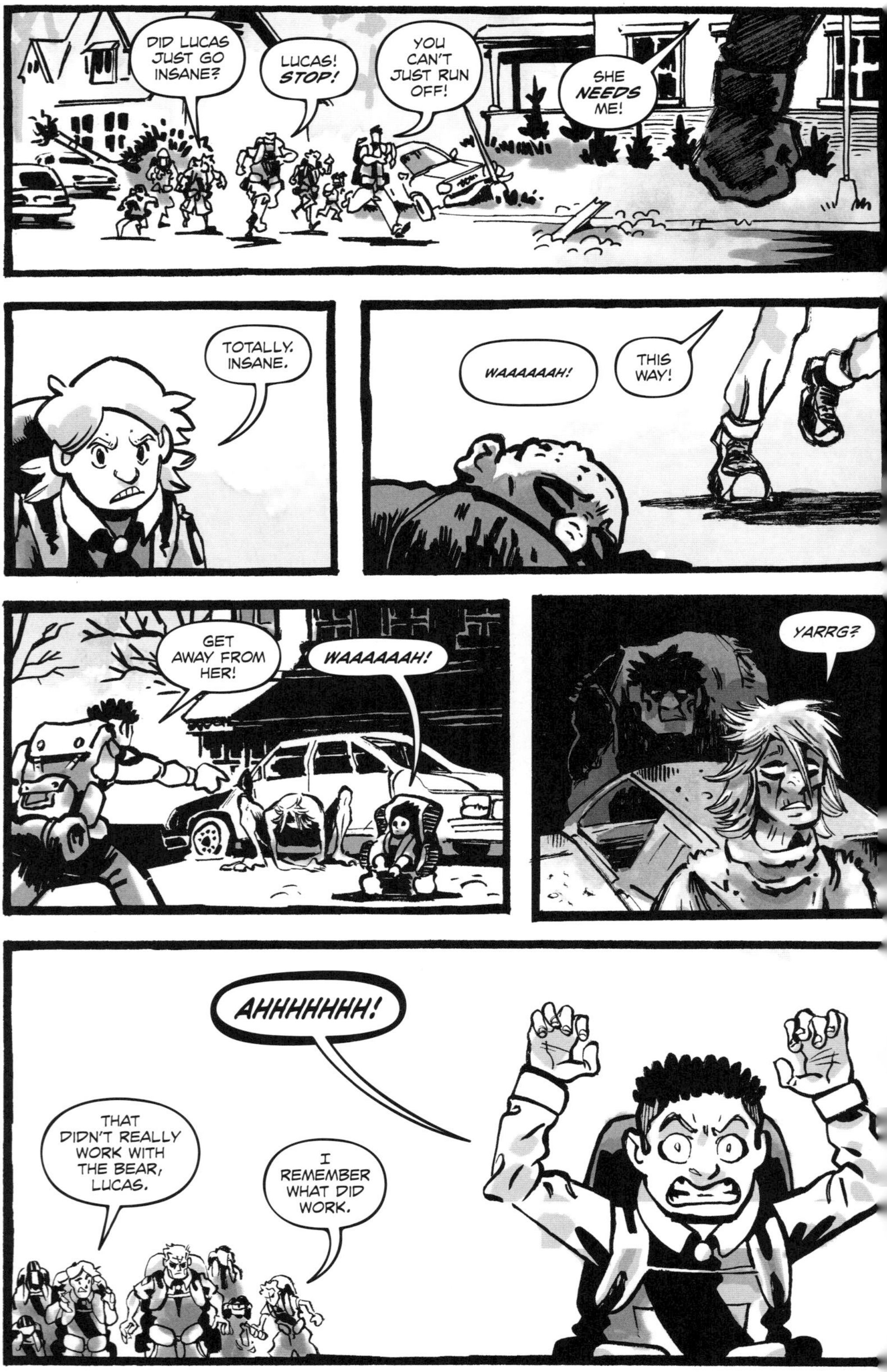
DID LUCAS JUST GO INSANE?
LUCAS! STOP!
YOU CAN'T JUST RUN OFF!
SHE NEEDS ME!
TOTALLY. INSANE.
WAAAAAAH!
THIS WAY!
GET AWAY FROM HER!
WAAAAAAH!
YARRG?
AHHHHHHH!
THAT DIDN'T REALLY WORK WITH THE BEAR, LUCAS.
I REMEMBER WHAT DID WORK.

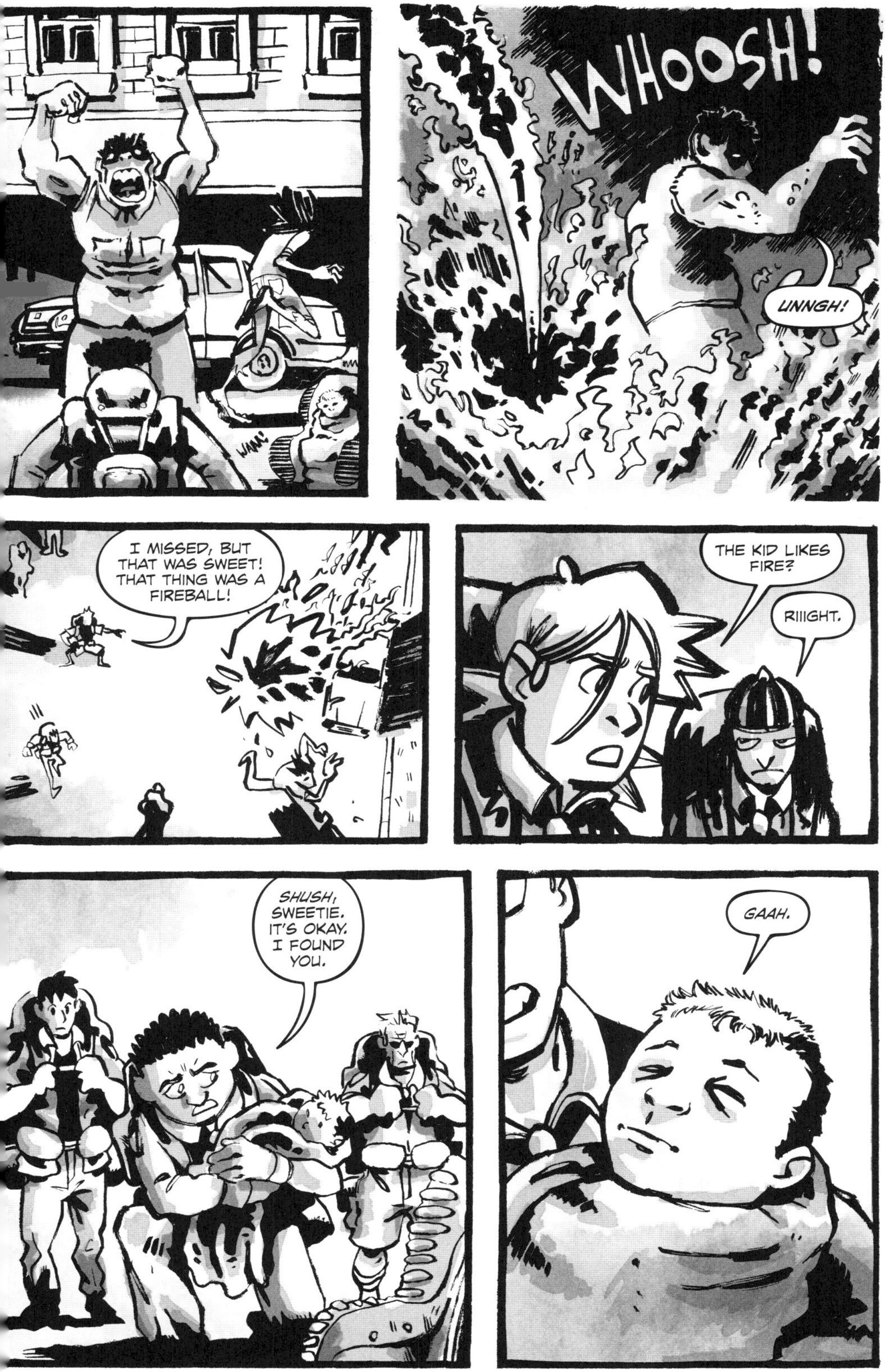
WHOOSH!
UNNGH!
I MISSED, BUT THAT WAS SWEET! THAT THING WAS A FIREBALL!
THE KID LIKES FIRE?
RIIIGHT.
SHUSH, SWEETIE. IT'S OKAY. I FOUND YOU.
GAAH.

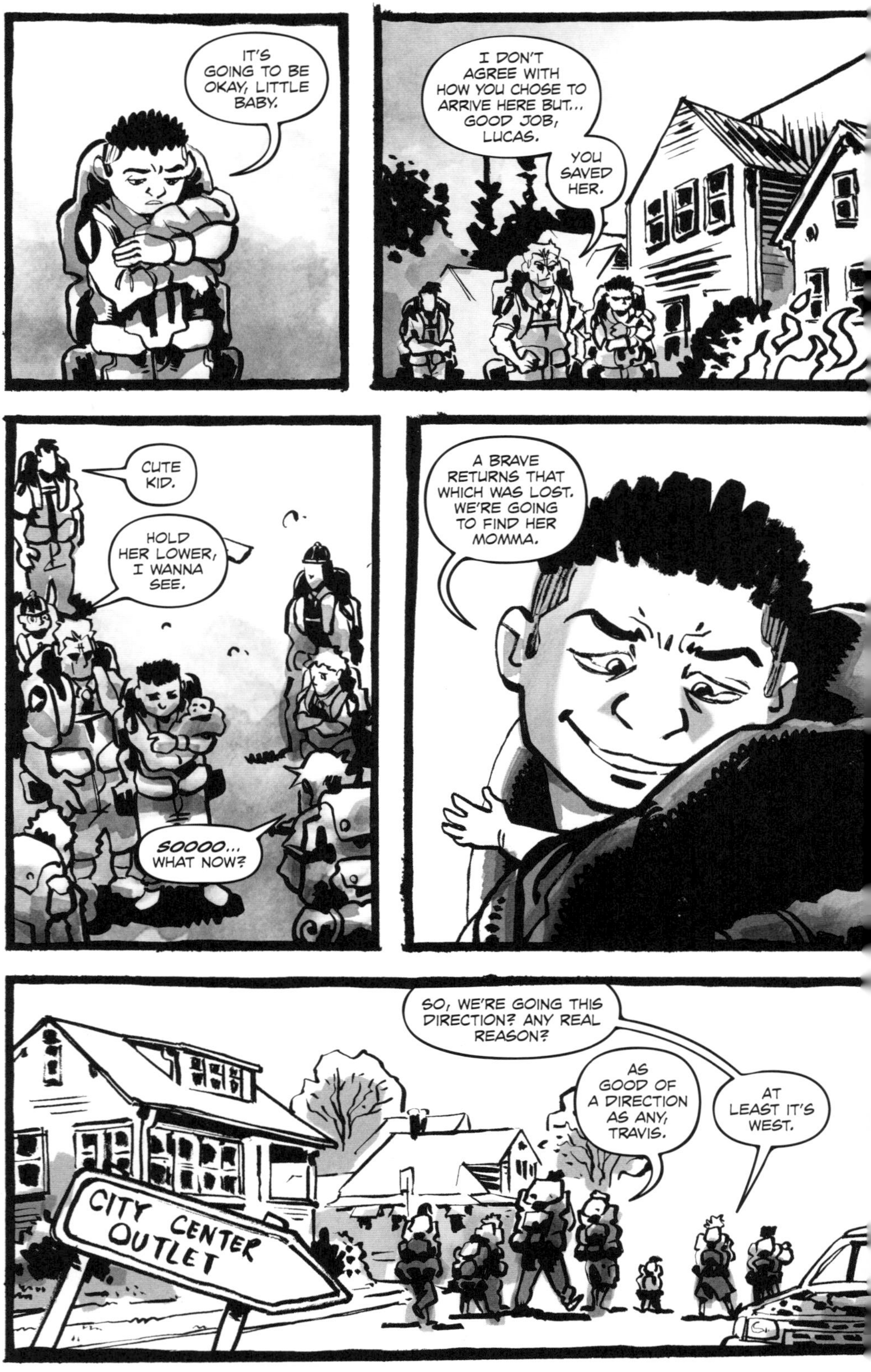
IT'S GOING TO BE OKAY, LITTLE BABY.
I DON'T AGREE WITH HOW YOU CHOSE TO ARRIVE HERE BUT... GOOD JOB, LUCAS.
YOU SAVED HER.
CUTE KID.
HOLD HER LOWER, I WANNA SEE.
SOOOO... WHAT NOW?
A BRAVE RETURNS THAT WHICH WAS LOST. WE'RE GOING TO FIND HER MOMMA.
CITY CENTER OUTLET
SO, WE'RE GOING THIS DIRECTION? ANY REAL REASON?
AS GOOD OF A DIRECTION AS ANY, TRAVIS.
AT LEAST IT'S WEST.

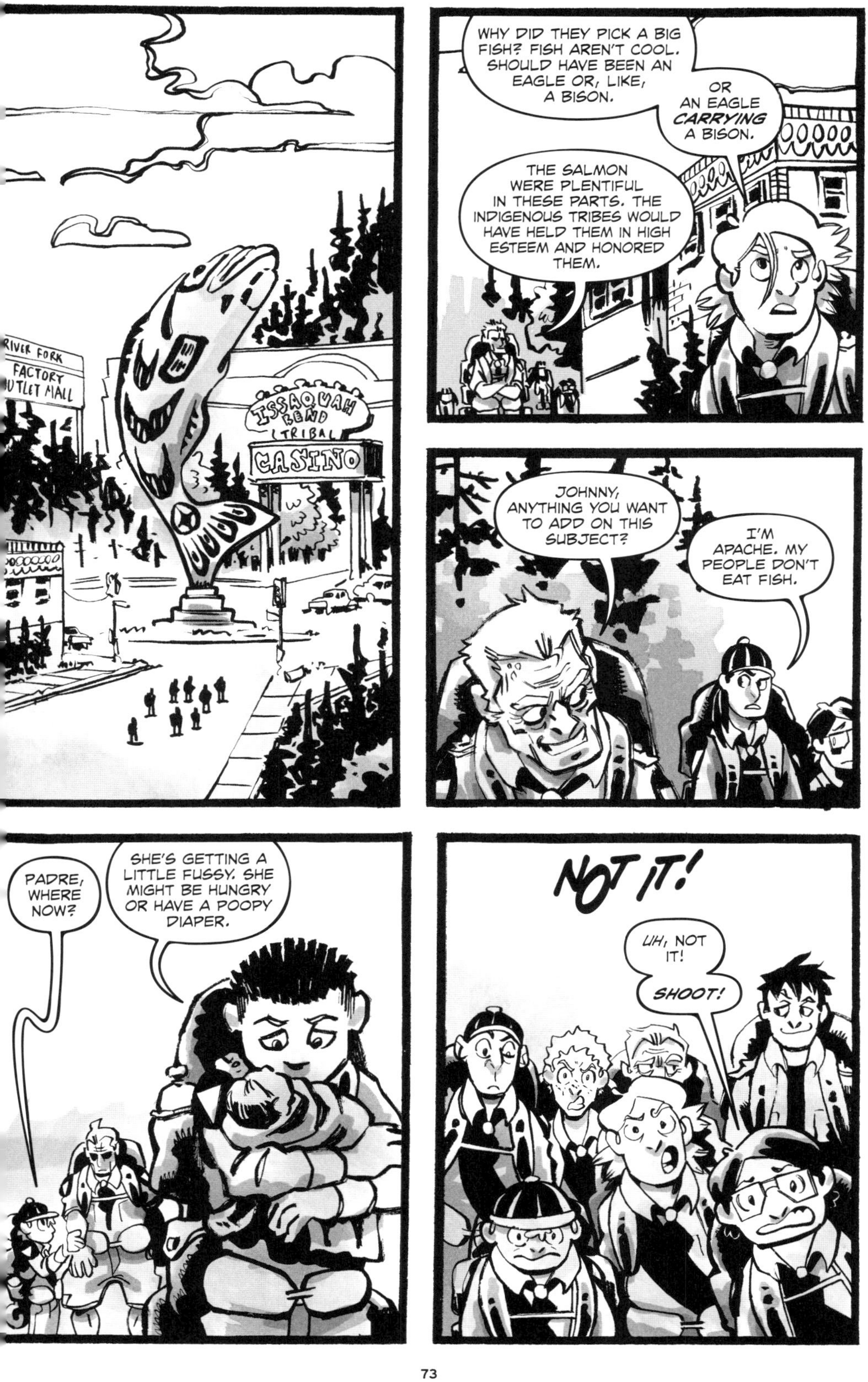
RIVER FORK
FACTORY
OUTLET MALL
ISSAQUAH BEND
TRIBAL
CASINO
WHY DID THEY PICK A BIG FISH? FISH AREN'T COOL. SHOULD HAVE BEEN AN EAGLE OR, LIKE, A BISON.
OR AN EAGLE *CARRYING* A BISON.
THE SALMON WERE PLENTIFUL IN THESE PARTS. THE INDIGENOUS TRIBES WOULD HAVE HELD THEM IN HIGH ESTEEM AND HONORED THEM.
JOHNNY, ANYTHING YOU WANT TO ADD ON THIS SUBJECT?
I'M APACHE. MY PEOPLE DON'T EAT FISH.
PADRE, WHERE NOW?
SHE'S GETTING A LITTLE FUSSY. SHE MIGHT BE HUNGRY OR HAVE A POOPY DIAPER.
NOT IT!
UH, NOT IT!
SHOOT!

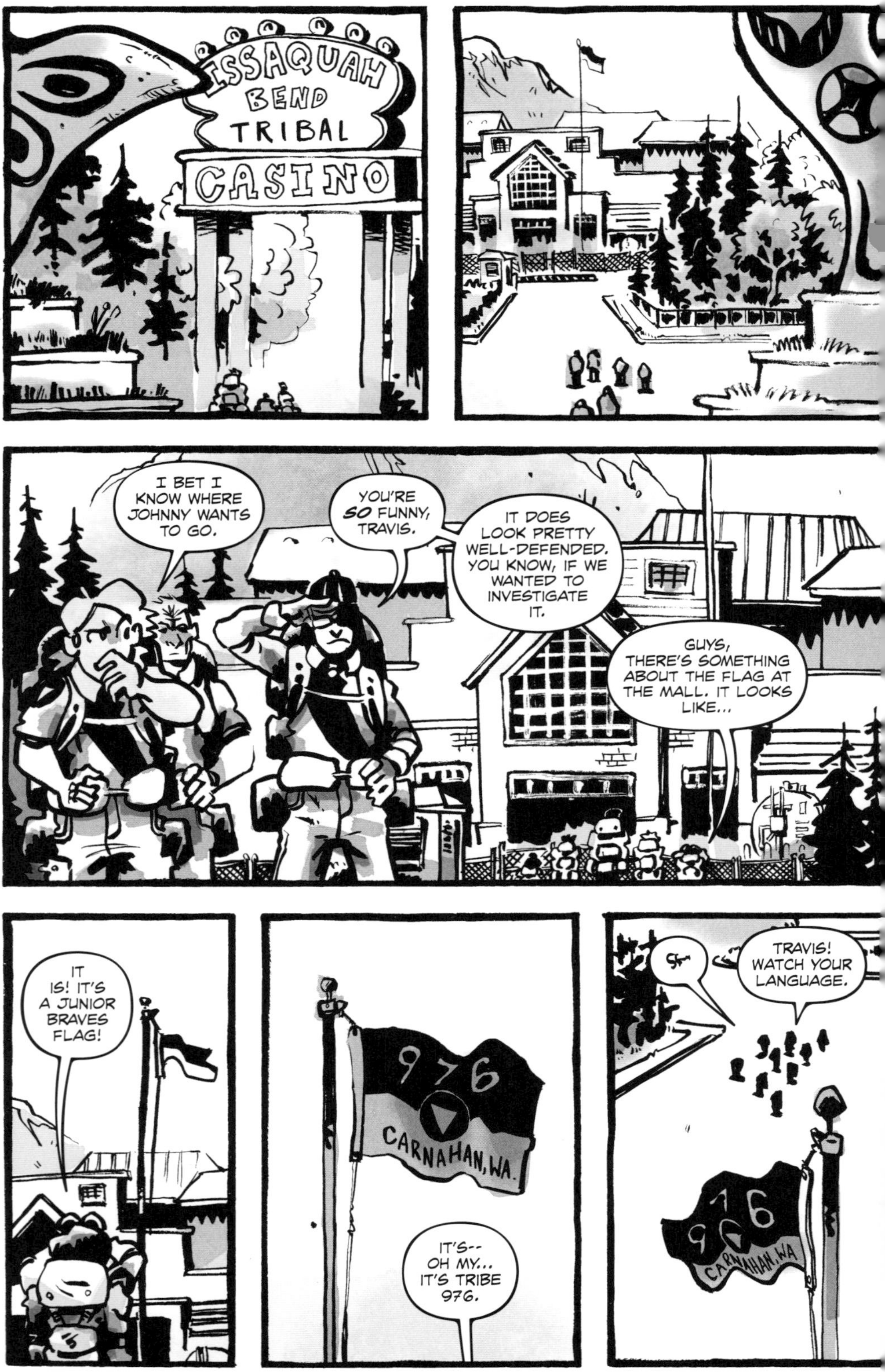
ISSAQUAH BEND TRIBAL CASINO
I BET I KNOW WHERE JOHNNY WANTS TO GO.
YOU'RE *SO* FUNNY, TRAVIS.
IT DOES LOOK PRETTY WELL-DEFENDED. YOU KNOW, IF WE WANTED TO INVESTIGATE IT.
GUYS, THERE'S SOMETHING ABOUT THE FLAG AT THE MALL. IT LOOKS LIKE...
IT IS! IT'S A JUNIOR BRAVES FLAG!
976
CARNAHAN, WA.
IT'S-- OH MY... IT'S TRIBE 976.
TRAVIS! WATCH YOUR LANGUAGE.
976
CARNAHAN, WA

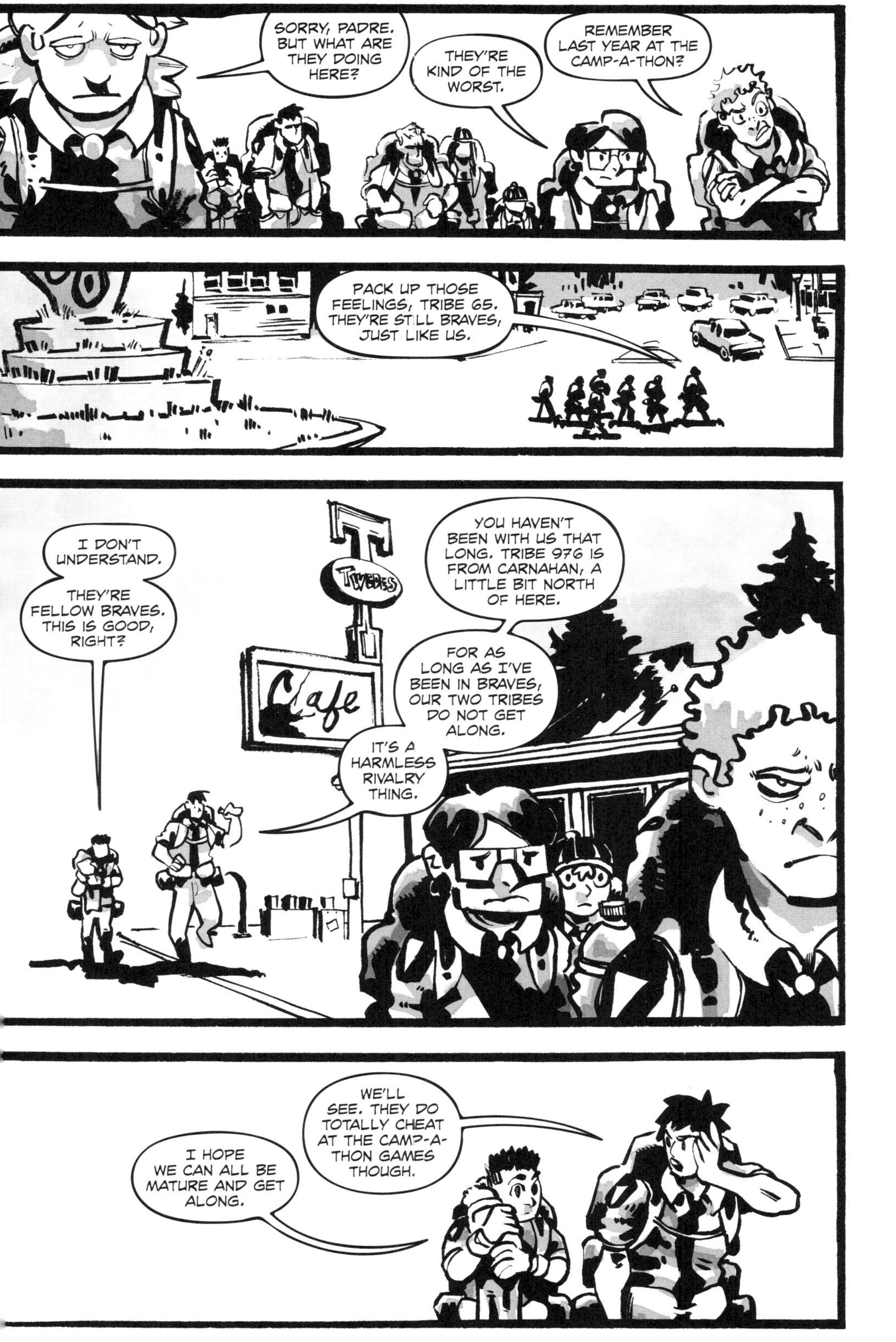
SORRY, PADRE. BUT WHAT ARE THEY DOING HERE?
THEY'RE KIND OF THE WORST.
REMEMBER LAST YEAR AT THE CAMP-A-THON?
PACK UP THOSE FEELINGS, TRIBE 65. THEY'RE STILL BRAVES, JUST LIKE US.
I DON'T UNDERSTAND.
THEY'RE FELLOW BRAVES. THIS IS GOOD, RIGHT?
YOU HAVEN'T BEEN WITH US THAT LONG. TRIBE 976 IS FROM CARNAHAN, A LITTLE BIT NORTH OF HERE.
FOR AS LONG AS I'VE BEEN IN BRAVES, OUR TWO TRIBES DO NOT GET ALONG.
IT'S A HARMLESS RIVALRY THING.
Cafe
I HOPE WE CAN ALL BE MATURE AND GET ALONG.
WE'LL SEE. THEY DO TOTALLY CHEAT AT THE CAMP-A-THON GAMES THOUGH.

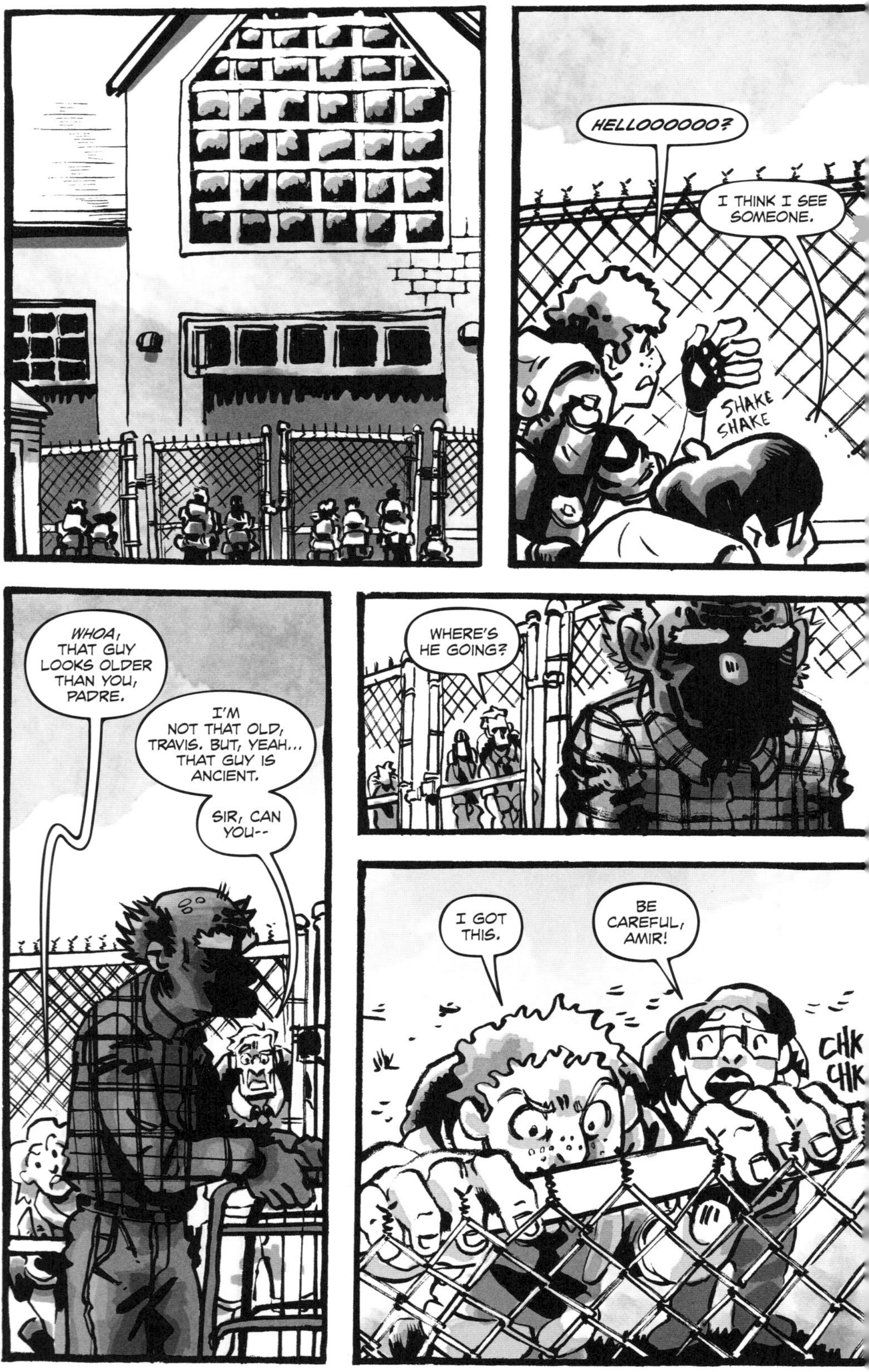
HELLOOOOOO?
I THINK I SEE SOMEONE.
SHAKE SHAKE
WHOA, THAT GUY LOOKS OLDER THAN YOU, PADRE.
I'M NOT THAT OLD, TRAVIS. BUT, YEAH... THAT GUY IS ANCIENT.
SIR, CAN YOU--
WHERE'S HE GOING?
I GOT THIS.
BE CAREFUL, AMIR!
CHK CHK

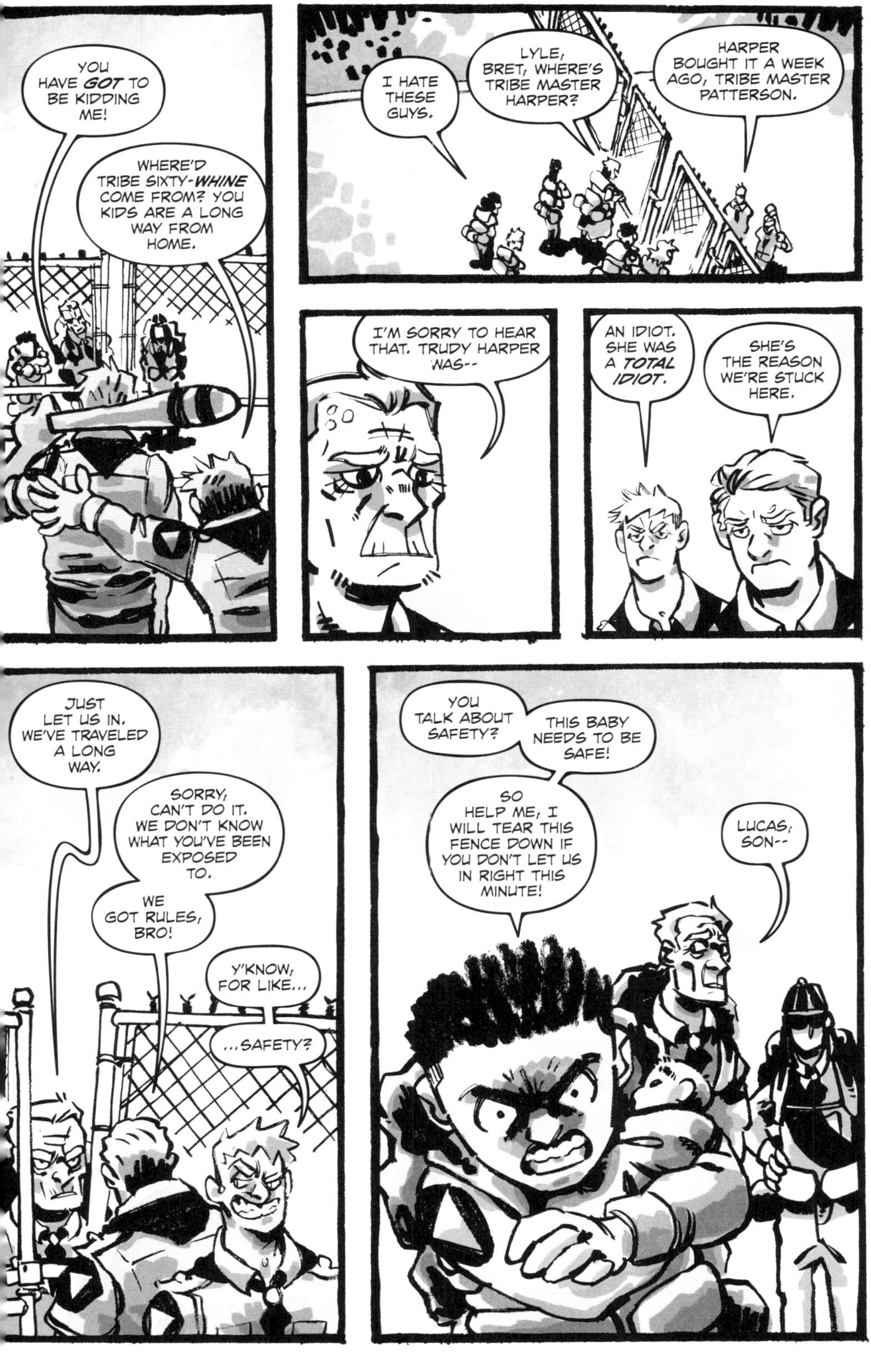
YOU HAVE GOT TO BE KIDDING ME!
WHERE'D TRIBE SIXTY-WHINE COME FROM? YOU KIDS ARE A LONG WAY FROM HOME.
I HATE THESE GUYS.
LYLE, BRET, WHERE'S TRIBE MASTER HARPER?
HARPER BOUGHT IT A WEEK AGO, TRIBE MASTER PATTERSON.
I'M SORRY TO HEAR THAT. TRUDY HARPER WAS--
AN IDIOT. SHE WAS A TOTAL IDIOT.
SHE'S THE REASON WE'RE STUCK HERE.
JUST LET US IN. WE'VE TRAVELED A LONG WAY.
SORRY, CAN'T DO IT. WE DON'T KNOW WHAT YOU'VE BEEN EXPOSED TO.
WE GOT RULES, BRO!
Y'KNOW, FOR LIKE...
...SAFETY?
YOU TALK ABOUT SAFETY?
THIS BABY NEEDS TO BE SAFE!
SO HELP ME, I WILL TEAR THIS FENCE DOWN IF YOU DON'T LET US IN RIGHT THIS MINUTE!
LUCAS, SON--

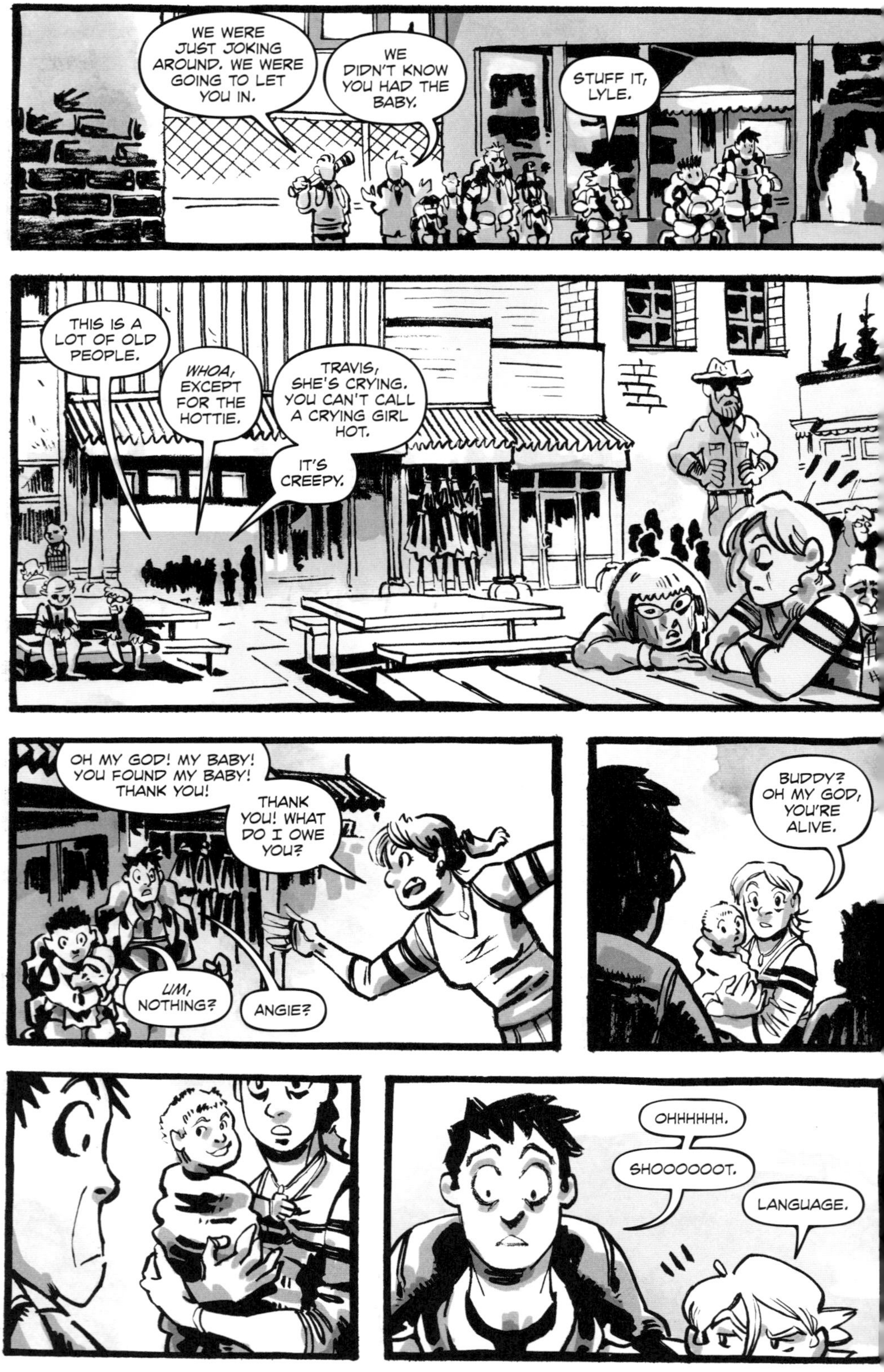
WE WERE JUST JOKING AROUND. WE WERE GOING TO LET YOU IN.
WE DIDN'T KNOW YOU HAD THE BABY.
STUFF IT, LYLE.
THIS IS A LOT OF OLD PEOPLE.
WHOA, EXCEPT FOR THE HOTTIE.
TRAVIS, SHE'S CRYING. YOU CAN'T CALL A CRYING GIRL HOT.
IT'S CREEPY.
OH MY GOD! MY BABY! YOU FOUND MY BABY! THANK YOU!
THANK YOU! WHAT DO I OWE YOU?
UM, NOTHING?
ANGIE?
BUDDY? OH MY GOD, YOU'RE ALIVE.
OHHHHHH.
SHOOOOOOT.
LANGUAGE.

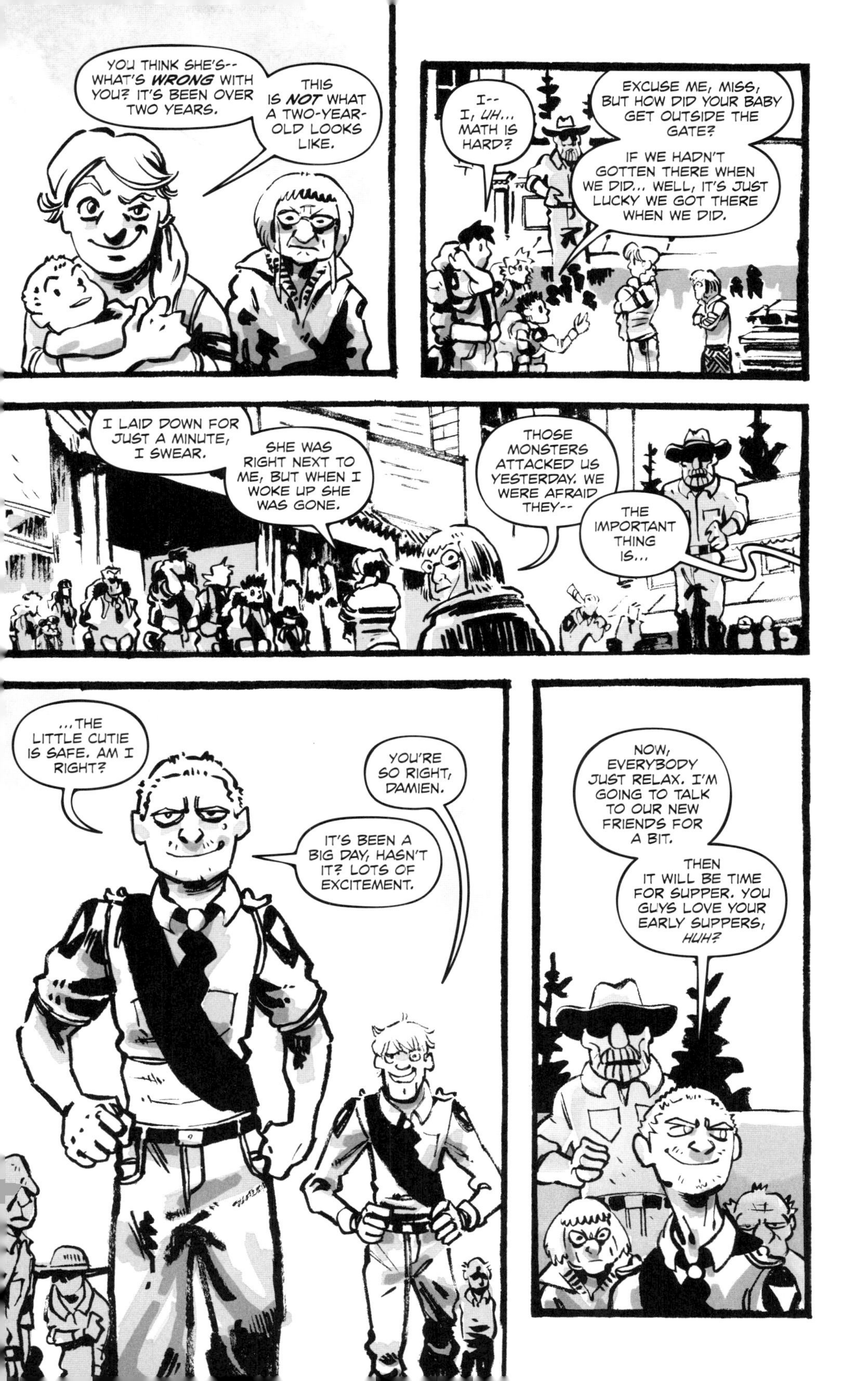
YOU THINK SHE'S-- WHAT'S **WRONG** WITH YOU? IT'S BEEN OVER TWO YEARS.
THIS IS **NOT** WHAT A TWO-YEAR-OLD LOOKS LIKE.
I-- I, *UH*... MATH IS HARD?
EXCUSE ME, MISS, BUT HOW DID YOUR BABY GET OUTSIDE THE GATE?
IF WE HADN'T GOTTEN THERE WHEN WE DID... WELL, IT'S JUST LUCKY WE GOT THERE WHEN WE DID.
I LAID DOWN FOR JUST A MINUTE, I SWEAR.
SHE WAS RIGHT NEXT TO ME, BUT WHEN I WOKE UP SHE WAS GONE.
THOSE MONSTERS ATTACKED US YESTERDAY. WE WERE AFRAID THEY--
THE IMPORTANT THING IS...
...THE LITTLE CUTIE IS SAFE. AM I RIGHT?
YOU'RE SO RIGHT, DAMIEN.
IT'S BEEN A BIG DAY, HASN'T IT? LOTS OF EXCITEMENT.
NOW, EVERYBODY JUST RELAX. I'M GOING TO TALK TO OUR NEW FRIENDS FOR A BIT.
THEN IT WILL BE TIME FOR SUPPER. YOU GUYS LOVE YOUR EARLY SUPPERS, *HUH*?

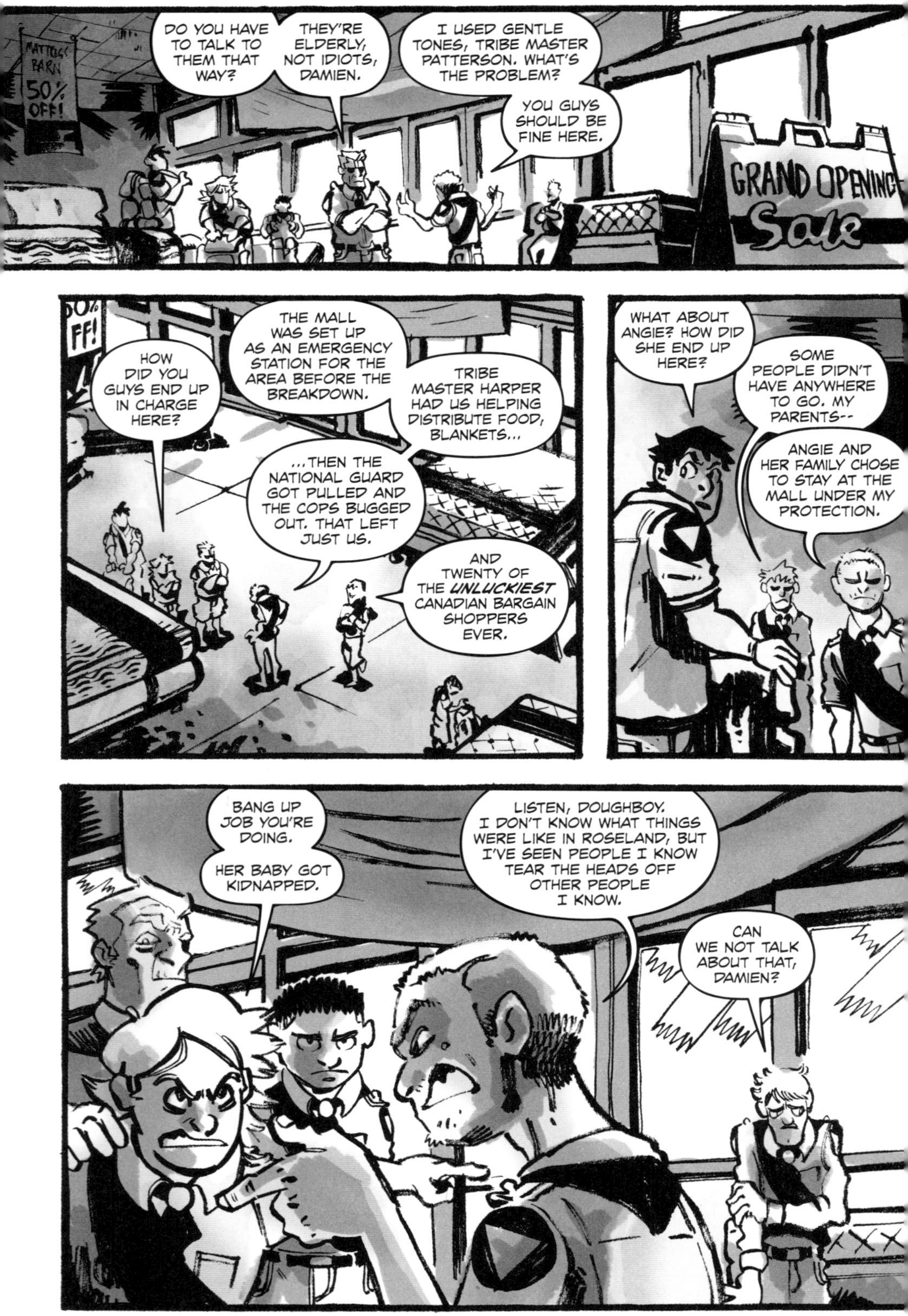
MATTRESS BARN 50% OFF!
DO YOU HAVE TO TALK TO THEM THAT WAY?
THEY'RE ELDERLY, NOT IDIOTS, DAMIEN.
I USED GENTLE TONES, TRIBE MASTER PATTERSON. WHAT'S THE PROBLEM?
YOU GUYS SHOULD BE FINE HERE.
GRAND OPENING Sale
HOW DID YOU GUYS END UP IN CHARGE HERE?
THE MALL WAS SET UP AS AN EMERGENCY STATION FOR THE AREA BEFORE THE BREAKDOWN.
TRIBE MASTER HARPER HAD US HELPING DISTRIBUTE FOOD, BLANKETS...
...THEN THE NATIONAL GUARD GOT PULLED AND THE COPS BUGGED OUT. THAT LEFT JUST US.
AND TWENTY OF THE *UNLUCKIEST* CANADIAN BARGAIN SHOPPERS EVER.
WHAT ABOUT ANGIE? HOW DID SHE END UP HERE?
SOME PEOPLE DIDN'T HAVE ANYWHERE TO GO. MY PARENTS--
ANGIE AND HER FAMILY CHOSE TO STAY AT THE MALL UNDER MY PROTECTION.
BANG UP JOB YOU'RE DOING.
HER BABY GOT KIDNAPPED.
LISTEN, DOUGHBOY. I DON'T KNOW WHAT THINGS WERE LIKE IN ROSELAND, BUT I'VE SEEN PEOPLE I KNOW TEAR THE HEADS OFF OTHER PEOPLE I KNOW.
CAN WE NOT TALK ABOUT THAT, DAMIEN?

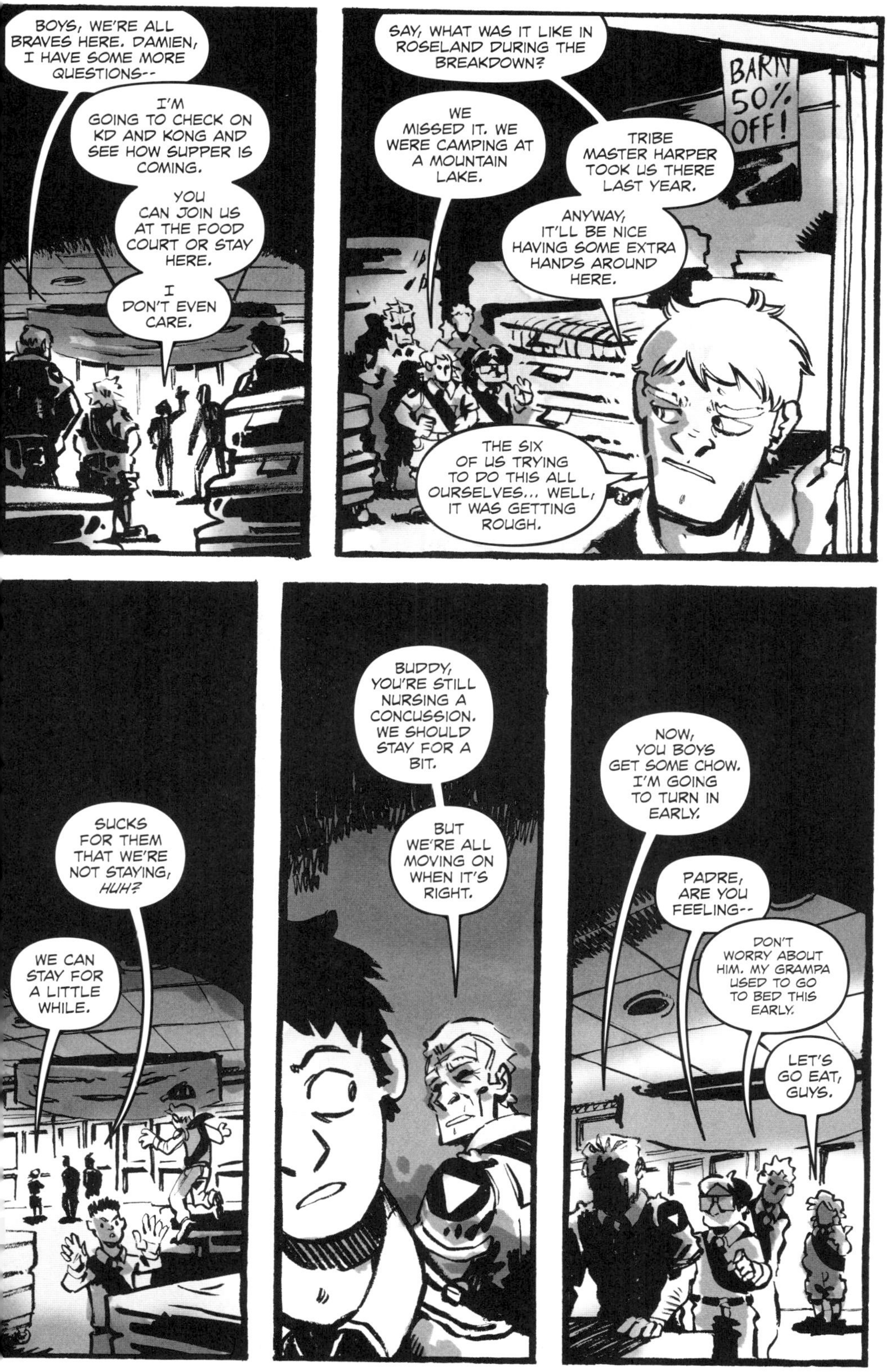
BOYS, WE'RE ALL BRAVES HERE. DAMIEN, I HAVE SOME MORE QUESTIONS--
I'M GOING TO CHECK ON KD AND KONG AND SEE HOW SUPPER IS COMING.
YOU CAN JOIN US AT THE FOOD COURT OR STAY HERE.
I DON'T EVEN CARE.
SAY, WHAT WAS IT LIKE IN ROSELAND DURING THE BREAKDOWN?
WE MISSED IT. WE WERE CAMPING AT A MOUNTAIN LAKE.
TRIBE MASTER HARPER TOOK US THERE LAST YEAR.
BARN 50% OFF!
ANYWAY, IT'LL BE NICE HAVING SOME EXTRA HANDS AROUND HERE.
THE SIX OF US TRYING TO DO THIS ALL OURSELVES... WELL, IT WAS GETTING ROUGH.
SUCKS FOR THEM THAT WE'RE NOT STAYING, *HUH?*
WE CAN STAY FOR A LITTLE WHILE.
BUDDY, YOU'RE STILL NURSING A CONCUSSION. WE SHOULD STAY FOR A BIT.
BUT WE'RE ALL MOVING ON WHEN IT'S RIGHT.
NOW, YOU BOYS GET SOME CHOW. I'M GOING TO TURN IN EARLY.
PADRE, ARE YOU FEELING--
DON'T WORRY ABOUT HIM. MY GRAMPA USED TO GO TO BED THIS EARLY.
LET'S GO EAT, GUYS.

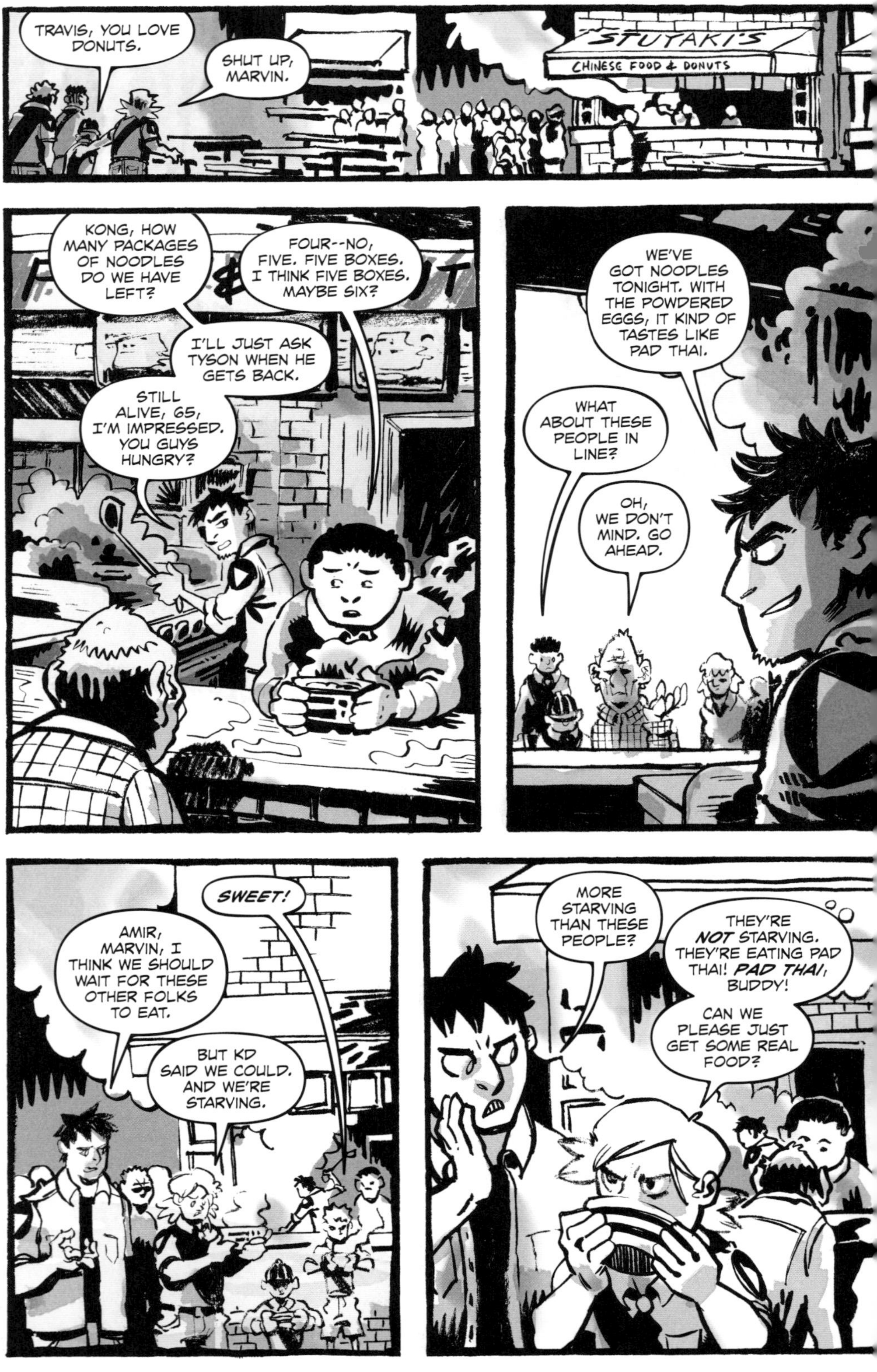

TRAVIS, YOU LOVE DONUTS.
SHUT UP, MARVIN.
STUTAKI'S
CHINESE FOOD & DONUTS
KONG, HOW MANY PACKAGES OF NOODLES DO WE HAVE LEFT?
FOUR--NO, FIVE. FIVE BOXES. I THINK FIVE BOXES. MAYBE SIX?
I'LL JUST ASK TYSON WHEN HE GETS BACK.
STILL ALIVE, 65, I'M IMPRESSED. YOU GUYS HUNGRY?
WE'VE GOT NOODLES TONIGHT. WITH THE POWDERED EGGS, IT KIND OF TASTES LIKE PAD THAI.
WHAT ABOUT THESE PEOPLE IN LINE?
OH, WE DON'T MIND. GO AHEAD.
AMIR, MARVIN, I THINK WE SHOULD WAIT FOR THESE OTHER FOLKS TO EAT.
SWEET!
BUT KD SAID WE COULD. AND WE'RE STARVING.
MORE STARVING THAN THESE PEOPLE?
THEY'RE NOT STARVING. THEY'RE EATING PAD THAI! PAD THAI, BUDDY!
CAN WE PLEASE JUST GET SOME REAL FOOD?

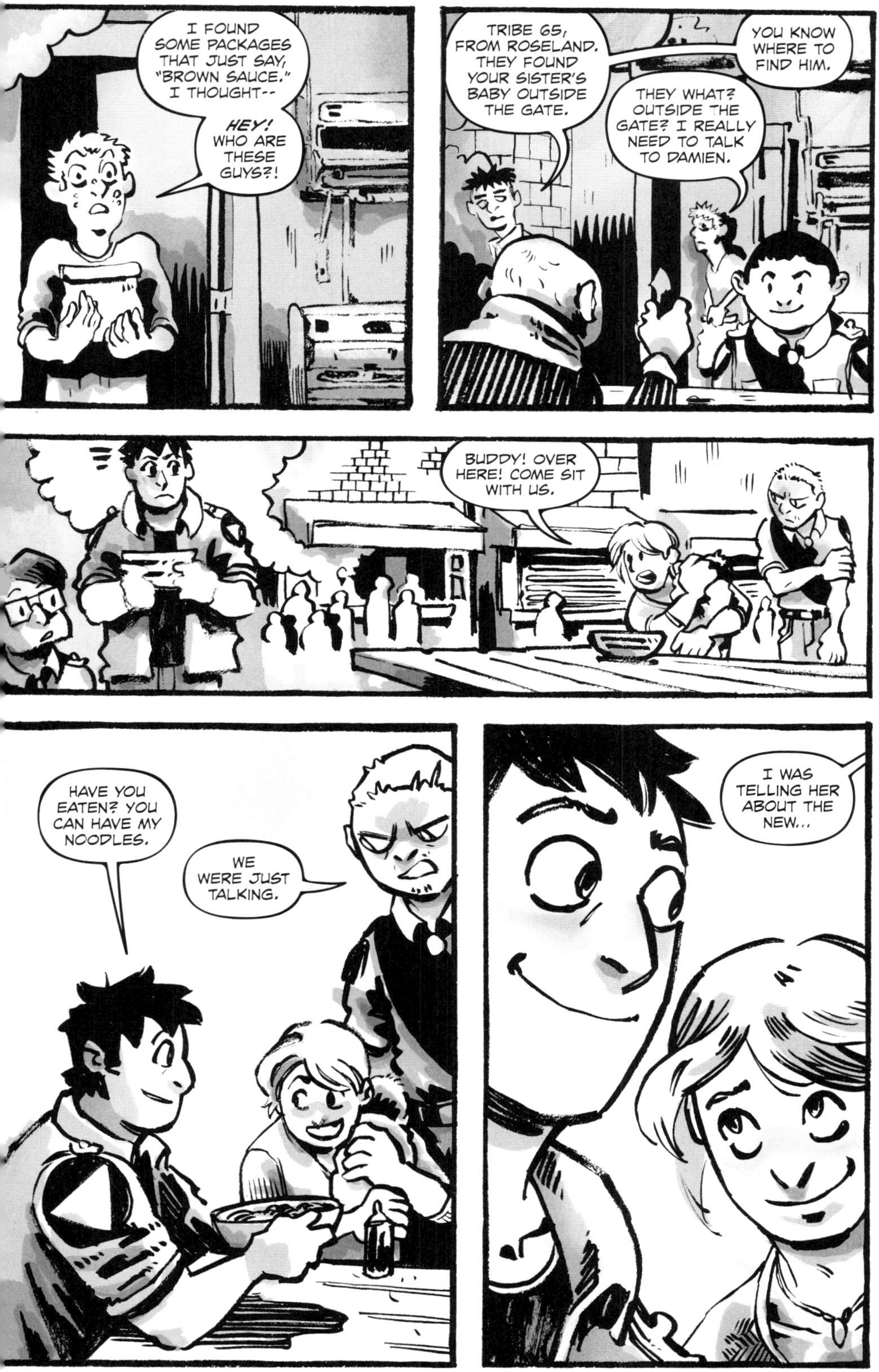

I FOUND SOME PACKAGES THAT JUST SAY, "BROWN SAUCE." I THOUGHT--
HEY! WHO ARE THESE GUYS?!
TRIBE 65, FROM ROSELAND. THEY FOUND YOUR SISTER'S BABY OUTSIDE THE GATE.
YOU KNOW WHERE TO FIND HIM.
THEY WHAT? OUTSIDE THE GATE? I REALLY NEED TO TALK TO DAMIEN.
BUDDY! OVER HERE! COME SIT WITH US.
HAVE YOU EATEN? YOU CAN HAVE MY NOODLES.
WE WERE JUST TALKING.
I WAS TELLING HER ABOUT THE NEW...

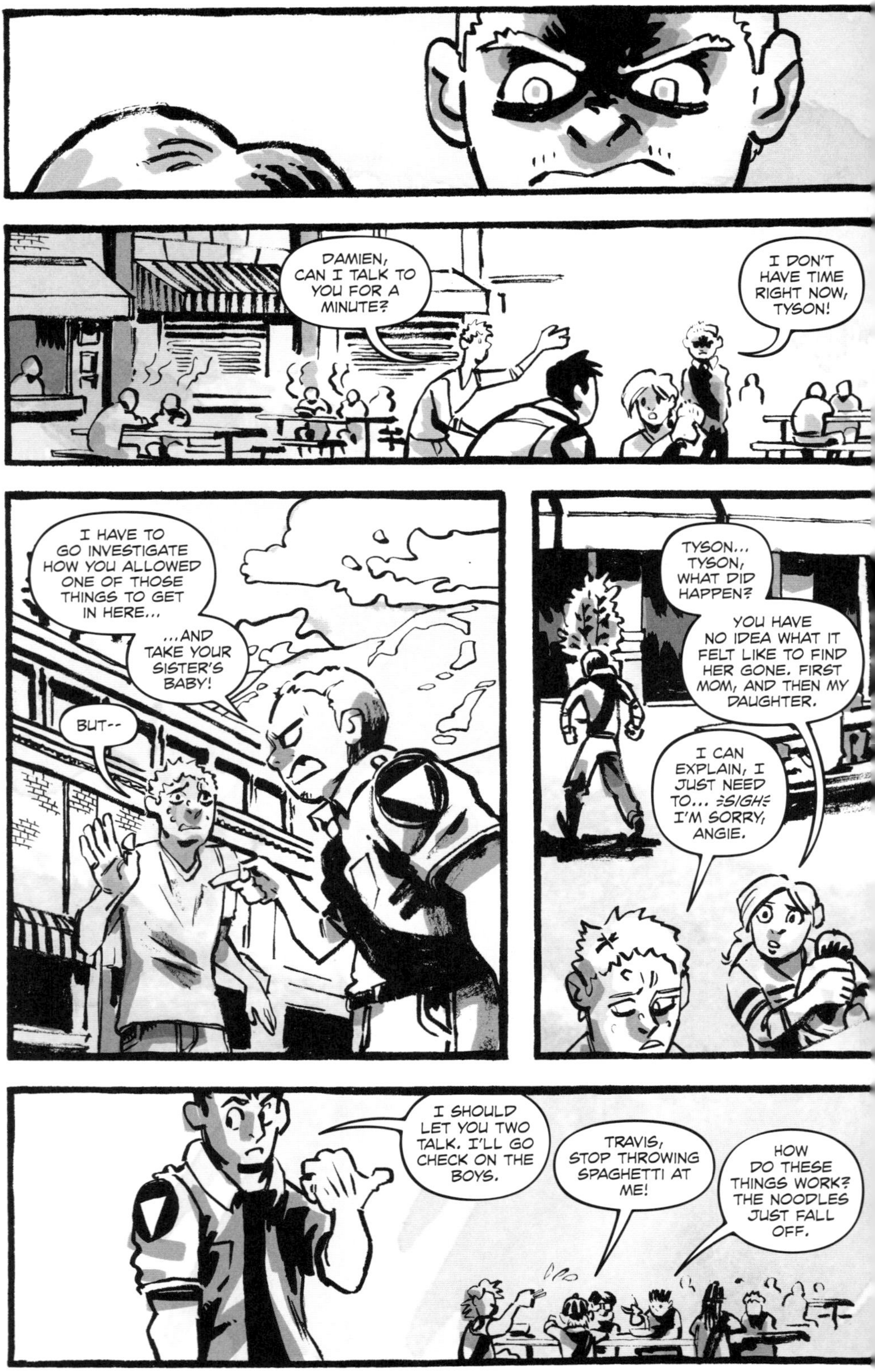
DAMIEN, CAN I TALK TO YOU FOR A MINUTE?
I DON'T HAVE TIME RIGHT NOW, TYSON!
I HAVE TO GO INVESTIGATE HOW YOU ALLOWED ONE OF THOSE THINGS TO GET IN HERE...
...AND TAKE YOUR SISTER'S BABY!
BUT--
TYSON... TYSON, WHAT DID HAPPEN?
YOU HAVE NO IDEA WHAT IT FELT LIKE TO FIND HER GONE. FIRST MOM, AND THEN MY DAUGHTER.
I CAN EXPLAIN, I JUST NEED TO... =SIGH= I'M SORRY, ANGIE.
I SHOULD LET YOU TWO TALK. I'LL GO CHECK ON THE BOYS.
TRAVIS, STOP THROWING SPAGHETTI AT ME!
HOW DO THESE THINGS WORK? THE NOODLES JUST FALL OFF.

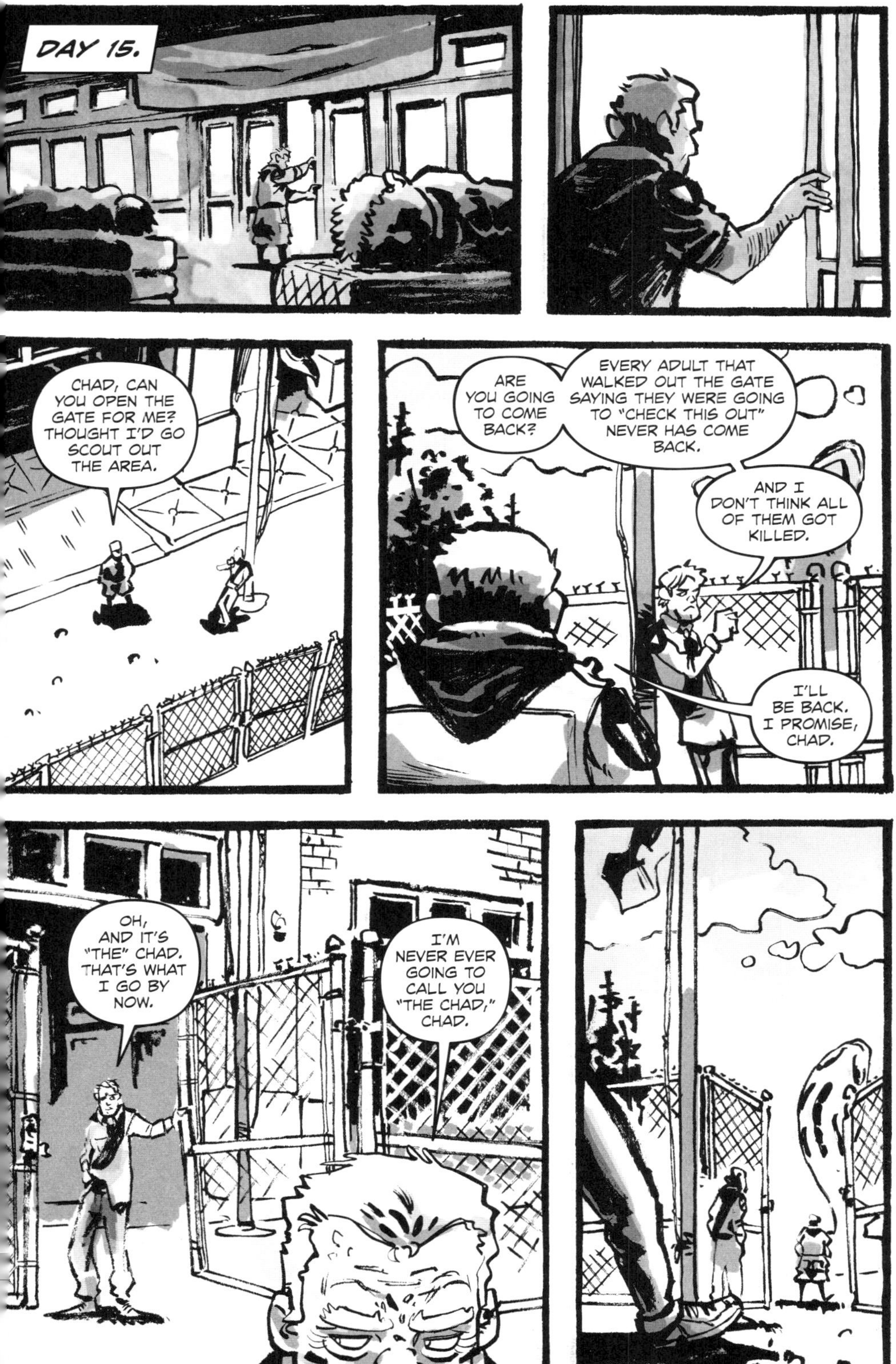
DAY 15.
CHAD, CAN YOU OPEN THE GATE FOR ME? THOUGHT I'D GO SCOUT OUT THE AREA.
ARE YOU GOING TO COME BACK?
EVERY ADULT THAT WALKED OUT THE GATE SAYING THEY WERE GOING TO "CHECK THIS OUT" NEVER HAS COME BACK.
AND I DON'T THINK ALL OF THEM GOT KILLED.
I'LL BE BACK. I PROMISE, CHAD.
OH, AND IT'S "THE" CHAD. THAT'S WHAT I GO BY NOW.
I'M NEVER EVER GOING TO CALL YOU "THE CHAD," CHAD.

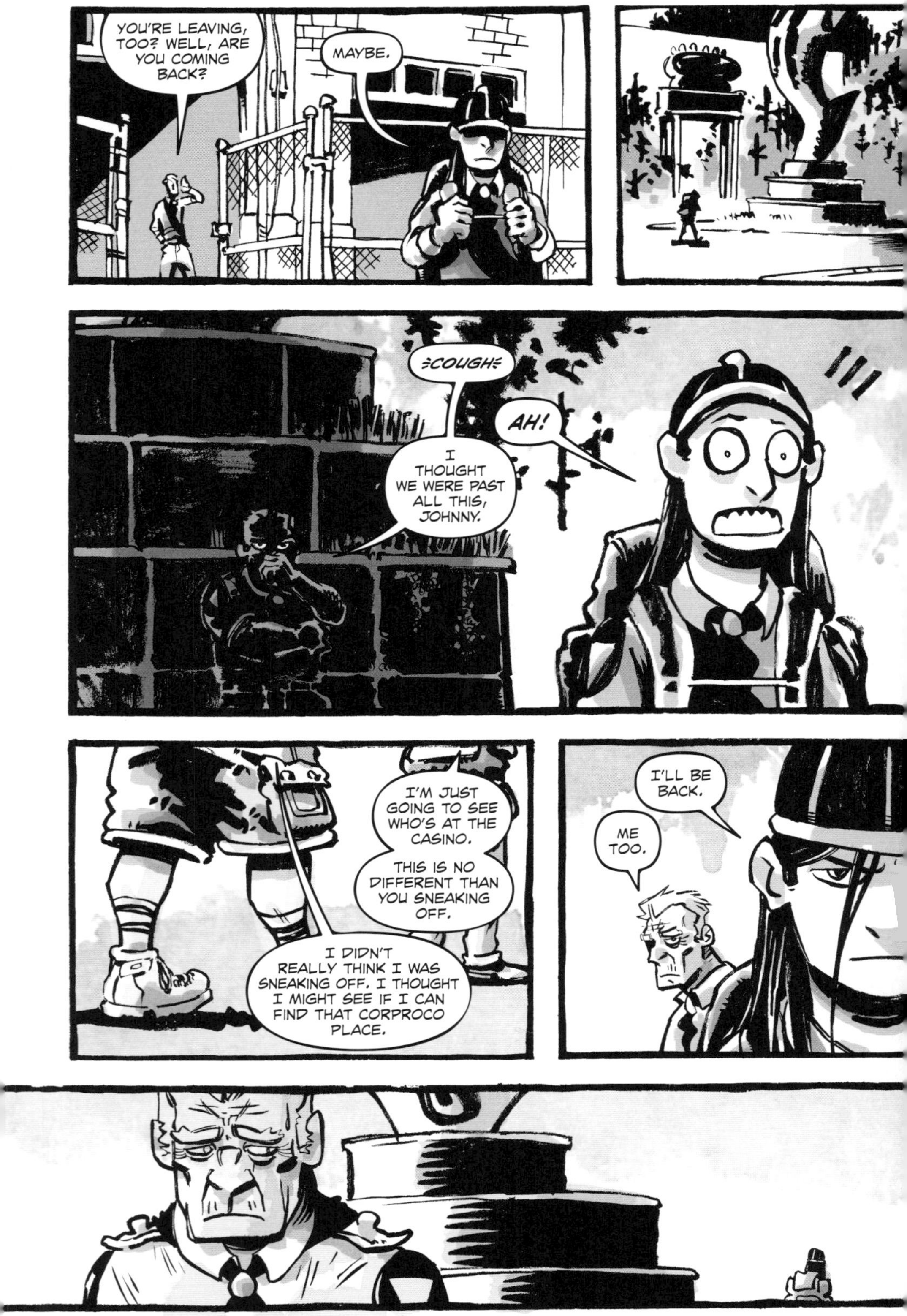
YOU'RE LEAVING, TOO? WELL, ARE YOU COMING BACK?
MAYBE.
=COUGH=
AH!
I THOUGHT WE WERE PAST ALL THIS, JOHNNY.
I'M JUST GOING TO SEE WHO'S AT THE CASINO.
THIS IS NO DIFFERENT THAN YOU SNEAKING OFF.
I DIDN'T REALLY THINK I WAS SNEAKING OFF. I THOUGHT I MIGHT SEE IF I CAN FIND THAT CORPROCO PLACE.
I'LL BE BACK.
ME TOO.

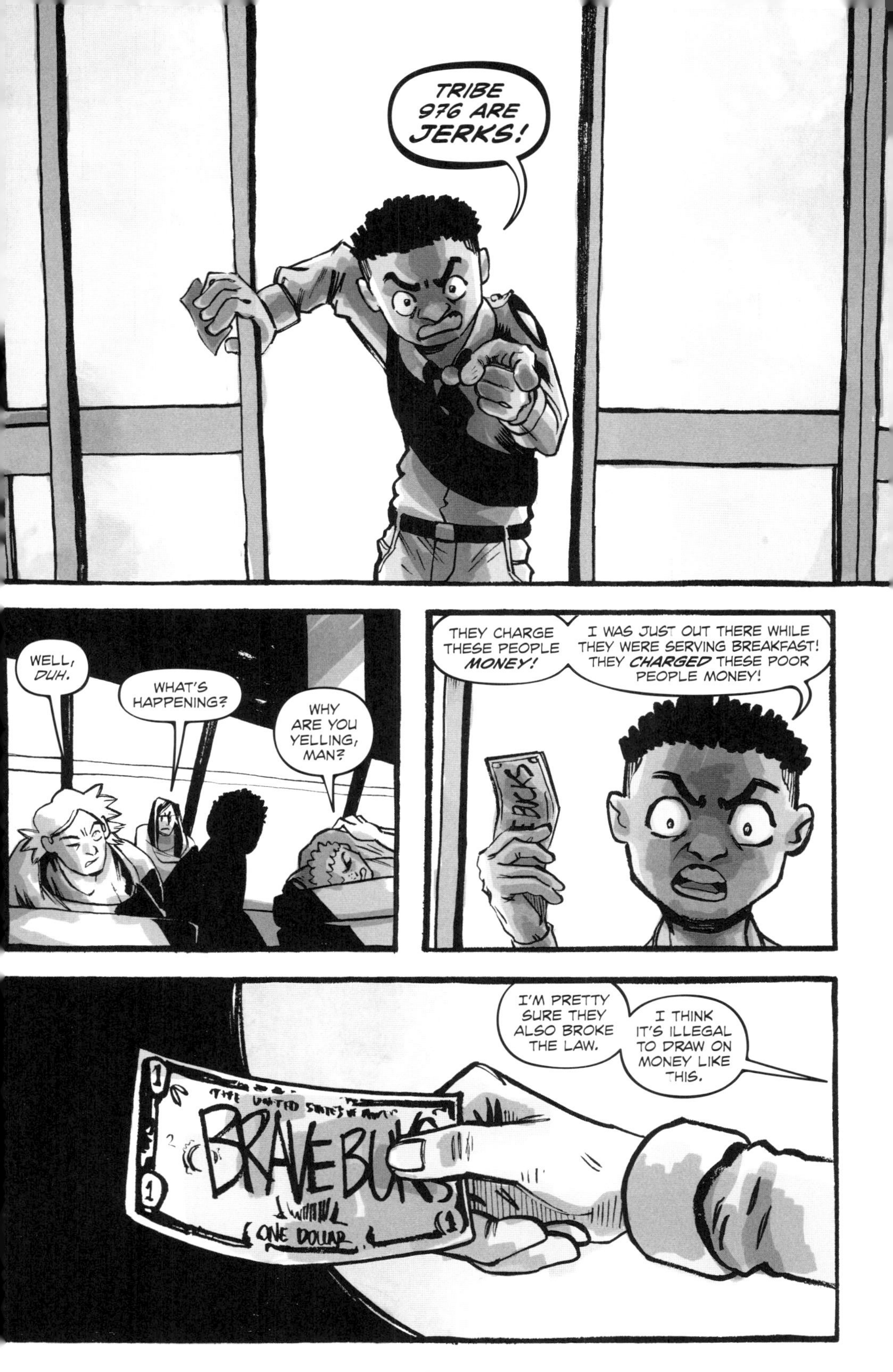
TRIBE 976 ARE JERKS!
WELL, DUH.
WHAT'S HAPPENING?
WHY ARE YOU YELLING, MAN?
THEY CHARGE THESE PEOPLE MONEY!
I WAS JUST OUT THERE WHILE THEY WERE SERVING BREAKFAST! THEY CHARGED THESE POOR PEOPLE MONEY!
I'M PRETTY SURE THEY ALSO BROKE THE LAW.
I THINK IT'S ILLEGAL TO DRAW ON MONEY LIKE THIS.
BRAVE BUCKS
ONE DOLLAR

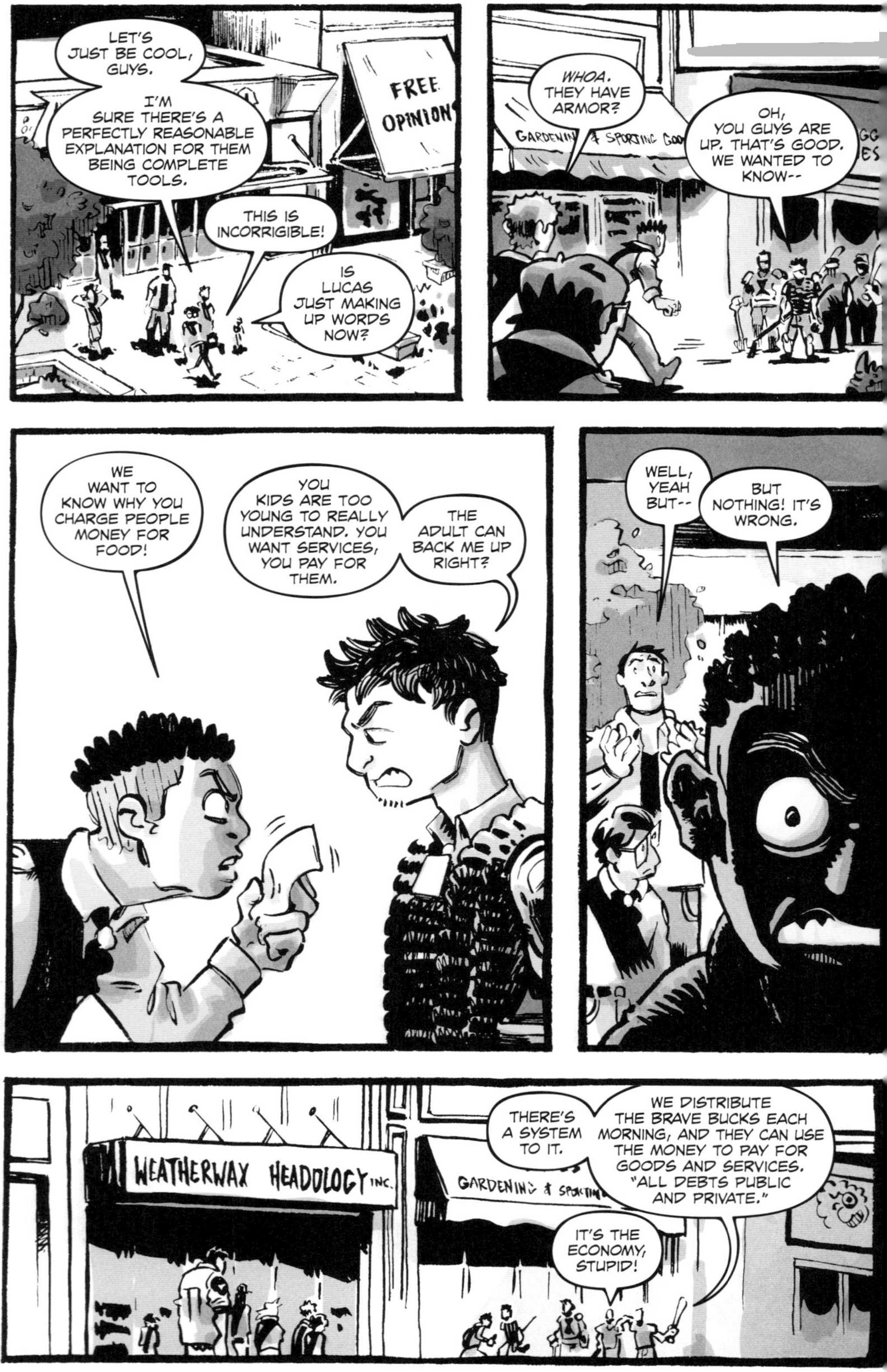
LET'S JUST BE COOL, GUYS.
I'M SURE THERE'S A PERFECTLY REASONABLE EXPLANATION FOR THEM BEING COMPLETE TOOLS.
FREE OPINION
THIS IS INCORRIGIBLE!
IS LUCAS JUST MAKING UP WORDS NOW?
WHOA. THEY HAVE ARMOR?
GARDENING & SPORTING GOODS
OH, YOU GUYS ARE UP. THAT'S GOOD. WE WANTED TO KNOW--
WE WANT TO KNOW WHY YOU CHARGE PEOPLE MONEY FOR FOOD!
YOU KIDS ARE TOO YOUNG TO REALLY UNDERSTAND. YOU WANT SERVICES, YOU PAY FOR THEM.
THE ADULT CAN BACK ME UP RIGHT?
WELL, YEAH BUT--
BUT NOTHING! IT'S WRONG.
WEATHERWAX HEADOLOGY INC.
GARDENING & SPORTING
THERE'S A SYSTEM TO IT.
WE DISTRIBUTE THE BRAVE BUCKS EACH MORNING, AND THEY CAN USE THE MONEY TO PAY FOR GOODS AND SERVICES. "ALL DEBTS PUBLIC AND PRIVATE."
IT'S THE ECONOMY, STUPID!

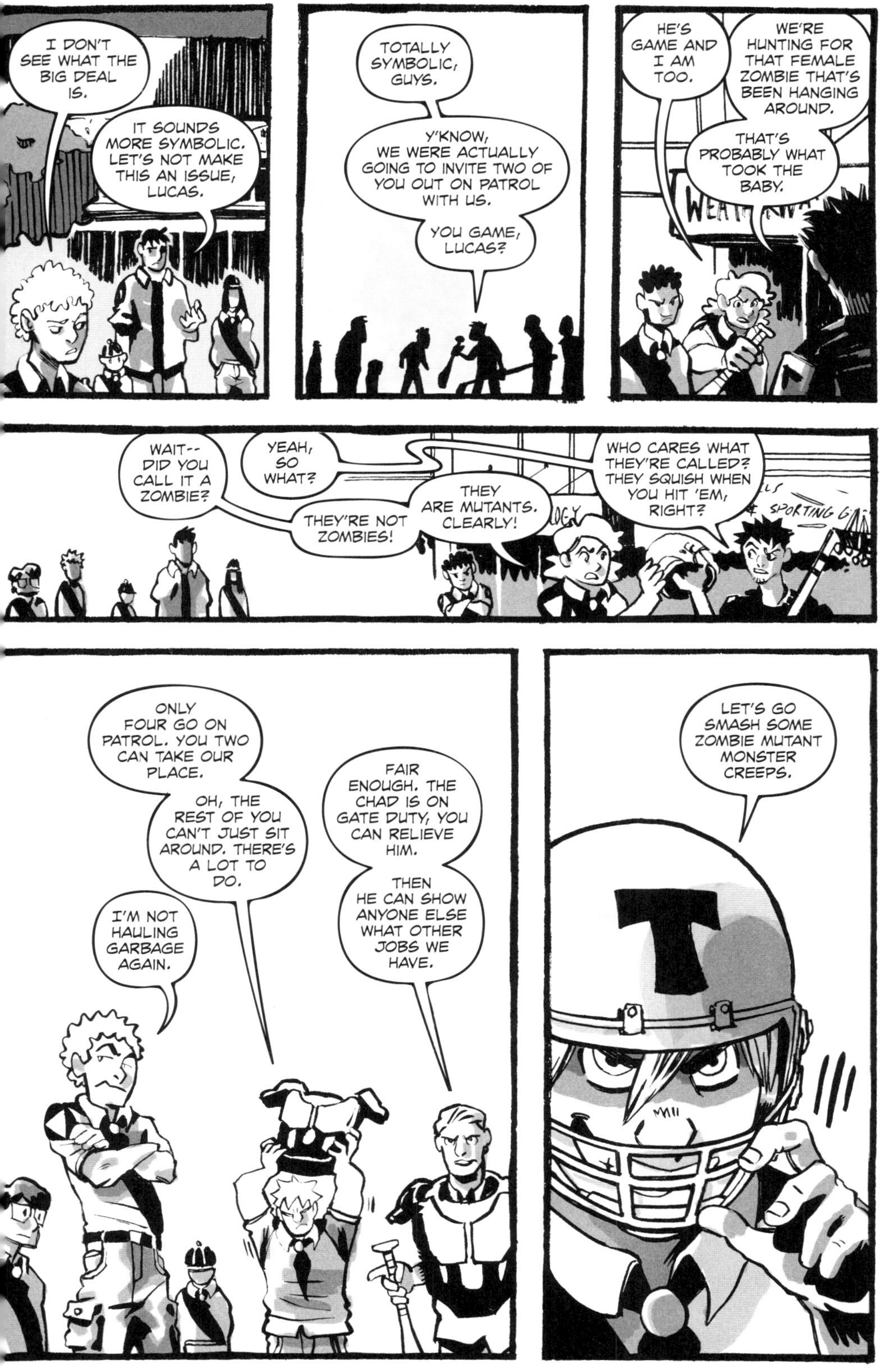
I DON'T SEE WHAT THE BIG DEAL IS.
IT SOUNDS MORE SYMBOLIC. LET'S NOT MAKE THIS AN ISSUE, LUCAS.
TOTALLY SYMBOLIC, GUYS.
Y'KNOW, WE WERE ACTUALLY GOING TO INVITE TWO OF YOU OUT ON PATROL WITH US.
YOU GAME, LUCAS?
HE'S GAME AND I AM TOO.
WE'RE HUNTING FOR THAT FEMALE ZOMBIE THAT'S BEEN HANGING AROUND.
THAT'S PROBABLY WHAT TOOK THE BABY.
WAIT-- DID YOU CALL IT A ZOMBIE?
YEAH, SO WHAT?
THEY'RE NOT ZOMBIES!
THEY ARE MUTANTS. CLEARLY!
WHO CARES WHAT THEY'RE CALLED? THEY SQUISH WHEN YOU HIT 'EM, RIGHT?
SPORTING G
ONLY FOUR GO ON PATROL. YOU TWO CAN TAKE OUR PLACE.
OH, THE REST OF YOU CAN'T JUST SIT AROUND. THERE'S A LOT TO DO.
I'M NOT HAULING GARBAGE AGAIN.
FAIR ENOUGH. THE CHAD IS ON GATE DUTY, YOU CAN RELIEVE HIM.
THEN HE CAN SHOW ANYONE ELSE WHAT OTHER JOBS WE HAVE.
LET'S GO SMASH SOME ZOMBIE MUTANT MONSTER CREEPS.

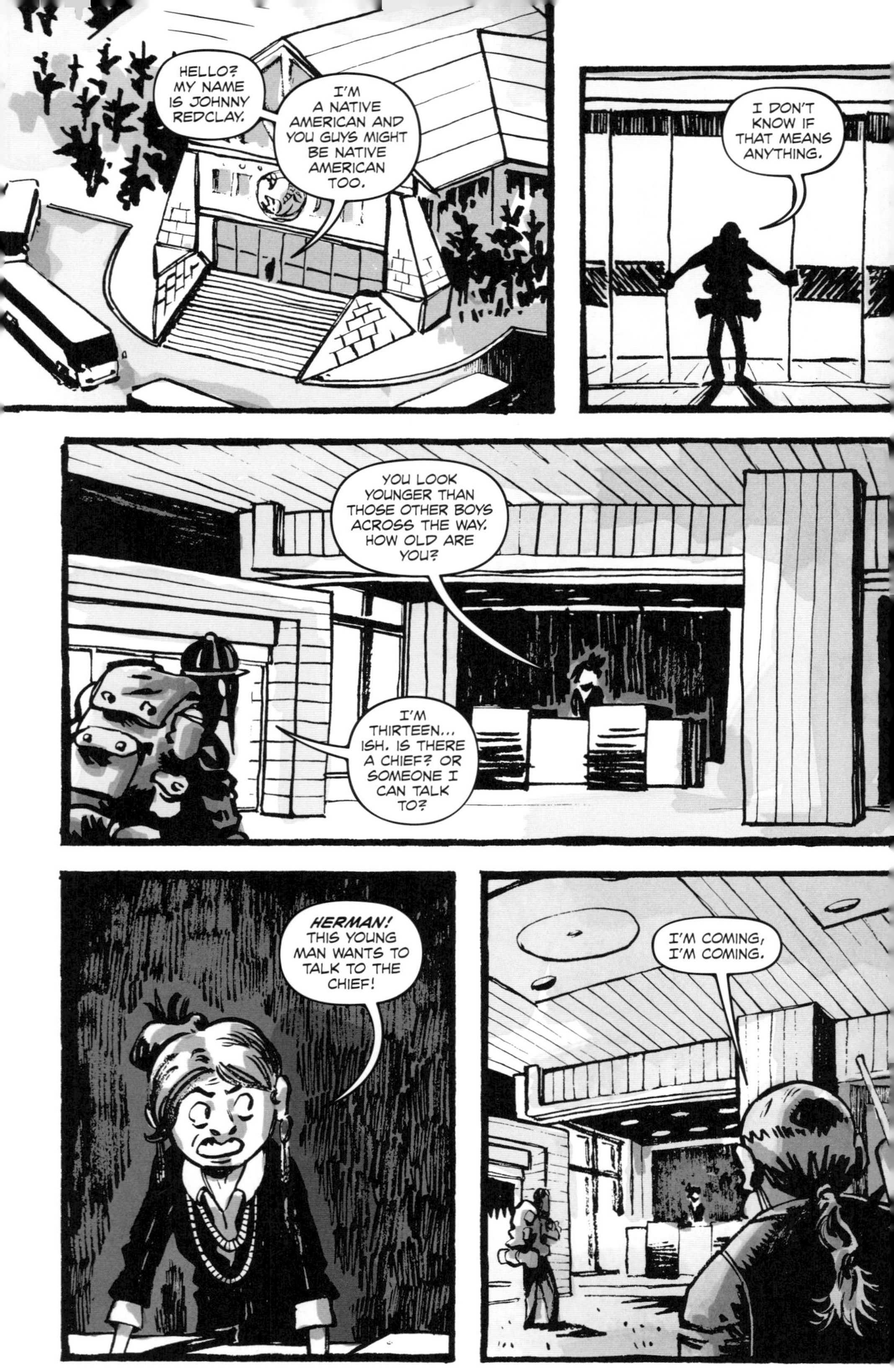
HELLO? MY NAME IS JOHNNY REDCLAY.
I'M A NATIVE AMERICAN AND YOU GUYS MIGHT BE NATIVE AMERICAN TOO.
I DON'T KNOW IF THAT MEANS ANYTHING.
YOU LOOK YOUNGER THAN THOSE OTHER BOYS ACROSS THE WAY. HOW OLD ARE YOU?
I'M THIRTEEN... ISH. IS THERE A CHIEF? OR SOMEONE I CAN TALK TO?
HERMAN! THIS YOUNG MAN WANTS TO TALK TO THE CHIEF!
I'M COMING, I'M COMING.

YOU'RE THE CHIEF?

I'M COUNCIL CHIEF HERMAN WHITTAKER.

WE'VE SEEN YOU JUNIOR BRAVES FROM ACROSS THE STREET THE PAST FEW WEEKS.

FUNNY, THEY SENT THEIR INDIAN KID OVER.

NO ONE *SENT* ME. I'M HERE ON MY OWN.

I'M LOOKING FOR MY PARENTS, I THINK THEY MIGHT HAVE ENDED UP HERE.

THEIR NAMES ARE LORETTA REDCLAY AND BENJAMIN REDCLAY.

THOSE NAMES DON'T SOUND--

SOMETIMES THEY GO BY NAICHE AND ONAWAH REDCLAY; OR RAYMOND DESCHAMP AND MIRABEL COLTER.

MY DAD IS TALL AND HAS LONG BLACK HAIR. HE USUALLY WEARS IT IN A PONYTAIL.

THAT'S HALF THE MEN HERE, AND ME TWENTY YEARS AGO.

I DON'T THINK THEY'RE HERE, JOHNNY. BUT YOU CAN STAY WITH US, AND WE CAN HELP YOU FIND THEM.

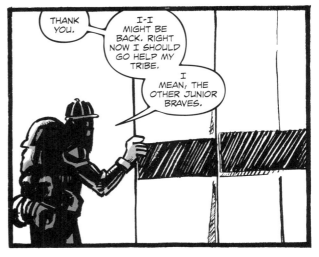

THANK YOU.

I-I MIGHT BE BACK. RIGHT NOW I SHOULD GO HELP MY TRIBE.

I MEAN, THE OTHER JUNIOR BRAVES.

I'M BORED OUT OF MY GOURD.

IT'S NOT SO BAD. WE'RE ACTUALLY DOING SOMETHING.

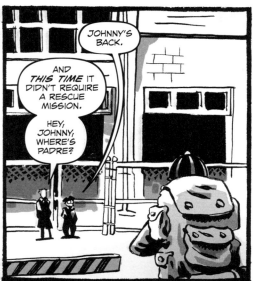

JOHNNY'S BACK.

AND *THIS TIME* IT DIDN'T REQUIRE A RESCUE MISSION.

HEY, JOHNNY, WHERE'S PADRE?

THE CHAD SAID YOU TWO LEFT TOGETHER.

SAME TIME, NOT TOGETHER.

HE WAS GOING TO GO CHECK OUT THE CORPROCO CAMPUS.

I WAS JUST... WALKING AROUND.

THAT'S A GREAT STORY.

WOULD YOU MIND BABYSITTING THE FENCING WITH PRABIR?

I'M GOING TO GO SEE WHAT ELSE THERE IS TO DO AROUND HERE.

YOU MISSED LUCAS GETTING MAD AT THE TRIBE 976 GUYS.

TRAVIS AND HIM WENT OUT TO FIGHT SOME ZOMBIE MUTANTS.

OH. I'M SURE THAT'S GOING WELL.

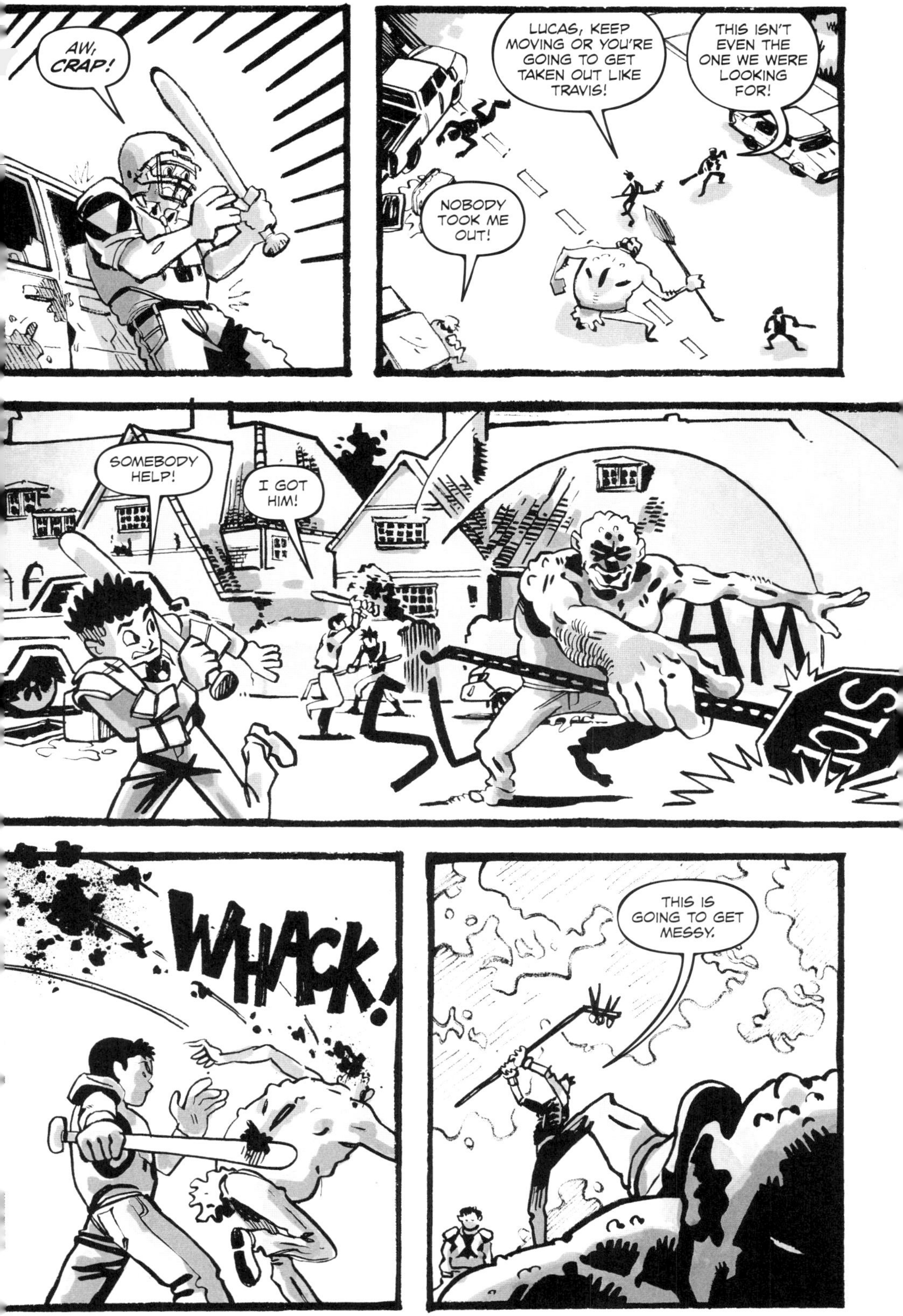
AW, CRAP!
LUCAS, KEEP MOVING OR YOU'RE GOING TO GET TAKEN OUT LIKE TRAVIS!
THIS ISN'T EVEN THE ONE WE WERE LOOKING FOR!
NOBODY TOOK ME OUT!
SOMEBODY HELP!
I GOT HIM!
SLAM
STOP
WHACK!
THIS IS GOING TO GET MESSY.

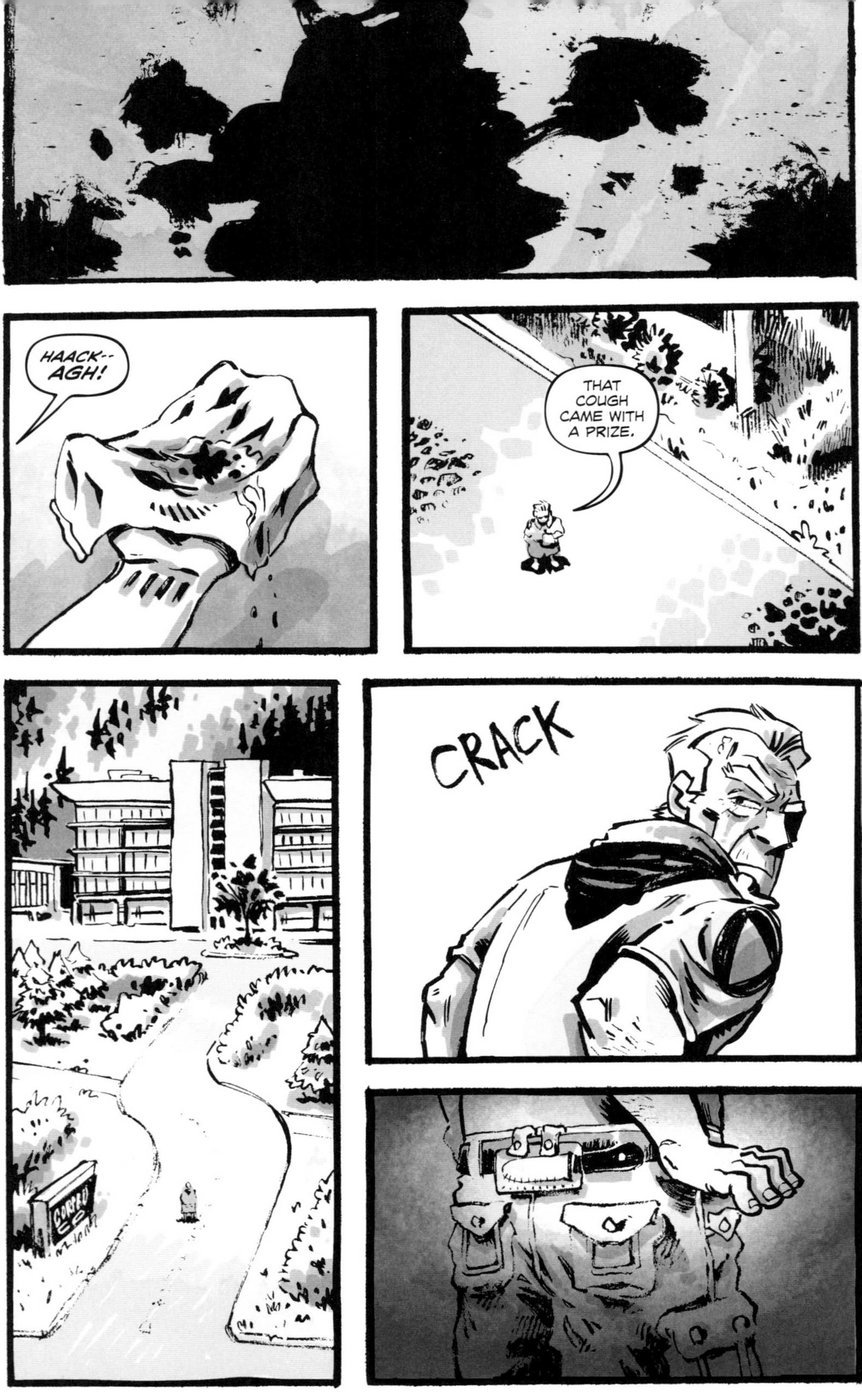
HAACK--
AGH!
THAT COUGH CAME WITH A PRIZE.
CRACK

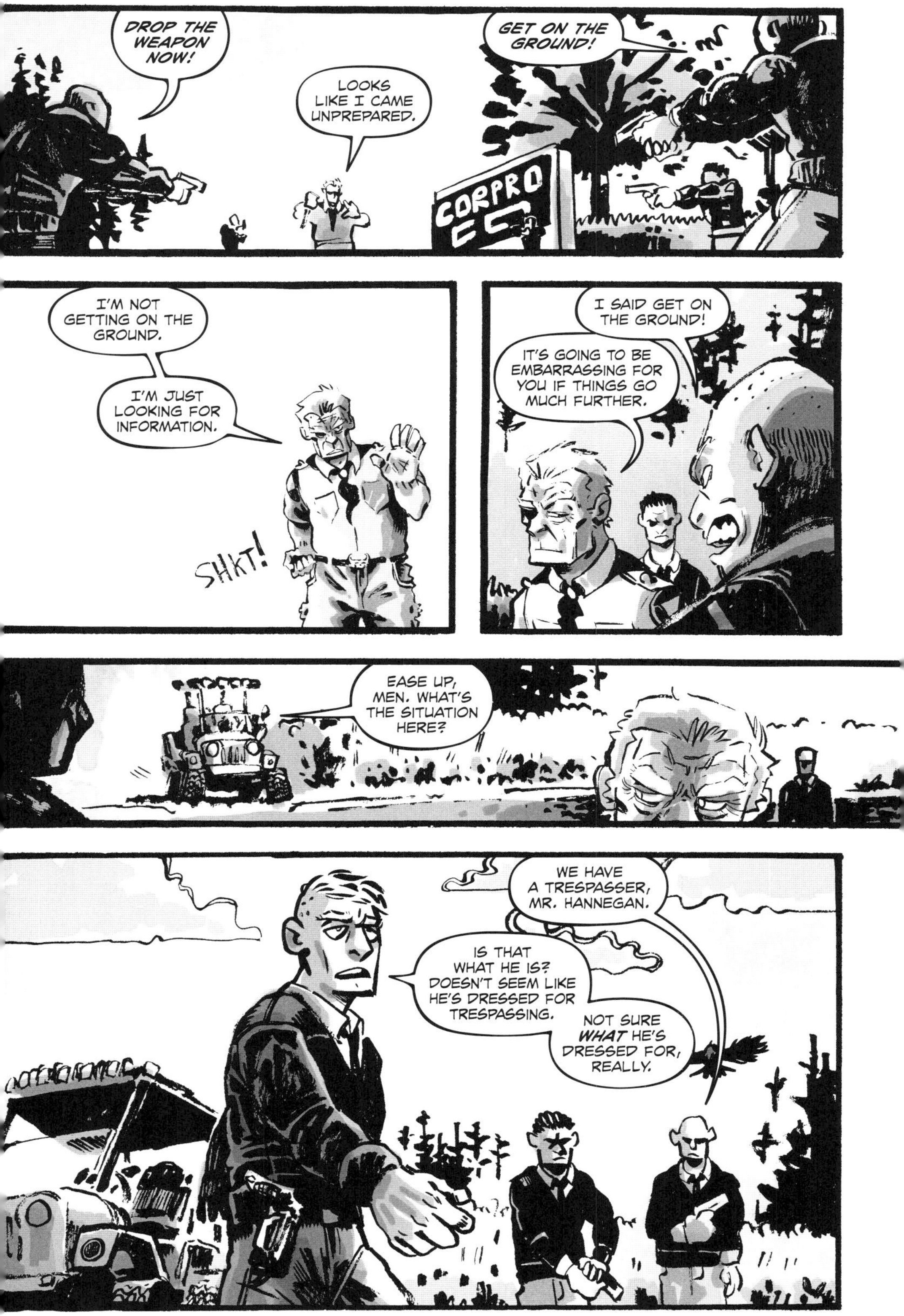
DROP THE WEAPON NOW!
LOOKS LIKE I CAME UNPREPARED.
GET ON THE GROUND!
CORPRO
I'M NOT GETTING ON THE GROUND.
I'M JUST LOOKING FOR INFORMATION.
SHKT!
I SAID GET ON THE GROUND!
IT'S GOING TO BE EMBARRASSING FOR YOU IF THINGS GO MUCH FURTHER.
EASE UP, MEN. WHAT'S THE SITUATION HERE?
WE HAVE A TRESPASSER, MR. HANNEGAN.
IS THAT WHAT HE IS? DOESN'T SEEM LIKE HE'S DRESSED FOR TRESPASSING.
NOT SURE *WHAT* HE'S DRESSED FOR, REALLY.

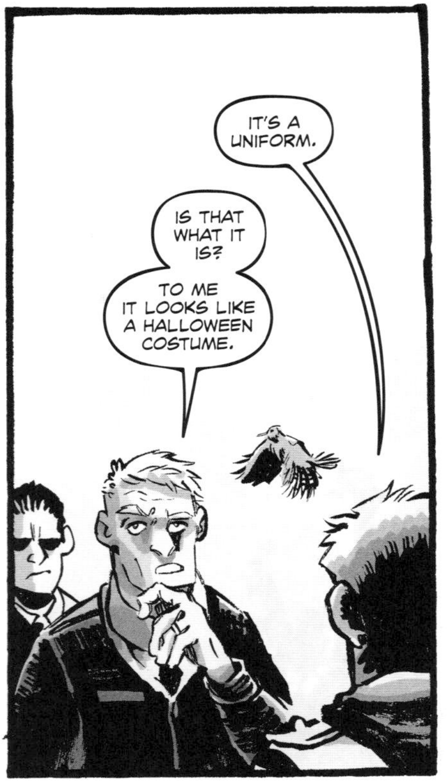
IT'S A UNIFORM.
IS THAT WHAT IT IS?
TO ME IT LOOKS LIKE A HALLOWEEN COSTUME.

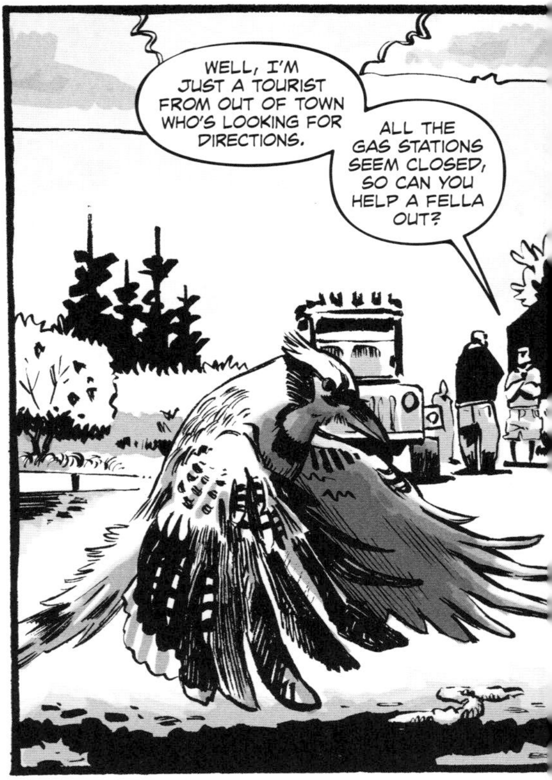
WELL, I'M JUST A TOURIST FROM OUT OF TOWN WHO'S LOOKING FOR DIRECTIONS.
ALL THE GAS STATIONS SEEM CLOSED, SO CAN YOU HELP A FELLA OUT?

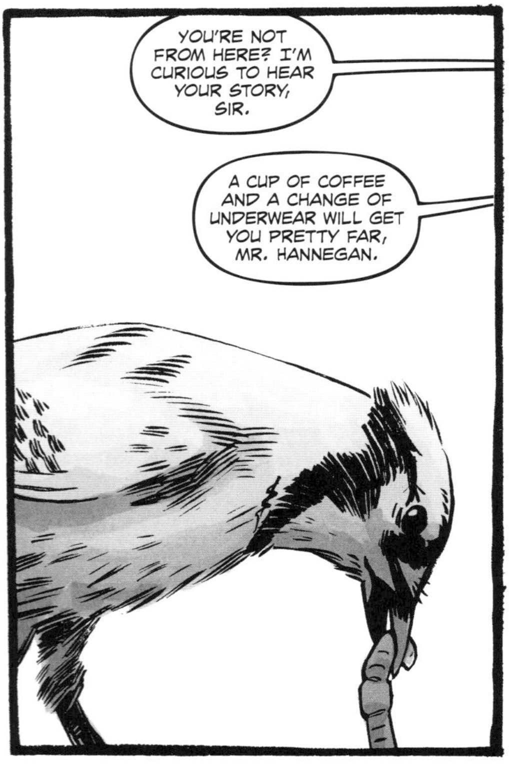
YOU'RE NOT FROM HERE? I'M CURIOUS TO HEAR YOUR STORY, SIR.
A CUP OF COFFEE AND A CHANGE OF UNDERWEAR WILL GET YOU PRETTY FAR, MR. HANNEGAN.

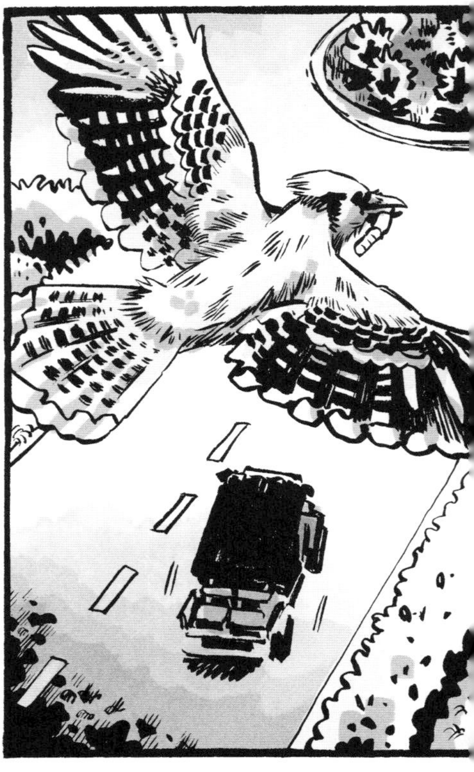

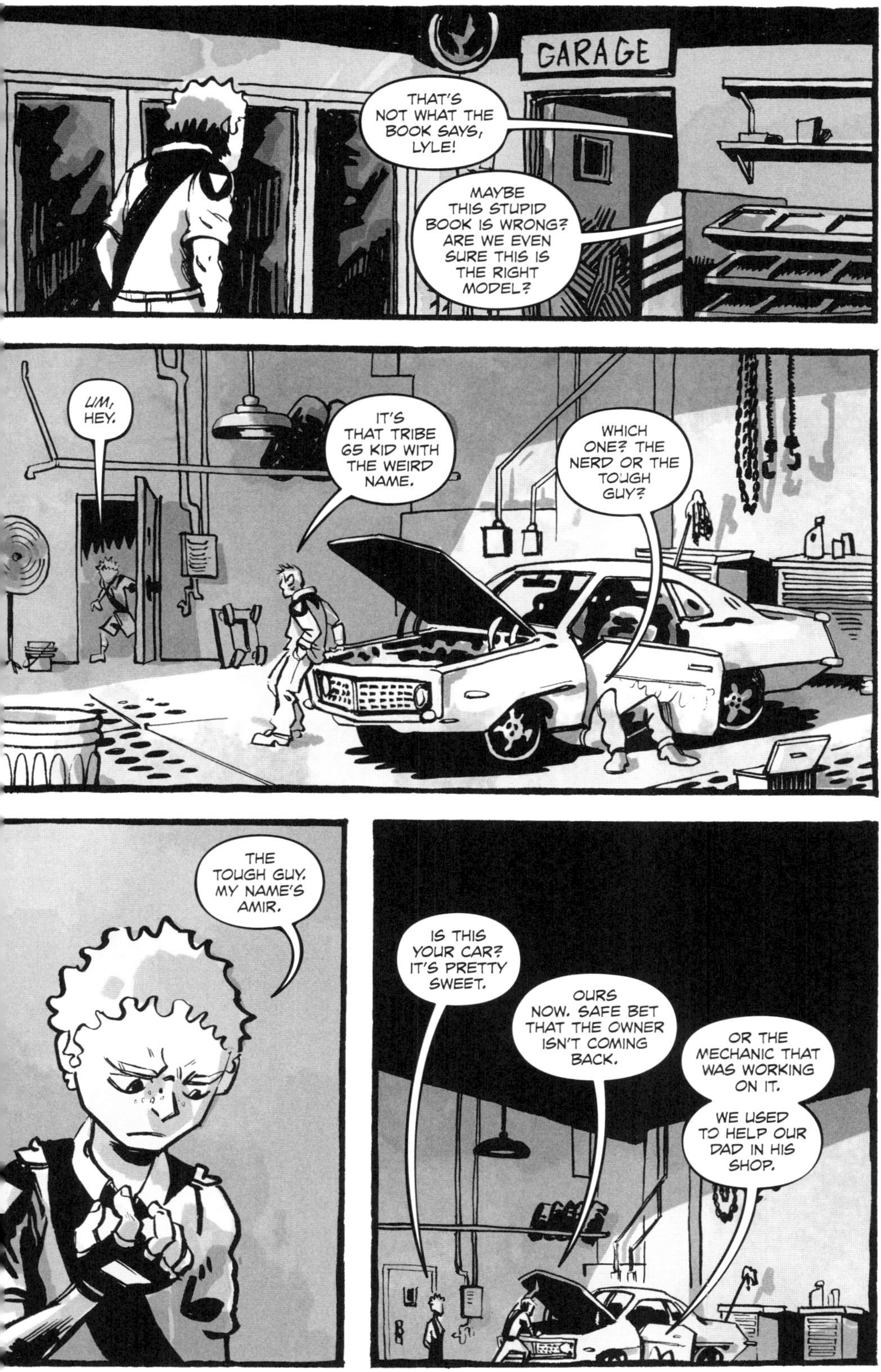
GARAGE
THAT'S NOT WHAT THE BOOK SAYS, LYLE!
MAYBE THIS STUPID BOOK IS WRONG? ARE WE EVEN SURE THIS IS THE RIGHT MODEL?
UM, HEY.
IT'S THAT TRIBE 65 KID WITH THE WEIRD NAME.
WHICH ONE? THE NERD OR THE TOUGH GUY?
THE TOUGH GUY. MY NAME'S AMIR.
IS THIS YOUR CAR? IT'S PRETTY SWEET.
OURS NOW. SAFE BET THAT THE OWNER ISN'T COMING BACK.
OR THE MECHANIC THAT WAS WORKING ON IT.
WE USED TO HELP OUR DAD IN HIS SHOP.

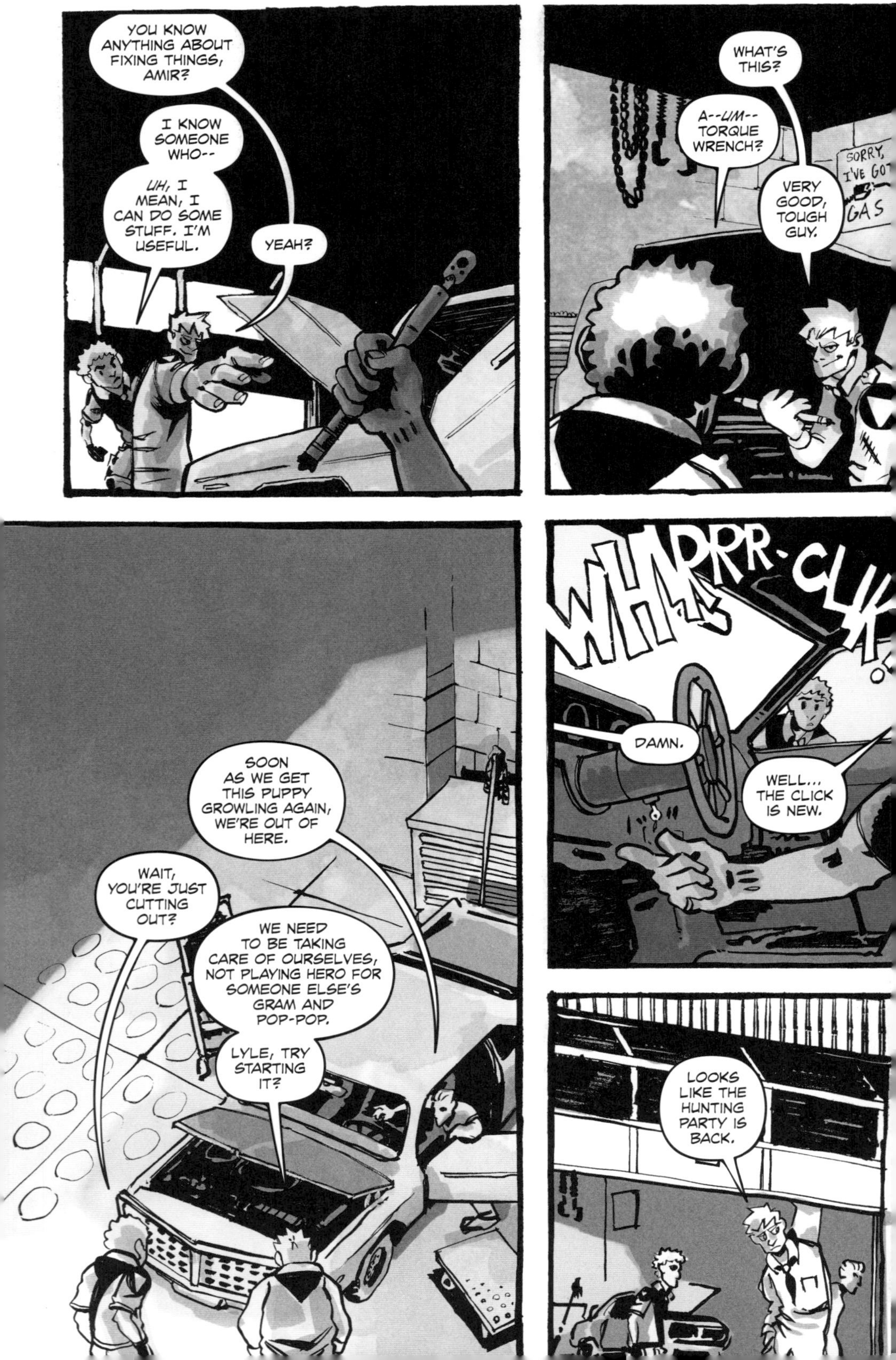
YOU KNOW ANYTHING ABOUT FIXING THINGS, AMIR?
I KNOW SOMEONE WHO--
UH, I MEAN, I CAN DO SOME STUFF. I'M USEFUL.
YEAH?
WHAT'S THIS?
A--*UM*--TORQUE WRENCH?
SORRY, I'VE GOT
GAS
VERY GOOD, TOUGH GUY.
SOON AS WE GET THIS PUPPY GROWLING AGAIN, WE'RE OUT OF HERE.
WAIT, YOU'RE JUST CUTTING OUT?
WE NEED TO BE TAKING CARE OF OURSELVES, NOT PLAYING HERO FOR SOMEONE ELSE'S GRAM AND POP-POP.
LYLE, TRY STARTING IT?
DAMN.
WELL... THE CLICK IS NEW.
LOOKS LIKE THE HUNTING PARTY IS BACK.

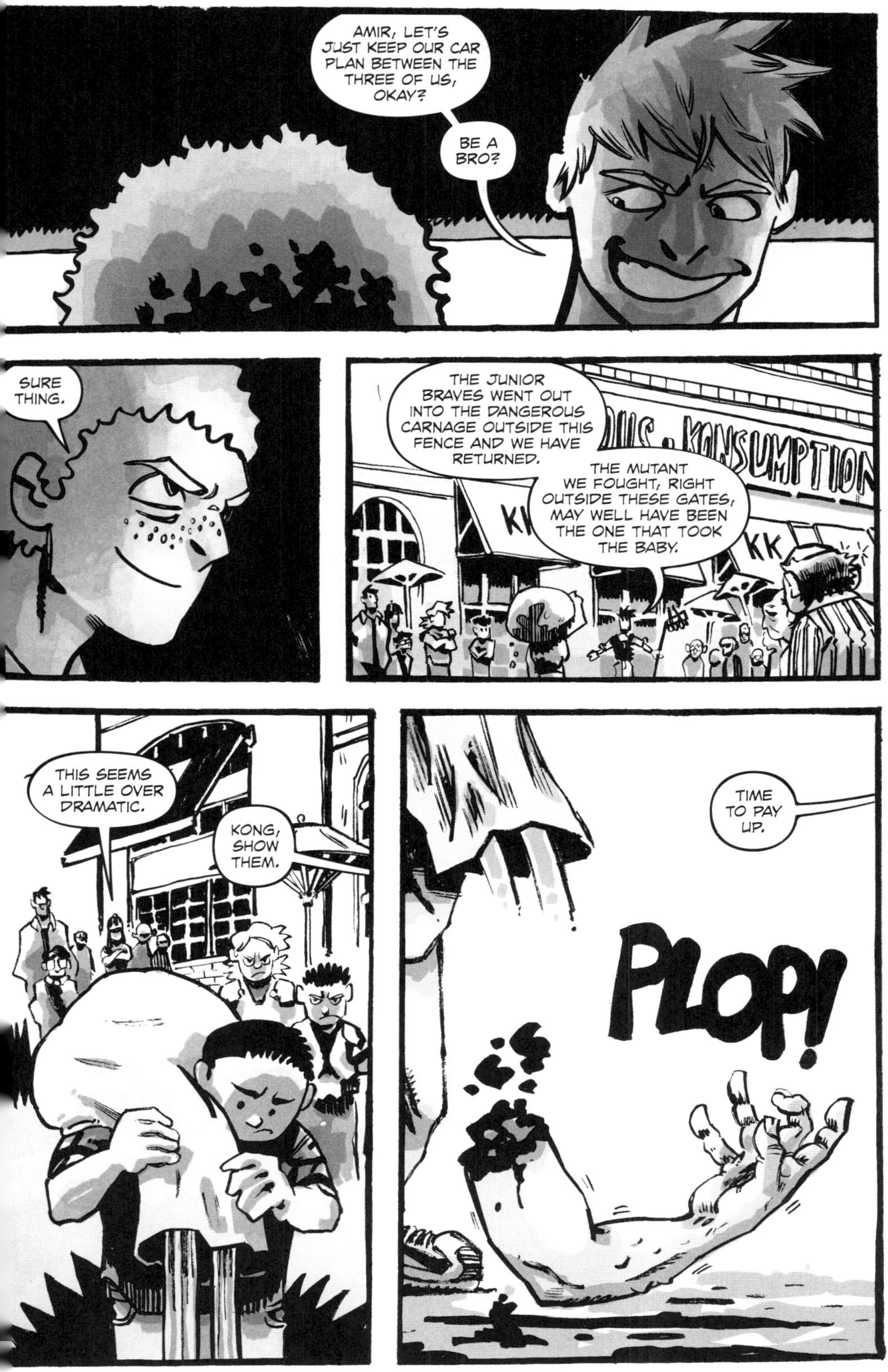
AMIR, LET'S JUST KEEP OUR CAR PLAN BETWEEN THE THREE OF US, OKAY?
BE A BRO?
SURE THING.
THE JUNIOR BRAVES WENT OUT INTO THE DANGEROUS CARNAGE OUTSIDE THIS FENCE AND WE HAVE RETURNED.
KONSUMPTION
KK
THE MUTANT WE FOUGHT, RIGHT OUTSIDE THESE GATES, MAY WELL HAVE BEEN THE ONE THAT TOOK THE BABY.
KK
THIS SEEMS A LITTLE OVER DRAMATIC.
KONG, SHOW THEM.
TIME TO PAY UP.
PLOP!

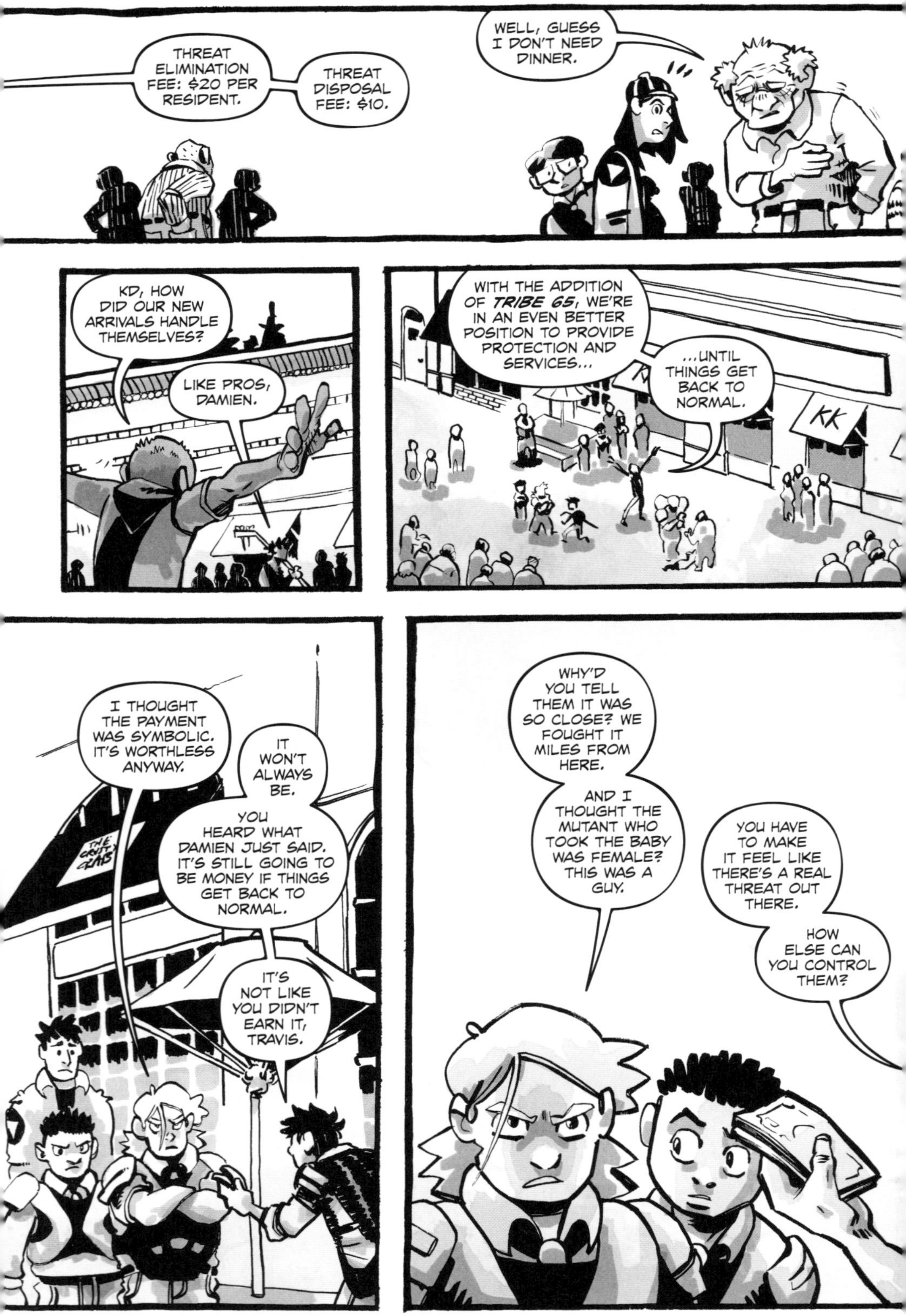
THREAT ELIMINATION FEE: $20 PER RESIDENT.
THREAT DISPOSAL FEE: $10.
WELL, GUESS I DON'T NEED DINNER.
KD, HOW DID OUR NEW ARRIVALS HANDLE THEMSELVES?
LIKE PROS, DAMIEN.
WITH THE ADDITION OF *TRIBE 65*, WE'RE IN AN EVEN BETTER POSITION TO PROVIDE PROTECTION AND SERVICES...
...UNTIL THINGS GET BACK TO NORMAL.
KK
I THOUGHT THE PAYMENT WAS SYMBOLIC. IT'S WORTHLESS ANYWAY.
IT WON'T ALWAYS BE.
YOU HEARD WHAT DAMIEN JUST SAID. IT'S STILL GOING TO BE MONEY IF THINGS GET BACK TO NORMAL.
IT'S NOT LIKE YOU DIDN'T EARN IT, TRAVIS.
WHY'D YOU TELL THEM IT WAS SO CLOSE? WE FOUGHT IT MILES FROM HERE.
AND I THOUGHT THE MUTANT WHO TOOK THE BABY WAS FEMALE? THIS WAS A GUY.
YOU HAVE TO MAKE IT FEEL LIKE THERE'S A REAL THREAT OUT THERE.
HOW ELSE CAN YOU CONTROL THEM?

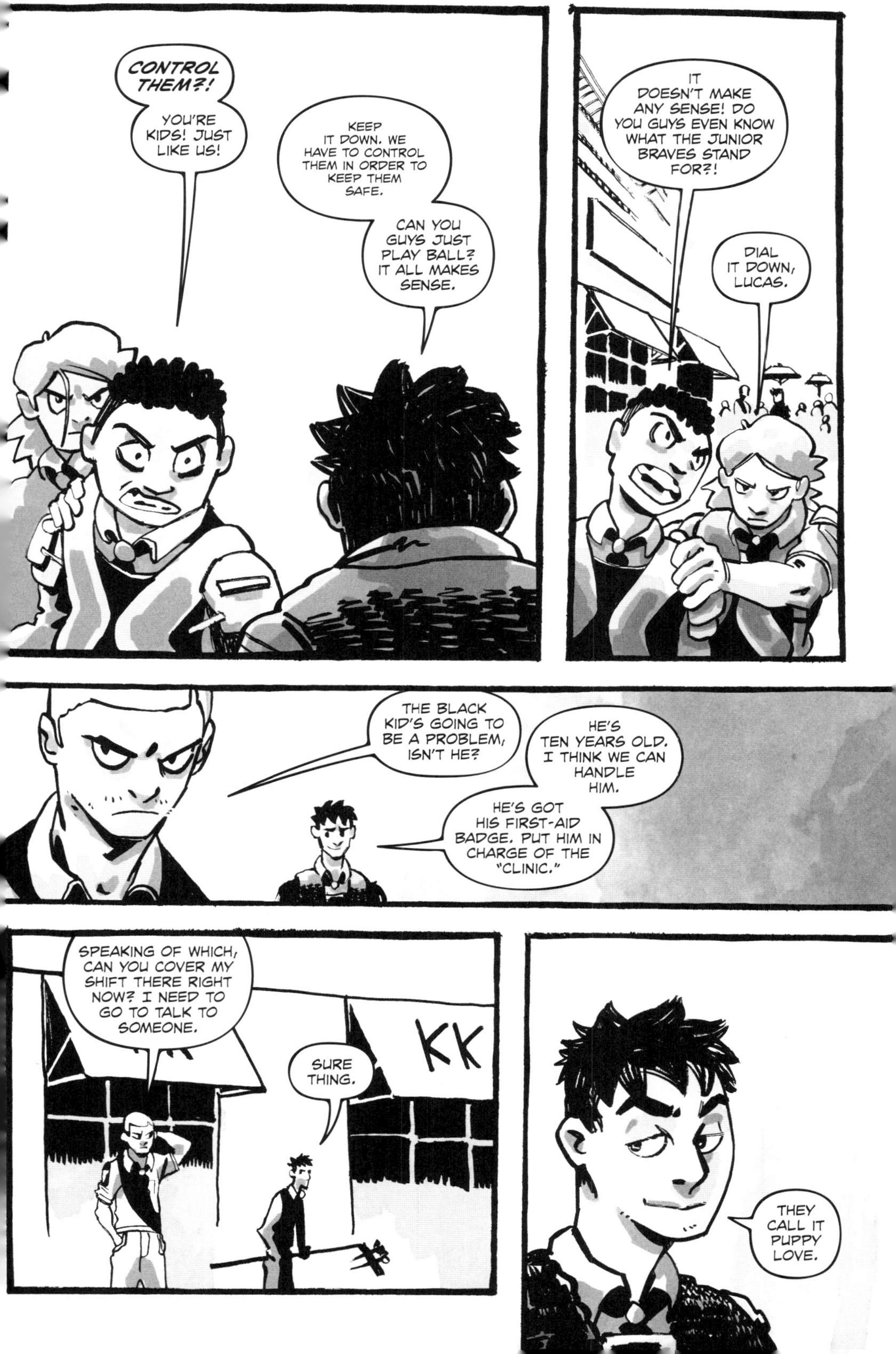
CONTROL THEM?!
YOU'RE KIDS! JUST LIKE US!
KEEP IT DOWN. WE HAVE TO CONTROL THEM IN ORDER TO KEEP THEM SAFE.
CAN YOU GUYS JUST PLAY BALL? IT ALL MAKES SENSE.
IT DOESN'T MAKE ANY SENSE! DO YOU GUYS EVEN KNOW WHAT THE JUNIOR BRAVES STAND FOR?!
DIAL IT DOWN, LUCAS.
THE BLACK KID'S GOING TO BE A PROBLEM, ISN'T HE?
HE'S TEN YEARS OLD. I THINK WE CAN HANDLE HIM.
HE'S GOT HIS FIRST-AID BADGE. PUT HIM IN CHARGE OF THE "CLINIC."
SPEAKING OF WHICH, CAN YOU COVER MY SHIFT THERE RIGHT NOW? I NEED TO GO TO TALK TO SOMEONE.
KK
SURE THING.
THEY CALL IT PUPPY LOVE.

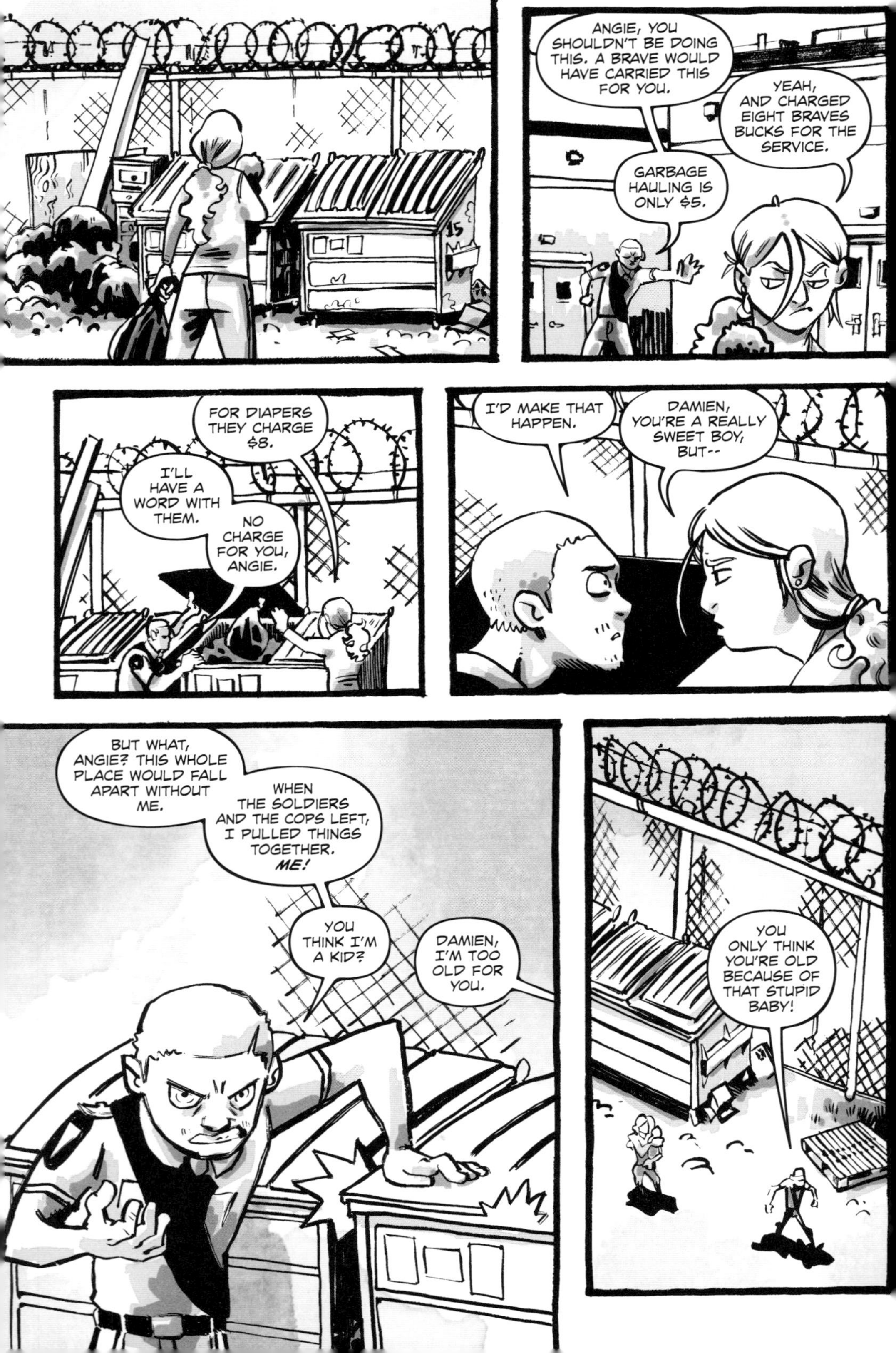
ANGIE, YOU SHOULDN'T BE DOING THIS. A BRAVE WOULD HAVE CARRIED THIS FOR YOU.
YEAH, AND CHARGED EIGHT BRAVES BUCKS FOR THE SERVICE.
GARBAGE HAULING IS ONLY $5.
FOR DIAPERS THEY CHARGE $8.
I'LL HAVE A WORD WITH THEM.
NO CHARGE FOR YOU, ANGIE.
I'D MAKE THAT HAPPEN.
DAMIEN, YOU'RE A REALLY SWEET BOY, BUT--
BUT WHAT, ANGIE? THIS WHOLE PLACE WOULD FALL APART WITHOUT ME.
WHEN THE SOLDIERS AND THE COPS LEFT, I PULLED THINGS TOGETHER. ME!
DAMIEN, I'M TOO OLD FOR YOU.
YOU THINK I'M A KID?
YOU ONLY THINK YOU'RE OLD BECAUSE OF THAT STUPID BABY!

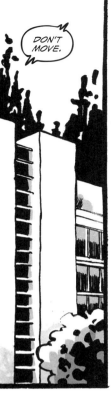

DON'T MOVE.

I'M NOT.

MR. PATTERSON, THIS WILL BE OVER IN A MINUTE.

YOU'RE NOT GOING TO TELL ME ANYTHING I DON'T ALREADY KNOW.

LATER.

SIR, MY NAME'S THOMAS THADDEUS. I'M ASSISTANT DIRECTOR HERE AT CORPROCO.

I'M ALSO PROBABLY THE ONLY SURVIVING MEMBER OF THE SENIOR STAFF. MIND IF I COME IN?

I THINK YOU GET TO COME IN REGARDLESS OF MY ANSWER, SINCE APPARENTLY THIS IS YOUR BUILDING NOW.

CLICK!

YOU ARE FASCINATING TO ME. FROM WHAT I'M TOLD, YOU HAVE NO IDEA ABOUT, WELL, ANYTHING THAT HAPPENED THE LAST TWO WEEKS.

SO I HAVE A PROPOSITION FOR YOU. I'LL ANSWER ONE OF YOUR QUESTIONS IF YOU ANSWER ONE OF MINE. DEAL?

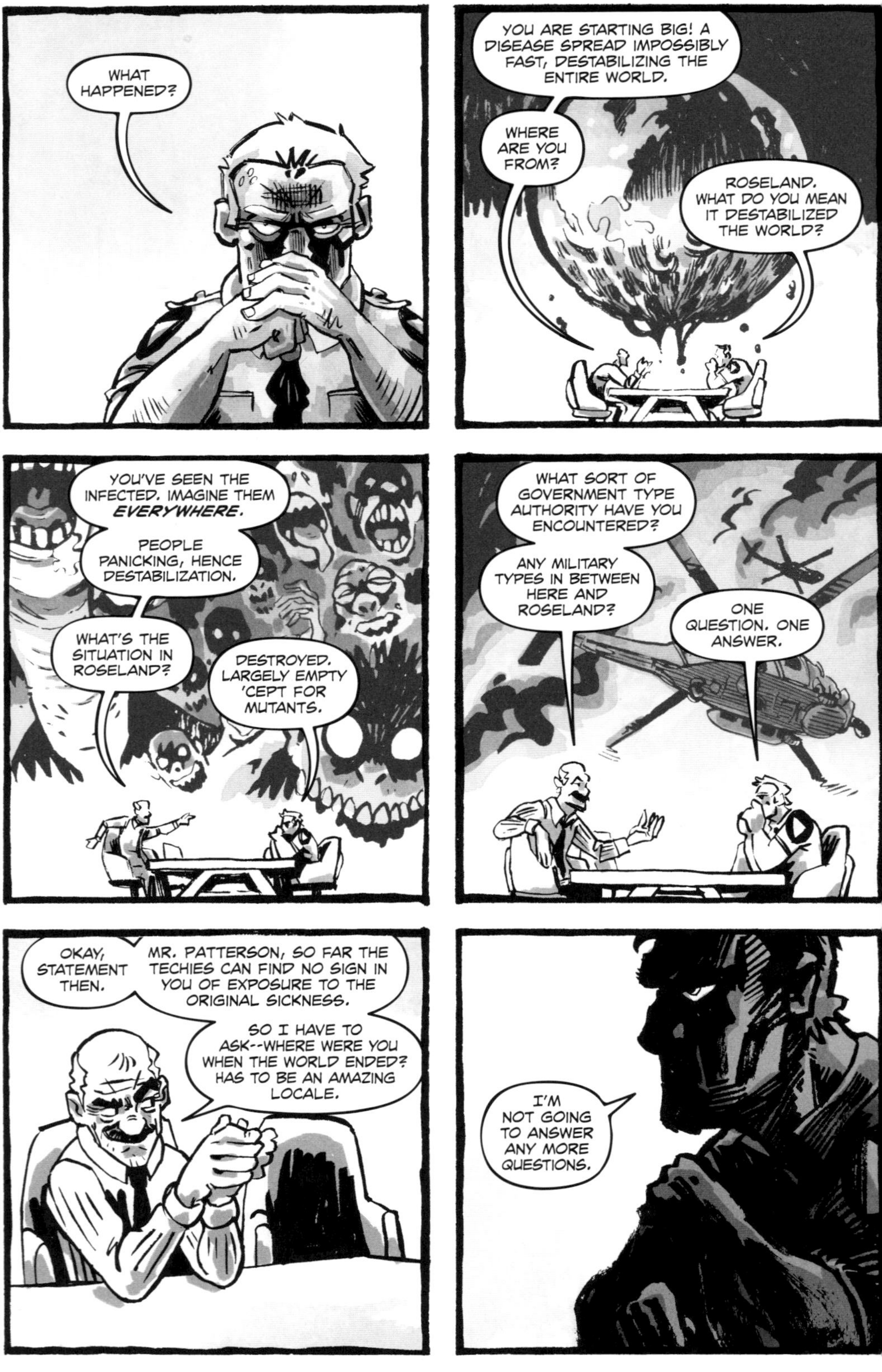
WHAT HAPPENED?
YOU ARE STARTING BIG! A DISEASE SPREAD IMPOSSIBLY FAST, DESTABILIZING THE ENTIRE WORLD.
WHERE ARE YOU FROM?
ROSELAND. WHAT DO YOU MEAN IT DESTABILIZED THE WORLD?
YOU'VE SEEN THE INFECTED. IMAGINE THEM *EVERYWHERE*.
PEOPLE PANICKING, HENCE DESTABILIZATION.
WHAT'S THE SITUATION IN ROSELAND?
DESTROYED. LARGELY EMPTY 'CEPT FOR MUTANTS.
WHAT SORT OF GOVERNMENT TYPE AUTHORITY HAVE YOU ENCOUNTERED?
ANY MILITARY TYPES IN BETWEEN HERE AND ROSELAND?
ONE QUESTION. ONE ANSWER.
OKAY, STATEMENT THEN.
MR. PATTERSON, SO FAR THE TECHIES CAN FIND NO SIGN IN YOU OF EXPOSURE TO THE ORIGINAL SICKNESS.
SO I HAVE TO ASK--WHERE WERE YOU WHEN THE WORLD ENDED? HAS TO BE AN AMAZING LOCALE.
I'M NOT GOING TO ANSWER ANY MORE QUESTIONS.

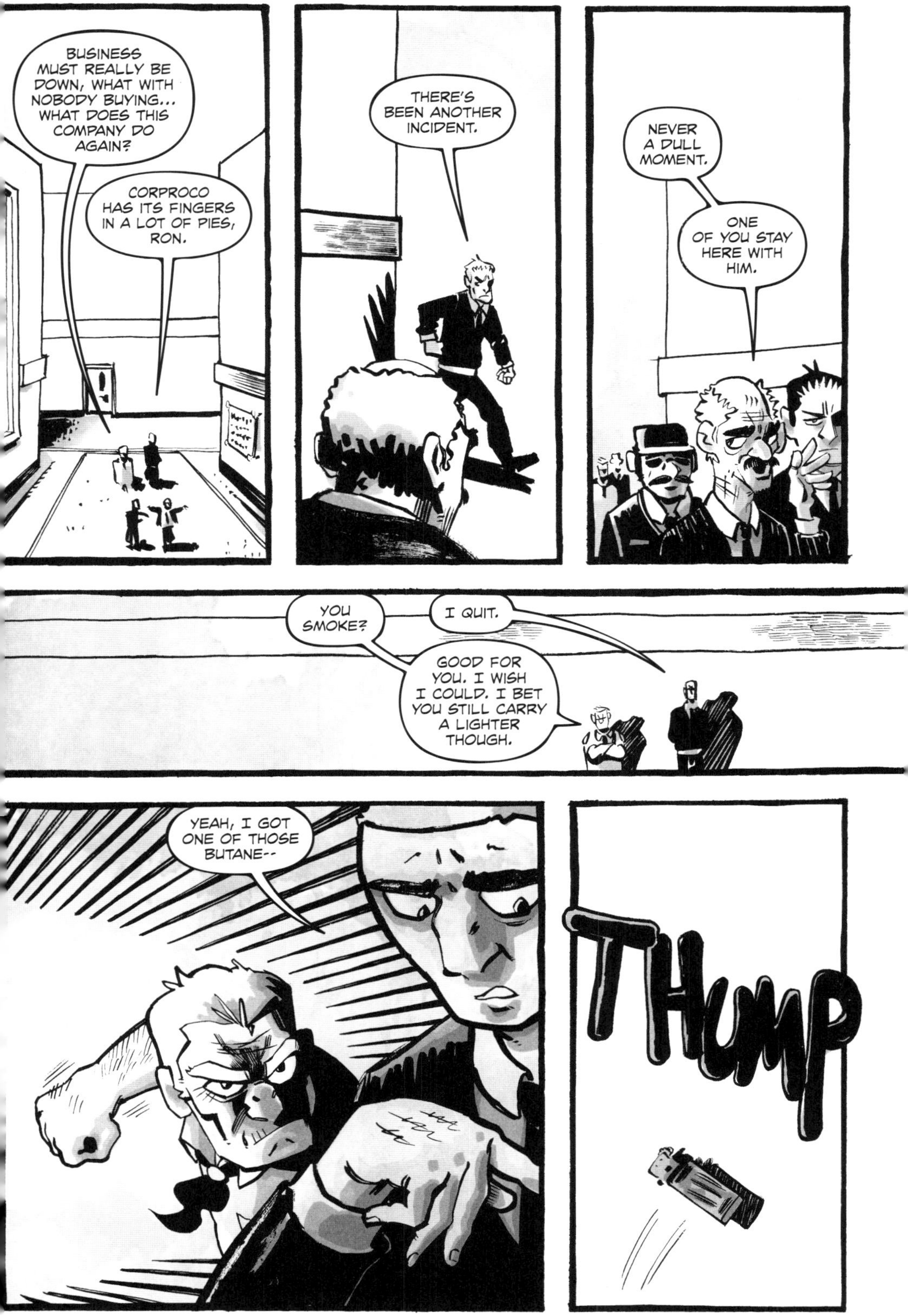
BUSINESS MUST REALLY BE DOWN, WHAT WITH NOBODY BUYING... WHAT DOES THIS COMPANY DO AGAIN?
CORPROCO HAS ITS FINGERS IN A LOT OF PIES, RON.
THERE'S BEEN ANOTHER INCIDENT.
NEVER A DULL MOMENT.
ONE OF YOU STAY HERE WITH HIM.
YOU SMOKE?
I QUIT.
GOOD FOR YOU. I WISH I COULD. I BET YOU STILL CARRY A LIGHTER THOUGH.
YEAH, I GOT ONE OF THOSE BUTANE--
THUMP

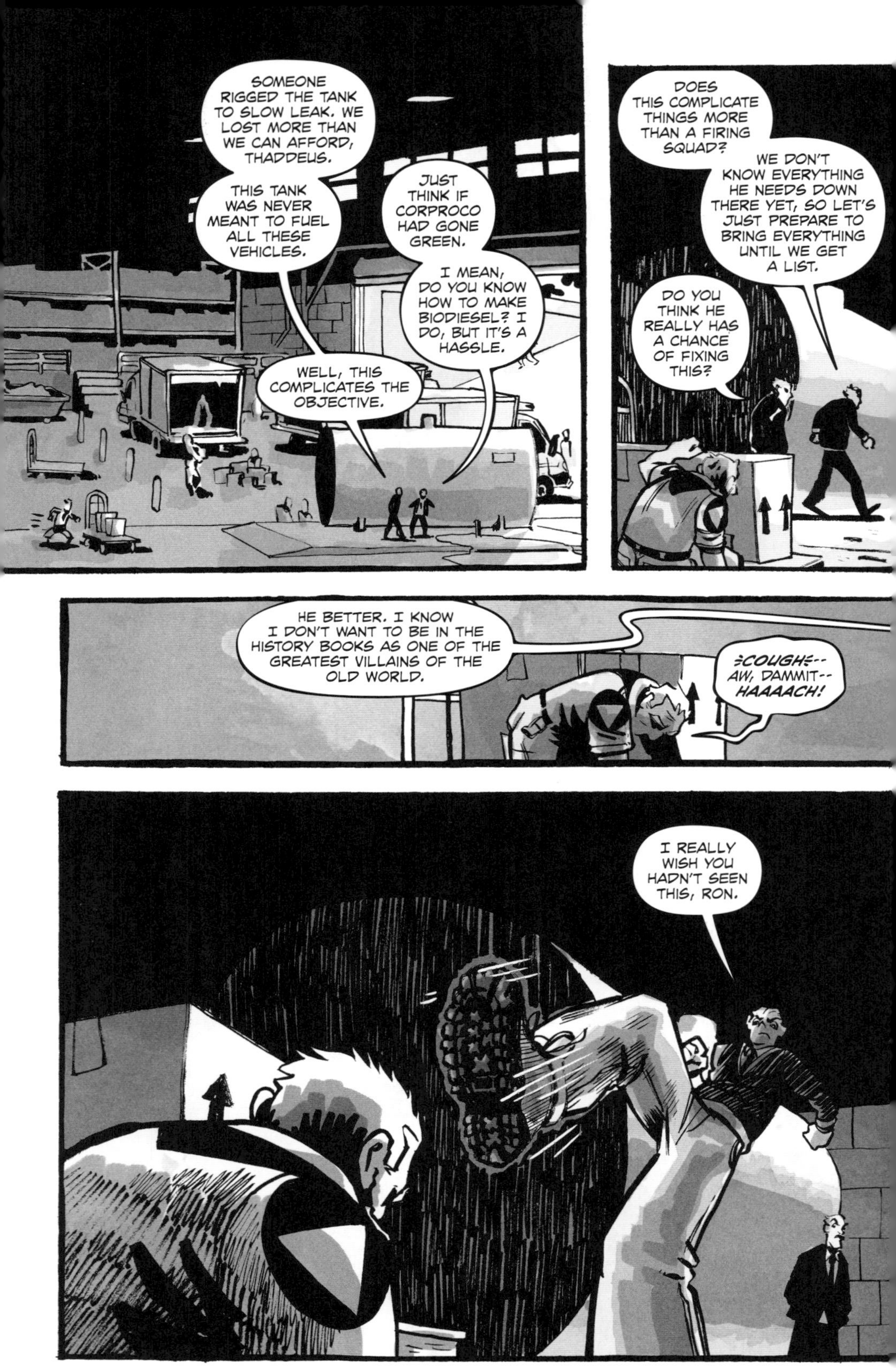
SOMEONE RIGGED THE TANK TO SLOW LEAK. WE LOST MORE THAN WE CAN AFFORD, THADDEUS.
THIS TANK WAS NEVER MEANT TO FUEL ALL THESE VEHICLES.
JUST THINK IF CORPROCO HAD GONE GREEN.
I MEAN, DO YOU KNOW HOW TO MAKE BIODIESEL? I DO, BUT IT'S A HASSLE.
WELL, THIS COMPLICATES THE OBJECTIVE.
DOES THIS COMPLICATE THINGS MORE THAN A FIRING SQUAD?
WE DON'T KNOW EVERYTHING HE NEEDS DOWN THERE YET, SO LET'S JUST PREPARE TO BRING EVERYTHING UNTIL WE GET A LIST.
DO YOU THINK HE REALLY HAS A CHANCE OF FIXING THIS?
HE BETTER. I KNOW I DON'T WANT TO BE IN THE HISTORY BOOKS AS ONE OF THE GREATEST VILLAINS OF THE OLD WORLD.
COUGH-- AW, DAMMIT-- HAAAACH!
I REALLY WISH YOU HADN'T SEEN THIS, RON.

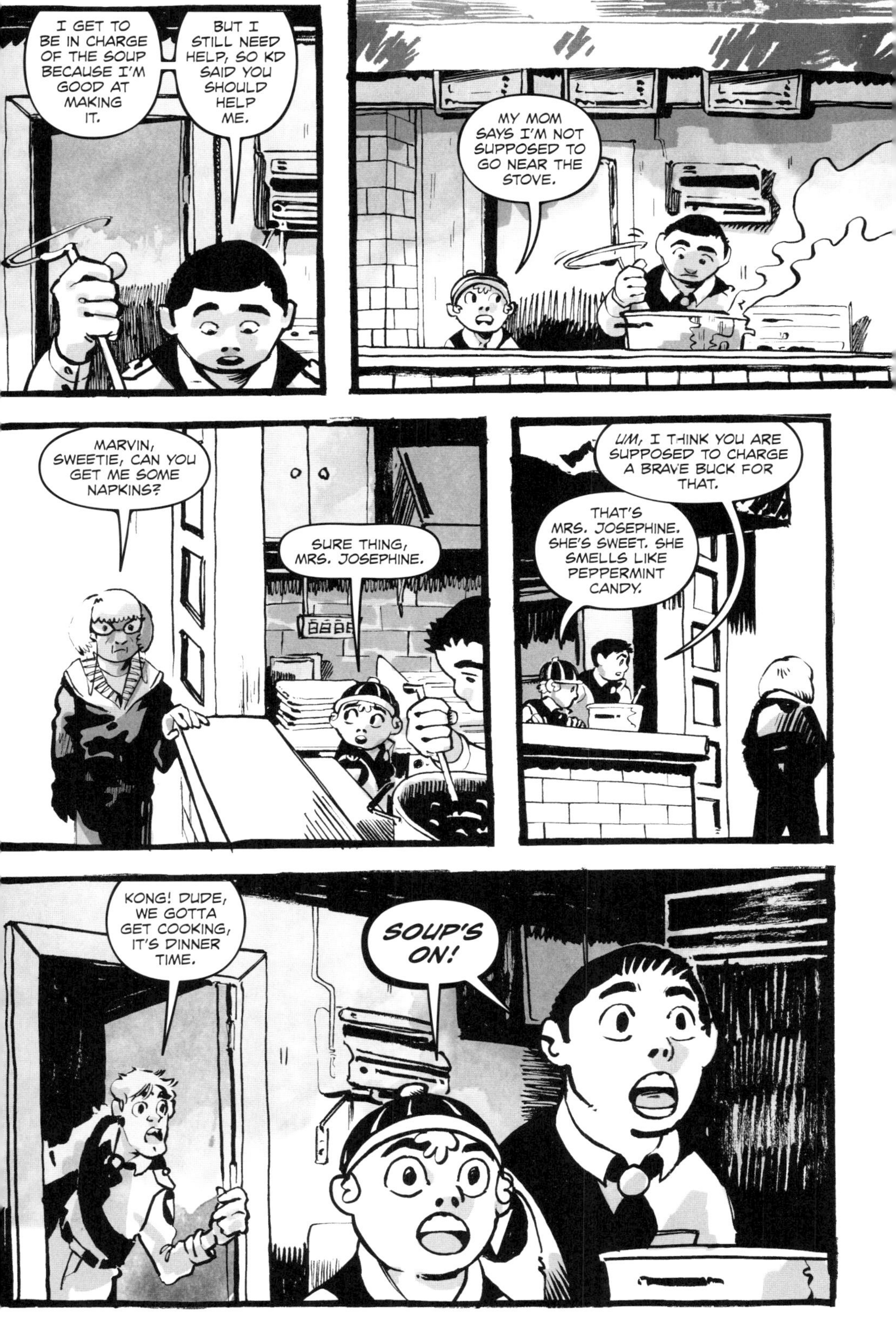
I GET TO BE IN CHARGE OF THE SOUP BECAUSE I'M GOOD AT MAKING IT.
BUT I STILL NEED HELP, SO KD SAID YOU SHOULD HELP ME.
MY MOM SAYS I'M NOT SUPPOSED TO GO NEAR THE STOVE.
MARVIN, SWEETIE, CAN YOU GET ME SOME NAPKINS?
SURE THING, MRS. JOSEPHINE.
UM, I THINK YOU ARE SUPPOSED TO CHARGE A BRAVE BUCK FOR THAT.
THAT'S MRS. JOSEPHINE. SHE'S SWEET. SHE SMELLS LIKE PEPPERMINT CANDY.
KONG! DUDE, WE GOTTA GET COOKING, IT'S DINNER TIME.
SOUP'S ON!

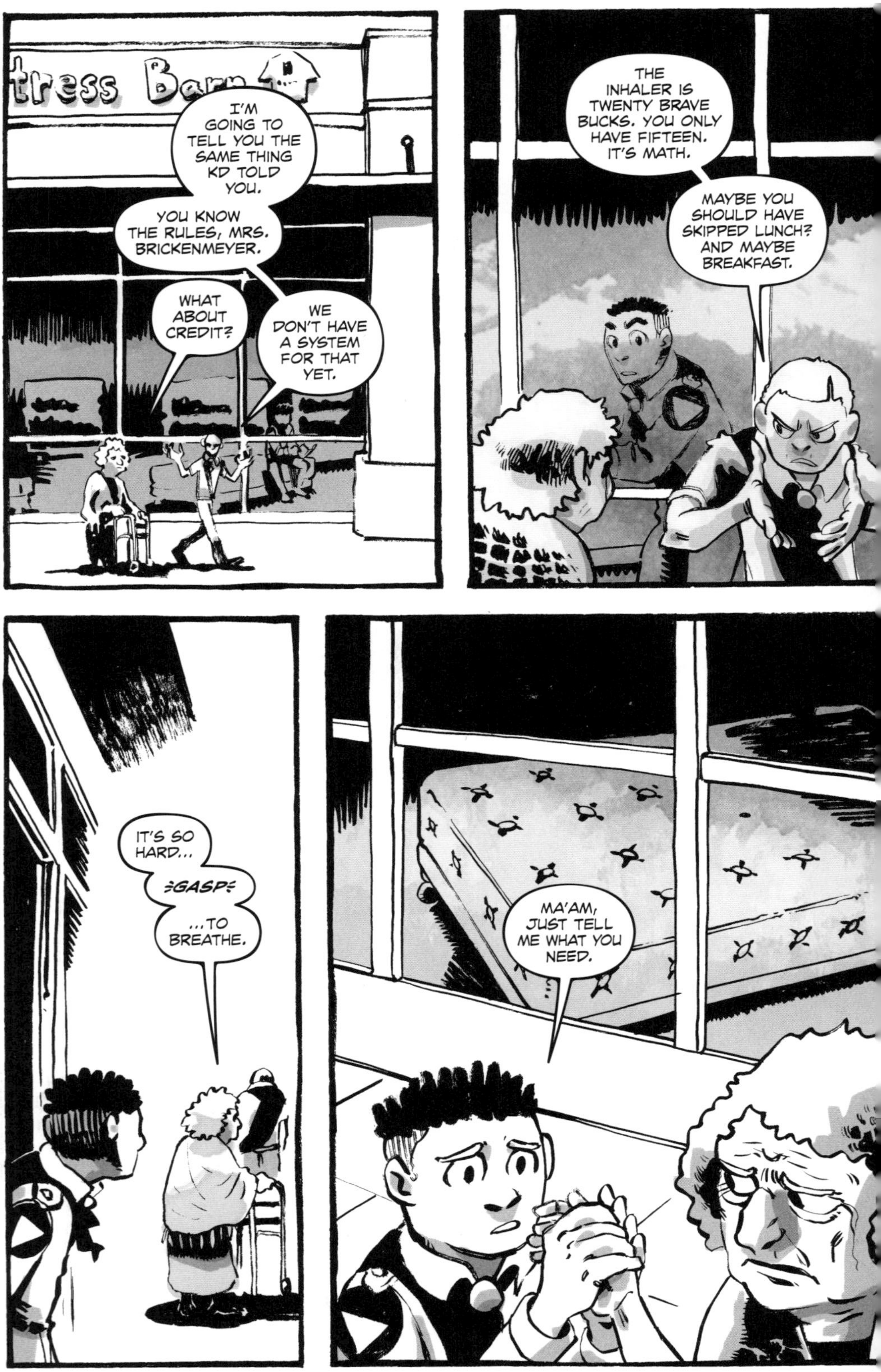
tress Barn
I'M GOING TO TELL YOU THE SAME THING KD TOLD YOU.
YOU KNOW THE RULES, MRS. BRICKENMEYER.
WHAT ABOUT CREDIT?
WE DON'T HAVE A SYSTEM FOR THAT YET.
THE INHALER IS TWENTY BRAVE BUCKS. YOU ONLY HAVE FIFTEEN. IT'S MATH.
MAYBE YOU SHOULD HAVE SKIPPED LUNCH? AND MAYBE BREAKFAST.
IT'S SO HARD...
GASP
...TO BREATHE.
MA'AM, JUST TELL ME WHAT YOU NEED.

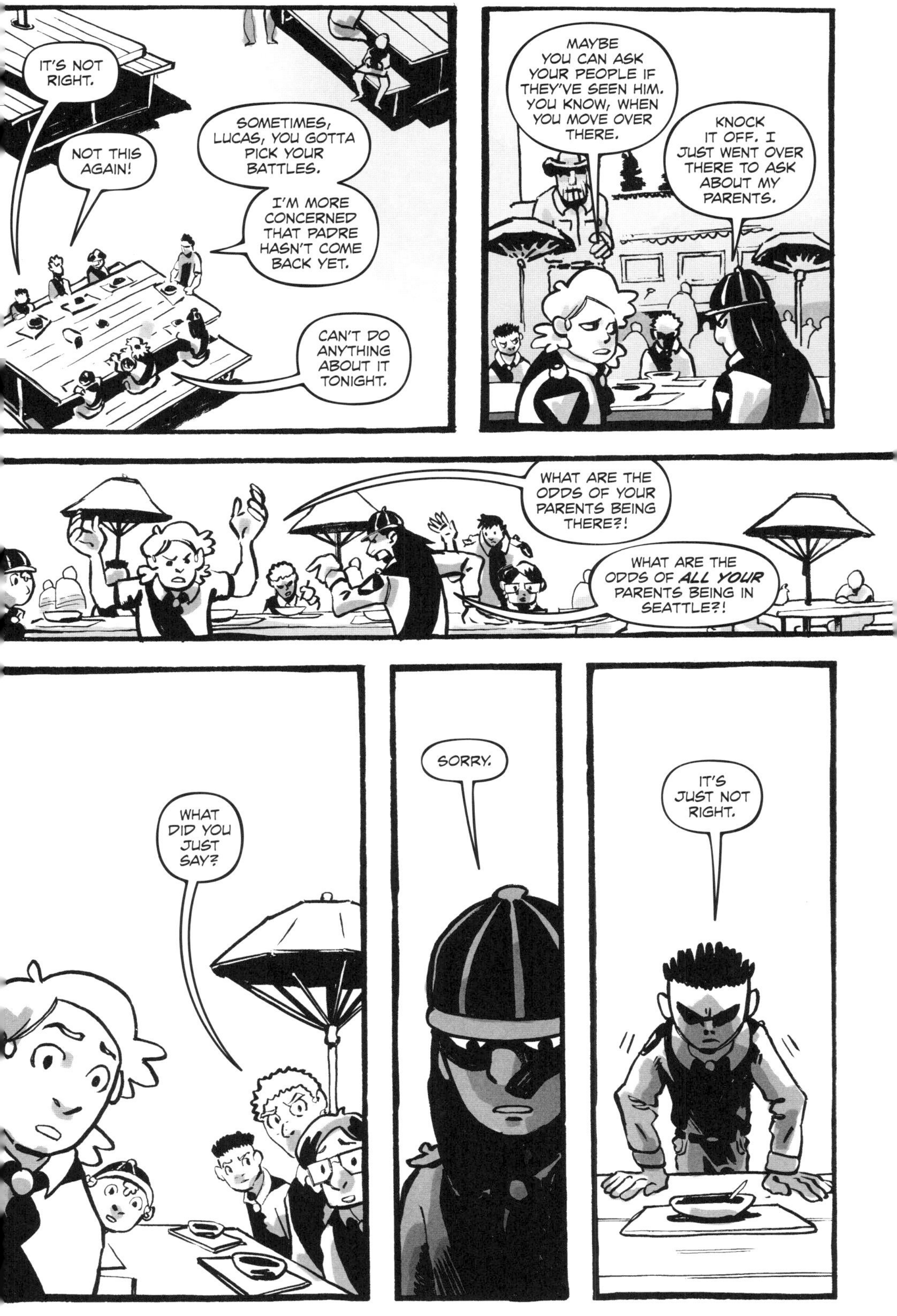
IT'S NOT RIGHT.
NOT THIS AGAIN!
SOMETIMES, LUCAS, YOU GOTTA PICK YOUR BATTLES.
I'M MORE CONCERNED THAT PADRE HASN'T COME BACK YET.
CAN'T DO ANYTHING ABOUT IT TONIGHT.
MAYBE YOU CAN ASK YOUR PEOPLE IF THEY'VE SEEN HIM. YOU KNOW, WHEN YOU MOVE OVER THERE.
KNOCK IT OFF. I JUST WENT OVER THERE TO ASK ABOUT MY PARENTS.
WHAT ARE THE ODDS OF YOUR PARENTS BEING THERE?!
WHAT ARE THE ODDS OF ***ALL YOUR*** PARENTS BEING IN SEATTLE?!
WHAT DID YOU JUST SAY?
SORRY.
IT'S JUST NOT RIGHT.

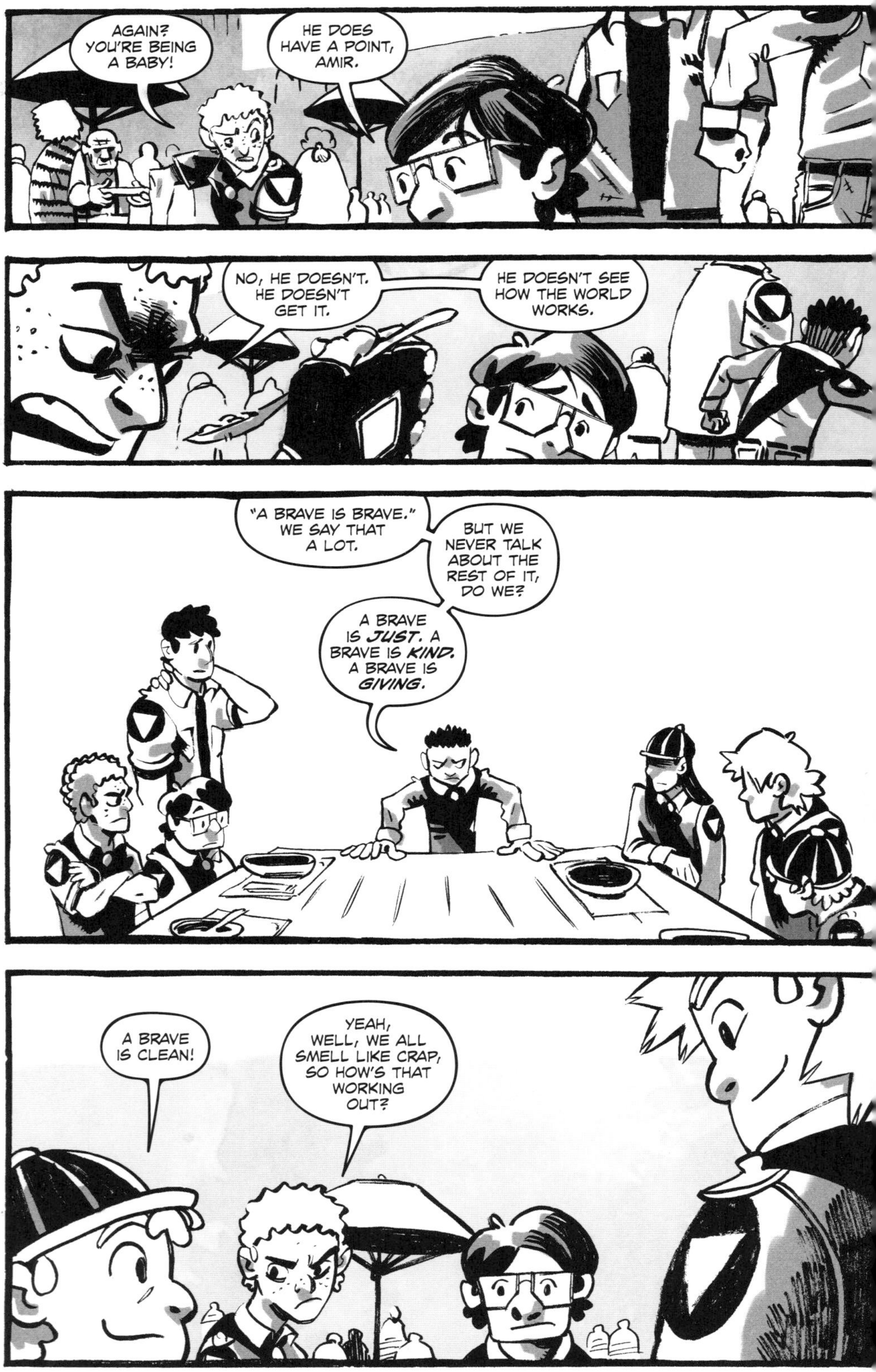
AGAIN? YOU'RE BEING A BABY!
HE DOES HAVE A POINT, AMIR.
NO, HE DOESN'T. HE DOESN'T GET IT.
HE DOESN'T SEE HOW THE WORLD WORKS.
"A BRAVE IS BRAVE." WE SAY THAT A LOT.
BUT WE NEVER TALK ABOUT THE REST OF IT, DO WE?
A BRAVE IS *JUST*. A BRAVE IS *KIND*. A BRAVE IS *GIVING*.
A BRAVE IS CLEAN!
YEAH, WELL, WE ALL SMELL LIKE CRAP, SO HOW'S THAT WORKING OUT?

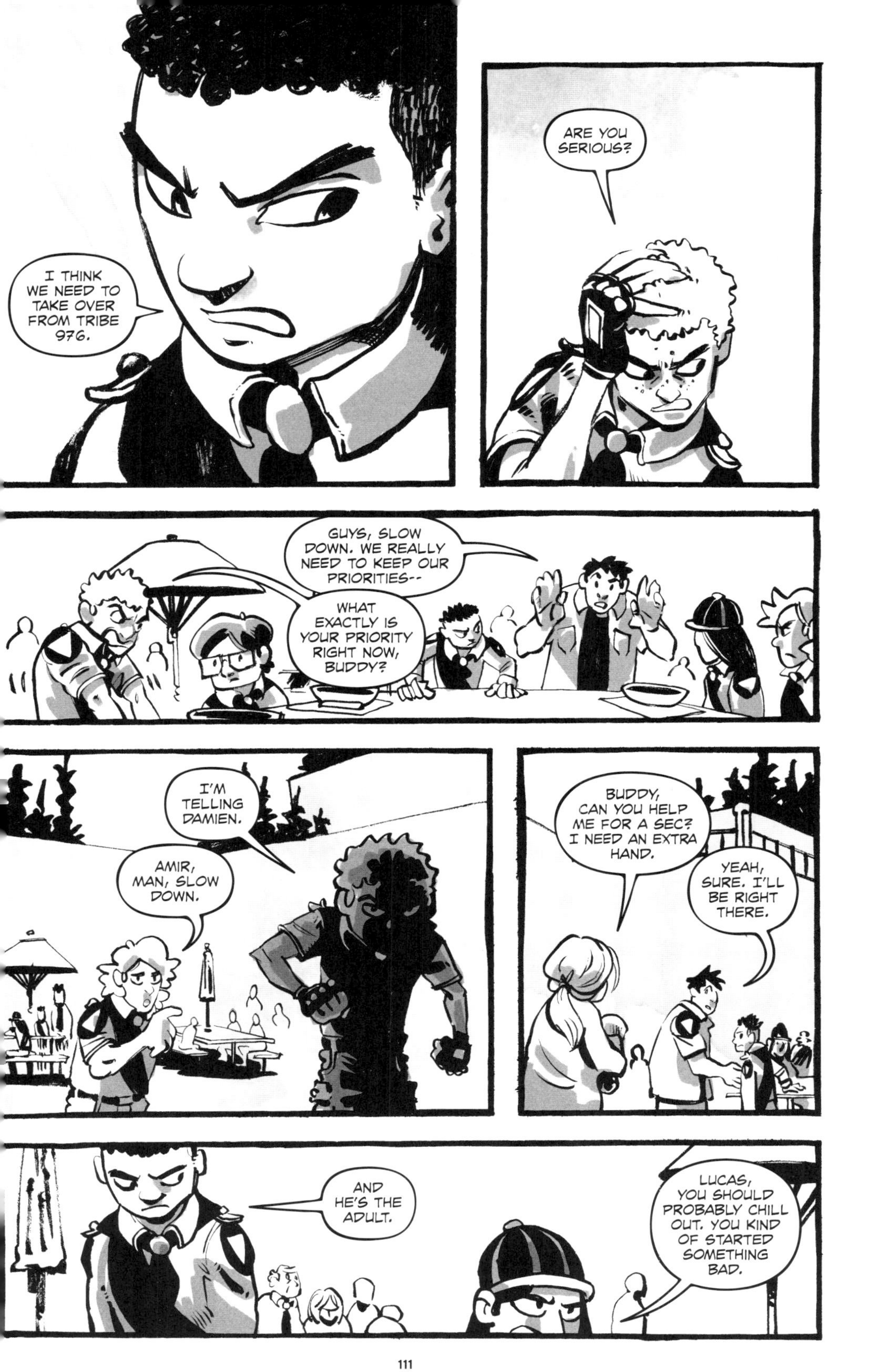
I THINK WE NEED TO TAKE OVER FROM TRIBE 976.
ARE YOU SERIOUS?
GUYS, SLOW DOWN. WE REALLY NEED TO KEEP OUR PRIORITIES--
WHAT EXACTLY IS YOUR PRIORITY RIGHT NOW, BUDDY?
I'M TELLING DAMIEN.
AMIR, MAN, SLOW DOWN.
BUDDY, CAN YOU HELP ME FOR A SEC? I NEED AN EXTRA HAND.
YEAH, SURE. I'LL BE RIGHT THERE.
AND HE'S THE ADULT.
LUCAS, YOU SHOULD PROBABLY CHILL OUT. YOU KIND OF STARTED SOMETHING BAD.

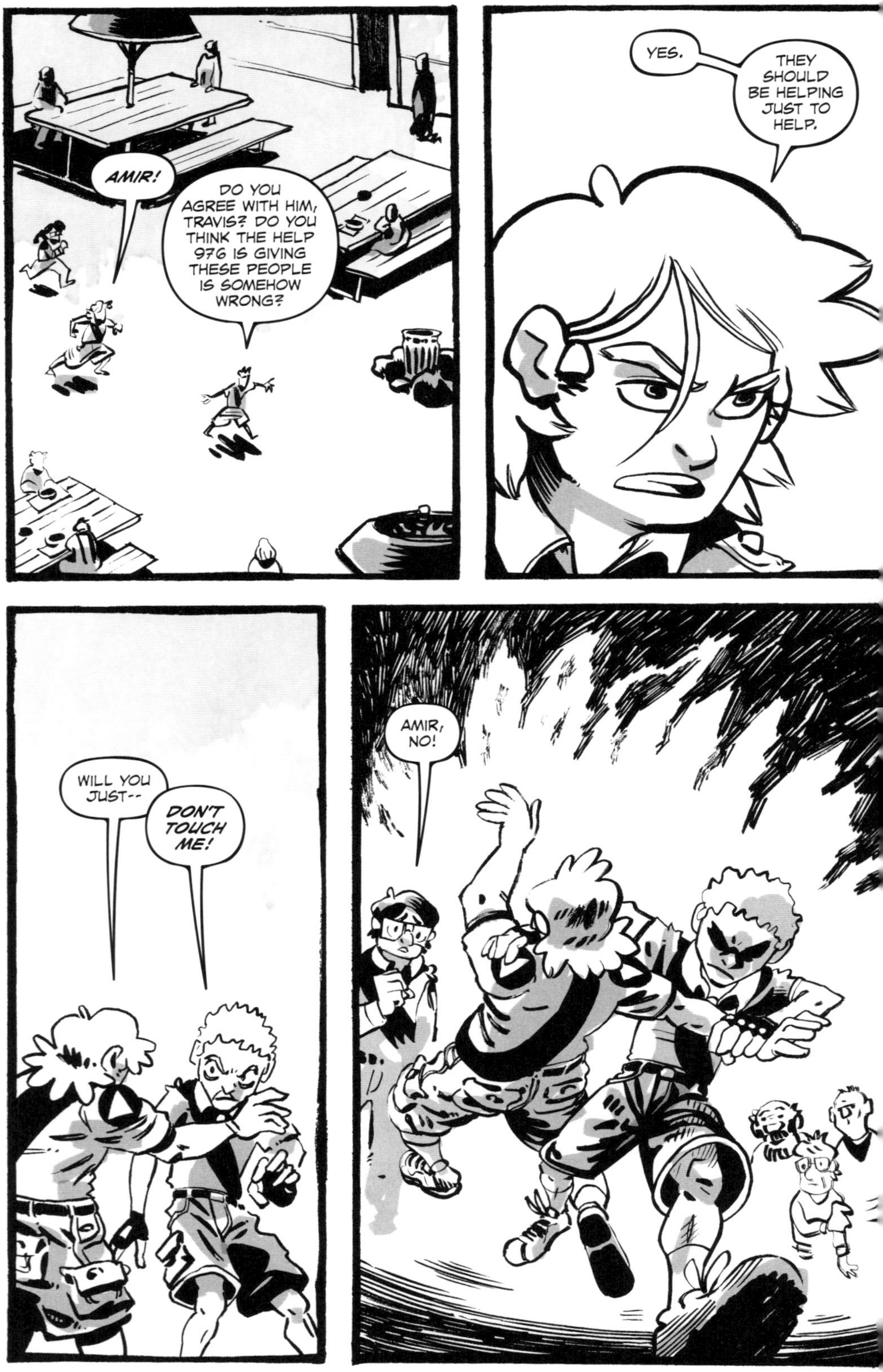
AMIR!
DO YOU AGREE WITH HIM, TRAVIS? DO YOU THINK THE HELP 976 IS GIVING THESE PEOPLE IS SOMEHOW WRONG?
YES.
THEY SHOULD BE HELPING JUST TO HELP.
WILL YOU JUST--
DON'T TOUCH ME!
AMIR, NO!

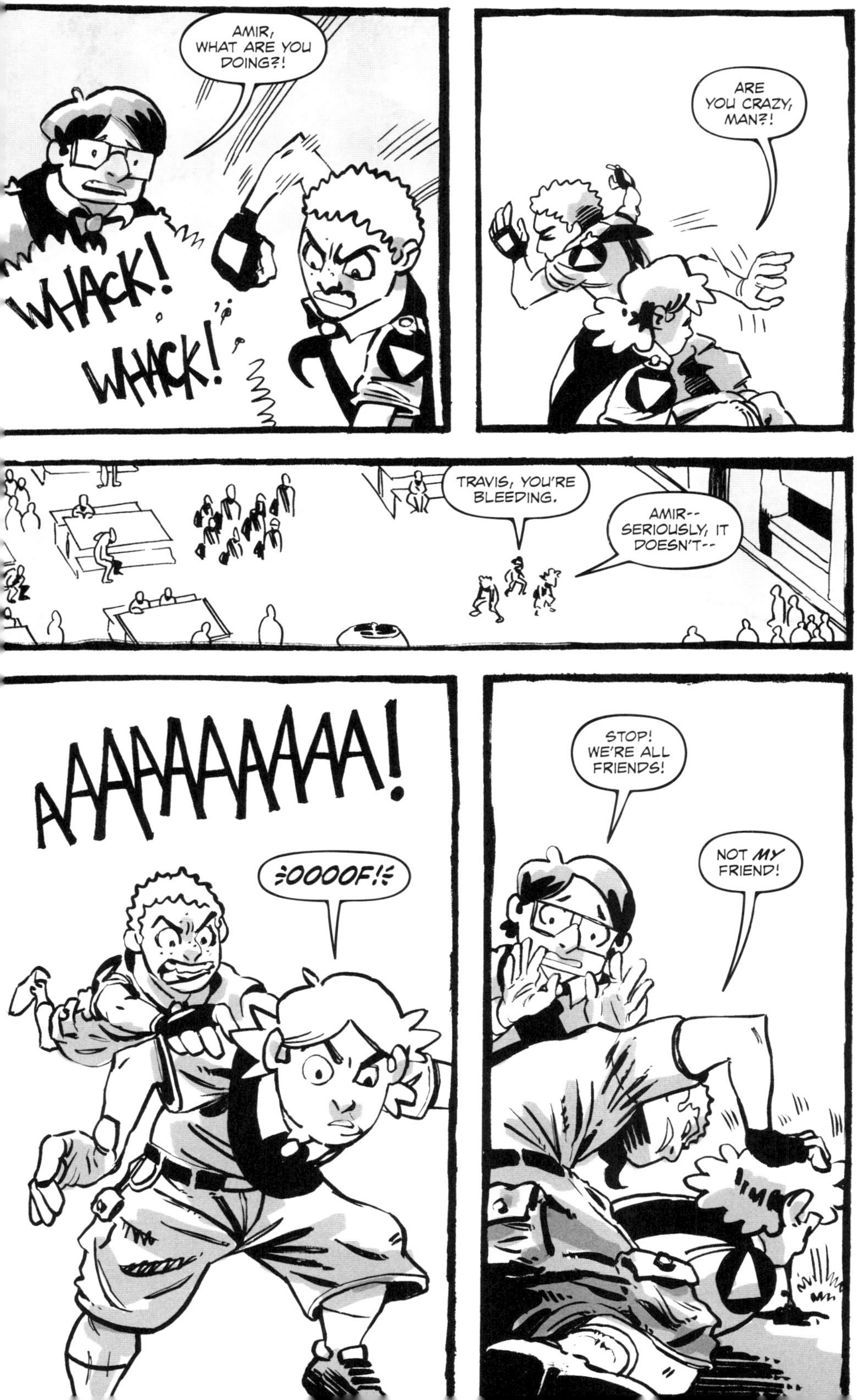
AMIR, WHAT ARE YOU DOING?!
WHACK! WHACK!
ARE YOU CRAZY, MAN?!
TRAVIS, YOU'RE BLEEDING.
AMIR-- SERIOUSLY, IT DOESN'T--
AAAAAAAAAA!
OOOOF!
STOP! WE'RE ALL FRIENDS!
NOT *MY* FRIEND!

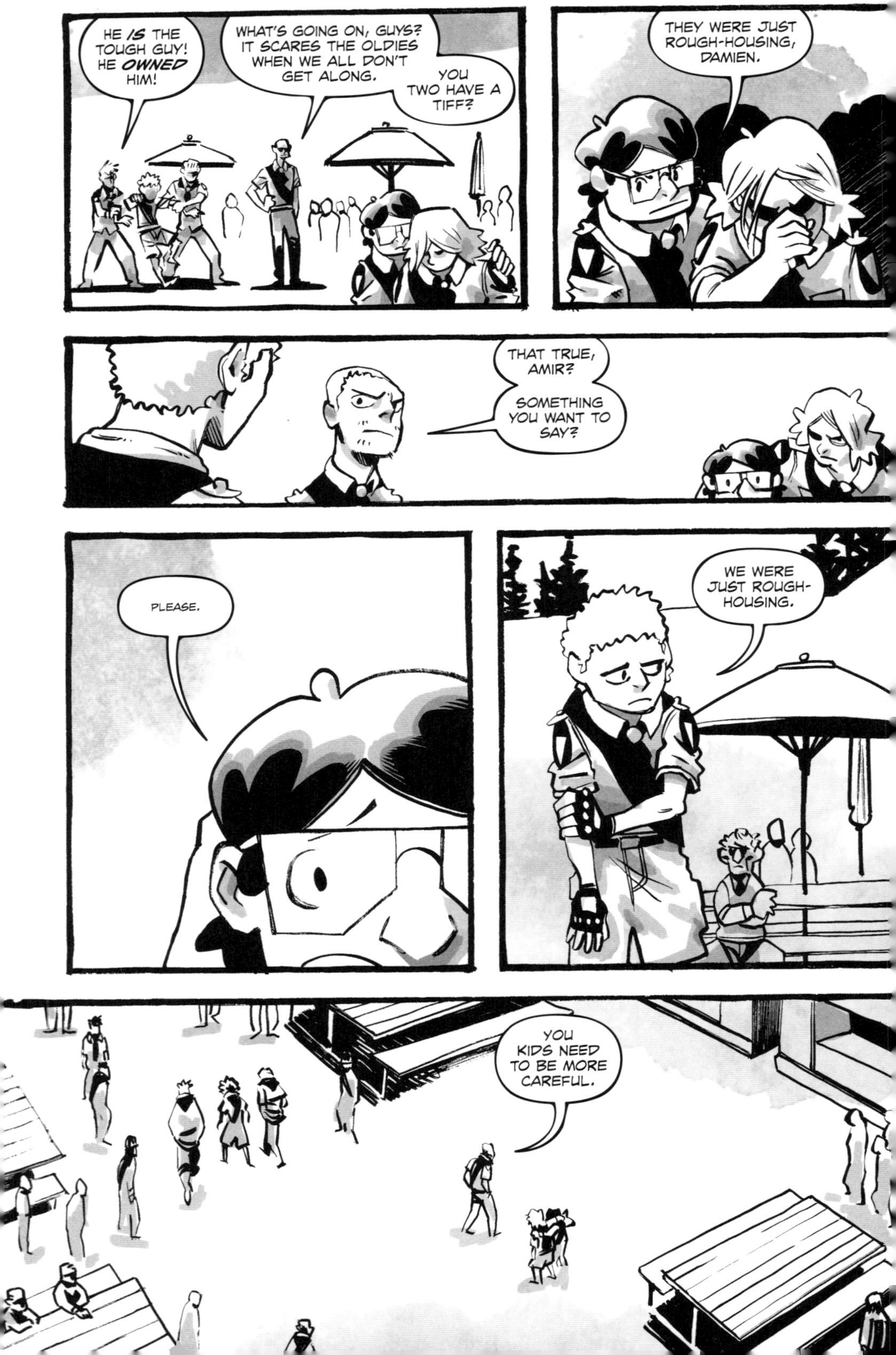
HE *IS* THE TOUGH GUY! HE ***OWNED*** HIM!
WHAT'S GOING ON, GUYS? IT SCARES THE OLDIES WHEN WE ALL DON'T GET ALONG.
YOU TWO HAVE A TIFF?
THEY WERE JUST ROUGH-HOUSING, DAMIEN.
THAT TRUE, AMIR?
SOMETHING YOU WANT TO SAY?
PLEASE.
WE WERE JUST ROUGH-HOUSING.
YOU KIDS NEED TO BE MORE CAREFUL.

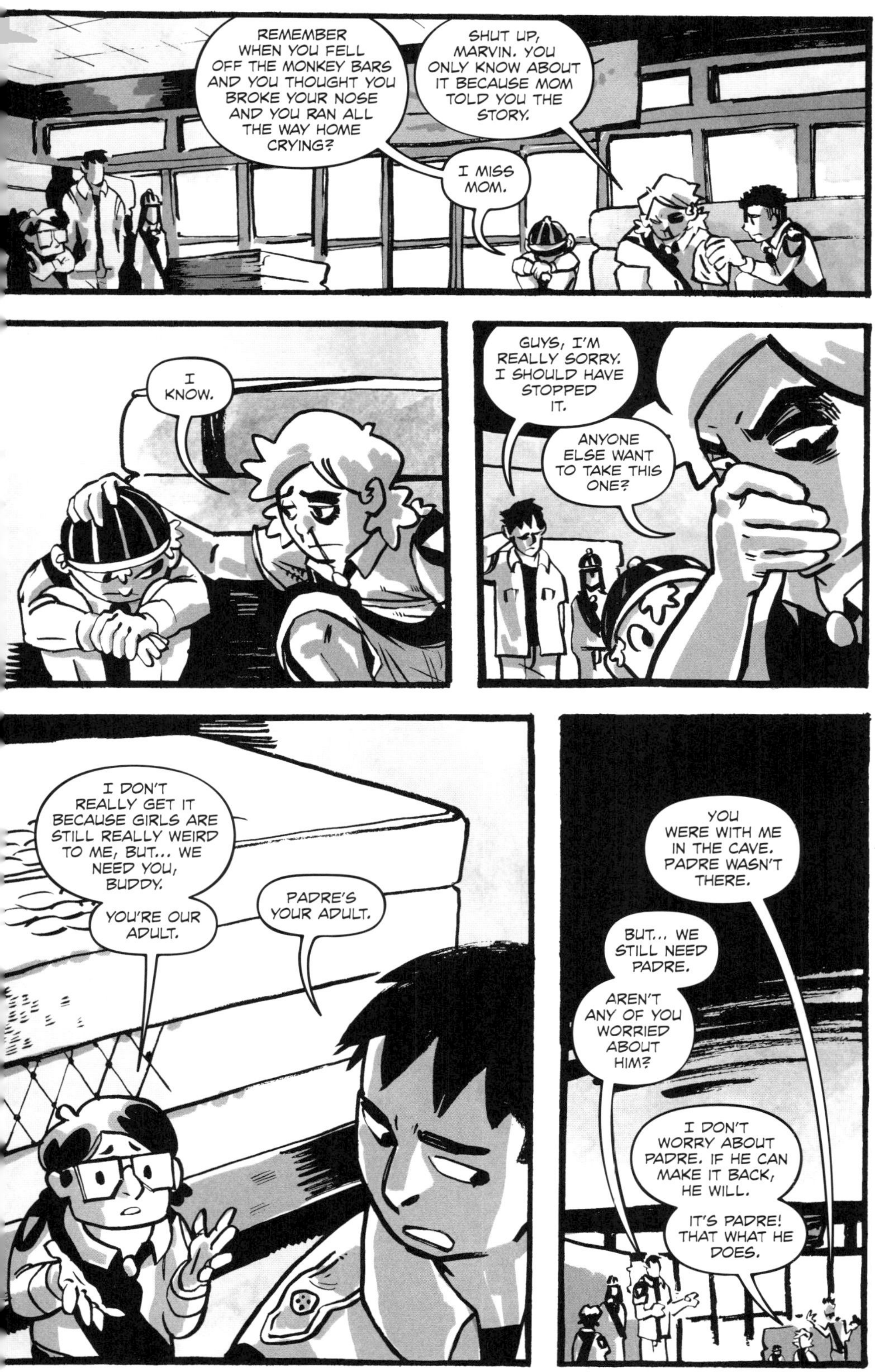
REMEMBER WHEN YOU FELL OFF THE MONKEY BARS AND YOU THOUGHT YOU BROKE YOUR NOSE AND YOU RAN ALL THE WAY HOME CRYING?
SHUT UP, MARVIN. YOU ONLY KNOW ABOUT IT BECAUSE MOM TOLD YOU THE STORY.
I MISS MOM.
I KNOW.
GUYS, I'M REALLY SORRY. I SHOULD HAVE STOPPED IT.
ANYONE ELSE WANT TO TAKE THIS ONE?
I DON'T REALLY GET IT BECAUSE GIRLS ARE STILL REALLY WEIRD TO ME, BUT... WE NEED YOU, BUDDY.
YOU'RE OUR ADULT.
PADRE'S YOUR ADULT.
YOU WERE WITH ME IN THE CAVE. PADRE WASN'T THERE.
BUT... WE STILL NEED PADRE.
AREN'T ANY OF YOU WORRIED ABOUT HIM?
I DON'T WORRY ABOUT PADRE. IF HE CAN MAKE IT BACK, HE WILL.
IT'S PADRE! THAT WHAT HE DOES.

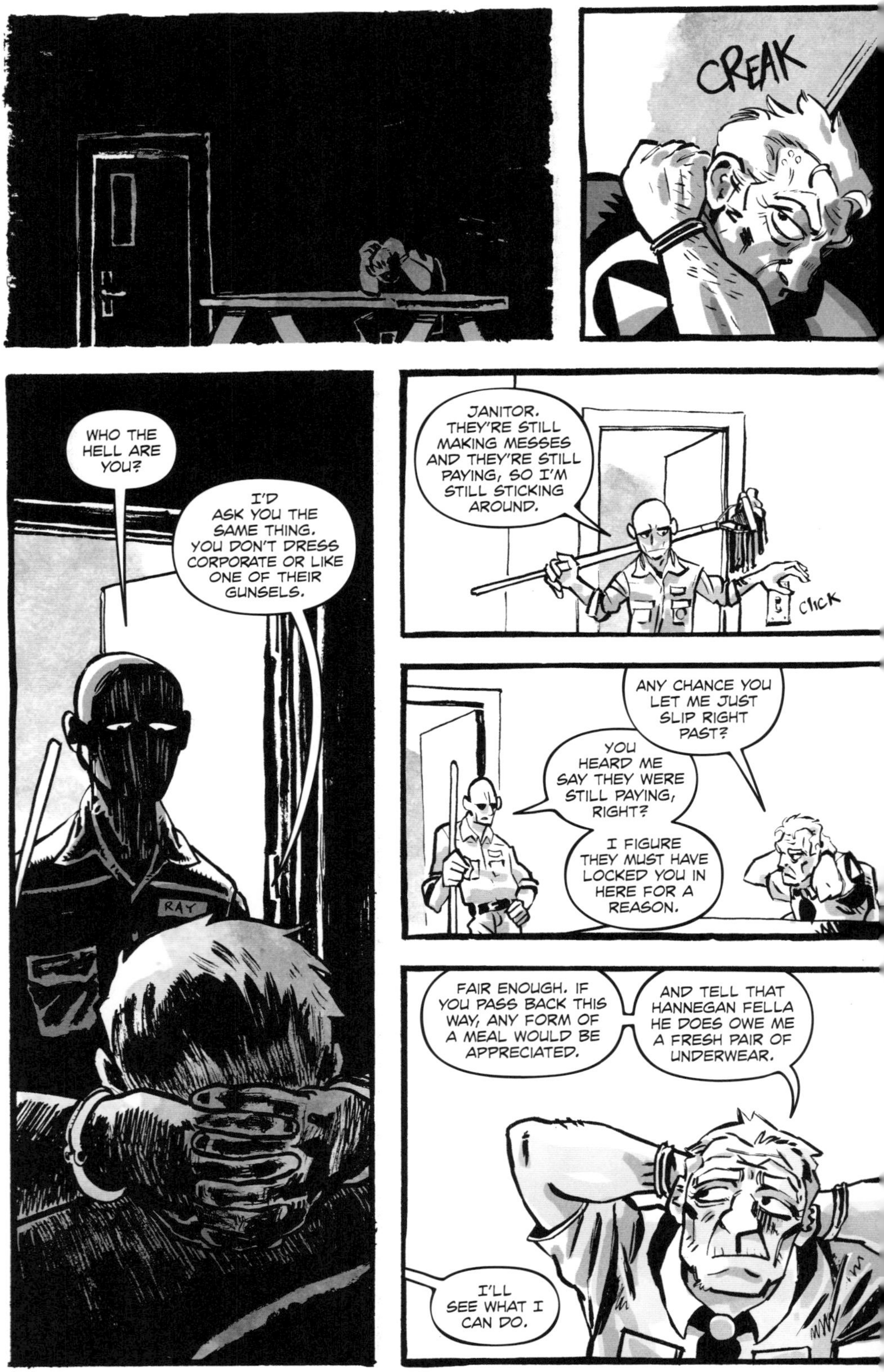
CREAK
WHO THE HELL ARE YOU?
I'D ASK YOU THE SAME THING. YOU DON'T DRESS CORPORATE OR LIKE ONE OF THEIR GUNSELS.
RAY
JANITOR. THEY'RE STILL MAKING MESSES AND THEY'RE STILL PAYING, SO I'M STILL STICKING AROUND.
CLICK
ANY CHANCE YOU LET ME JUST SLIP RIGHT PAST?
YOU HEARD ME SAY THEY WERE STILL PAYING, RIGHT?
I FIGURE THEY MUST HAVE LOCKED YOU IN HERE FOR A REASON.
FAIR ENOUGH. IF YOU PASS BACK THIS WAY, ANY FORM OF A MEAL WOULD BE APPRECIATED.
AND TELL THAT HANNEGAN FELLA HE DOES OWE ME A FRESH PAIR OF UNDERWEAR.
I'LL SEE WHAT I CAN DO.

CALL AND RESPONSE

This song is to be sung at camp with two Tribes. The Tribes would face each other and insert their Tribe Number and a rhyming response while alternating verses. See the below example:

Hands up! (they echo & do motion)

Wrists together! (they echo & do motion)

We are TRIBE 65

and we always look alive!

Look Alive! TRIBE 65

We are TRIBE 65

Hands Up! (echo)

Wrists together! (echo)

Elbows In! (echo)

(keep adding the motion)

We are TRIBE 65

and we always look alive!

Look Alive! TRIBE 65

We are TRIBE 65

Hands Up! (echo)

Wrists together! (echo)

Elbows In! (echo)

Head back! (echo)

We are TRIBE 65

and we always look alive!

Look Alive! TRIBE 65

We are TRIBE 65

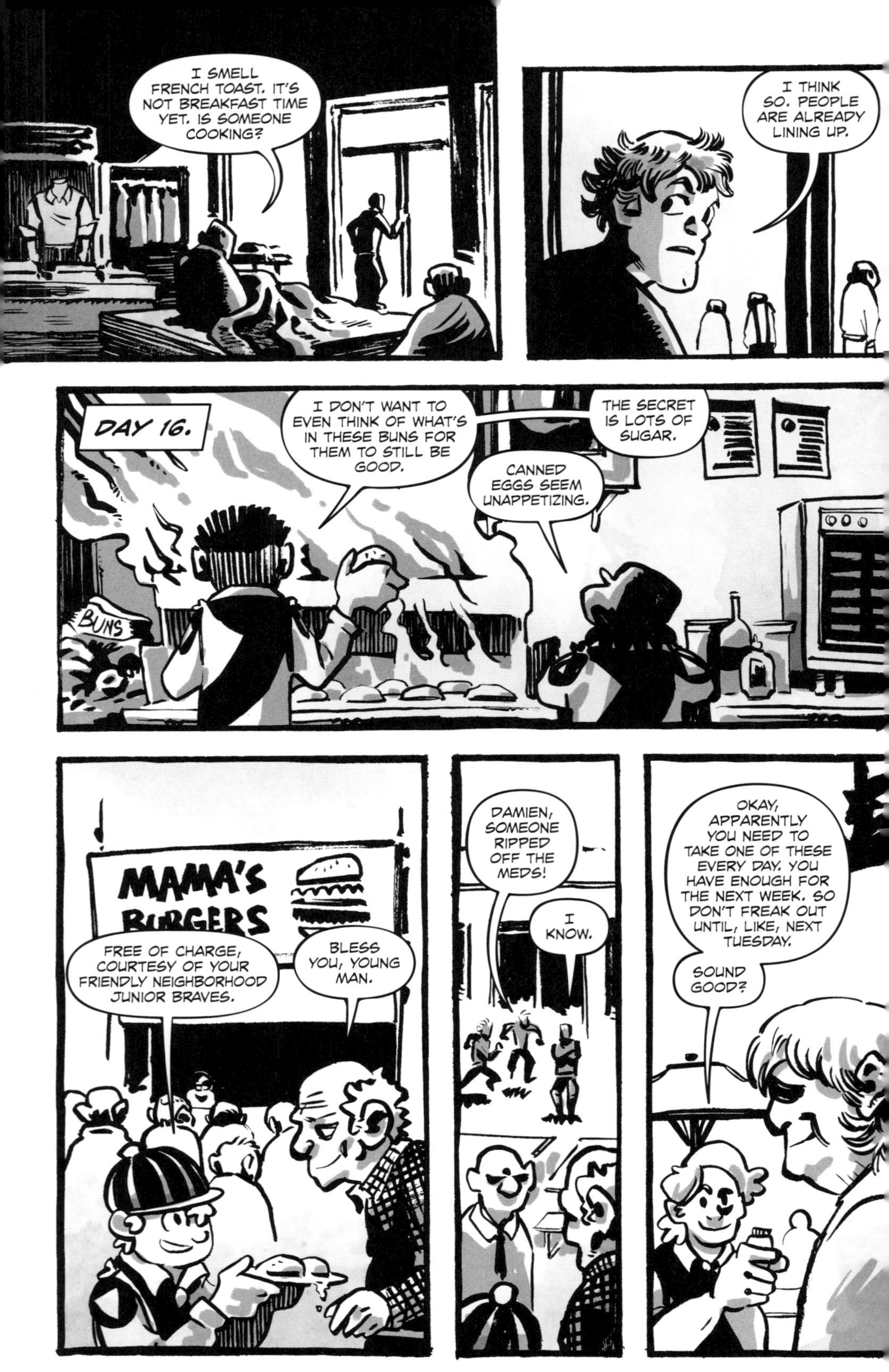
I SMELL FRENCH TOAST. IT'S NOT BREAKFAST TIME YET. IS SOMEONE COOKING?
I THINK SO. PEOPLE ARE ALREADY LINING UP.
DAY 16.
I DON'T WANT TO EVEN THINK OF WHAT'S IN THESE BUNS FOR THEM TO STILL BE GOOD.
THE SECRET IS LOTS OF SUGAR.
CANNED EGGS SEEM UNAPPETIZING.
BUNS
MAMA'S BURGERS
FREE OF CHARGE, COURTESY OF YOUR FRIENDLY NEIGHBORHOOD JUNIOR BRAVES.
BLESS YOU, YOUNG MAN.
DAMIEN, SOMEONE RIPPED OFF THE MEDS!
I KNOW.
OKAY, APPARENTLY YOU NEED TO TAKE ONE OF THESE EVERY DAY. YOU HAVE ENOUGH FOR THE NEXT WEEK. SO DON'T FREAK OUT UNTIL, LIKE, NEXT TUESDAY.
SOUND GOOD?

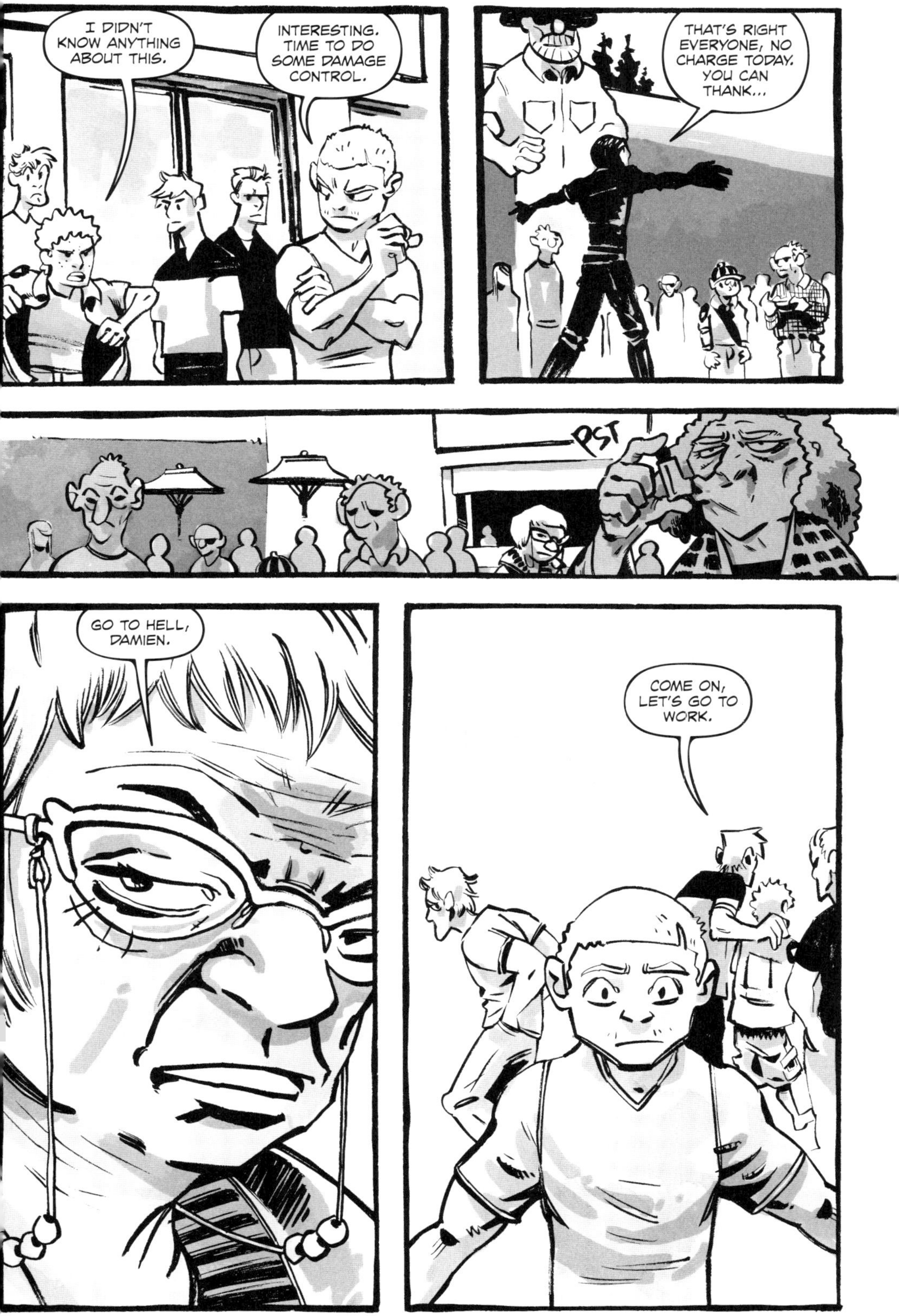

I DIDN'T KNOW ANYTHING ABOUT THIS.
INTERESTING. TIME TO DO SOME DAMAGE CONTROL.
THAT'S RIGHT EVERYONE, NO CHARGE TODAY. YOU CAN THANK...
PST
GO TO HELL, DAMIEN.
COME ON, LET'S GO TO WORK.

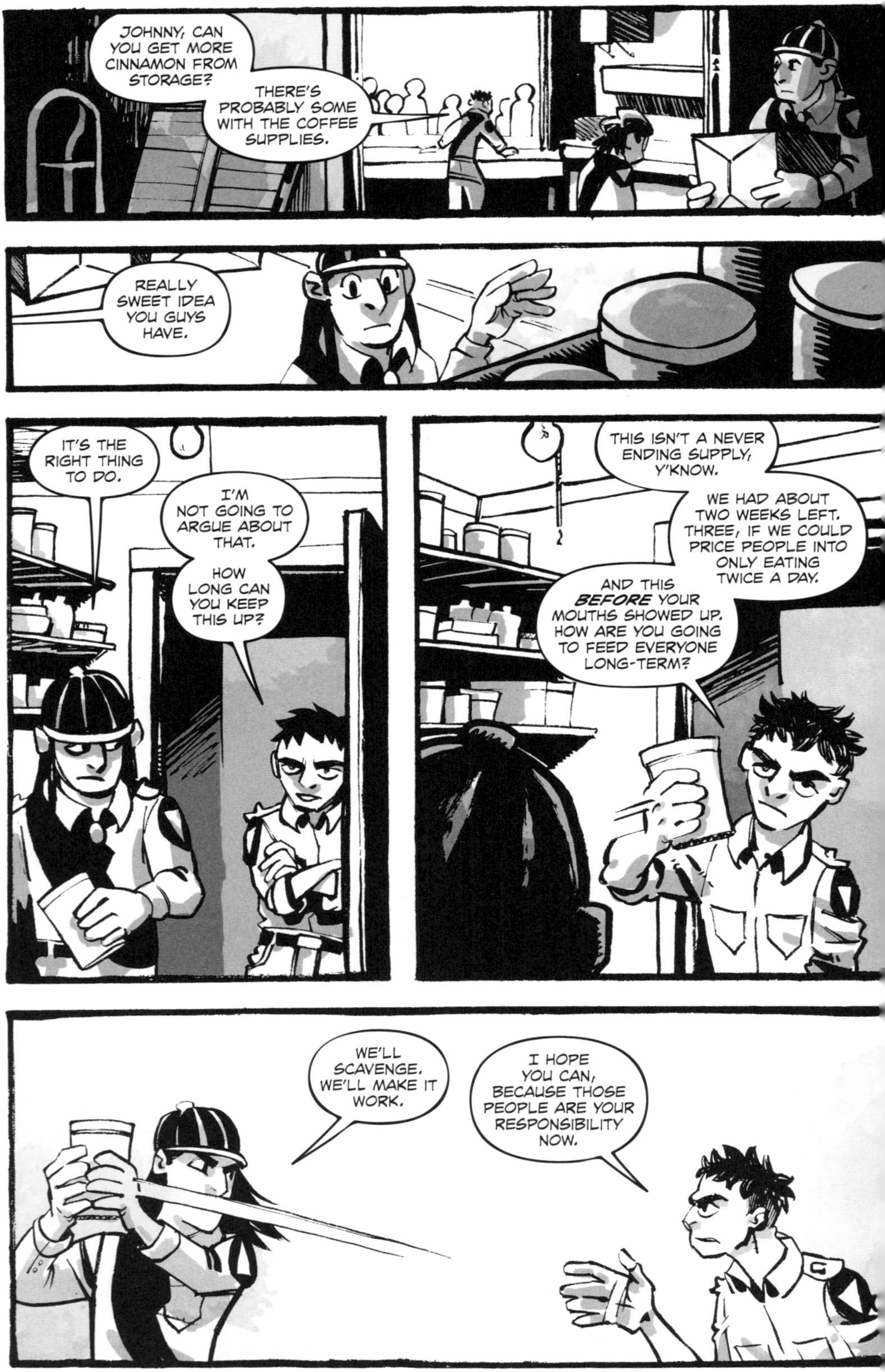
JOHNNY, CAN YOU GET MORE CINNAMON FROM STORAGE?
THERE'S PROBABLY SOME WITH THE COFFEE SUPPLIES.
REALLY SWEET IDEA YOU GUYS HAVE.
IT'S THE RIGHT THING TO DO.
I'M NOT GOING TO ARGUE ABOUT THAT.
HOW LONG CAN YOU KEEP THIS UP?
THIS ISN'T A NEVER ENDING SUPPLY, Y'KNOW.
WE HAD ABOUT TWO WEEKS LEFT. THREE, IF WE COULD PRICE PEOPLE INTO ONLY EATING TWICE A DAY.
AND THIS *BEFORE* YOUR MOUTHS SHOWED UP. HOW ARE YOU GOING TO FEED EVERYONE LONG-TERM?
WE'LL SCAVENGE. WE'LL MAKE IT WORK.
I HOPE YOU CAN, BECAUSE THOSE PEOPLE ARE YOUR RESPONSIBILITY NOW.

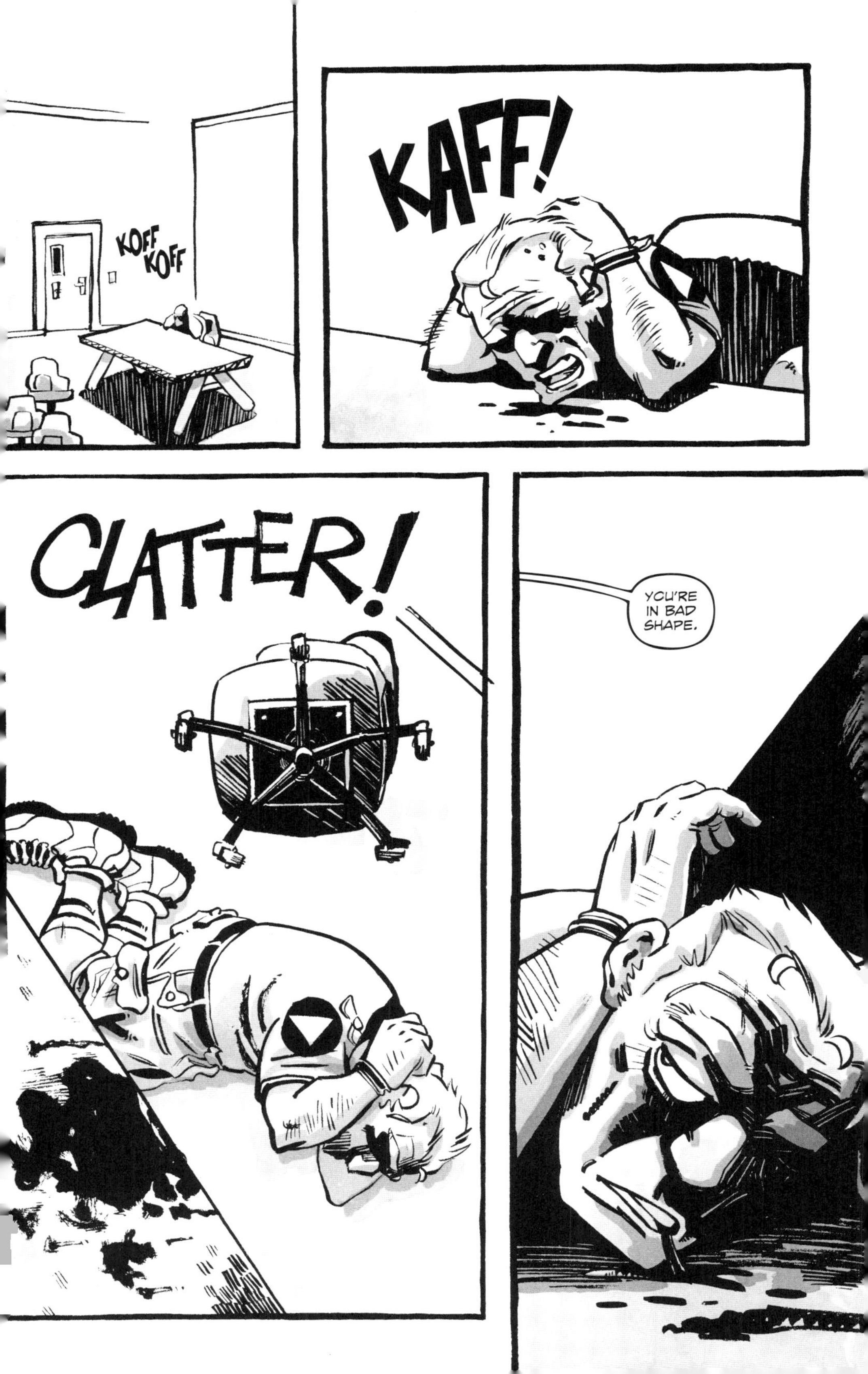
KOFF
KOFF
KAFF!
CLATTER!
YOU'RE IN BAD SHAPE.

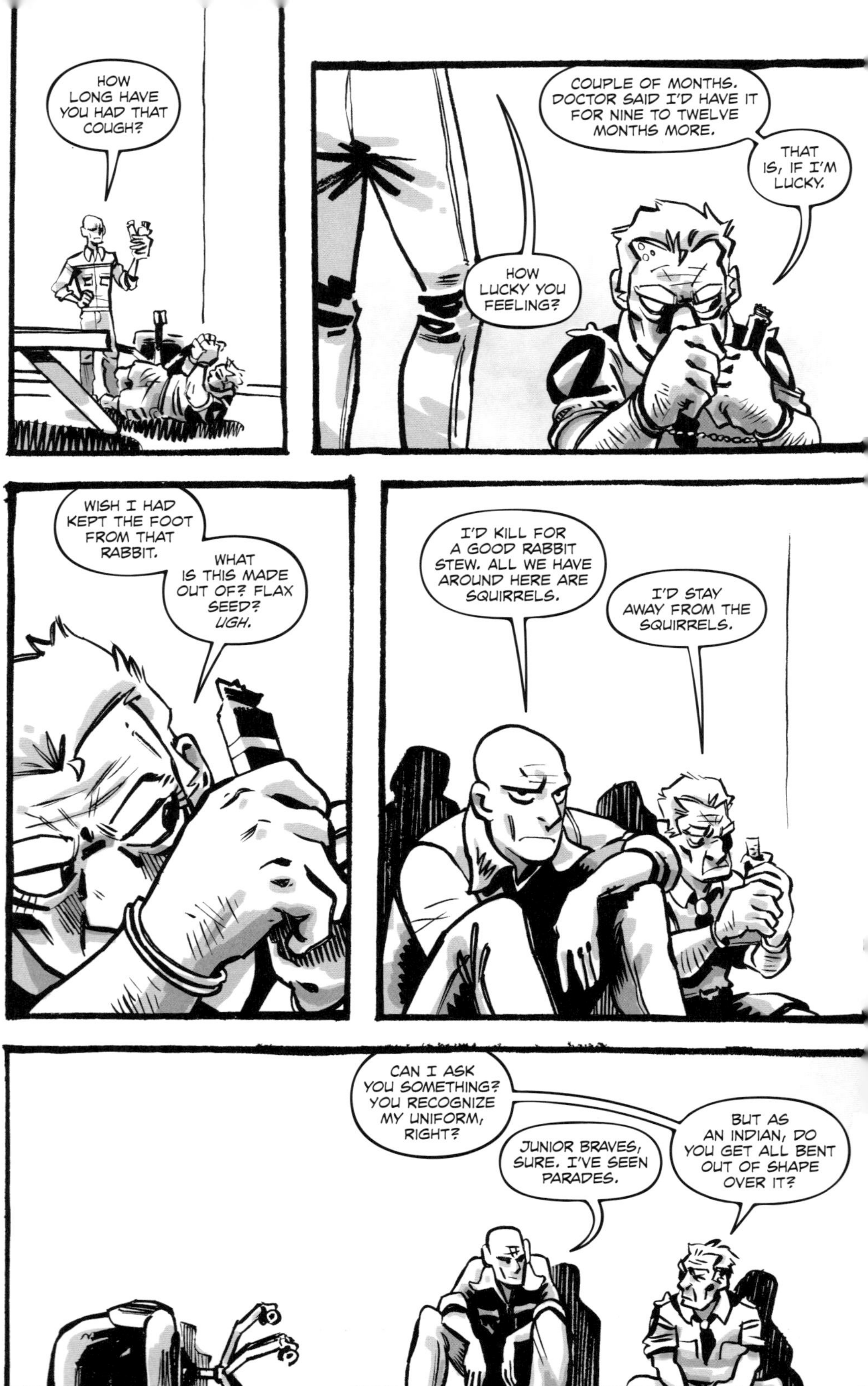
HOW LONG HAVE YOU HAD THAT COUGH?
COUPLE OF MONTHS. DOCTOR SAID I'D HAVE IT FOR NINE TO TWELVE MONTHS MORE.
THAT IS, IF I'M LUCKY.
HOW LUCKY YOU FEELING?
WISH I HAD KEPT THE FOOT FROM THAT RABBIT.
WHAT IS THIS MADE OUT OF? FLAX SEED? UGH.
I'D KILL FOR A GOOD RABBIT STEW. ALL WE HAVE AROUND HERE ARE SQUIRRELS.
I'D STAY AWAY FROM THE SQUIRRELS.
CAN I ASK YOU SOMETHING? YOU RECOGNIZE MY UNIFORM, RIGHT?
JUNIOR BRAVES, SURE. I'VE SEEN PARADES.
BUT AS AN INDIAN, DO YOU GET ALL BENT OUT OF SHAPE OVER IT?

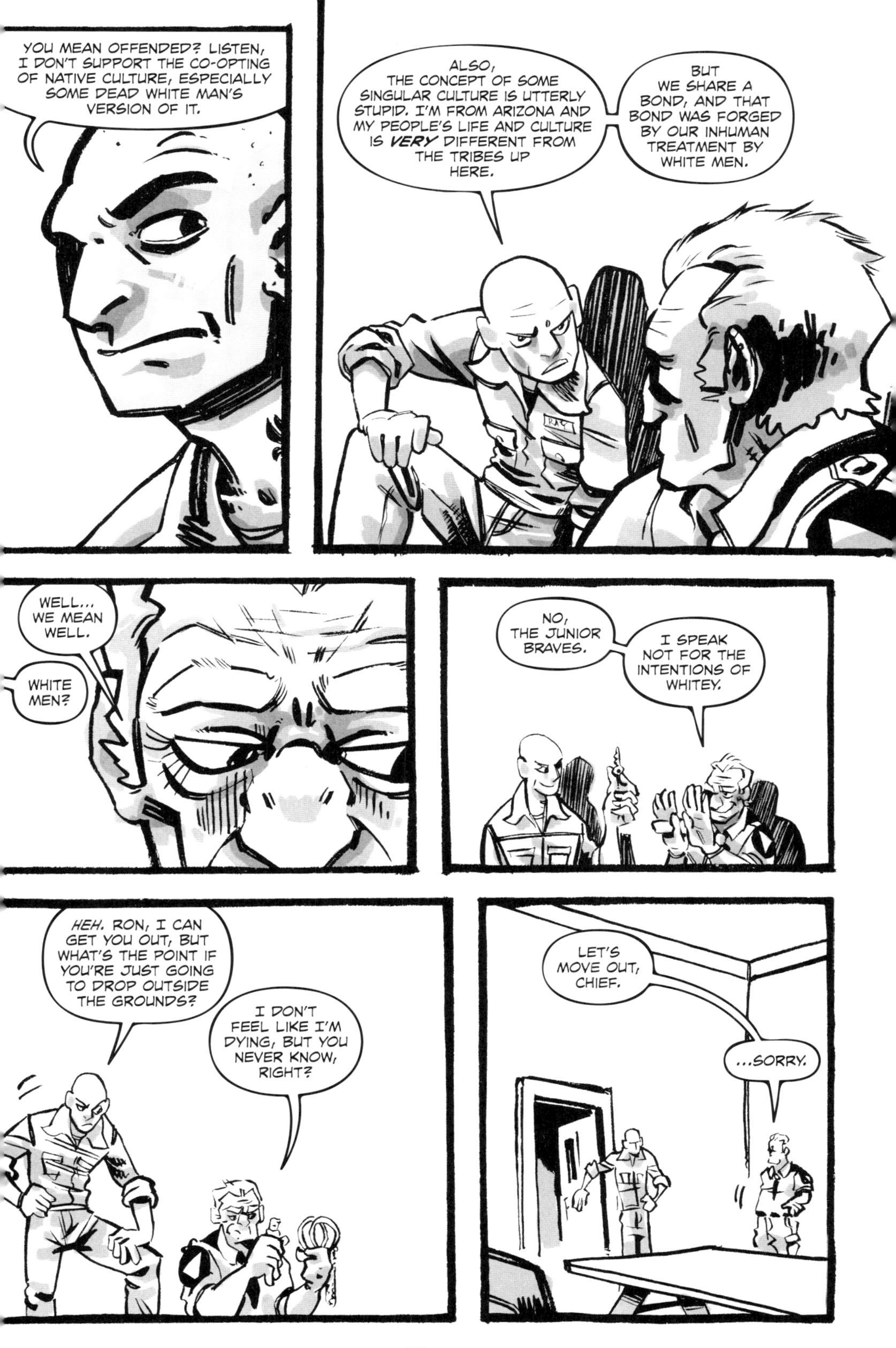
YOU MEAN OFFENDED? LISTEN, I DON'T SUPPORT THE CO-OPTING OF NATIVE CULTURE, ESPECIALLY SOME DEAD WHITE MAN'S VERSION OF IT.
ALSO, THE CONCEPT OF SOME SINGULAR CULTURE IS UTTERLY STUPID. I'M FROM ARIZONA AND MY PEOPLE'S LIFE AND CULTURE IS *VERY* DIFFERENT FROM THE TRIBES UP HERE.
BUT WE SHARE A BOND, AND THAT BOND WAS FORGED BY OUR INHUMAN TREATMENT BY WHITE MEN.
WELL... WE MEAN WELL.
WHITE MEN?
NO, THE JUNIOR BRAVES.
I SPEAK NOT FOR THE INTENTIONS OF WHITEY.
HEH. RON, I CAN GET YOU OUT, BUT WHAT'S THE POINT IF YOU'RE JUST GOING TO DROP OUTSIDE THE GROUNDS?
I DON'T FEEL LIKE I'M DYING, BUT YOU NEVER KNOW, RIGHT?
LET'S MOVE OUT, CHIEF.
...SORRY.

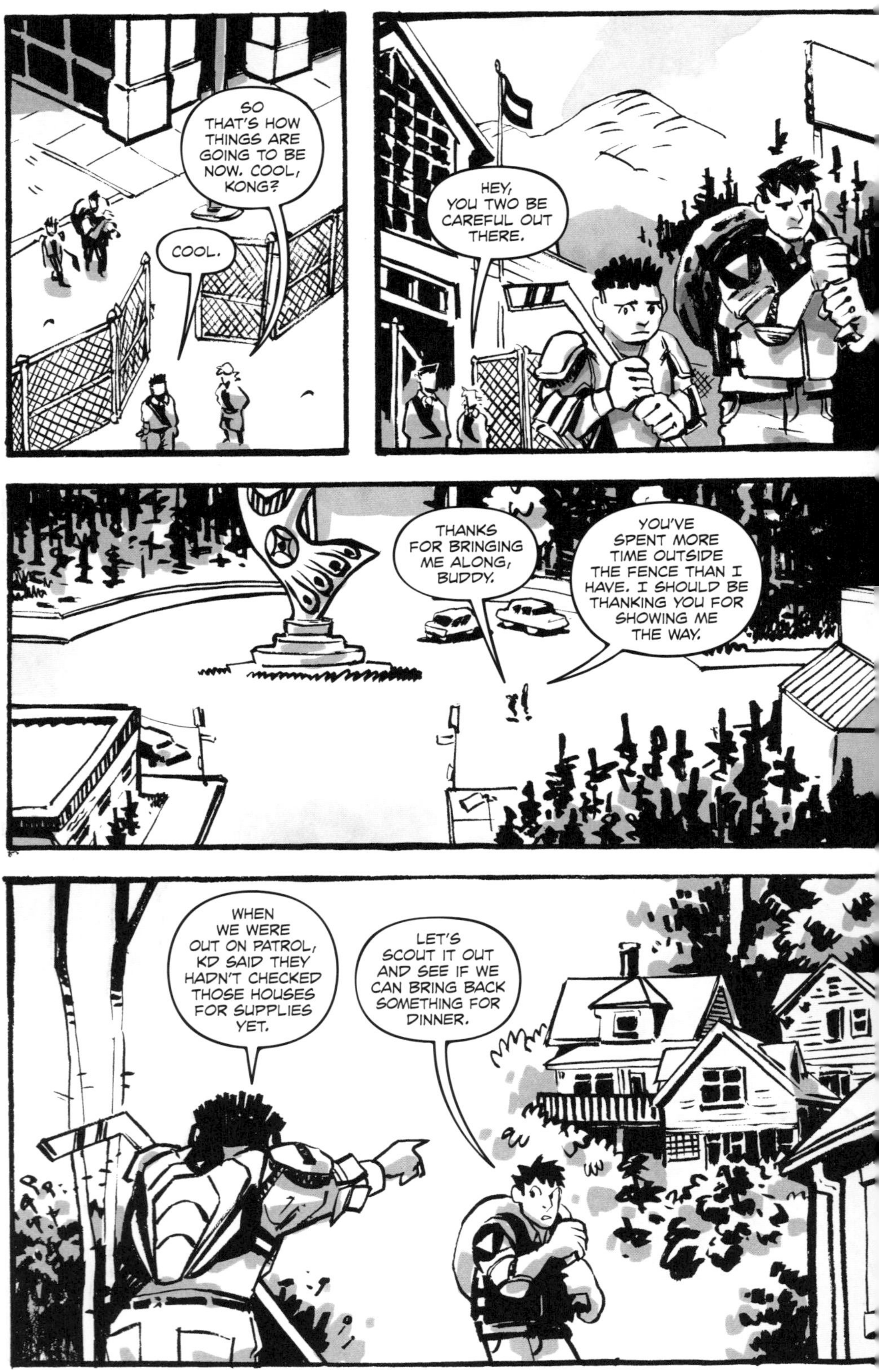
SO THAT'S HOW THINGS ARE GOING TO BE NOW. COOL, KONG?
COOL.
HEY, YOU TWO BE CAREFUL OUT THERE.
THANKS FOR BRINGING ME ALONG, BUDDY.
YOU'VE SPENT MORE TIME OUTSIDE THE FENCE THAN I HAVE. I SHOULD BE THANKING YOU FOR SHOWING ME THE WAY.
WHEN WE WERE OUT ON PATROL, KD SAID THEY HADN'T CHECKED THOSE HOUSES FOR SUPPLIES YET.
LET'S SCOUT IT OUT AND SEE IF WE CAN BRING BACK SOMETHING FOR DINNER.

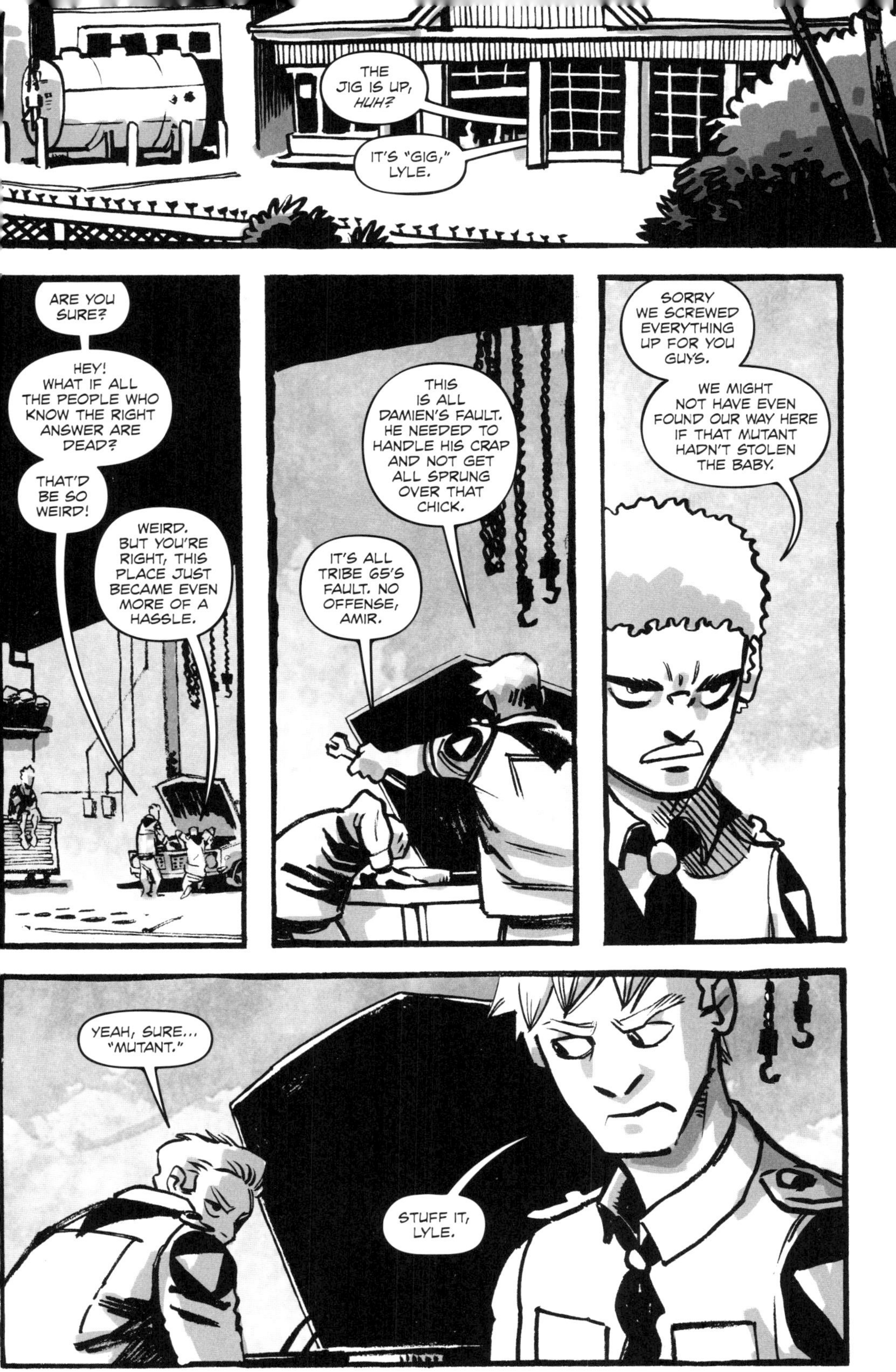
THE JIG IS UP, *HUH?*
IT'S "GIG," LYLE.
ARE YOU SURE?
HEY! WHAT IF ALL THE PEOPLE WHO KNOW THE RIGHT ANSWER ARE DEAD?
THAT'D BE SO WEIRD!
WEIRD. BUT YOU'RE RIGHT, THIS PLACE JUST BECAME EVEN MORE OF A HASSLE.
THIS IS ALL DAMIEN'S FAULT. HE NEEDED TO HANDLE HIS CRAP AND NOT GET ALL SPRUNG OVER THAT CHICK.
IT'S ALL TRIBE 65'S FAULT. NO OFFENSE, AMIR.
SORRY WE SCREWED EVERYTHING UP FOR YOU GUYS.
WE MIGHT NOT HAVE EVEN FOUND OUR WAY HERE IF THAT MUTANT HADN'T STOLEN THE BABY.
YEAH, SURE... "MUTANT."
STUFF IT, LYLE.

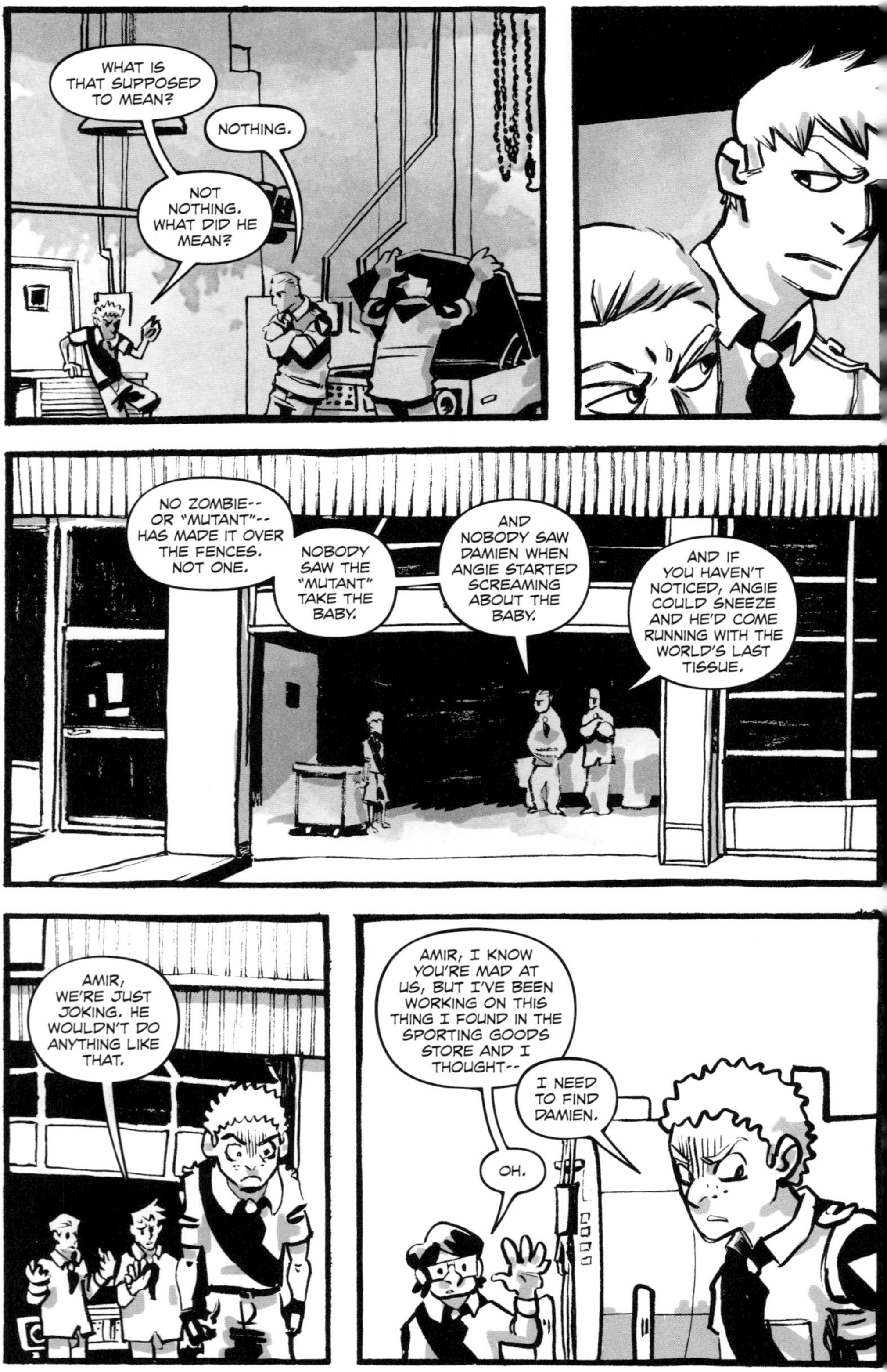
WHAT IS THAT SUPPOSED TO MEAN?
NOTHING.
NOT NOTHING. WHAT DID HE MEAN?
NO ZOMBIE-- OR "MUTANT"-- HAS MADE IT OVER THE FENCES. NOT ONE.
NOBODY SAW THE "MUTANT" TAKE THE BABY.
AND NOBODY SAW DAMIEN WHEN ANGIE STARTED SCREAMING ABOUT THE BABY.
AND IF YOU HAVEN'T NOTICED, ANGIE COULD SNEEZE AND HE'D COME RUNNING WITH THE WORLD'S LAST TISSUE.
AMIR, WE'RE JUST JOKING. HE WOULDN'T DO ANYTHING LIKE THAT.
AMIR, I KNOW YOU'RE MAD AT US, BUT I'VE BEEN WORKING ON THIS THING I FOUND IN THE SPORTING GOODS STORE AND I THOUGHT--
I NEED TO FIND DAMIEN.
OH.

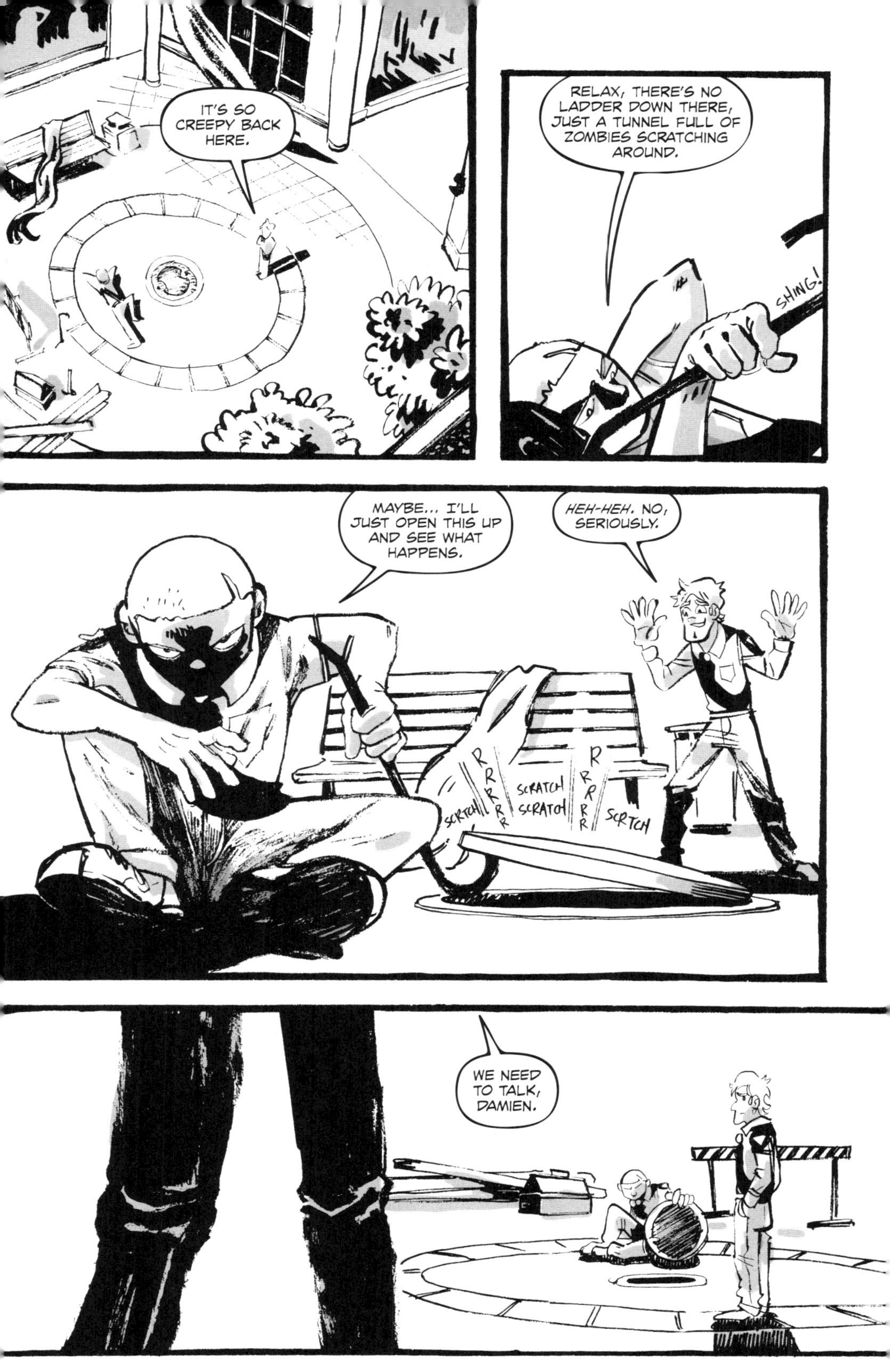
IT'S SO CREEPY BACK HERE.
RELAX, THERE'S NO LADDER DOWN THERE, JUST A TUNNEL FULL OF ZOMBIES SCRATCHING AROUND.
SHING!
MAYBE... I'LL JUST OPEN THIS UP AND SEE WHAT HAPPENS.
HEH-HEH. NO, SERIOUSLY.
SCRTCH
RRRRR
SCRATCH SCRATCH
RRRRRR
SCRTCH
WE NEED TO TALK, DAMIEN.

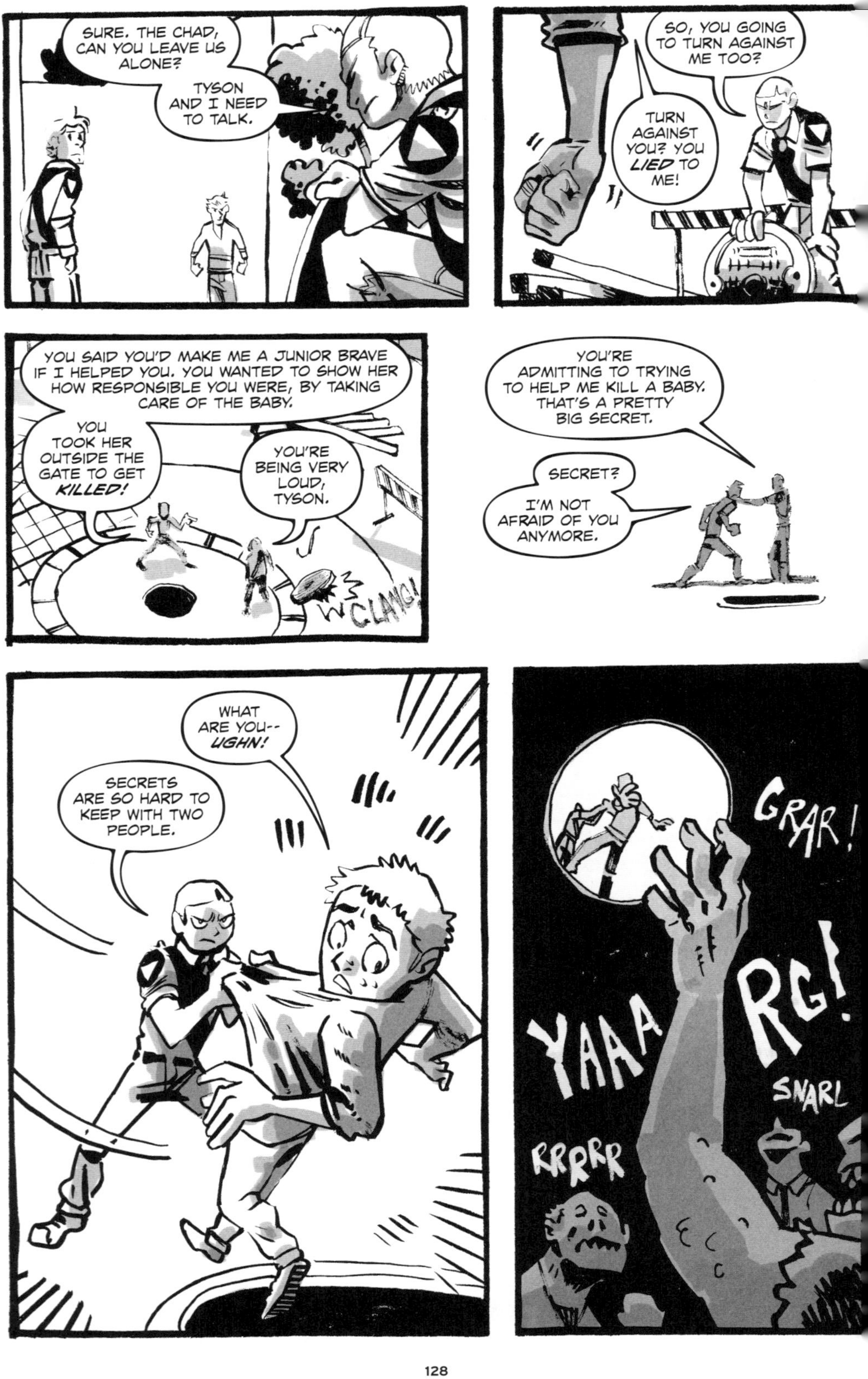

SURE. THE CHAD, CAN YOU LEAVE US ALONE?
TYSON AND I NEED TO TALK.
SO, YOU GOING TO TURN AGAINST ME TOO?
TURN AGAINST YOU? YOU LIED TO ME!
YOU SAID YOU'D MAKE ME A JUNIOR BRAVE IF I HELPED YOU. YOU WANTED TO SHOW HER HOW RESPONSIBLE YOU WERE, BY TAKING CARE OF THE BABY.
YOU TOOK HER OUTSIDE THE GATE TO GET KILLED!
YOU'RE BEING VERY LOUD, TYSON.
CLANG!
YOU'RE ADMITTING TO TRYING TO HELP ME KILL A BABY. THAT'S A PRETTY BIG SECRET.
SECRET?
I'M NOT AFRAID OF YOU ANYMORE.
WHAT ARE YOU-- UGHN!
SECRETS ARE SO HARD TO KEEP WITH TWO PEOPLE.
GRAR!
YAAARG!
SNARL
RRRRR

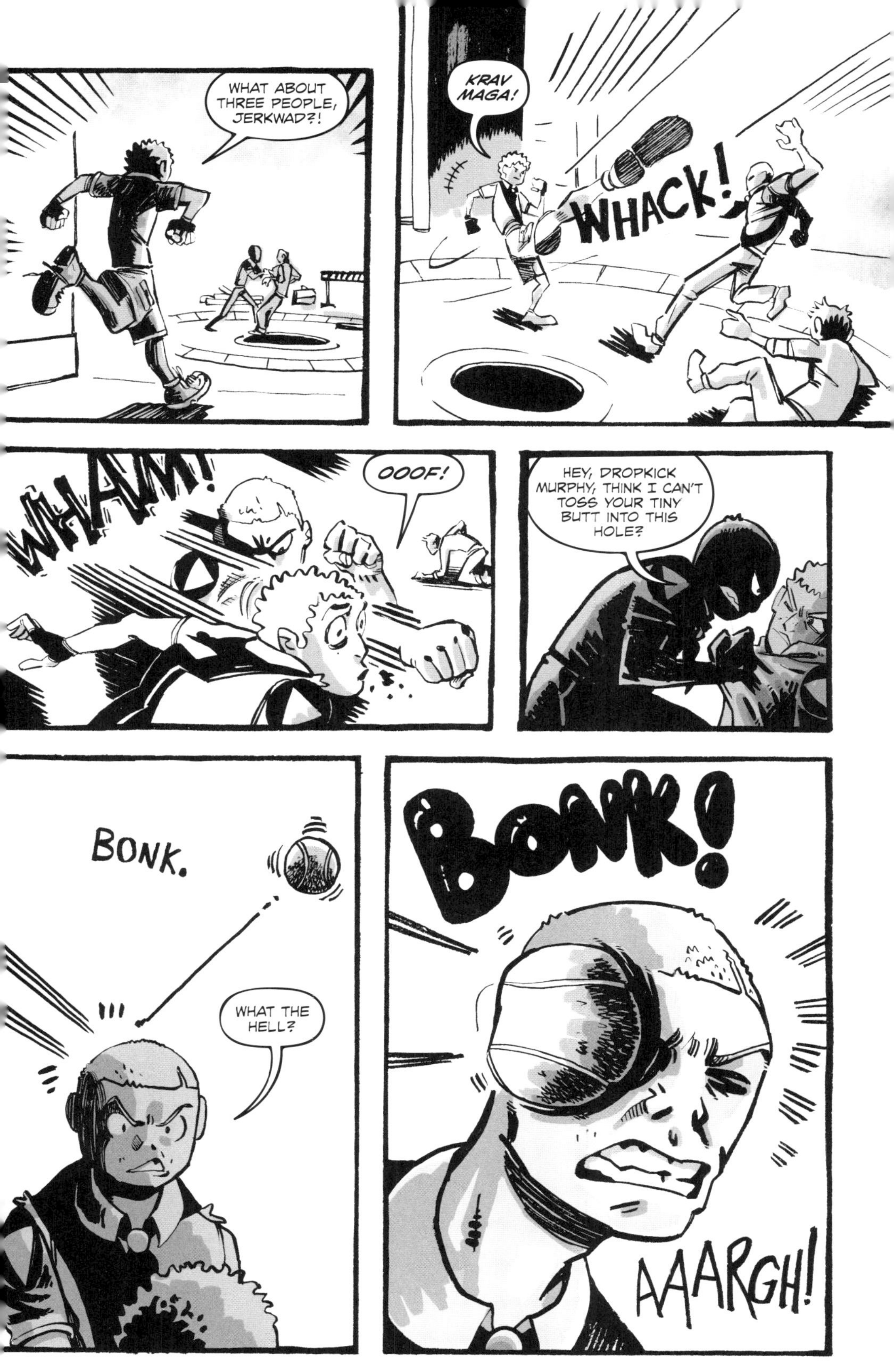
WHAT ABOUT THREE PEOPLE, JERKWAD?!
KRAV MAGA!
WHACK!
WHAM!
OOOF!
HEY, DROPKICK MURPHY, THINK I CAN'T TOSS YOUR TINY BUTT INTO THIS HOLE?
BONK.
WHAT THE HELL?
BONK!
AAARGH!

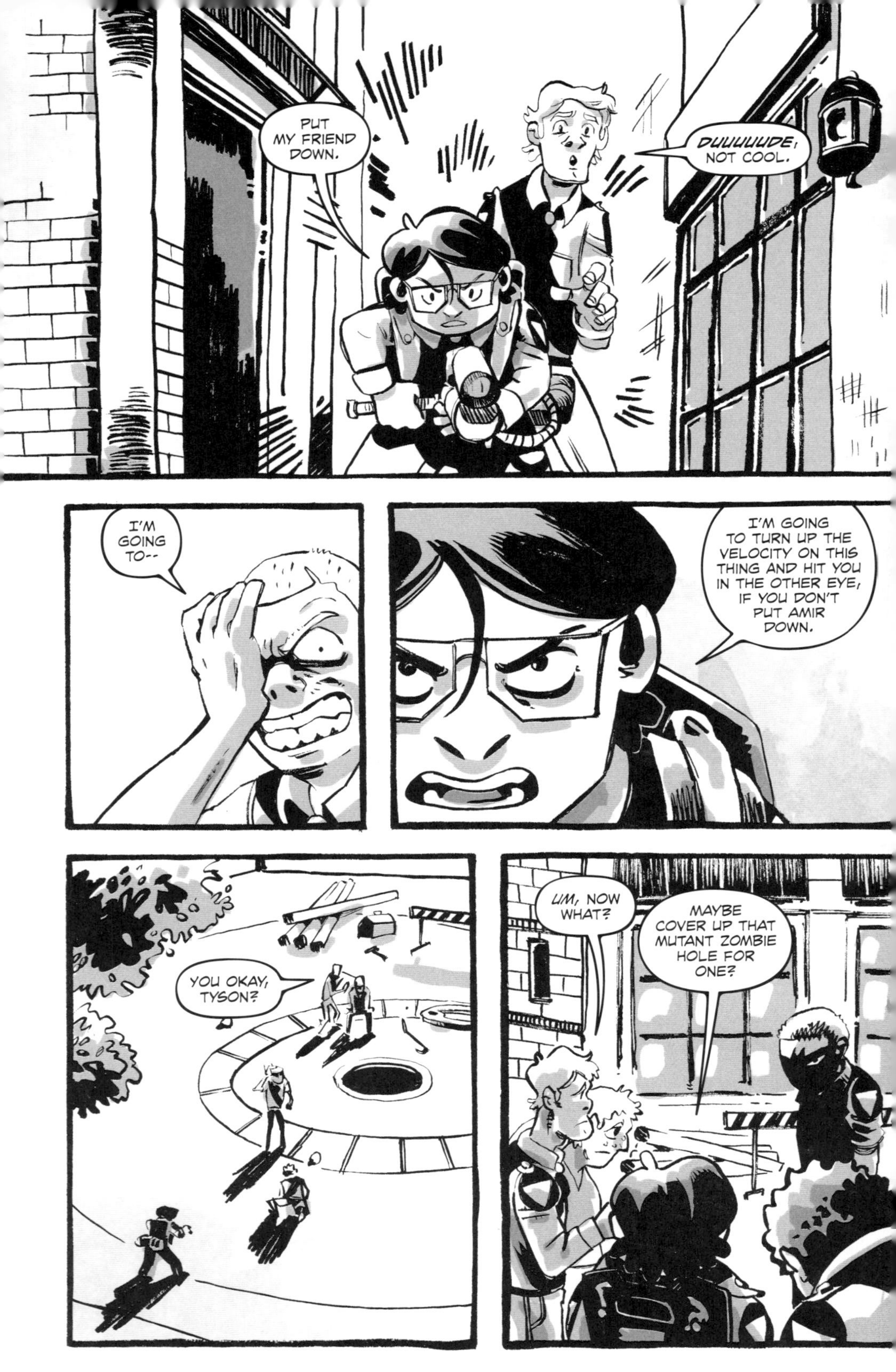
PUT MY FRIEND DOWN.
DUUUUUDE, NOT COOL.
I'M GOING TO--
I'M GOING TO TURN UP THE VELOCITY ON THIS THING AND HIT YOU IN THE OTHER EYE, IF YOU DON'T PUT AMIR DOWN.
YOU OKAY, TYSON?
UM, NOW WHAT?
MAYBE COVER UP THAT MUTANT ZOMBIE HOLE FOR ONE?

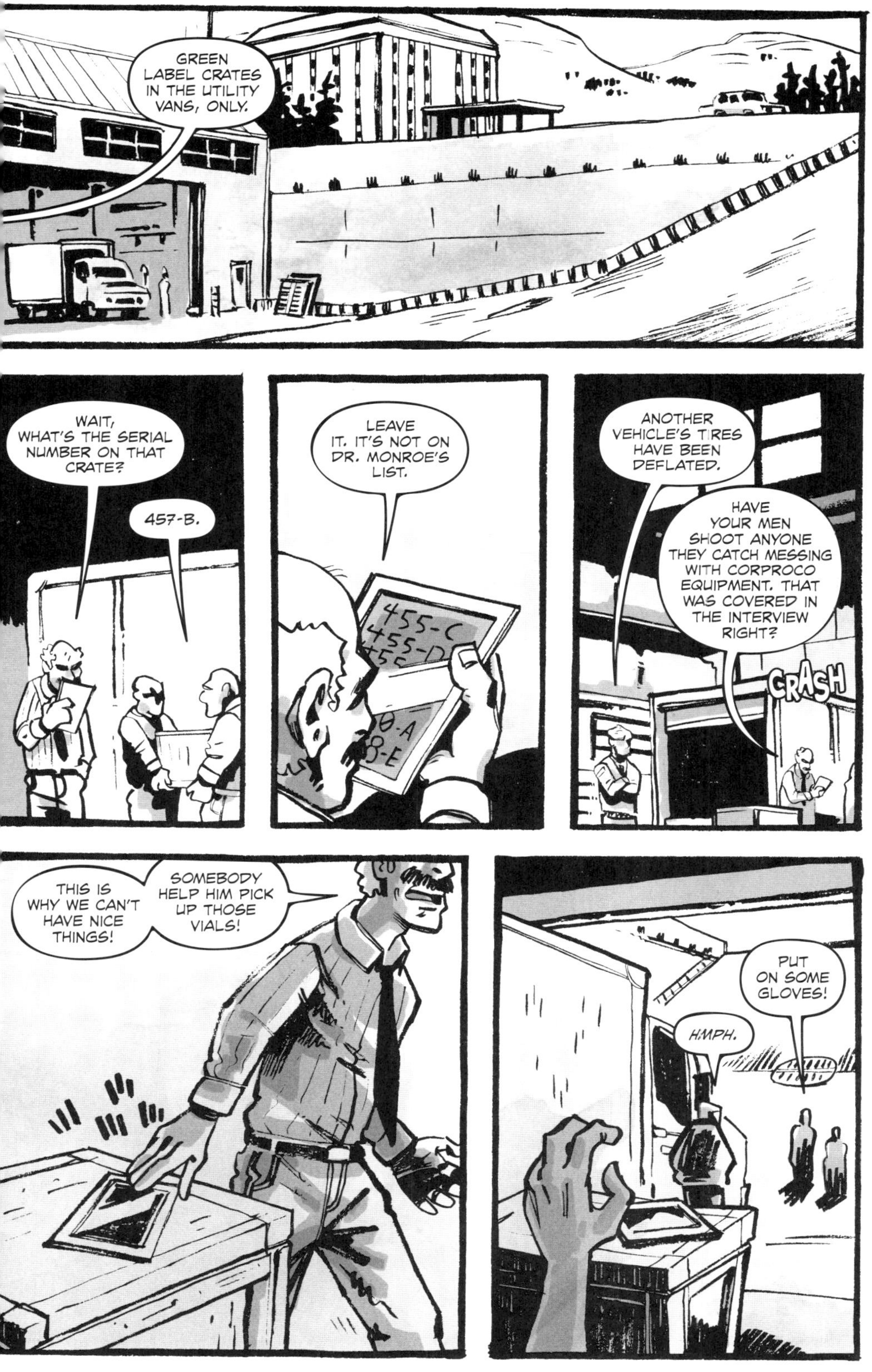
GREEN LABEL CRATES IN THE UTILITY VANS, ONLY.
WAIT, WHAT'S THE SERIAL NUMBER ON THAT CRATE?
457-B.
LEAVE IT. IT'S NOT ON DR. MONROE'S LIST.
455-C
455-D
ANOTHER VEHICLE'S TIRES HAVE BEEN DEFLATED.
HAVE YOUR MEN SHOOT ANYONE THEY CATCH MESSING WITH CORPROCO EQUIPMENT. THAT WAS COVERED IN THE INTERVIEW RIGHT?
CRASH
THIS IS WHY WE CAN'T HAVE NICE THINGS!
SOMEBODY HELP HIM PICK UP THOSE VIALS!
PUT ON SOME GLOVES!
HMPH.

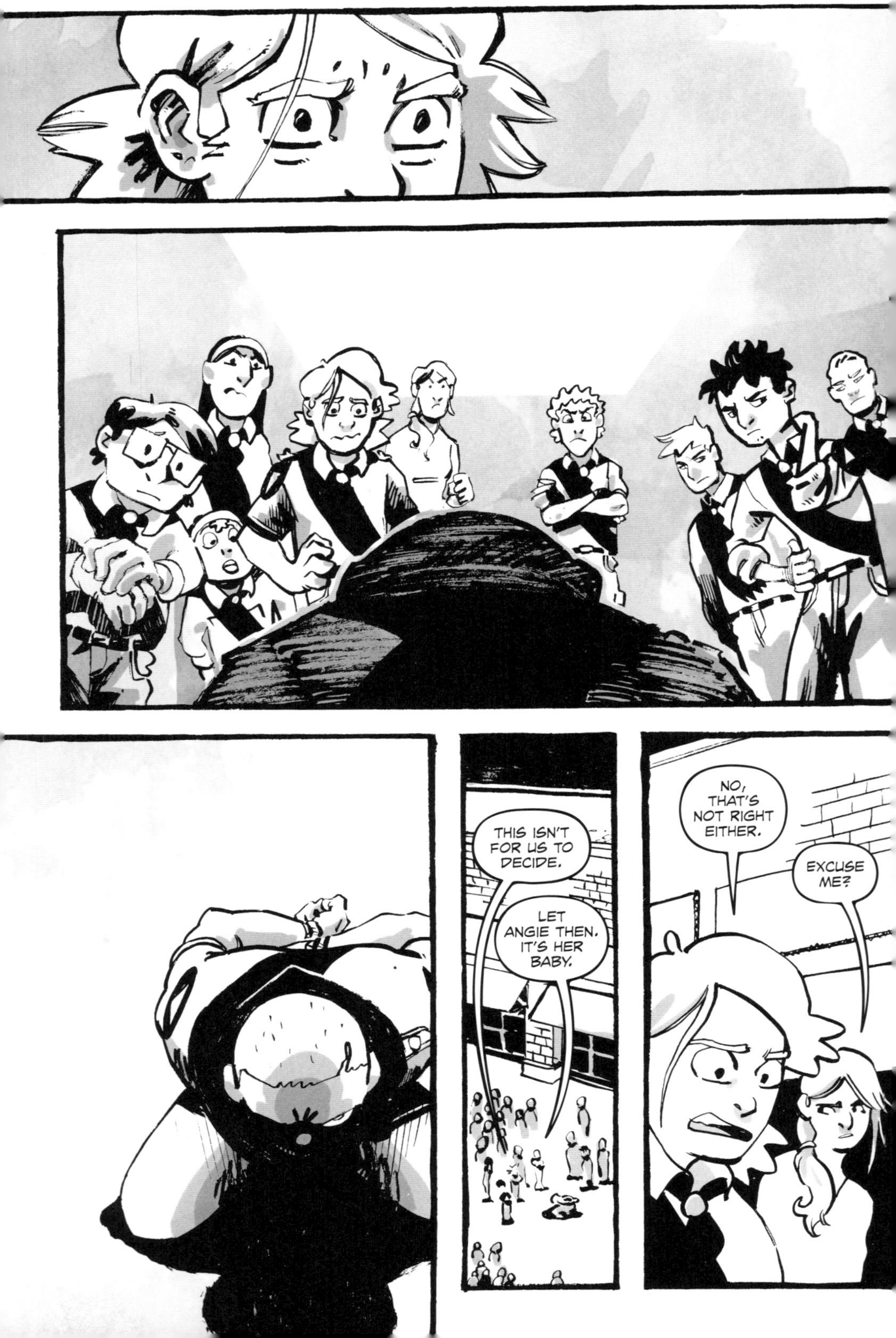
THIS ISN'T FOR US TO DECIDE.
LET ANGIE THEN. IT'S HER BABY.
NO, THAT'S NOT RIGHT EITHER.
EXCUSE ME?

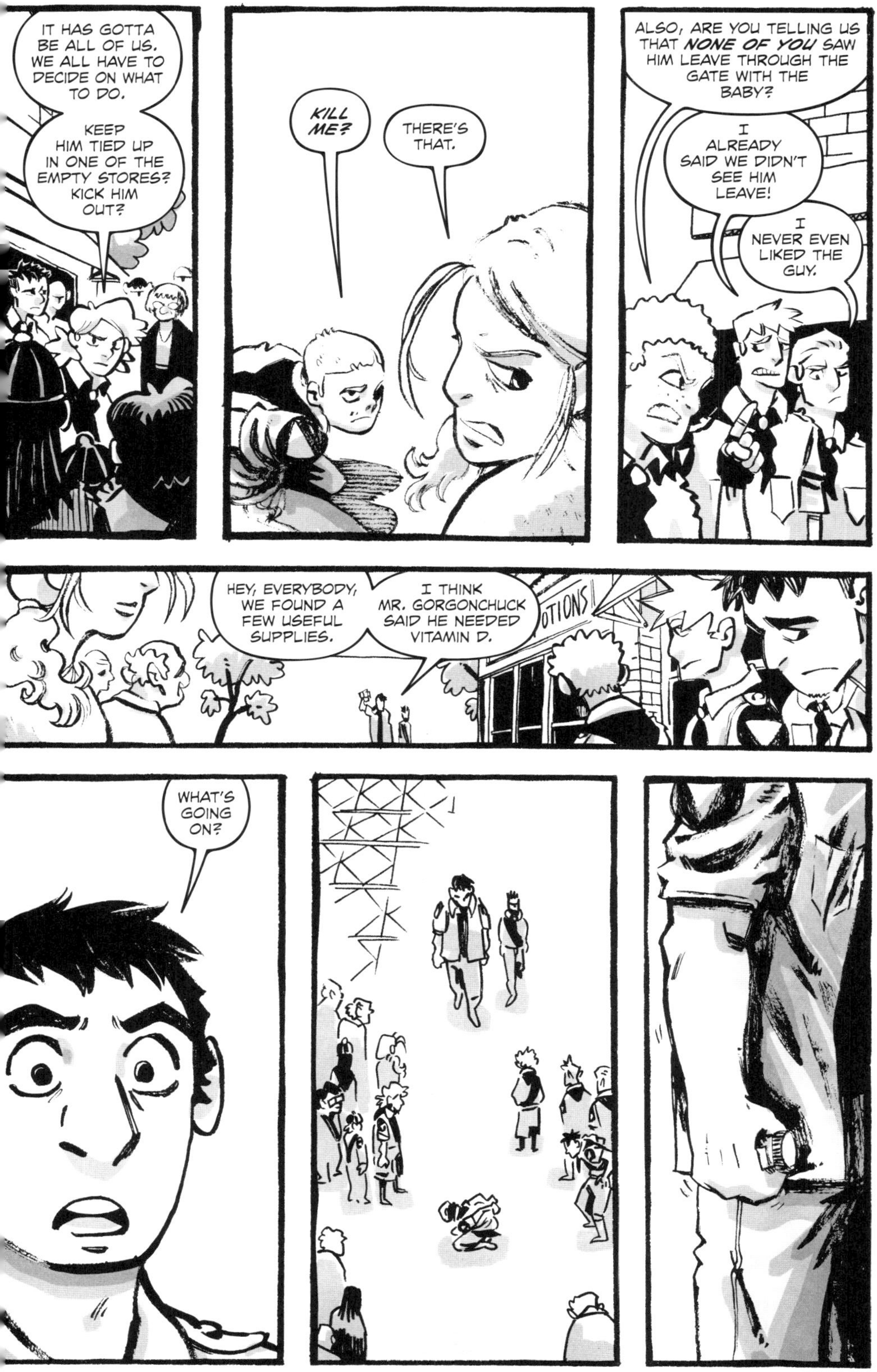

IT HAS GOTTA BE ALL OF US. WE ALL HAVE TO DECIDE ON WHAT TO DO.
KEEP HIM TIED UP IN ONE OF THE EMPTY STORES? KICK HIM OUT?
KILL ME?
THERE'S THAT.
ALSO, ARE YOU TELLING US THAT NONE OF YOU SAW HIM LEAVE THROUGH THE GATE WITH THE BABY?
I ALREADY SAID WE DIDN'T SEE HIM LEAVE!
I NEVER EVEN LIKED THE GUY.
HEY, EVERYBODY, WE FOUND A FEW USEFUL SUPPLIES.
I THINK MR. GORGONCHUCK SAID HE NEEDED VITAMIN D.
OTIONS
WHAT'S GOING ON?

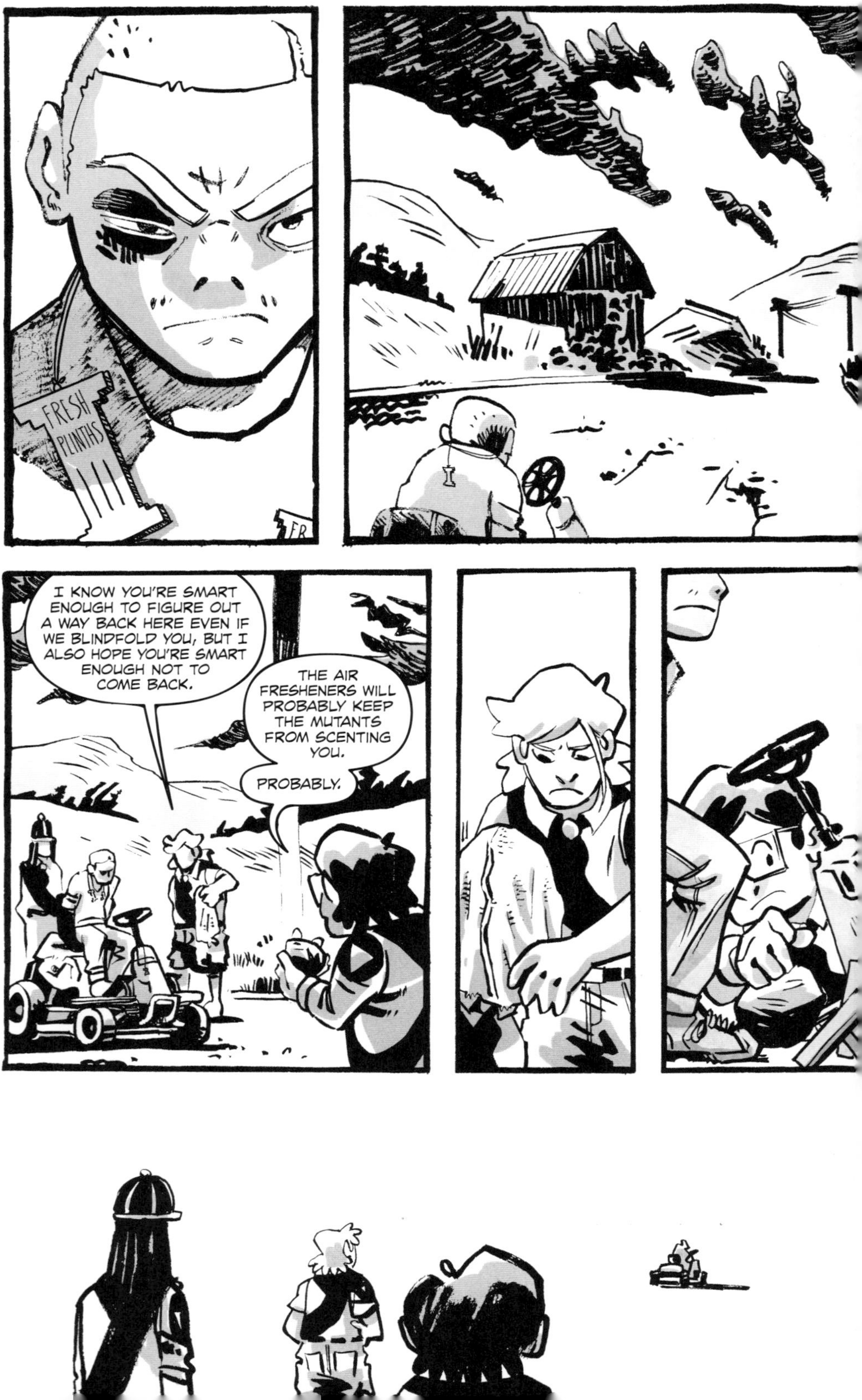
FRESH PLINTHS
I KNOW YOU'RE SMART ENOUGH TO FIGURE OUT A WAY BACK HERE EVEN IF WE BLINDFOLD YOU, BUT I ALSO HOPE YOU'RE SMART ENOUGH NOT TO COME BACK.
THE AIR FRESHENERS WILL PROBABLY KEEP THE MUTANTS FROM SCENTING YOU.
PROBABLY.

TRAVIS, HOW LONG UNTIL YOU FORGIVE AMIR FOR BEATING YOU UP?

...

OKAY. WHAT SHOULD WE DO WITH DAMIEN'S UNIFORM?

KEEP IT FOR REPLACEMENT PARTS. I KNOW I NEED SOME NEW BUTTONS.

DID YOU THINK ANY MORE ABOUT WHAT KD SAID?

YEAH. DID YOU THINK ANY MORE ABOUT WHAT I SAID?

COME ON, TRAVIS.

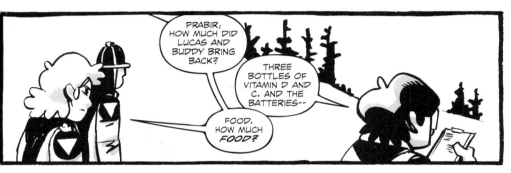

PRABIR, HOW MUCH DID LUCAS AND BUDDY BRING BACK?

THREE BOTTLES OF VITAMIN D AND C. AND THE BATTERIES--

FOOD. HOW MUCH *FOOD?*

NOT ENOUGH. NOT NEARLY ENOUGH.

THAT WAS ONE AFTERNOON AND ONLY TWO OF US. AND ONE OF THEM WAS LUCAS, SO...

YOU'VE ALREADY BEEN OVER THERE. GET THEM TO HELP. JUST ASK THEM IF THEY COULD HELP THESE PEOPLE.

WE NEED TO GET TO SEATTLE, WE CAN'T STAY HERE MUCH LONGER.

FINE. NO PROMISES.

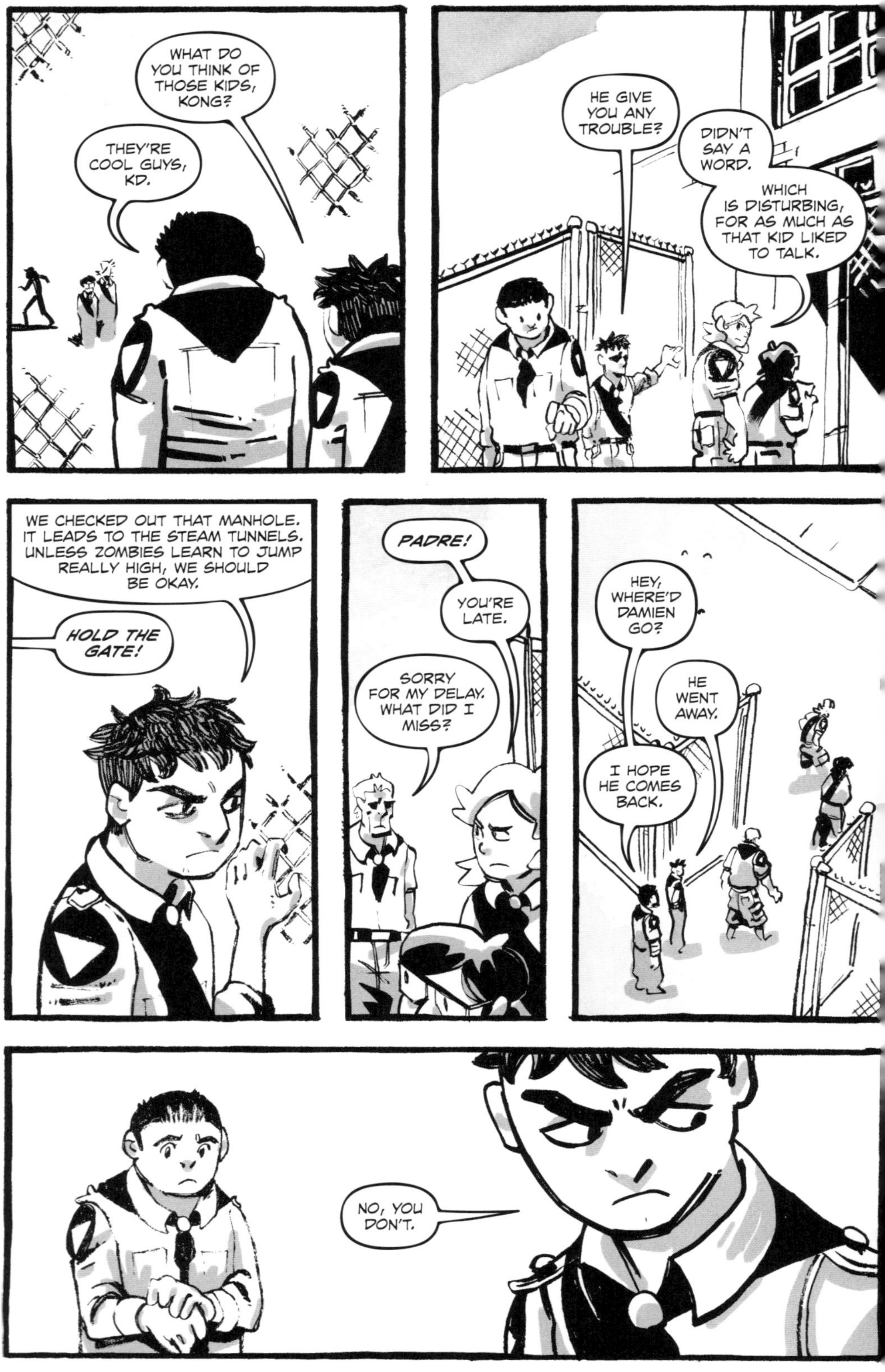

WHAT DO YOU THINK OF THOSE KIDS, KONG?
THEY'RE COOL GUYS, KD.
HE GIVE YOU ANY TROUBLE?
DIDN'T SAY A WORD.
WHICH IS DISTURBING, FOR AS MUCH AS THAT KID LIKED TO TALK.
WE CHECKED OUT THAT MANHOLE. IT LEADS TO THE STEAM TUNNELS. UNLESS ZOMBIES LEARN TO JUMP REALLY HIGH, WE SHOULD BE OKAY.
HOLD THE GATE!
PADRE!
YOU'RE LATE.
SORRY FOR MY DELAY. WHAT DID I MISS?
HEY, WHERE'D DAMIEN GO?
HE WENT AWAY.
I HOPE HE COMES BACK.
NO, YOU DON'T.

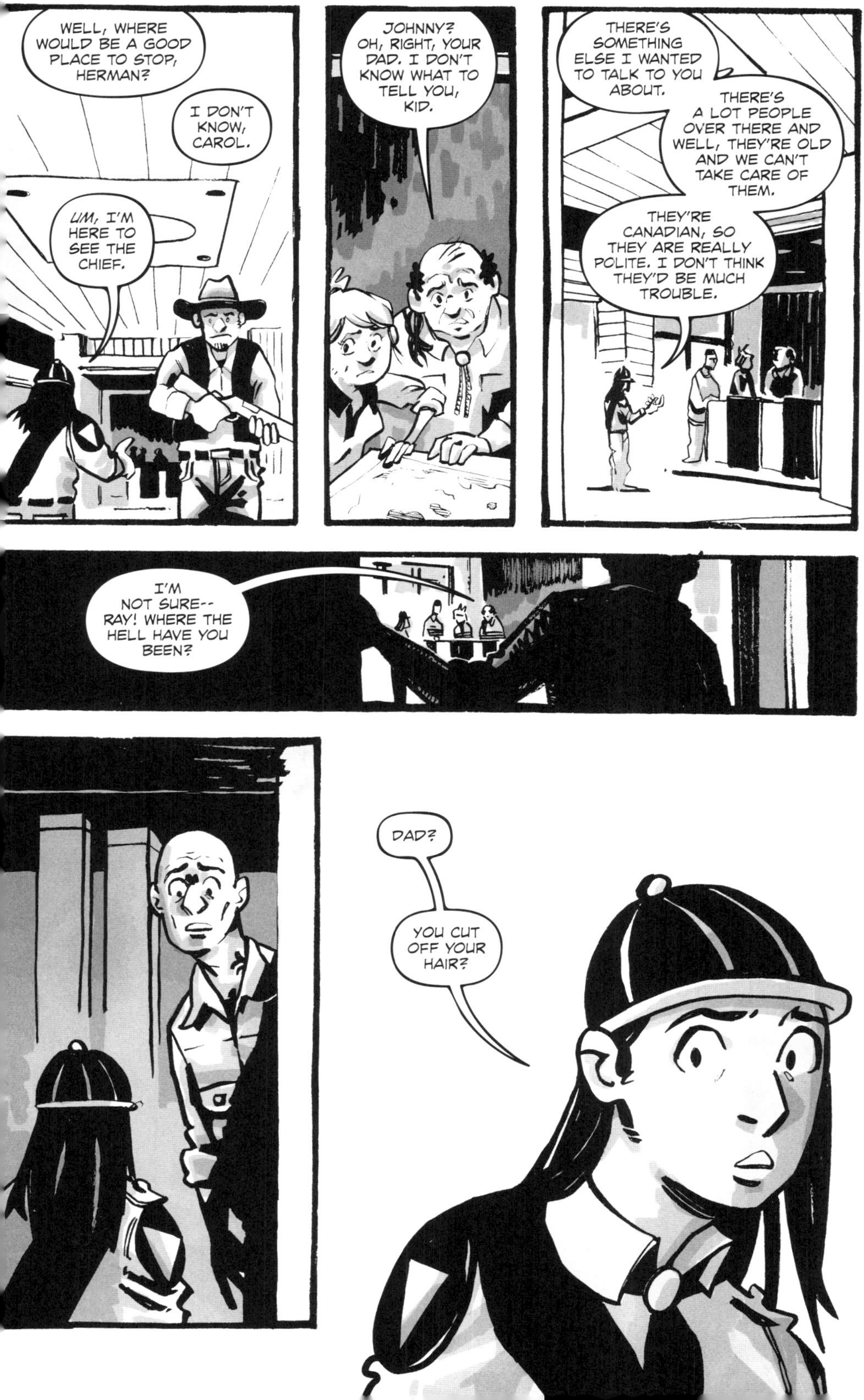
WELL, WHERE WOULD BE A GOOD PLACE TO STOP, HERMAN?
I DON'T KNOW, CAROL.
UM, I'M HERE TO SEE THE CHIEF.
JOHNNY? OH, RIGHT, YOUR DAD. I DON'T KNOW WHAT TO TELL YOU, KID.
THERE'S SOMETHING ELSE I WANTED TO TALK TO YOU ABOUT.
THERE'S A LOT PEOPLE OVER THERE AND WELL, THEY'RE OLD AND WE CAN'T TAKE CARE OF THEM.
THEY'RE CANADIAN, SO THEY ARE REALLY POLITE. I DON'T THINK THEY'D BE MUCH TROUBLE.
I'M NOT SURE-- RAY! WHERE THE HELL HAVE YOU BEEN?
DAD?
YOU CUT OFF YOUR HAIR?

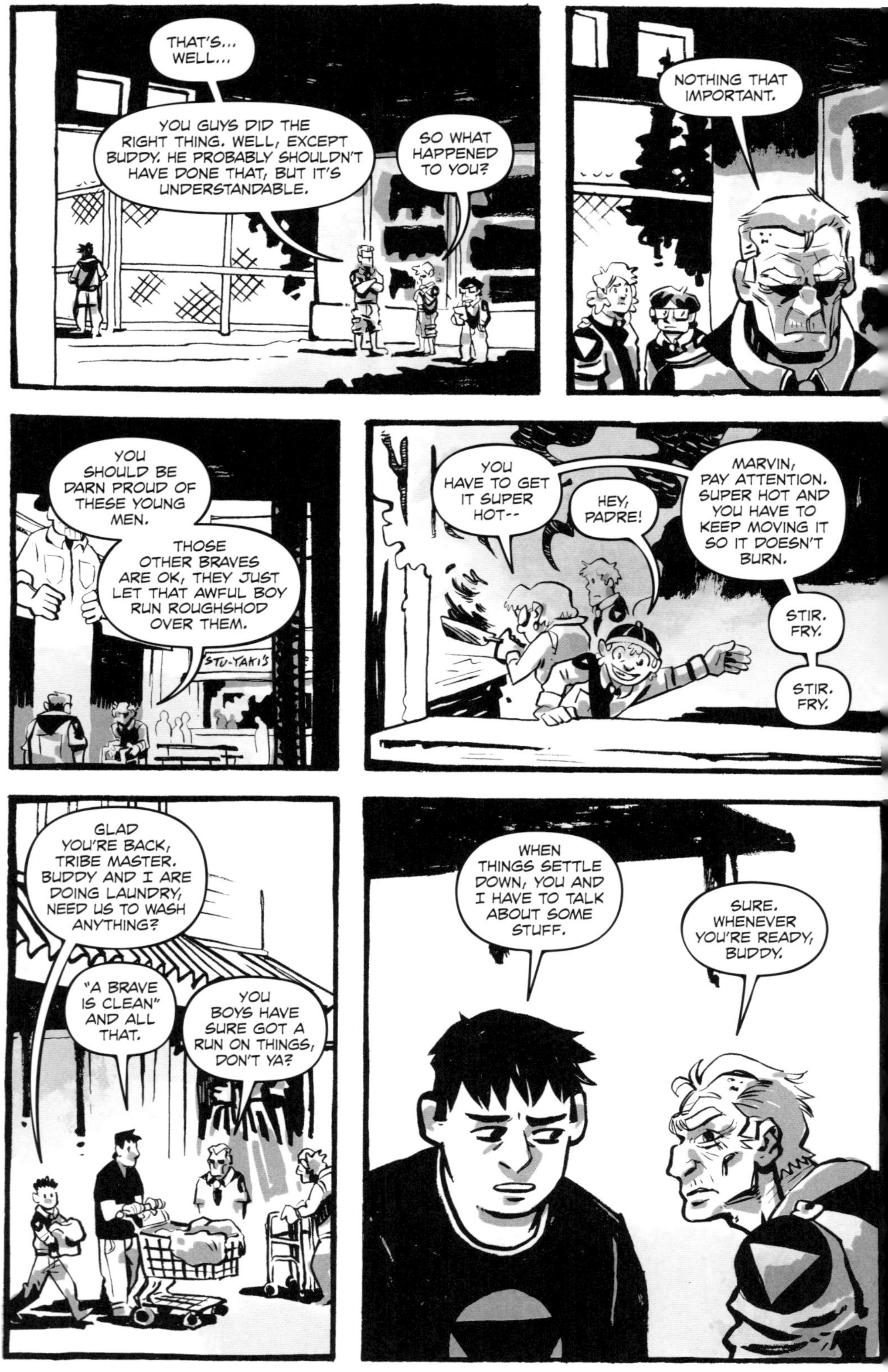
THAT'S... WELL...
YOU GUYS DID THE RIGHT THING. WELL, EXCEPT BUDDY. HE PROBABLY SHOULDN'T HAVE DONE THAT, BUT IT'S UNDERSTANDABLE.
SO WHAT HAPPENED TO YOU?
NOTHING THAT IMPORTANT.
YOU SHOULD BE DARN PROUD OF THESE YOUNG MEN.
THOSE OTHER BRAVES ARE OK, THEY JUST LET THAT AWFUL BOY RUN ROUGHSHOD OVER THEM.
STU-YAKI'S
YOU HAVE TO GET IT SUPER HOT--
HEY, PADRE!
MARVIN, PAY ATTENTION. SUPER HOT AND YOU HAVE TO KEEP MOVING IT SO IT DOESN'T BURN.
STIR. FRY.
STIR. FRY.
GLAD YOU'RE BACK, TRIBE MASTER. BUDDY AND I ARE DOING LAUNDRY, NEED US TO WASH ANYTHING?
"A BRAVE IS CLEAN" AND ALL THAT.
YOU BOYS HAVE SURE GOT A RUN ON THINGS, DON'T YA?
WHEN THINGS SETTLE DOWN, YOU AND I HAVE TO TALK ABOUT SOME STUFF.
SURE. WHENEVER YOU'RE READY, BUDDY.

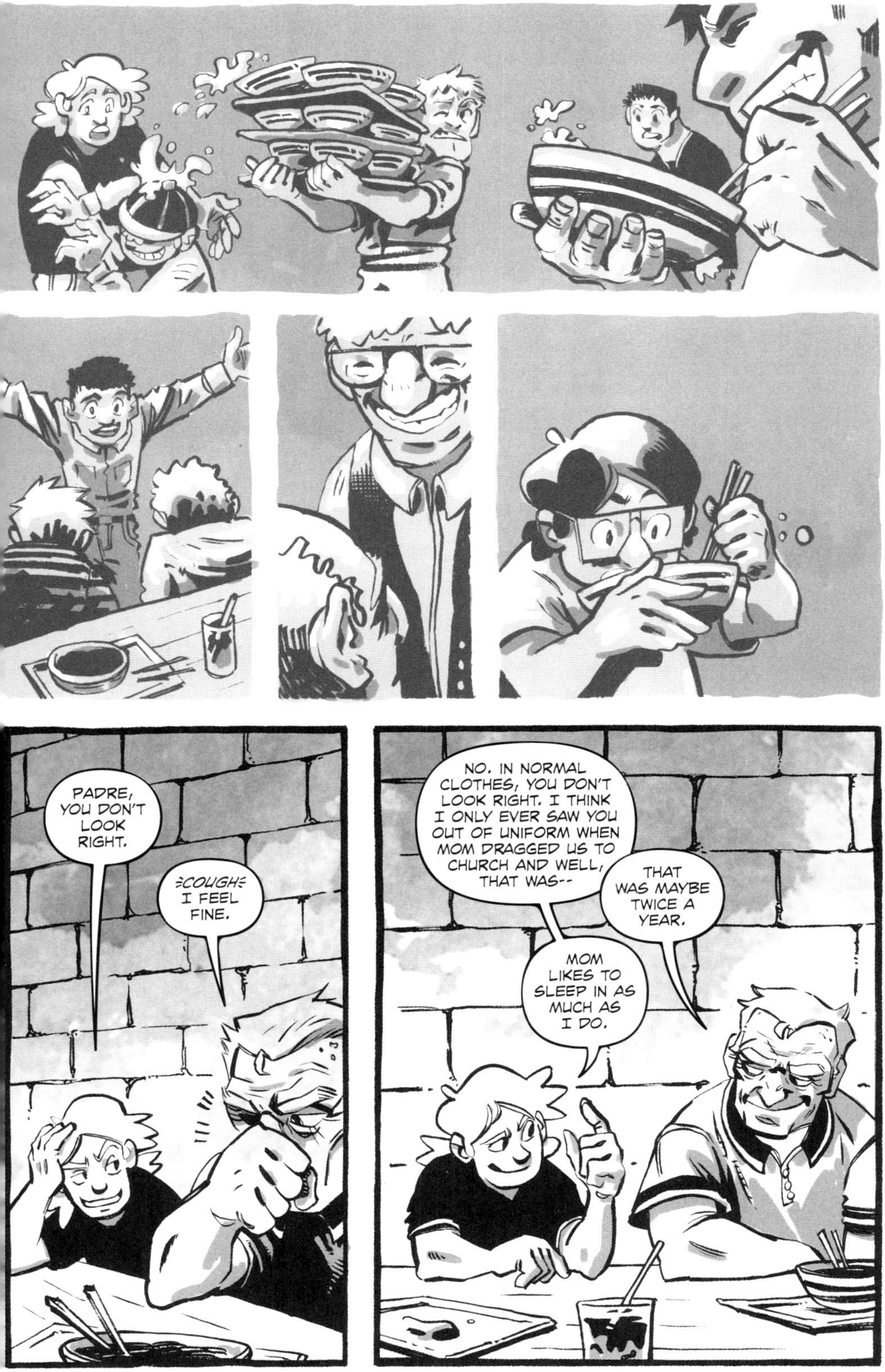
PADRE, YOU DON'T LOOK RIGHT.
=COUGH= I FEEL FINE.
NO. IN NORMAL CLOTHES, YOU DON'T LOOK RIGHT. I THINK I ONLY EVER SAW YOU OUT OF UNIFORM WHEN MOM DRAGGED US TO CHURCH AND WELL, THAT WAS--
THAT WAS MAYBE TWICE A YEAR.
MOM LIKES TO SLEEP IN AS MUCH AS I DO.

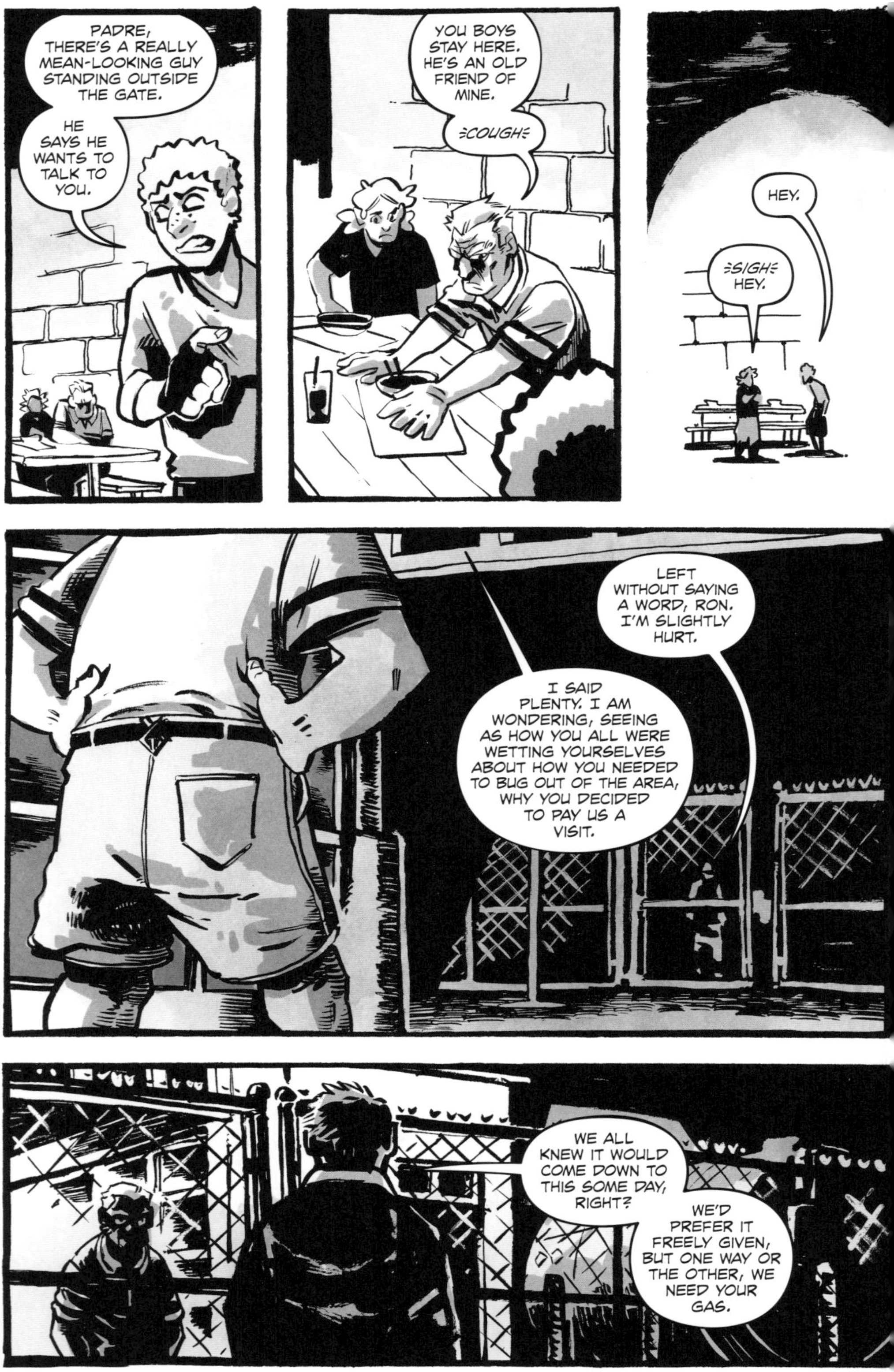
PADRE, THERE'S A REALLY MEAN-LOOKING GUY STANDING OUTSIDE THE GATE.
HE SAYS HE WANTS TO TALK TO YOU.
YOU BOYS STAY HERE. HE'S AN OLD FRIEND OF MINE.
≈COUGH≈
HEY.
≈SIGH≈ HEY.
LEFT WITHOUT SAYING A WORD, RON. I'M SLIGHTLY HURT.
I SAID PLENTY. I AM WONDERING, SEEING AS HOW YOU ALL WERE WETTING YOURSELVES ABOUT HOW YOU NEEDED TO BUG OUT OF THE AREA, WHY YOU DECIDED TO PAY US A VISIT.
WE ALL KNEW IT WOULD COME DOWN TO THIS SOME DAY, RIGHT?
WE'D PREFER IT FREELY GIVEN, BUT ONE WAY OR THE OTHER, WE NEED YOUR GAS.

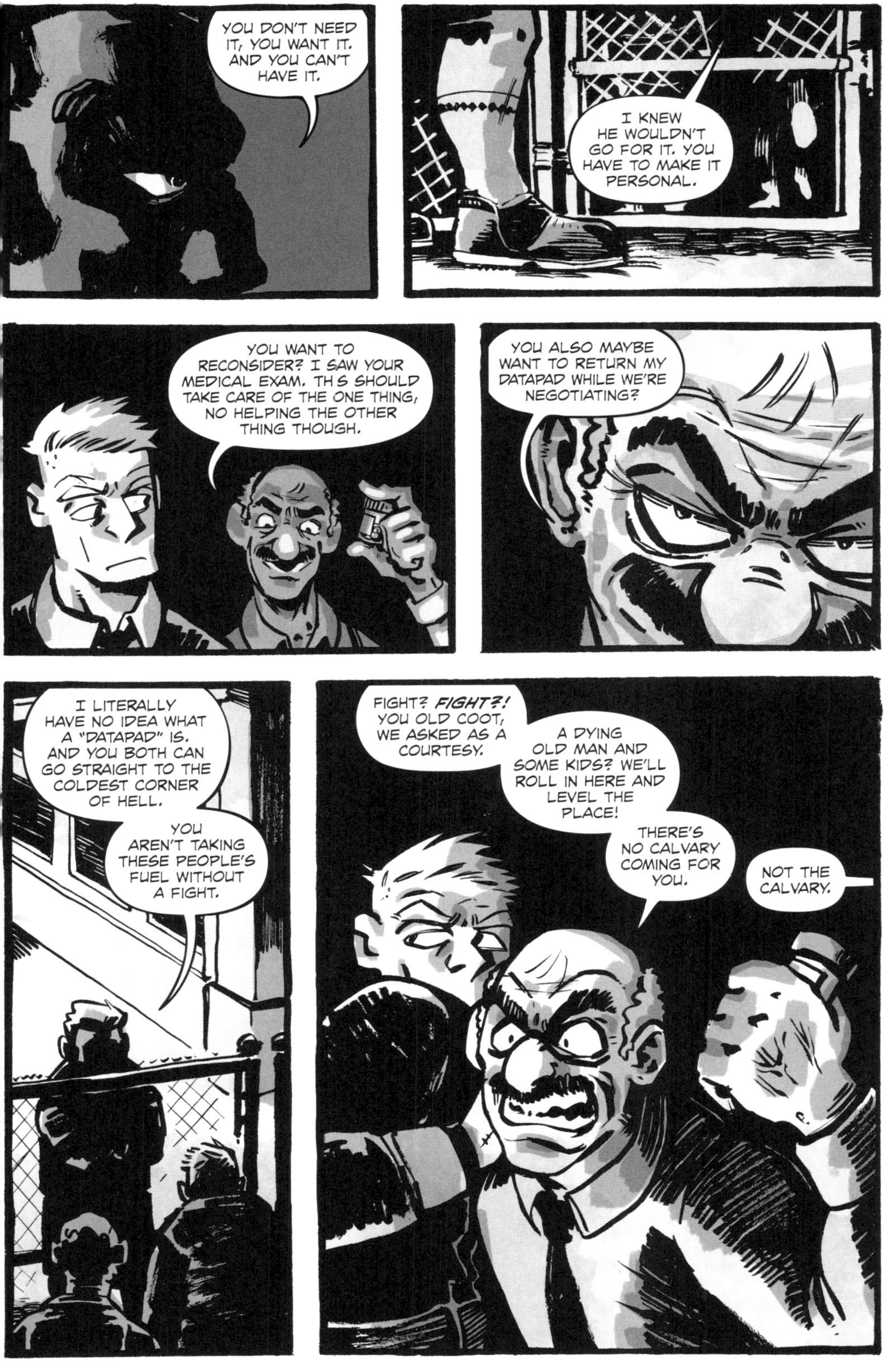
YOU DON'T NEED IT, YOU WANT IT. AND YOU CAN'T HAVE IT.
I KNEW HE WOULDN'T GO FOR IT. YOU HAVE TO MAKE IT PERSONAL.
YOU WANT TO RECONSIDER? I SAW YOUR MEDICAL EXAM. TH S SHOULD TAKE CARE OF THE ONE THING, NO HELPING THE OTHER THING THOUGH.
YOU ALSO MAYBE WANT TO RETURN MY DATAPAD WHILE WE'RE NEGOTIATING?
I LITERALLY HAVE NO IDEA WHAT A "DATAPAD" IS. AND YOU BOTH CAN GO STRAIGHT TO THE COLDEST CORNER OF HELL.
YOU AREN'T TAKING THESE PEOPLE'S FUEL WITHOUT A FIGHT.
FIGHT? *FIGHT?!* YOU OLD COOT, WE ASKED AS A COURTESY.
A DYING OLD MAN AND SOME KIDS? WE'LL ROLL IN HERE AND LEVEL THE PLACE!
THERE'S NO CALVARY COMING FOR YOU.
NOT THE CALVARY.

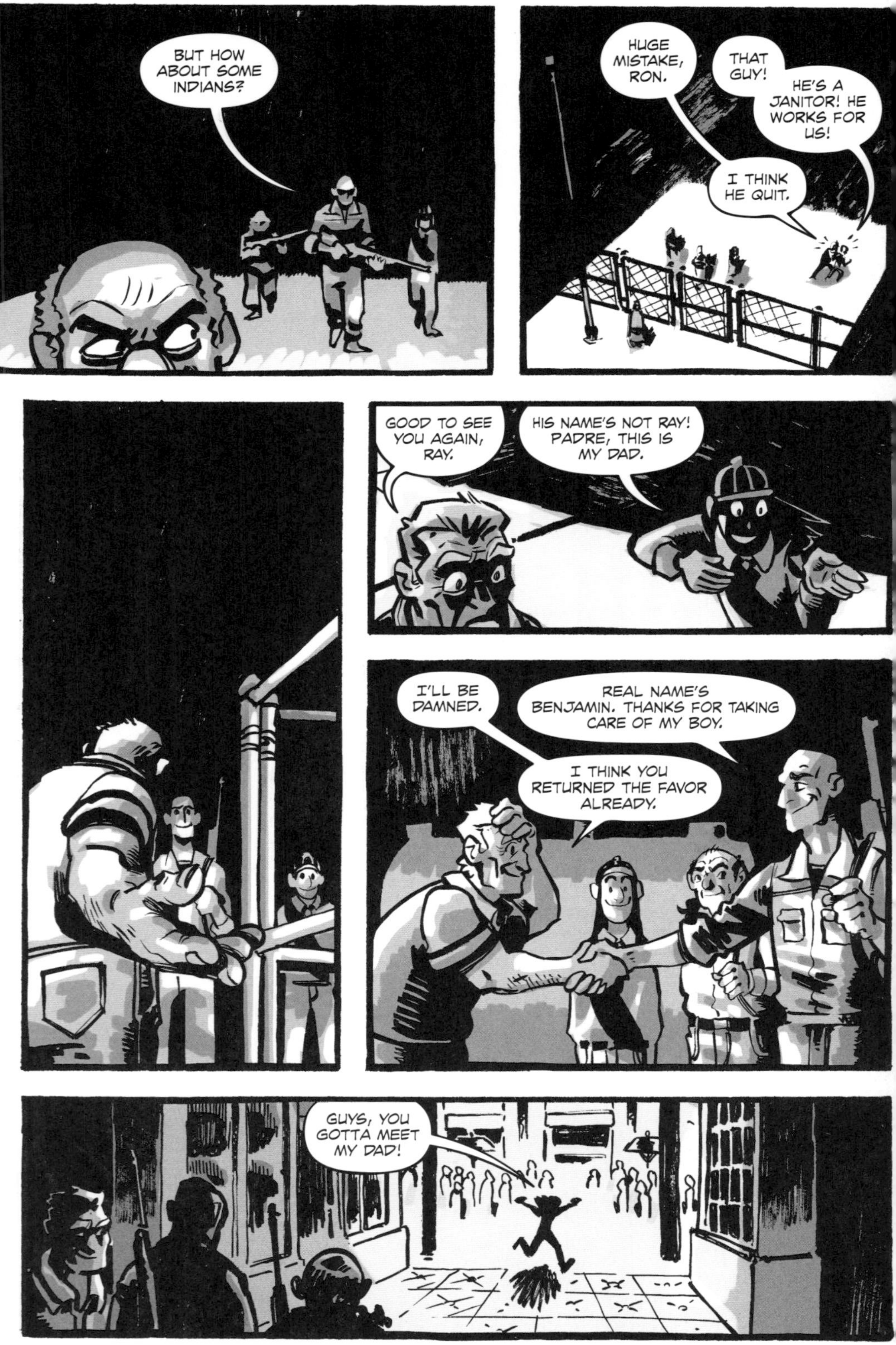
BUT HOW ABOUT SOME INDIANS?
HUGE MISTAKE, RON.
THAT GUY!
HE'S A JANITOR! HE WORKS FOR US!
I THINK HE QUIT.
GOOD TO SEE YOU AGAIN, RAY.
HIS NAME'S NOT RAY! PADRE, THIS IS MY DAD.
I'LL BE DAMNED.
REAL NAME'S BENJAMIN. THANKS FOR TAKING CARE OF MY BOY.
I THINK YOU RETURNED THE FAVOR ALREADY.
GUYS, YOU GOTTA MEET MY DAD!

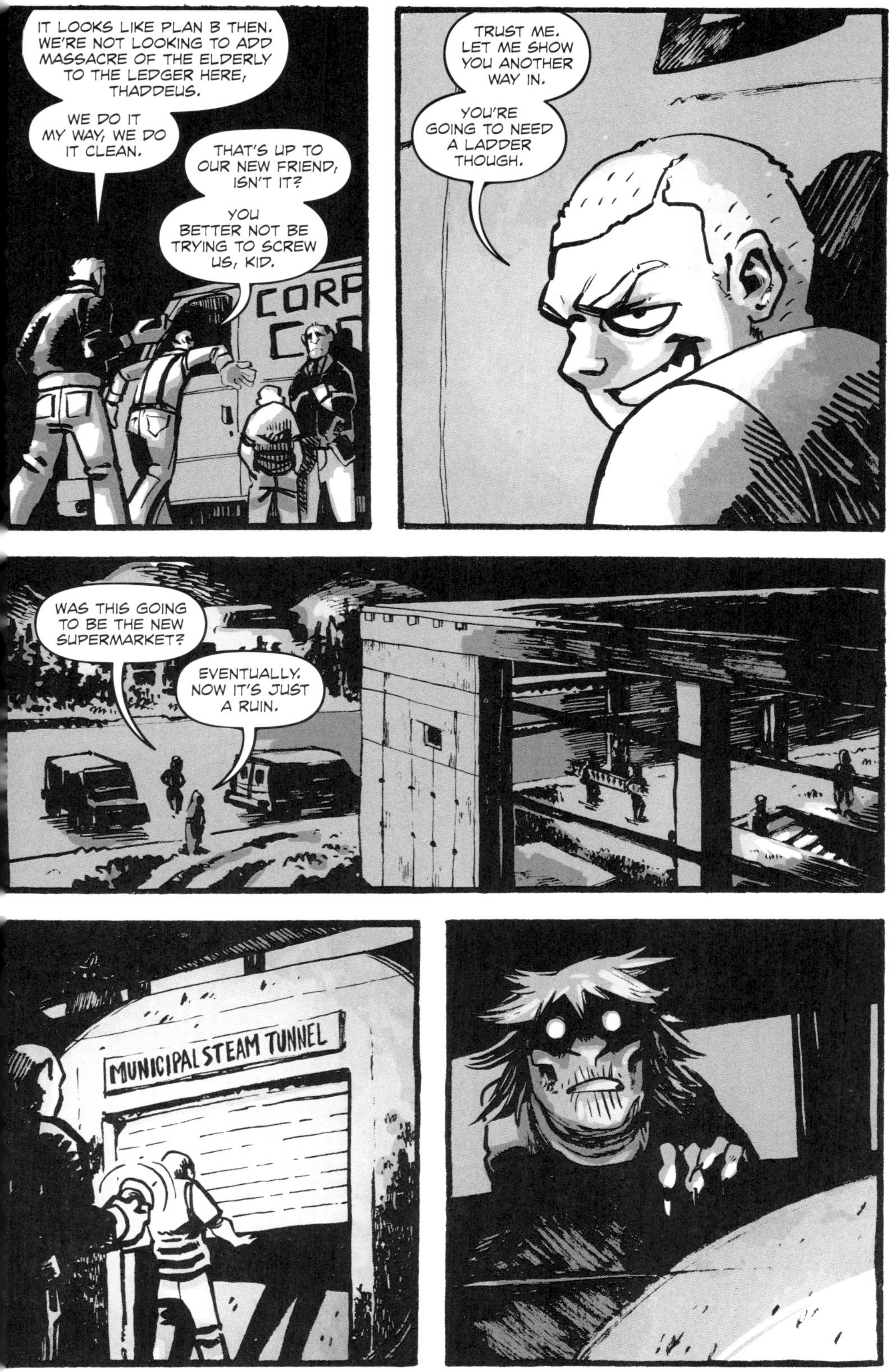
IT LOOKS LIKE PLAN B THEN. WE'RE NOT LOOKING TO ADD MASSACRE OF THE ELDERLY TO THE LEDGER HERE, THADDEUS.
WE DO IT MY WAY, WE DO IT CLEAN.
THAT'S UP TO OUR NEW FRIEND, ISN'T IT?
YOU BETTER NOT BE TRYING TO SCREW US, KID.
CORP
TRUST ME. LET ME SHOW YOU ANOTHER WAY IN.
YOU'RE GOING TO NEED A LADDER THOUGH.
WAS THIS GOING TO BE THE NEW SUPERMARKET?
EVENTUALLY. NOW IT'S JUST A RUIN.
MUNICIPAL STEAM TUNNEL

TENNIS BALL CANNON

BAD IDEA? OR BEST IDEA?
BAD BEST IDEA?

BASIC CONCEPT - HIGH PROPULSION BALL LAUNCHING
DAMAGE? MINIMAL
RANGE? 20 FEET EFFECTIVE

DAMAGE NOT IMPORTANT DISTRACTION TECHNIQUE?
HOW TO IMPROVE? SOAK TENNIS BALLS IN GARBAGE
                                              JUICE

LIKE PLAYING FETCH WITH MY DOG. IF MY
MOM LET ME HAVE A DOG.

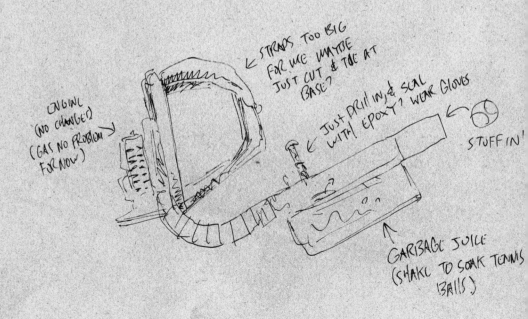

ENGINE
(NO CHANGES)
(GAS NO PROBLEM
FOR NOW)

← STRAPS TOO BIG
FOR ME MAYBE
JUST CUT & TIE AT
BASE?

← JUST DRILL IN & SEAL
WITH EPOXY? WEAR GLOVES

STUFF IN!

GARBAGE JUICE
(SHAKE TO SOAK TENNIS
BALLS)

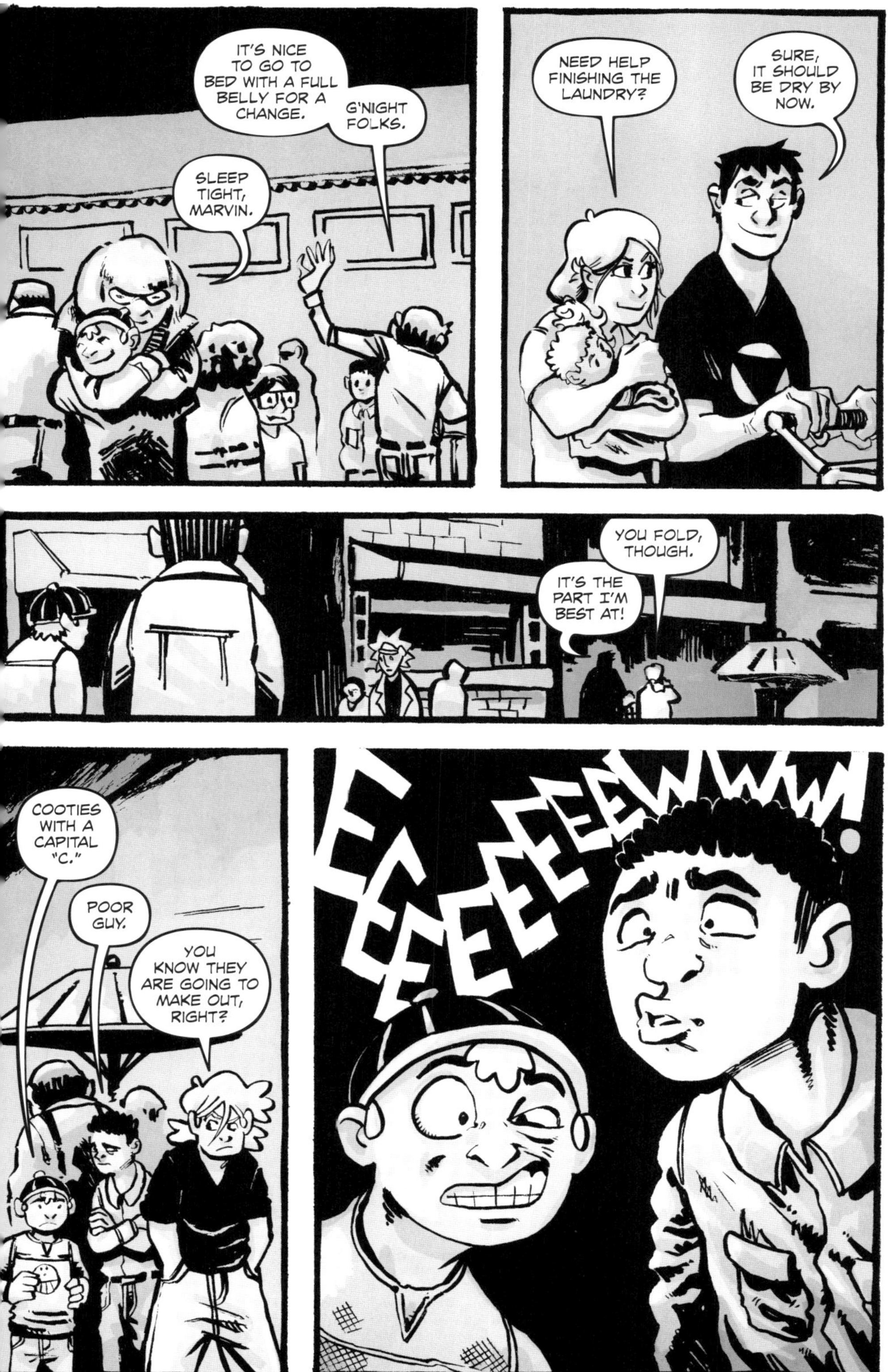
IT'S NICE TO GO TO BED WITH A FULL BELLY FOR A CHANGE.
G'NIGHT FOLKS.
SLEEP TIGHT, MARVIN.
NEED HELP FINISHING THE LAUNDRY?
SURE, IT SHOULD BE DRY BY NOW.
YOU FOLD, THOUGH.
IT'S THE PART I'M BEST AT!
COOTIES WITH A CAPITAL "C."
POOR GUY.
YOU KNOW THEY ARE GOING TO MAKE OUT, RIGHT?
EEEEEEEEWWWW!

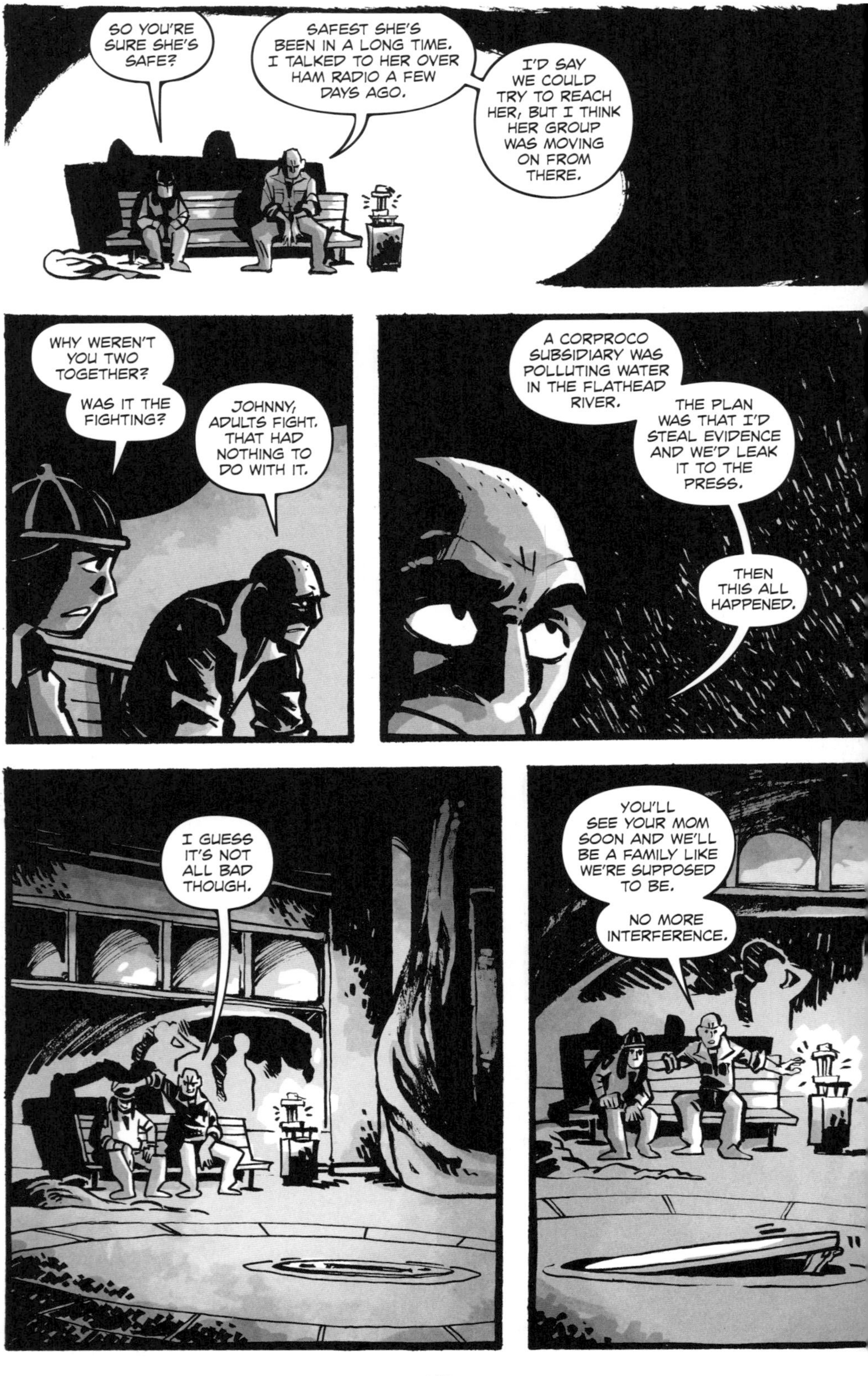

SO YOU'RE SURE SHE'S SAFE?
SAFEST SHE'S BEEN IN A LONG TIME. I TALKED TO HER OVER HAM RADIO A FEW DAYS AGO.
I'D SAY WE COULD TRY TO REACH HER, BUT I THINK HER GROUP WAS MOVING ON FROM THERE.
WHY WEREN'T YOU TWO TOGETHER?
WAS IT THE FIGHTING?
JOHNNY, ADULTS FIGHT. THAT HAD NOTHING TO DO WITH IT.
A CORPROCO SUBSIDIARY WAS POLLUTING WATER IN THE FLATHEAD RIVER.
THE PLAN WAS THAT I'D STEAL EVIDENCE AND WE'D LEAK IT TO THE PRESS.
THEN THIS ALL HAPPENED.
I GUESS IT'S NOT ALL BAD THOUGH.
YOU'LL SEE YOUR MOM SOON AND WE'LL BE A FAMILY LIKE WE'RE SUPPOSED TO BE.
NO MORE INTERFERENCE.

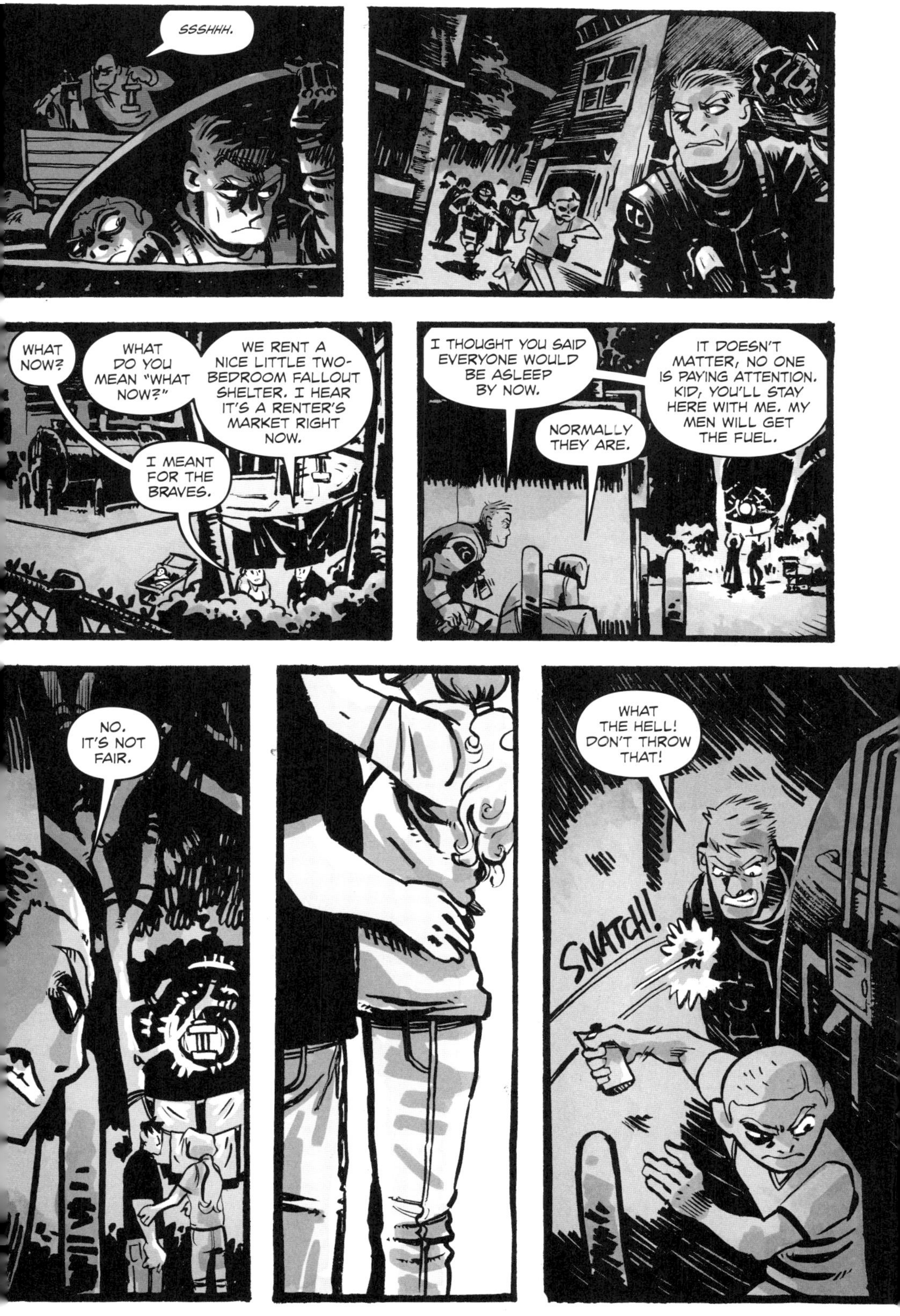

SSSHHH.
WHAT NOW?
WHAT DO YOU MEAN "WHAT NOW?"
WE RENT A NICE LITTLE TWO-BEDROOM FALLOUT SHELTER. I HEAR IT'S A RENTER'S MARKET RIGHT NOW.
I MEANT FOR THE BRAVES.
I THOUGHT YOU SAID EVERYONE WOULD BE ASLEEP BY NOW.
NORMALLY THEY ARE.
IT DOESN'T MATTER, NO ONE IS PAYING ATTENTION. KID, YOU'LL STAY HERE WITH ME. MY MEN WILL GET THE FUEL.
NO. IT'S NOT FAIR.
WHAT THE HELL! DON'T THROW THAT!
SNATCH!

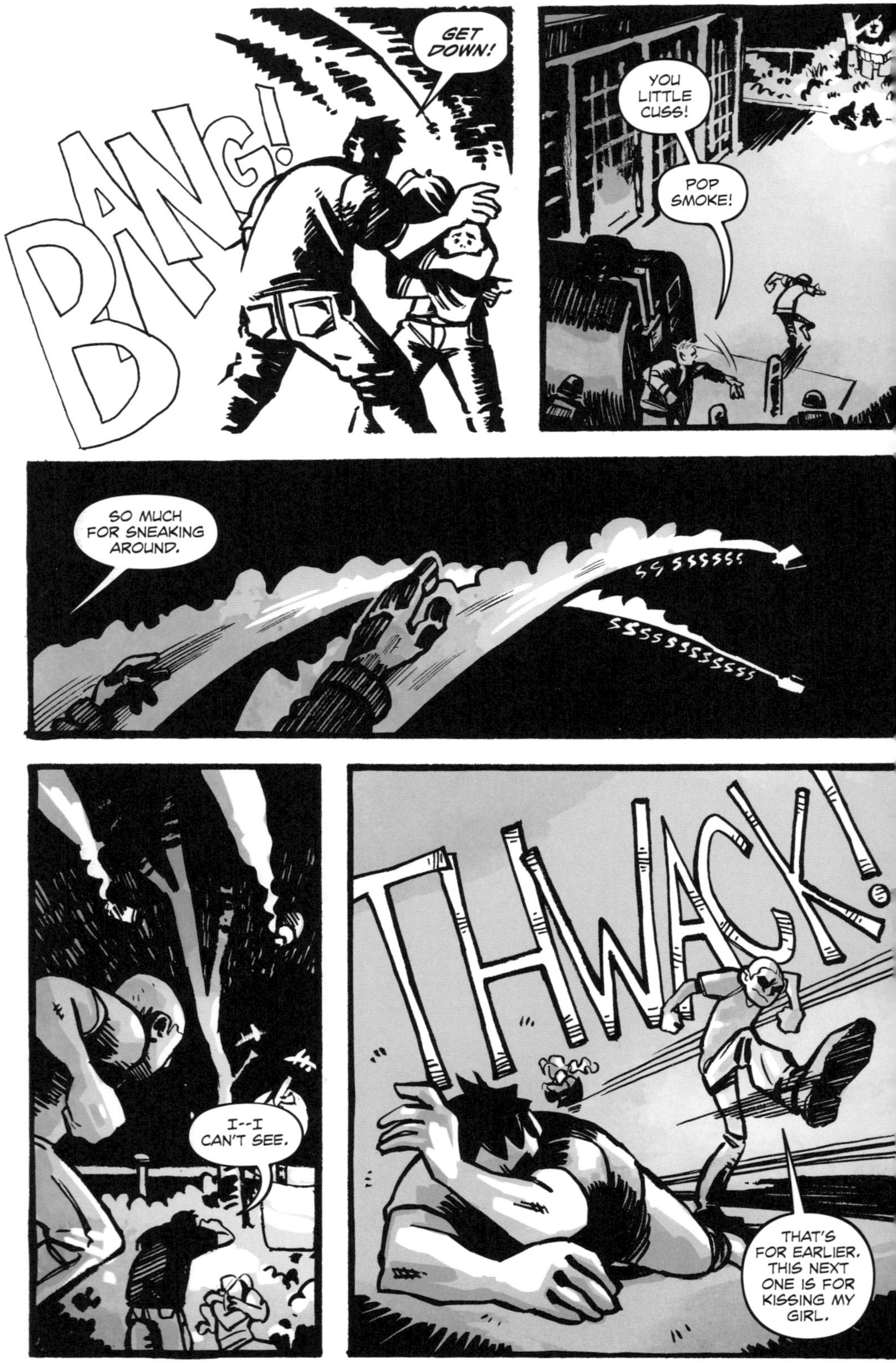
GET DOWN!
BANG!
YOU LITTLE CUSS!
POP SMOKE!
SO MUCH FOR SNEAKING AROUND.
I--I CAN'T SEE.
THWACK!
THAT'S FOR EARLIER. THIS NEXT ONE IS FOR KISSING MY GIRL.

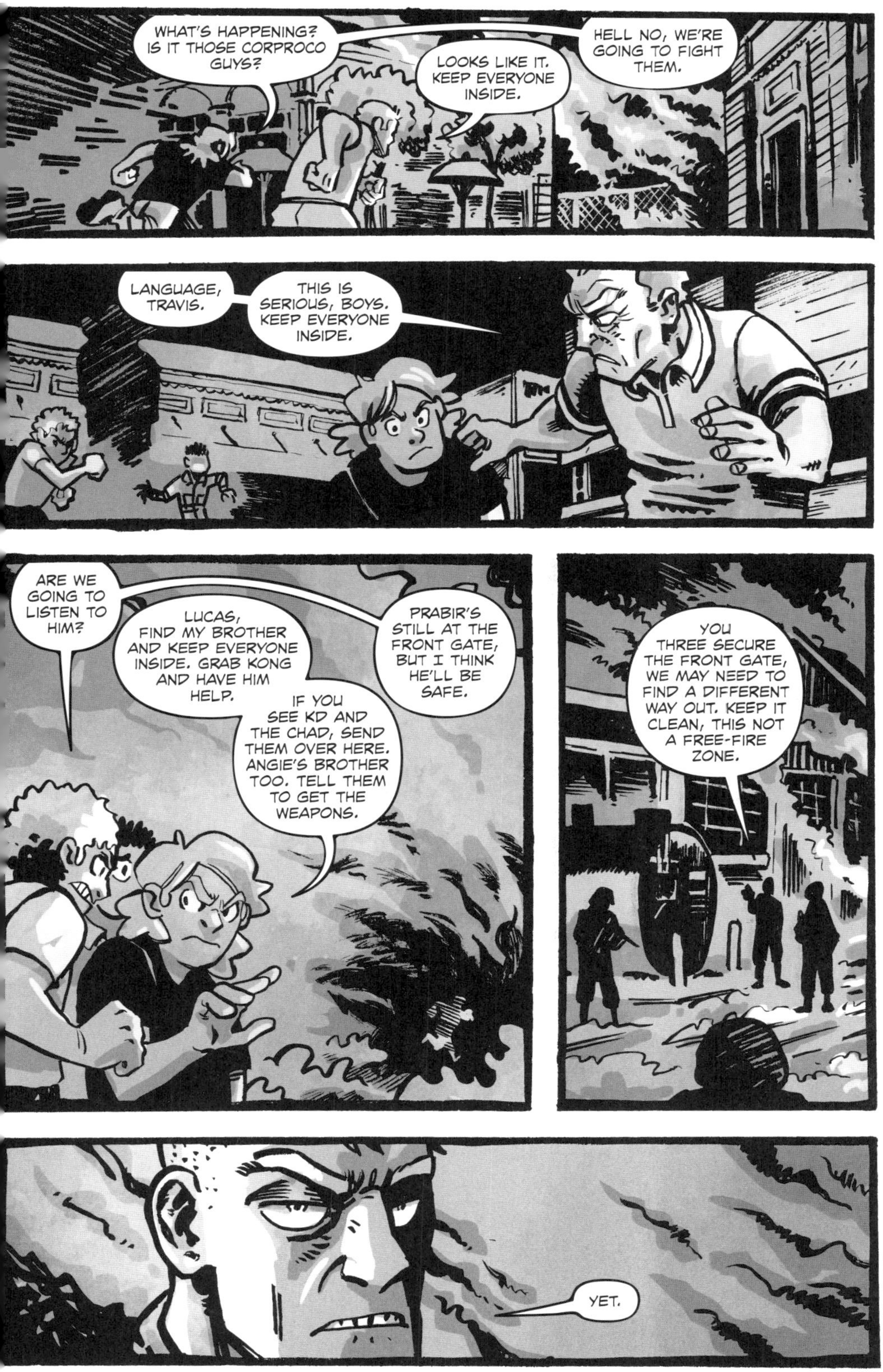
WHAT'S HAPPENING? IS IT THOSE CORPROCO GUYS?
LOOKS LIKE IT. KEEP EVERYONE INSIDE.
HELL NO, WE'RE GOING TO FIGHT THEM.
LANGUAGE, TRAVIS.
THIS IS SERIOUS, BOYS. KEEP EVERYONE INSIDE.
ARE WE GOING TO LISTEN TO HIM?
PRABIR'S STILL AT THE FRONT GATE, BUT I THINK HE'LL BE SAFE.
LUCAS, FIND MY BROTHER AND KEEP EVERYONE INSIDE. GRAB KONG AND HAVE HIM HELP.
IF YOU SEE KD AND THE CHAD, SEND THEM OVER HERE. ANGIE'S BROTHER TOO. TELL THEM TO GET THE WEAPONS.
YOU THREE SECURE THE FRONT GATE, WE MAY NEED TO FIND A DIFFERENT WAY OUT. KEEP IT CLEAN, THIS NOT A FREE-FIRE ZONE.
YET.

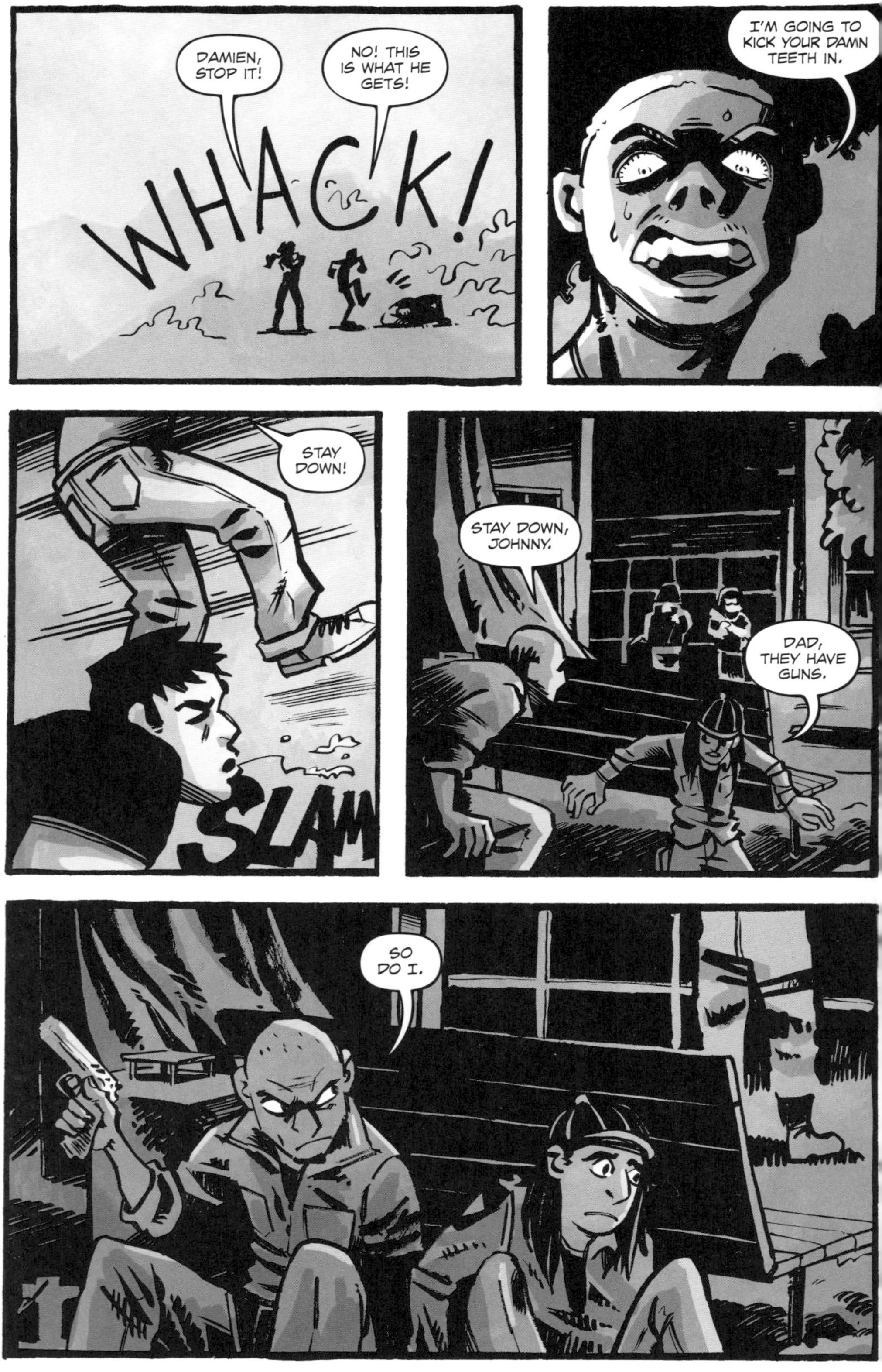
DAMIEN, STOP IT!
NO! THIS IS WHAT HE GETS!
WHACK!
I'M GOING TO KICK YOUR DAMN TEETH IN.
STAY DOWN!
SLAM
STAY DOWN, JOHNNY.
DAD, THEY HAVE GUNS.
SO DO I.

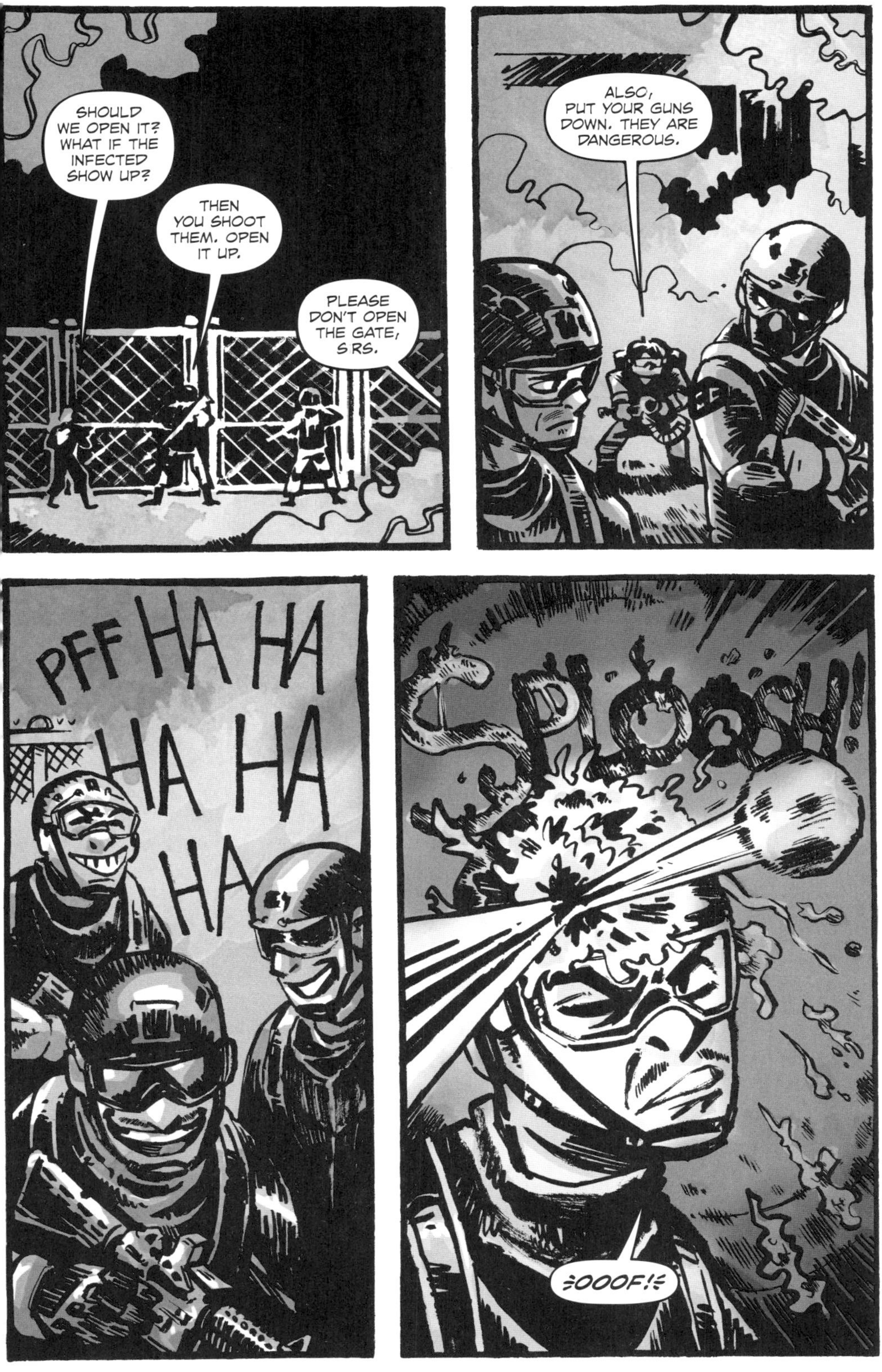
SHOULD WE OPEN IT? WHAT IF THE INFECTED SHOW UP?
THEN YOU SHOOT THEM. OPEN IT UP.
PLEASE DON'T OPEN THE GATE, S RS.
ALSO, PUT YOUR GUNS DOWN. THEY ARE DANGEROUS.
PFF HA HA HA HA HA
SPLOOSH!!
OOOF!

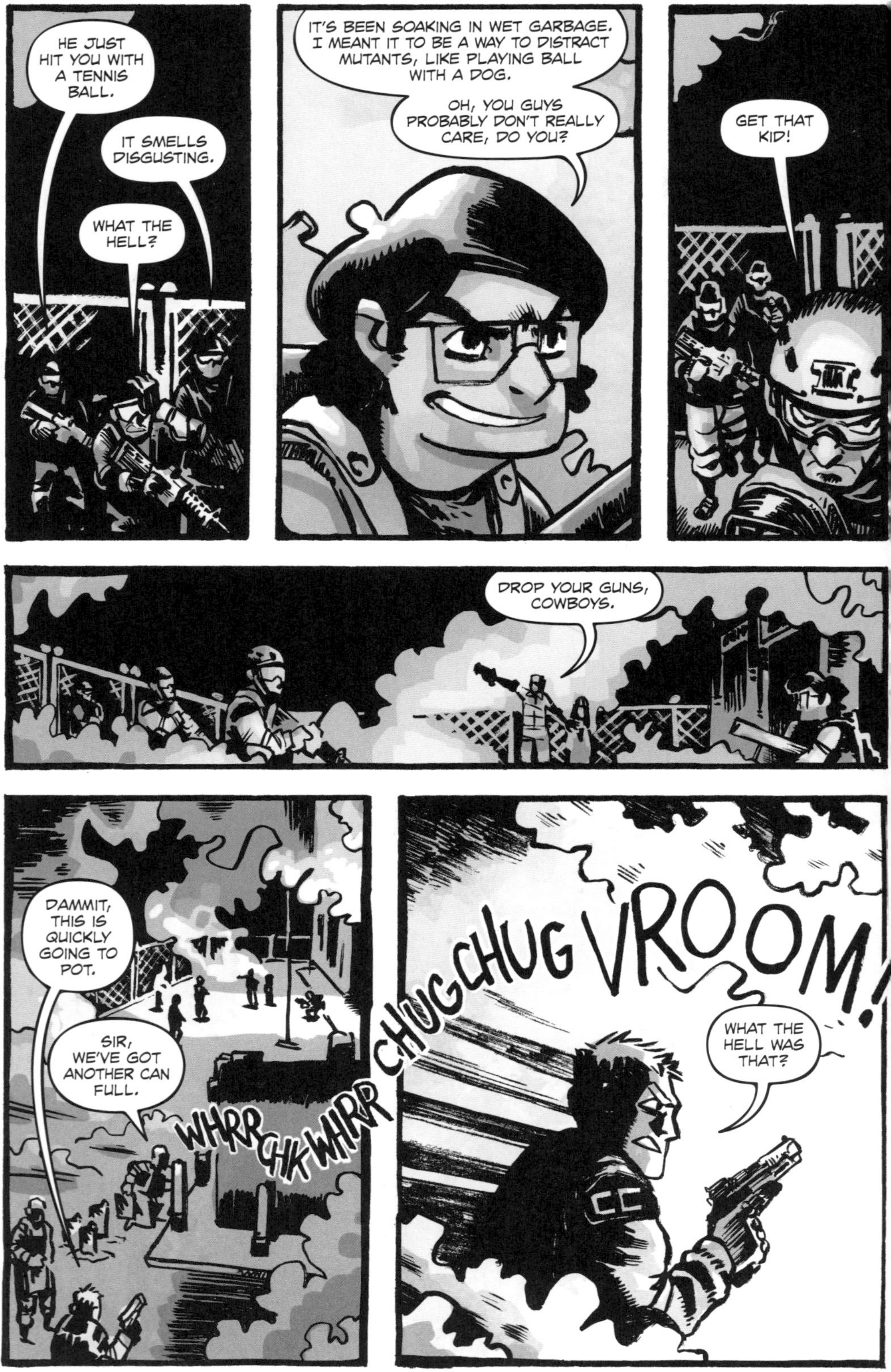
HE JUST HIT YOU WITH A TENNIS BALL.
IT SMELLS DISGUSTING.
WHAT THE HELL?
IT'S BEEN SOAKING IN WET GARBAGE. I MEANT IT TO BE A WAY TO DISTRACT MUTANTS, LIKE PLAYING BALL WITH A DOG.
OH, YOU GUYS PROBABLY DON'T REALLY CARE, DO YOU?
GET THAT KID!
DROP YOUR GUNS, COWBOYS.
DAMMIT, THIS IS QUICKLY GOING TO POT.
SIR, WE'VE GOT ANOTHER CAN FULL.
WHRR CHK WHRR CHUG CHUG CHUG VROOM!!
WHAT THE HELL WAS THAT?

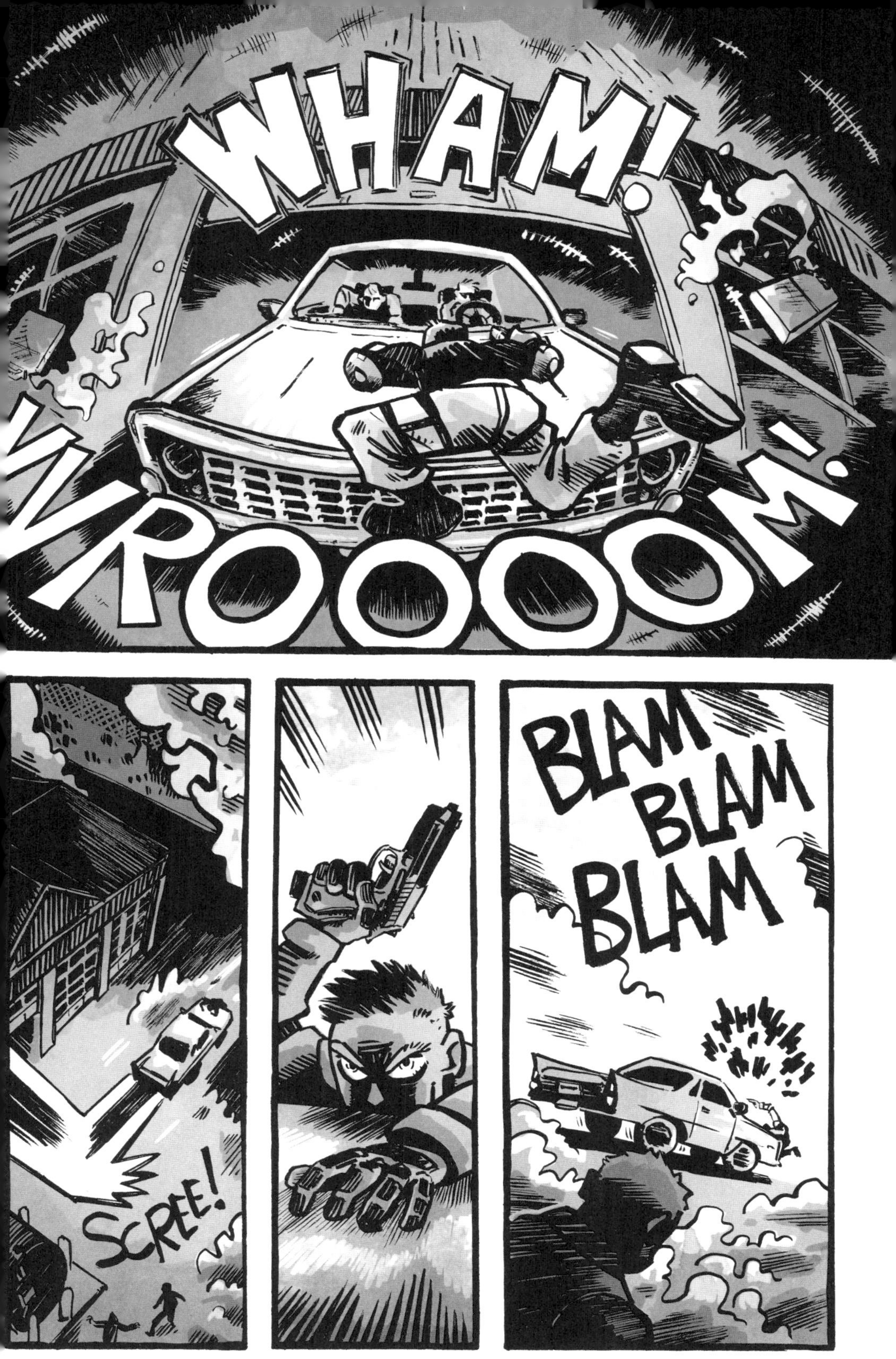
WHAM!
VROOOOM!
SCREE!
BLAM
BLAM
BLAM

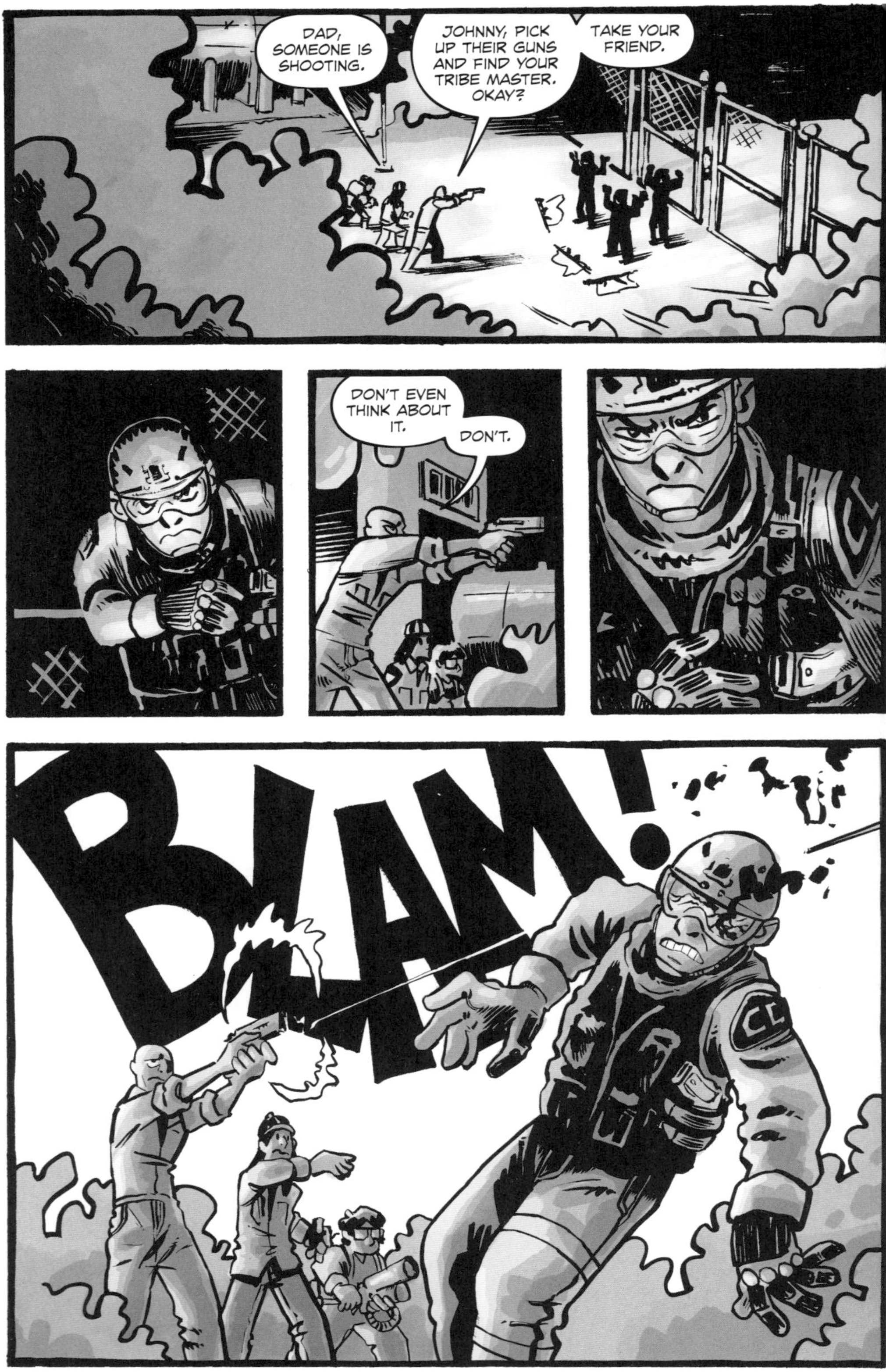
DAD, SOMEONE IS SHOOTING.
JOHNNY, PICK UP THEIR GUNS AND FIND YOUR TRIBE MASTER. OKAY?
TAKE YOUR FRIEND.
DON'T EVEN THINK ABOUT IT.
DON'T.
BLAM!

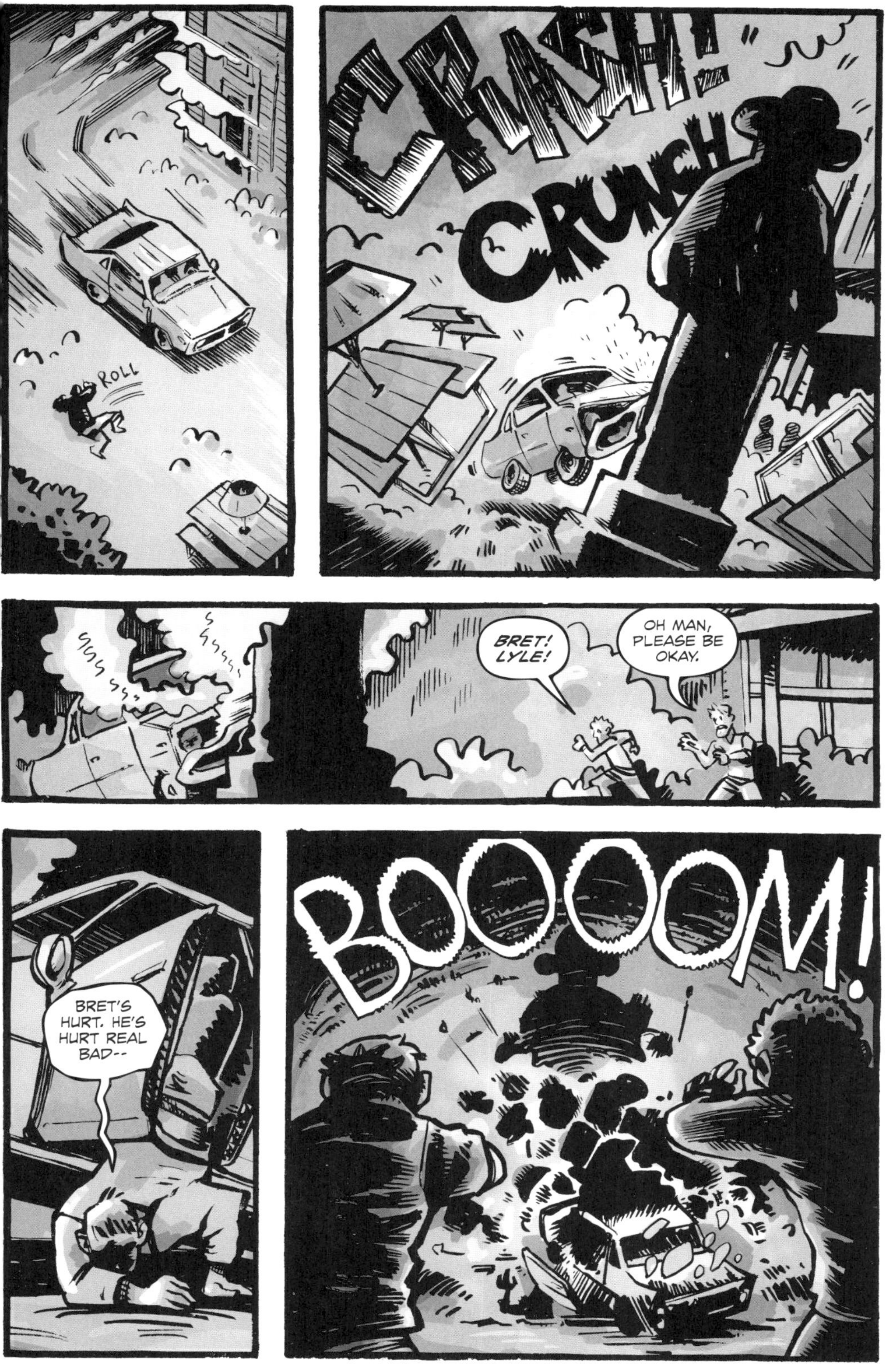
ROLL
CRASH!
CRUNCH
BRET! LYLE!
OH MAN, PLEASE BE OKAY.
BRET'S HURT. HE'S HURT REAL BAD--
BOOOOM!

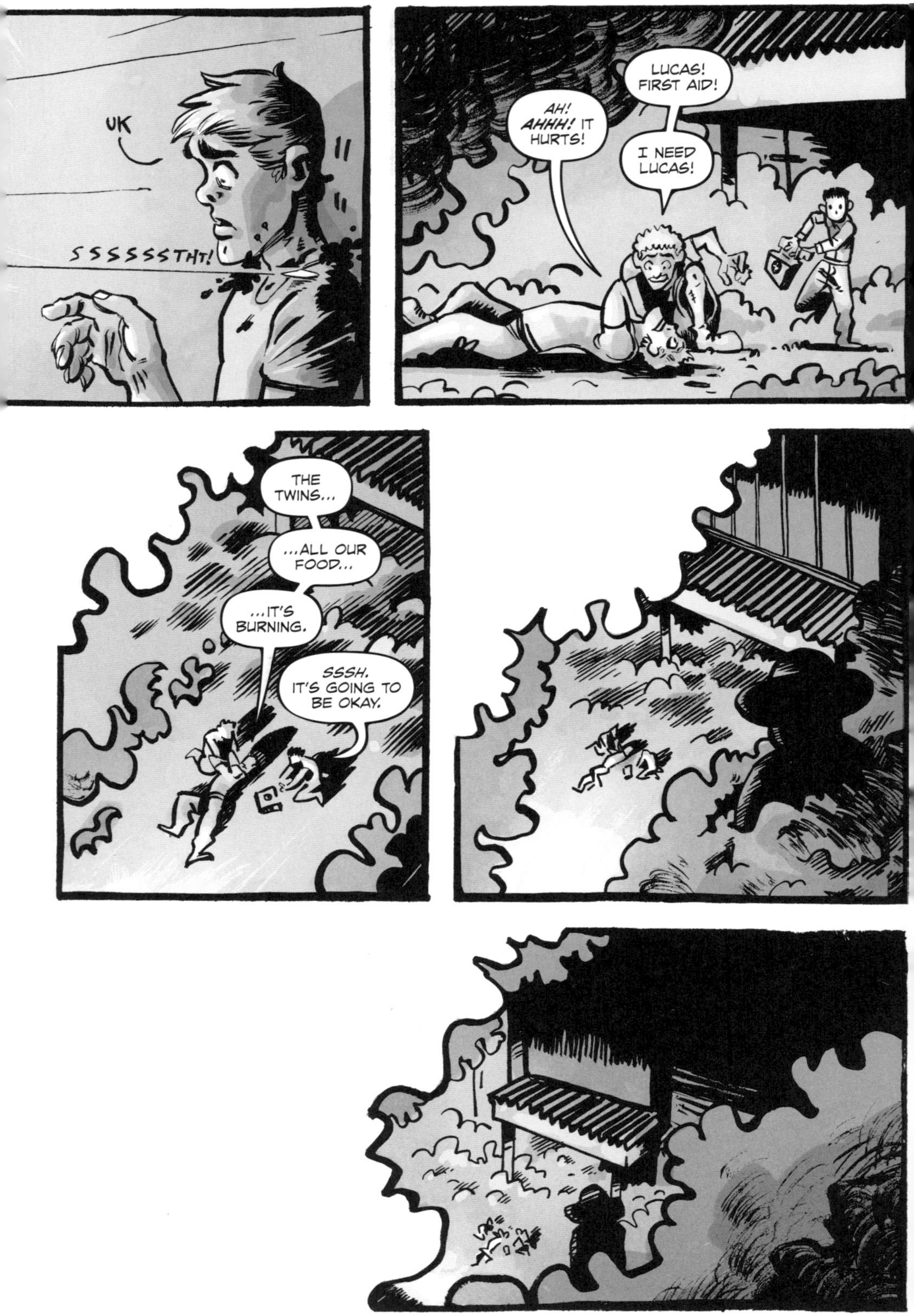
UK
SSSSSSTHT!
LUCAS! FIRST AID!
AH! AHHH! IT HURTS!
I NEED LUCAS!
THE TWINS...
...ALL OUR FOOD...
...IT'S BURNING.
SSSH. IT'S GOING TO BE OKAY.

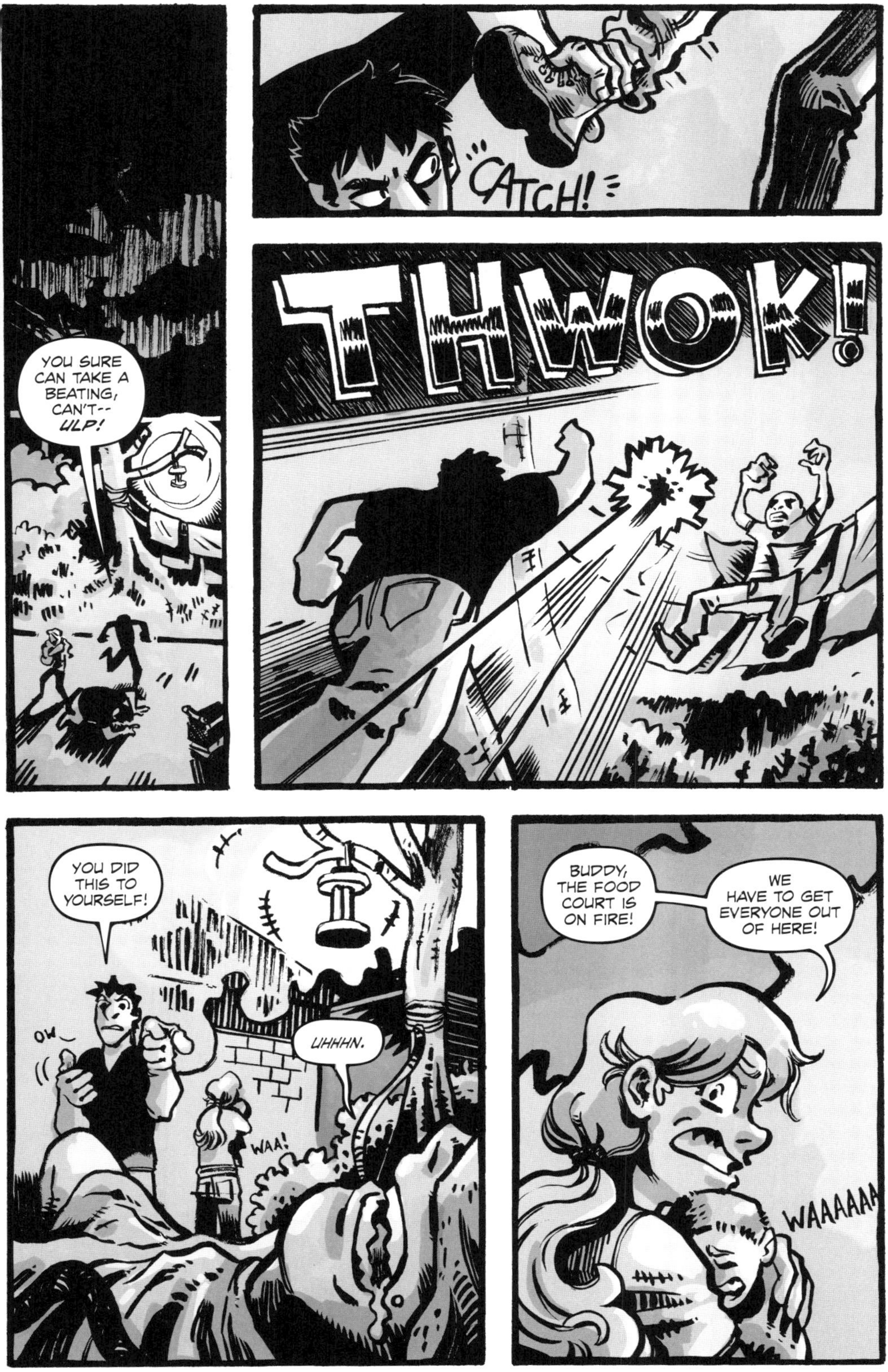
CATCH!
THWOK!
YOU SURE CAN TAKE A BEATING, CAN'T-- ULP!
YOU DID THIS TO YOURSELF!
OW
UHHHN.
WAA!
BUDDY, THE FOOD COURT IS ON FIRE!
WE HAVE TO GET EVERYONE OUT OF HERE!
WAAAAAA

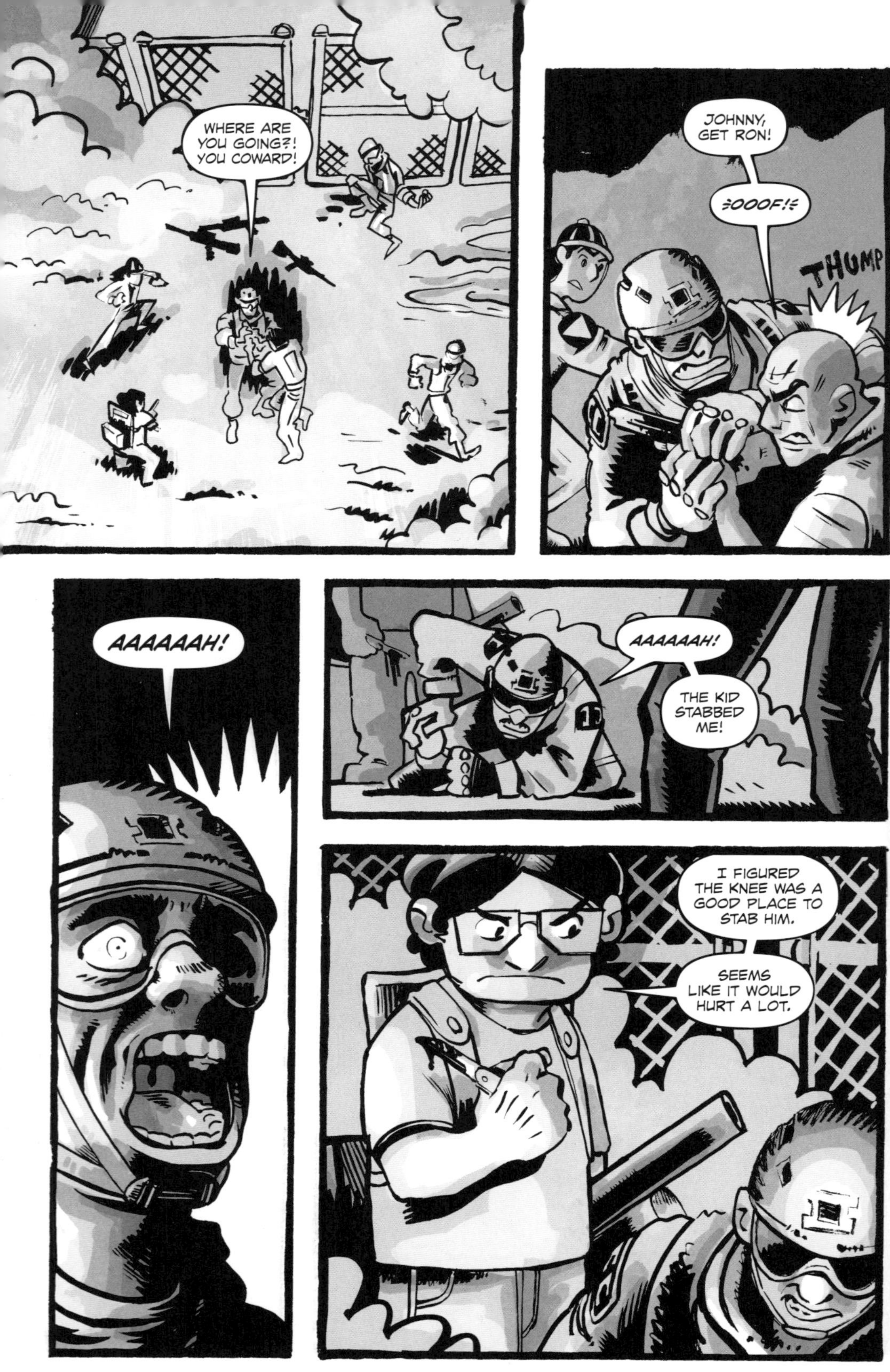
WHERE ARE YOU GOING?! YOU COWARD!
JOHNNY, GET RON!
OOOF!
THUMP
AAAAAAH!
AAAAAAH!
THE KID STABBED ME!
I FIGURED THE KNEE WAS A GOOD PLACE TO STAB HIM.
SEEMS LIKE IT WOULD HURT A LOT.

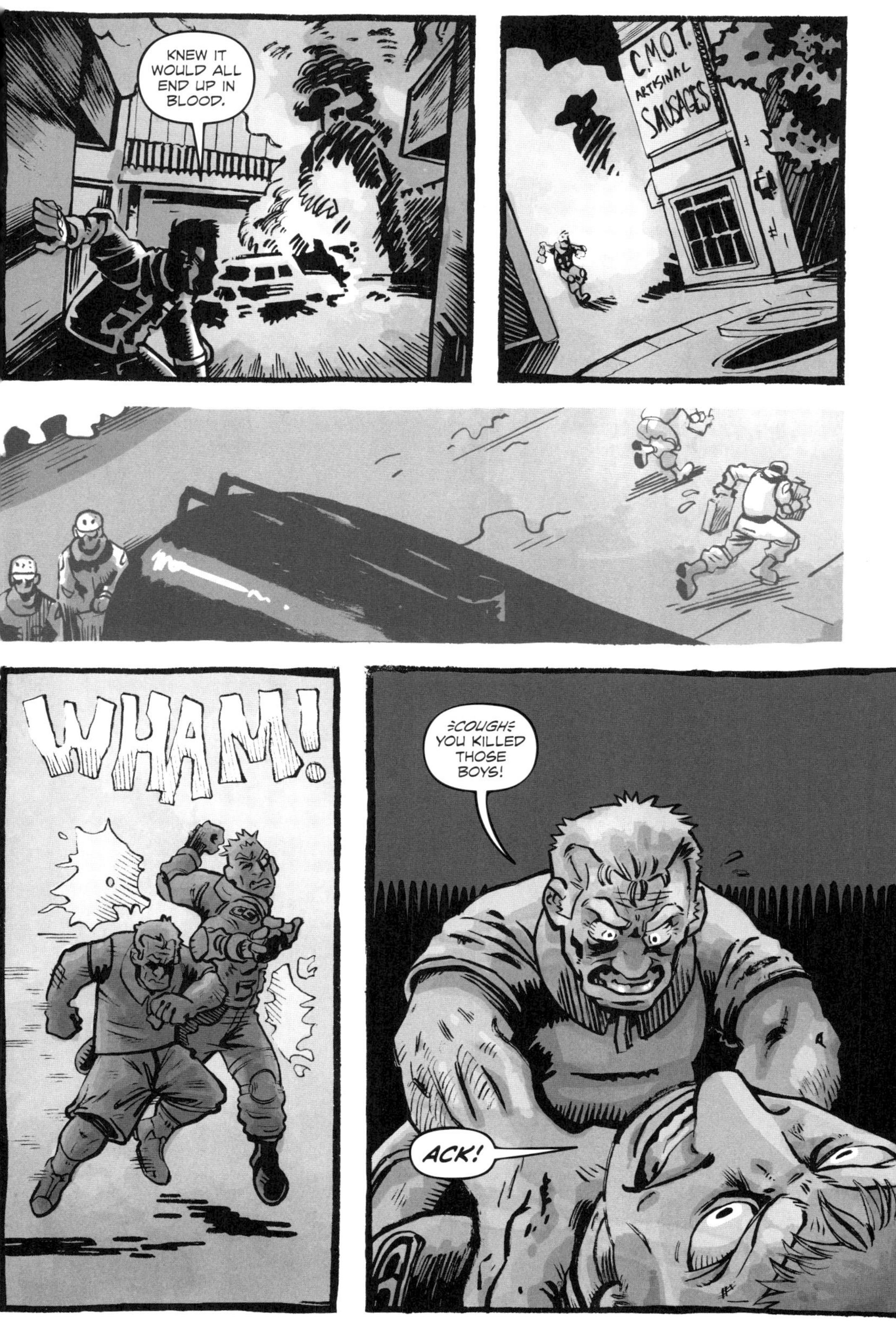
KNEW IT WOULD ALL END UP IN BLOOD.
C.M.O.T. ARTISINAL SAUSAGES
WHAM!
COUGH
YOU KILLED THOSE BOYS!
ACK!

ƎCOUGHƎ
ƎCOUGHƎ
ARRRG.

JUST DIE
ALREADY!

ƎCOUGHƎ
YOU'LL PAY,
HANNEGAN--
ƎCOUGHƎ

GOD
HELP ME.
ƎCOUGHƎ

RON!
ARE YOU
OKAY?

ƎCOUGHƎ
DON'T LET--
ƎCOUGHƎ--HIM
GET AWAY,
HE KILLED
THEM!

BLAM!
BLAM!

WAAAAAAA!

CLICK

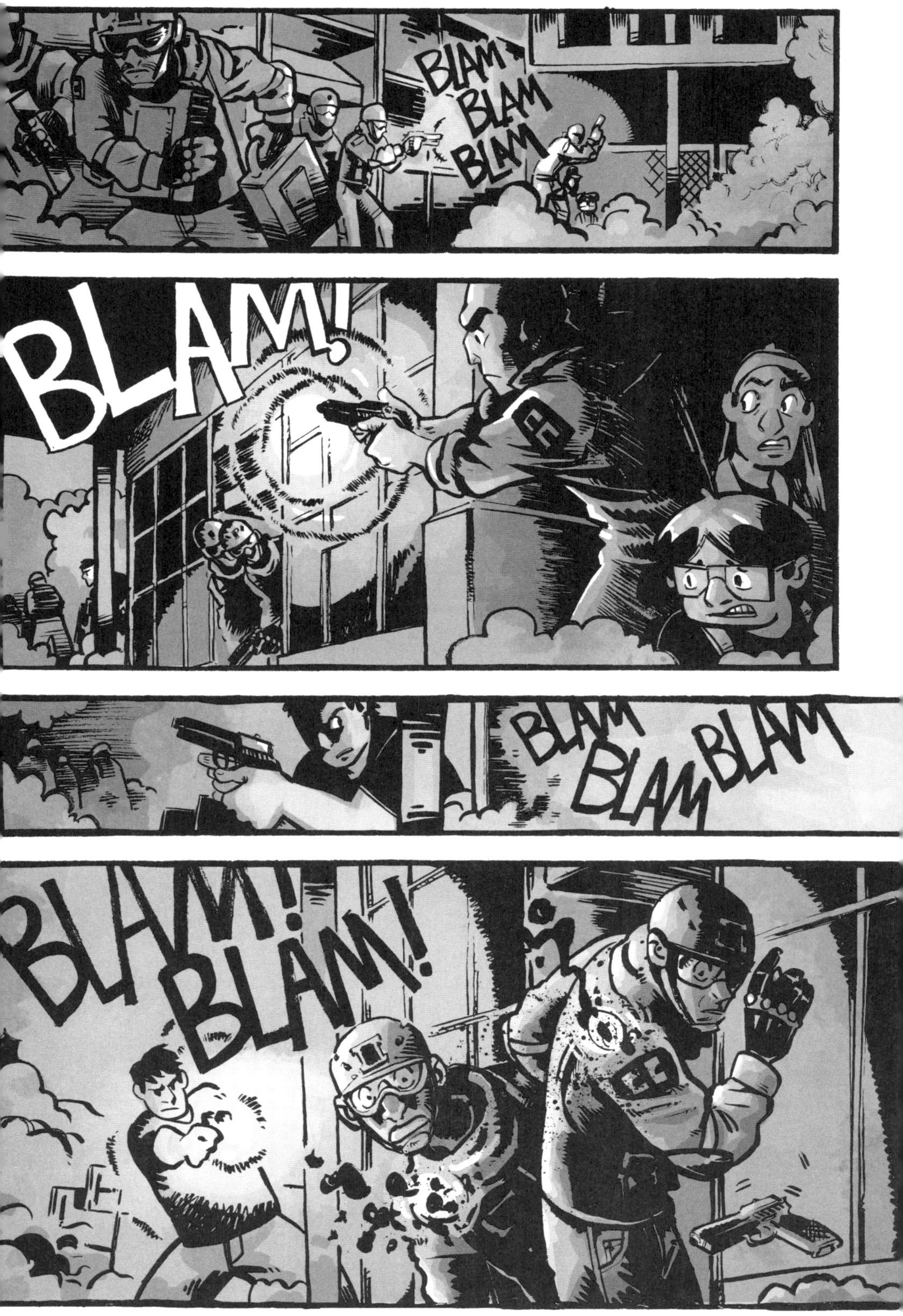
BLAM
BLAM
BLAM
BLAM!
BLAM
BLAM
BLAM
BLAM!
BLAM!

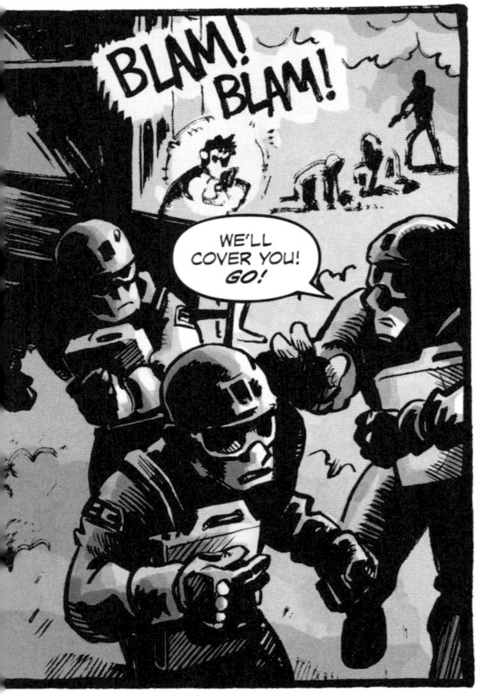
BLAM! BLAM!
WE'LL COVER YOU! *GO!*

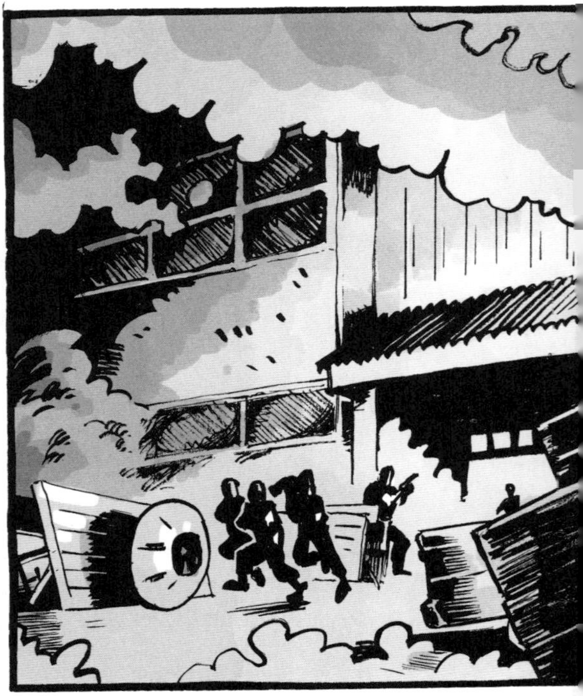

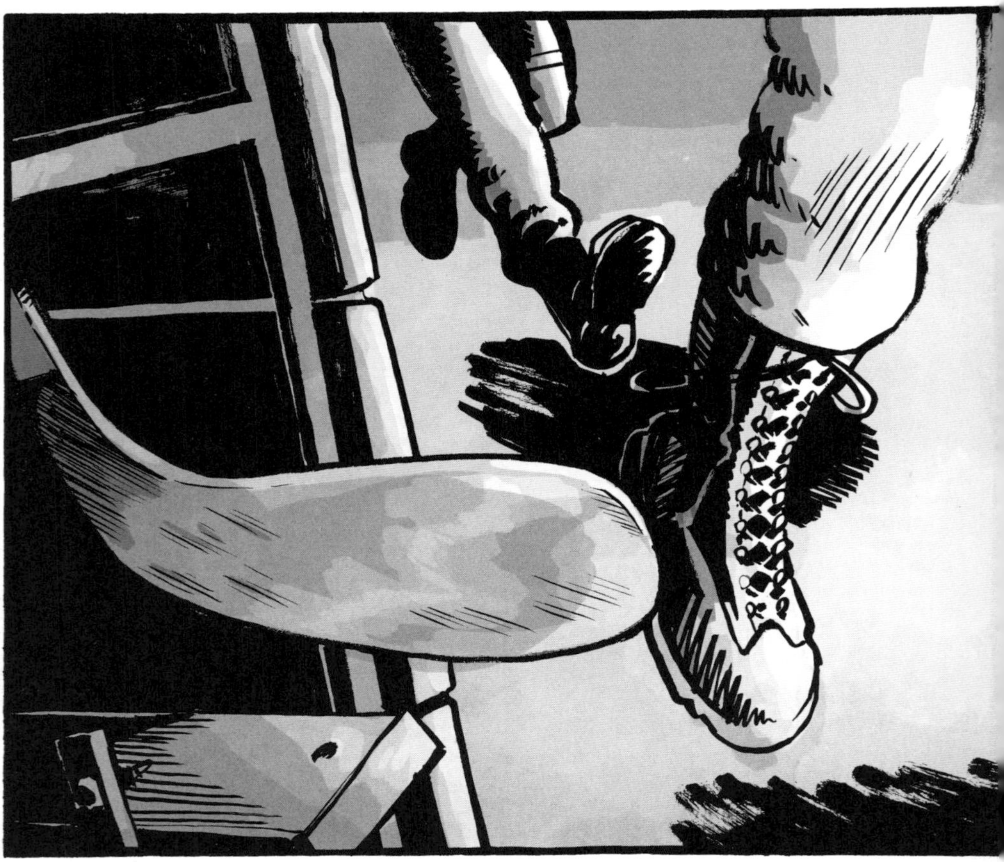

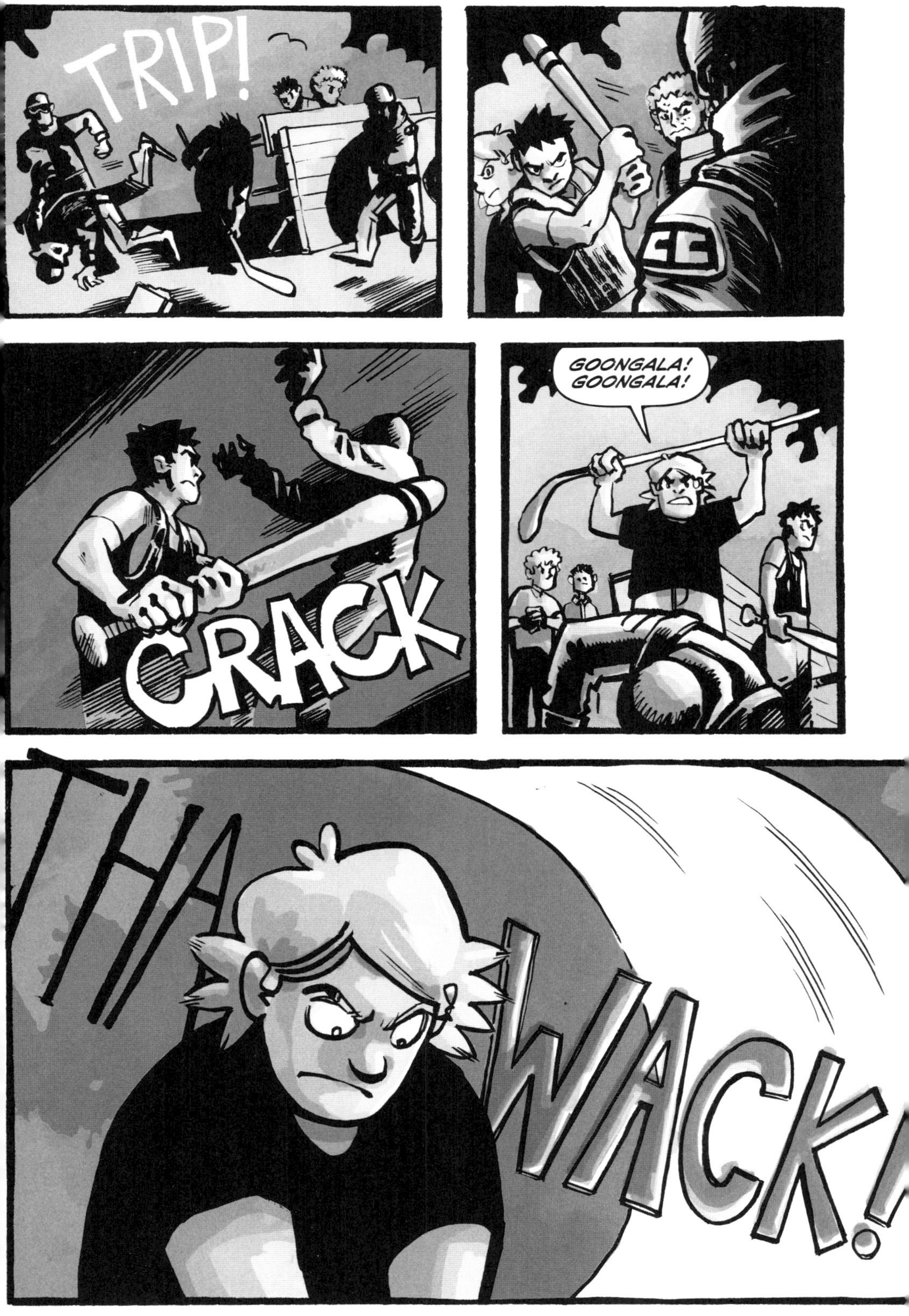
TRIP!
CRACK
GOONGALA! GOONGALA!
THA WACK!

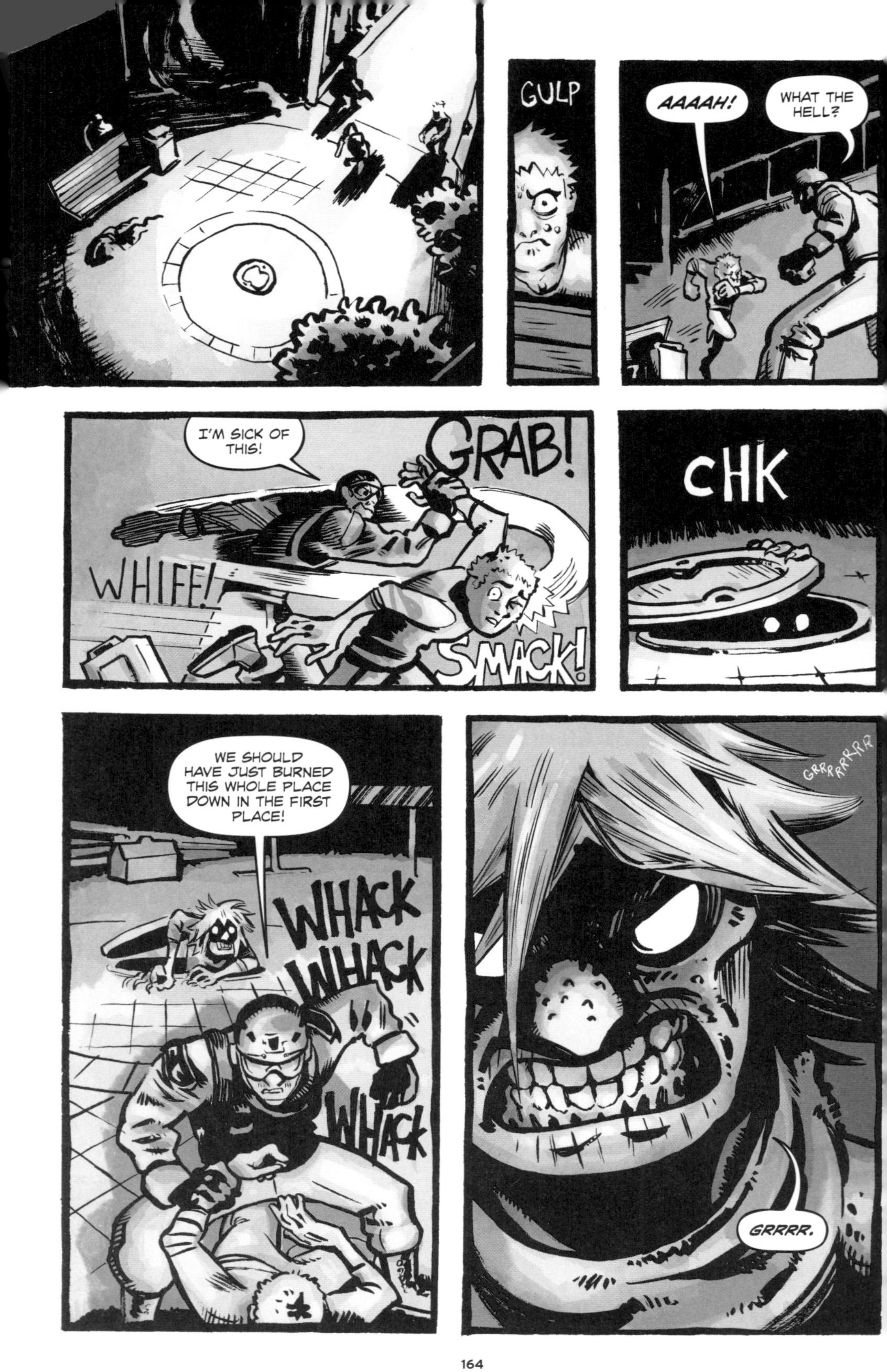
GULP
AAAAH!
WHAT THE HELL?
I'M SICK OF THIS!
GRAB!
WHIFF!
SMACK!
CHK
WE SHOULD HAVE JUST BURNED THIS WHOLE PLACE DOWN IN THE FIRST PLACE!
WHACK
WHACK
WHACK
GRRRRRRRR
GRRRR.

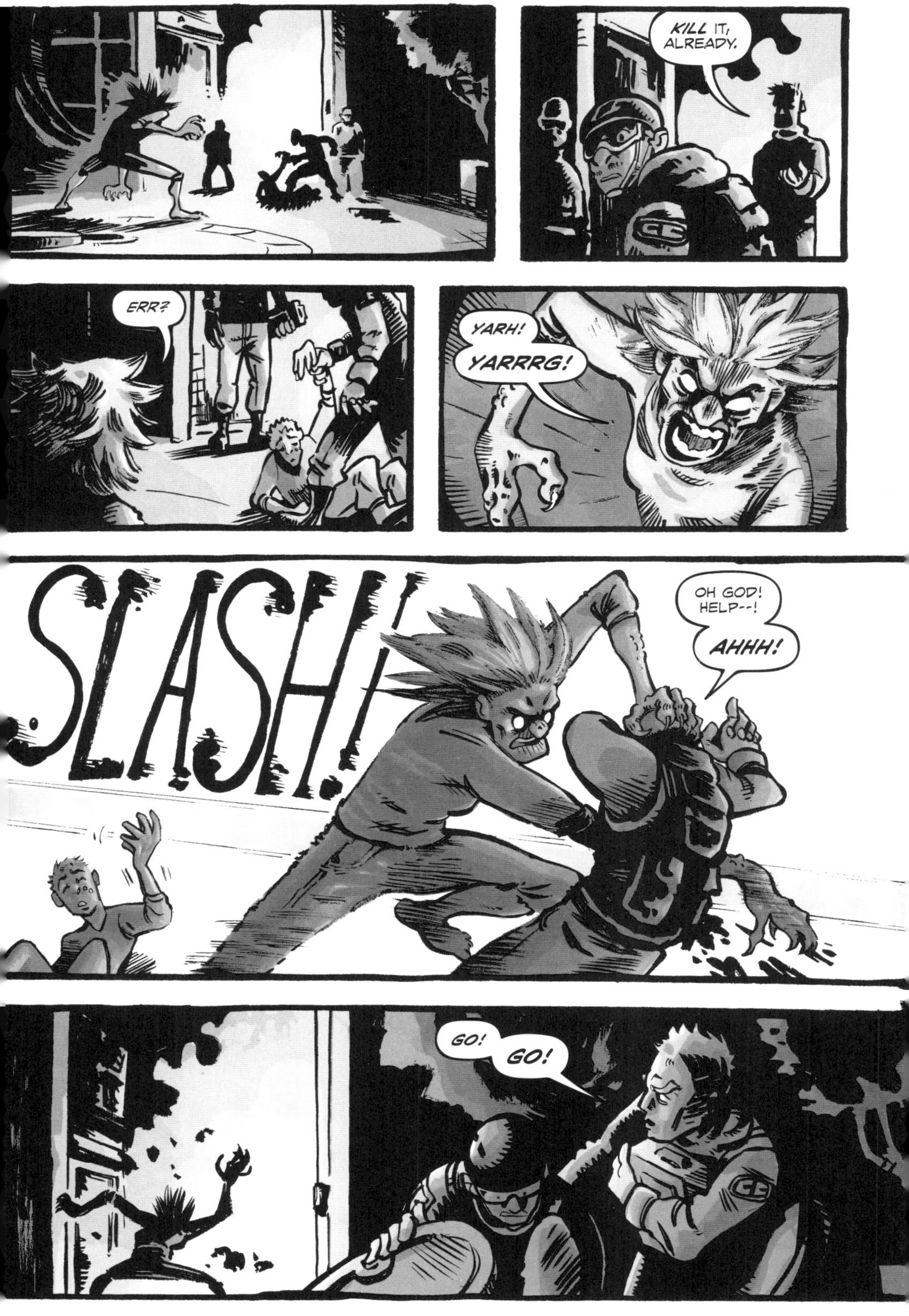
KILL IT, ALREADY.
ERR?
YARH!
YARRRG!
SLASH!
OH GOD! HELP--!
AHHH!
GO!
GO!

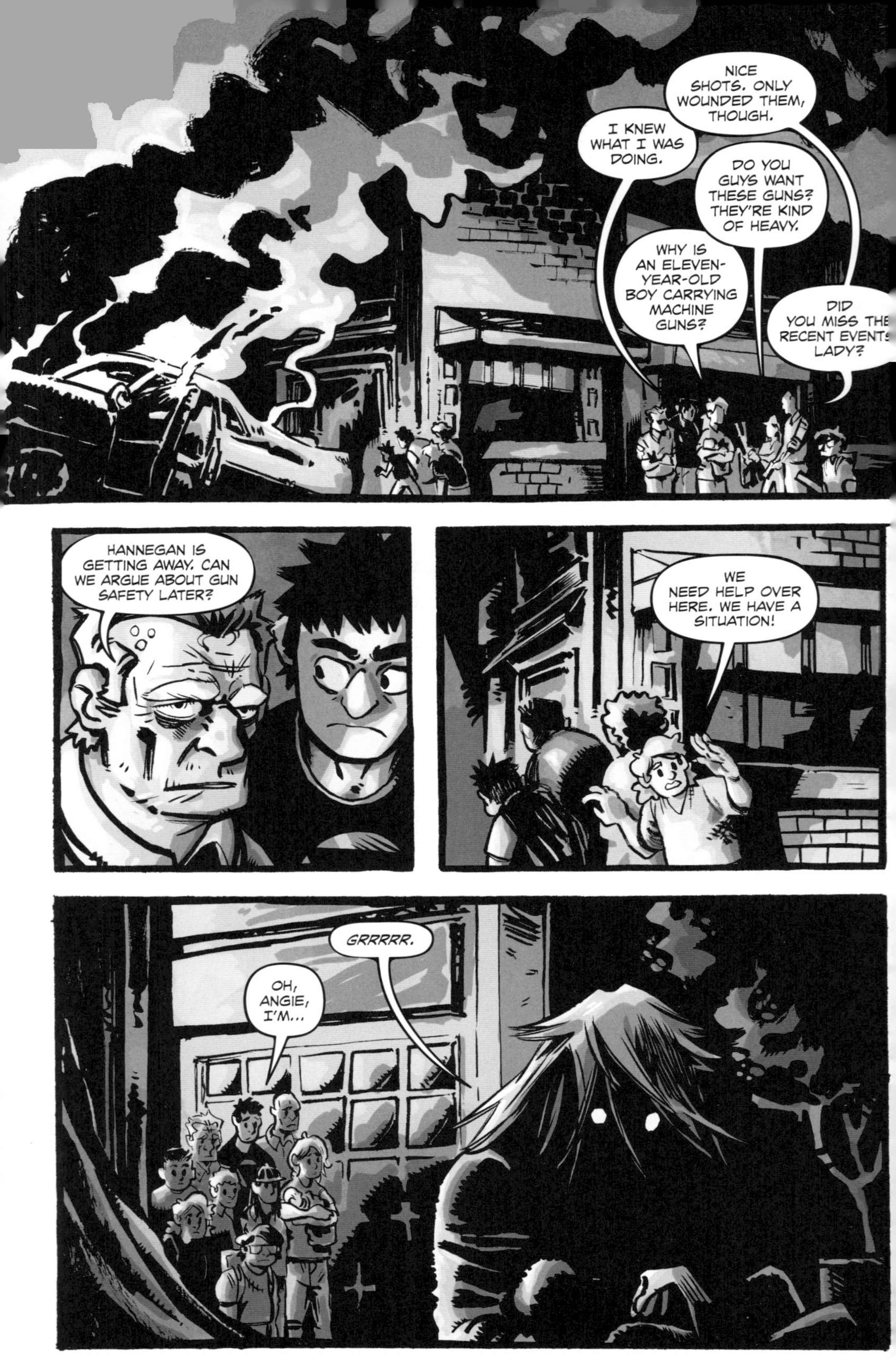
NICE SHOTS. ONLY WOUNDED THEM, THOUGH.
I KNEW WHAT I WAS DOING.
DO YOU GUYS WANT THESE GUNS? THEY'RE KIND OF HEAVY.
WHY IS AN ELEVEN-YEAR-OLD BOY CARRYING MACHINE GUNS?
DID YOU MISS THE RECENT EVENTS LADY?
HANNEGAN IS GETTING AWAY. CAN WE ARGUE ABOUT GUN SAFETY LATER?
WE NEED HELP OVER HERE. WE HAVE A SITUATION!
GRRRRR.
OH, ANGIE, I'M...

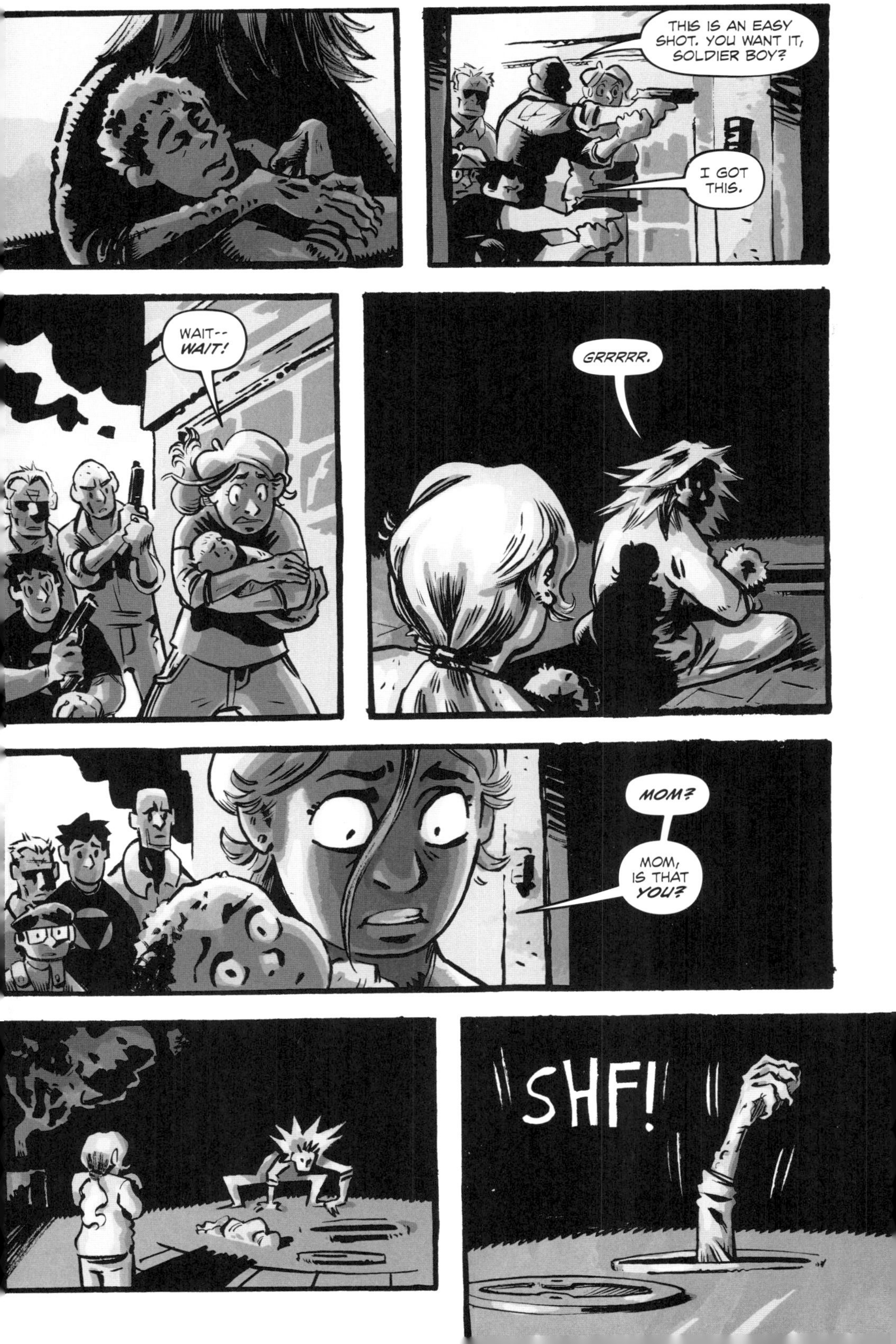
THIS IS AN EASY SHOT. YOU WANT IT, SOLDIER BOY?
I GOT THIS.
WAIT-- WAIT!
GRRRRR.
MOM?
MOM, IS THAT YOU?
SHF!

CHAPTER SIX

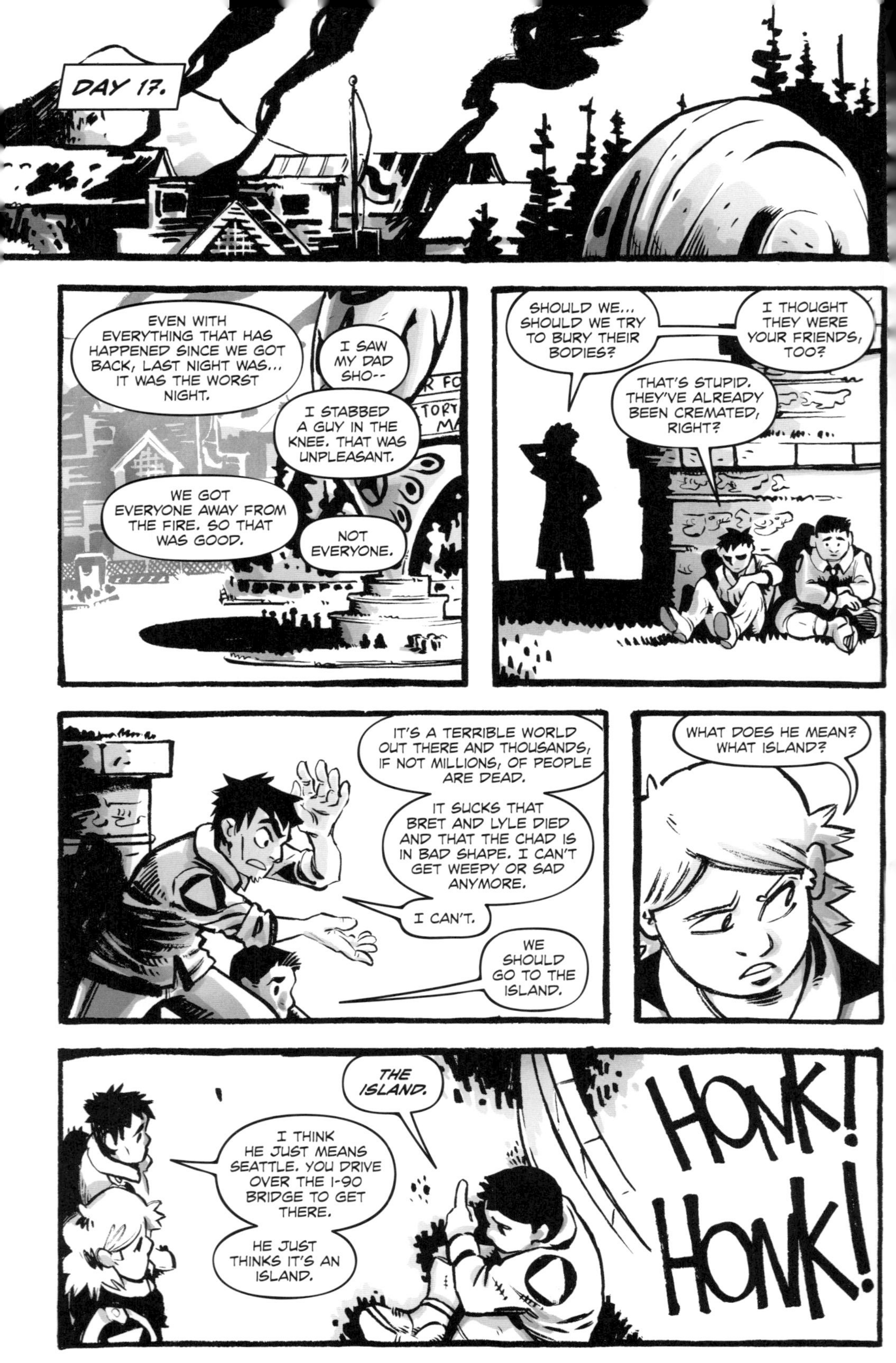
DAY 17.
EVEN WITH EVERYTHING THAT HAS HAPPENED SINCE WE GOT BACK, LAST NIGHT WAS... IT WAS THE WORST NIGHT.
I SAW MY DAD SHO--
I STABBED A GUY IN THE KNEE. THAT WAS UNPLEASANT.
WE GOT EVERYONE AWAY FROM THE FIRE. SO THAT WAS GOOD.
NOT EVERYONE.
SHOULD WE... SHOULD WE TRY TO BURY THEIR BODIES?
I THOUGHT THEY WERE YOUR FRIENDS, TOO?
THAT'S STUPID. THEY'VE ALREADY BEEN CREMATED, RIGHT?
IT'S A TERRIBLE WORLD OUT THERE AND THOUSANDS, IF NOT MILLIONS, OF PEOPLE ARE DEAD.
IT SUCKS THAT BRET AND LYLE DIED AND THAT THE CHAD IS IN BAD SHAPE. I CAN'T GET WEEPY OR SAD ANYMORE.
I CAN'T.
WE SHOULD GO TO THE ISLAND.
WHAT DOES HE MEAN? WHAT ISLAND?
THE ISLAND.
I THINK HE JUST MEANS SEATTLE. YOU DRIVE OVER THE I-90 BRIDGE TO GET THERE.
HE JUST THINKS IT'S AN ISLAND.
HONK! HONK!

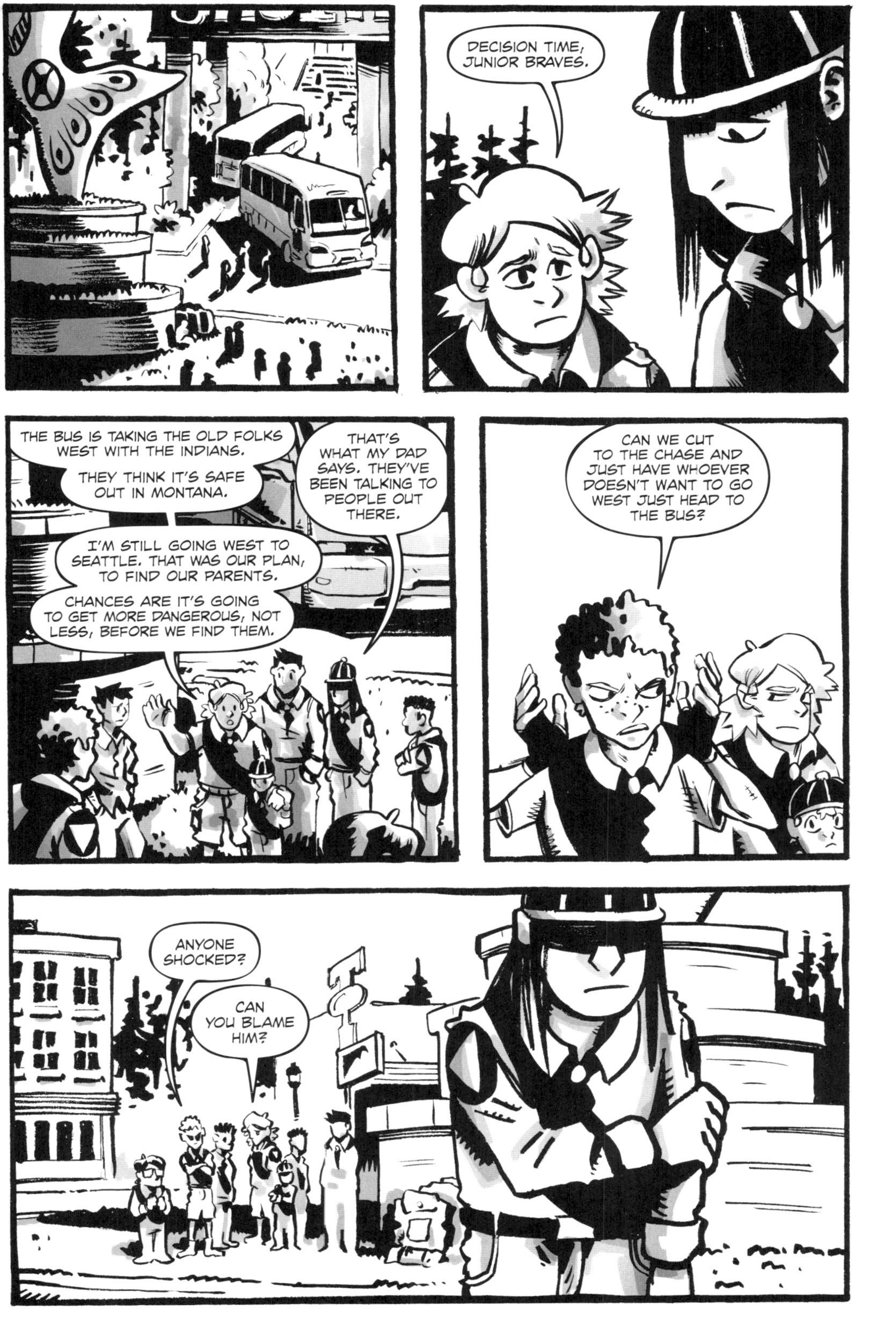
DECISION TIME, JUNIOR BRAVES.
THE BUS IS TAKING THE OLD FOLKS WEST WITH THE INDIANS.
THEY THINK IT'S SAFE OUT IN MONTANA.
THAT'S WHAT MY DAD SAYS. THEY'VE BEEN TALKING TO PEOPLE OUT THERE.
I'M STILL GOING WEST TO SEATTLE. THAT WAS OUR PLAN, TO FIND OUR PARENTS.
CHANCES ARE IT'S GOING TO GET MORE DANGEROUS, NOT LESS, BEFORE WE FIND THEM.
CAN WE CUT TO THE CHASE AND JUST HAVE WHOEVER DOESN'T WANT TO GO WEST JUST HEAD TO THE BUS?
ANYONE SHOCKED?
CAN YOU BLAME HIM?

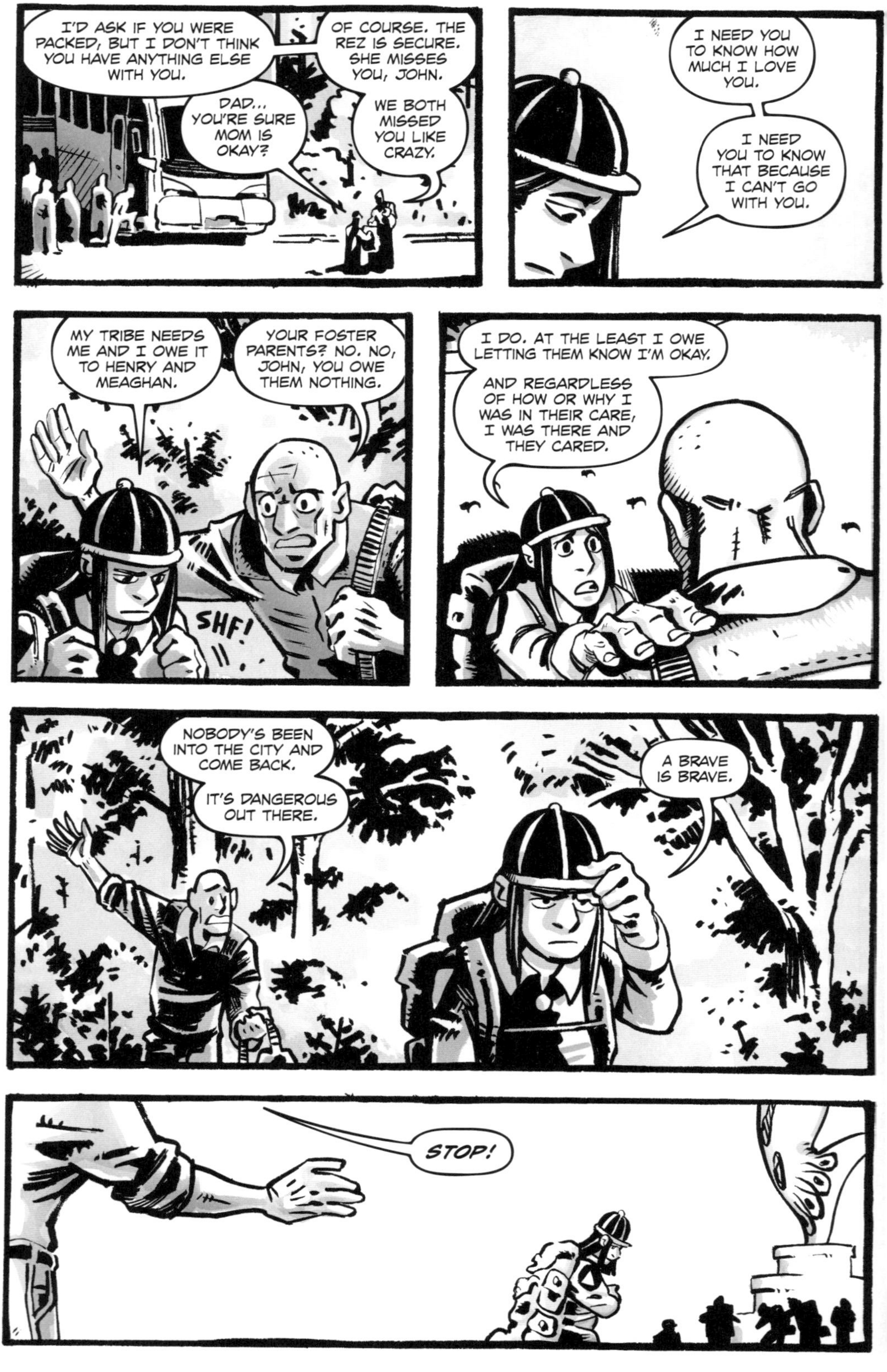
I'D ASK IF YOU WERE PACKED, BUT I DON'T THINK YOU HAVE ANYTHING ELSE WITH YOU.
OF COURSE. THE REZ IS SECURE. SHE MISSES YOU, JOHN.
DAD... YOU'RE SURE MOM IS OKAY?
WE BOTH MISSED YOU LIKE CRAZY.
I NEED YOU TO KNOW HOW MUCH I LOVE YOU.
I NEED YOU TO KNOW THAT BECAUSE I CAN'T GO WITH YOU.
MY TRIBE NEEDS ME AND I OWE IT TO HENRY AND MEAGHAN.
YOUR FOSTER PARENTS? NO. NO, JOHN, YOU OWE THEM NOTHING.
SHF!
I DO. AT THE LEAST I OWE LETTING THEM KNOW I'M OKAY.
AND REGARDLESS OF HOW OR WHY I WAS IN THEIR CARE, I WAS THERE AND THEY CARED.
NOBODY'S BEEN INTO THE CITY AND COME BACK.
IT'S DANGEROUS OUT THERE.
A BRAVE IS BRAVE.
STOP!

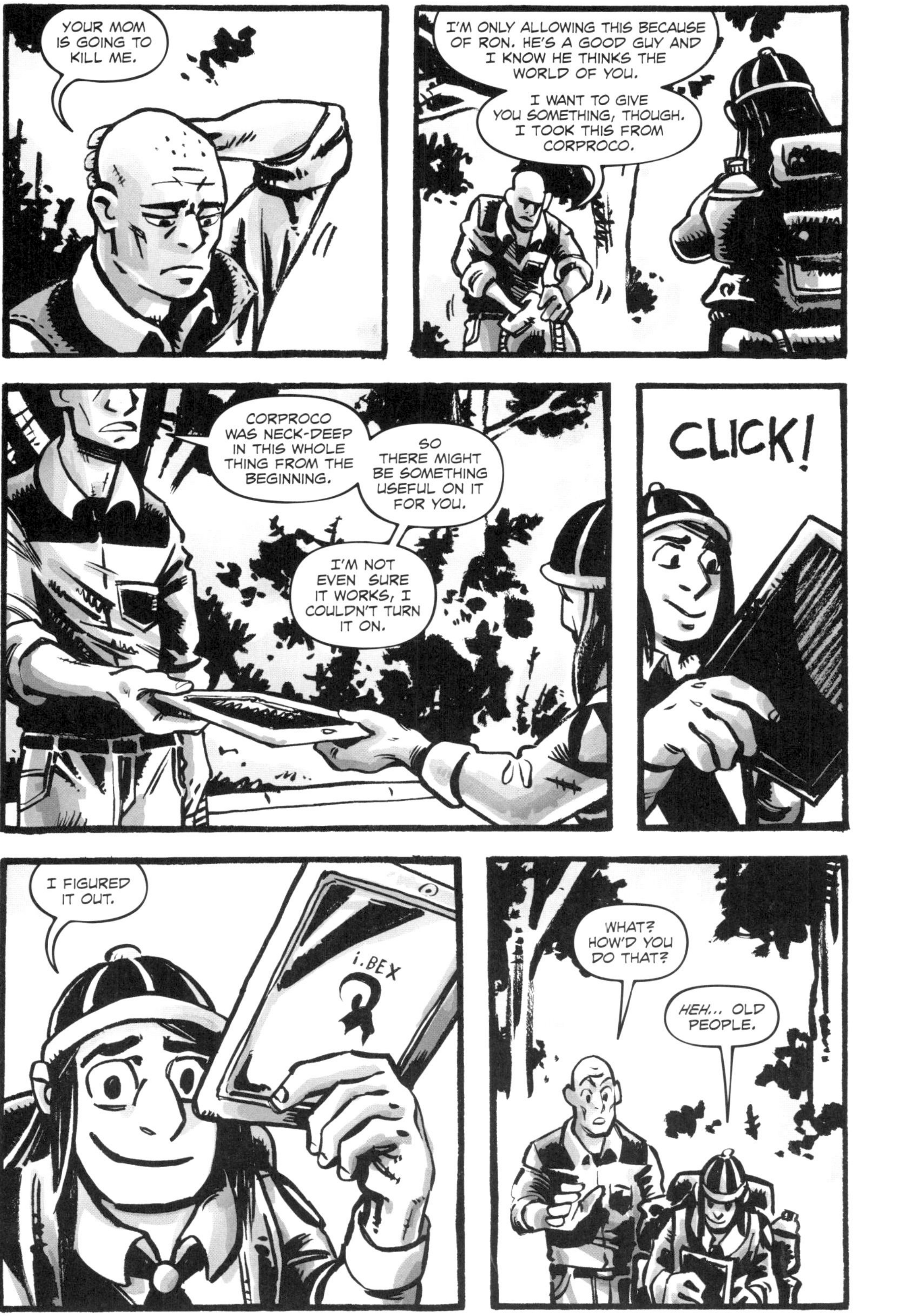
YOUR MOM IS GOING TO KILL ME.
I'M ONLY ALLOWING THIS BECAUSE OF RON. HE'S A GOOD GUY AND I KNOW HE THINKS THE WORLD OF YOU.
I WANT TO GIVE YOU SOMETHING, THOUGH. I TOOK THIS FROM CORPROCO.
CORPROCO WAS NECK-DEEP IN THIS WHOLE THING FROM THE BEGINNING.
SO THERE MIGHT BE SOMETHING USEFUL ON IT FOR YOU.
I'M NOT EVEN SURE IT WORKS, I COULDN'T TURN IT ON.
CLICK!
I FIGURED IT OUT.
i.BEX
WHAT? HOW'D YOU DO THAT?
HEH... OLD PEOPLE.

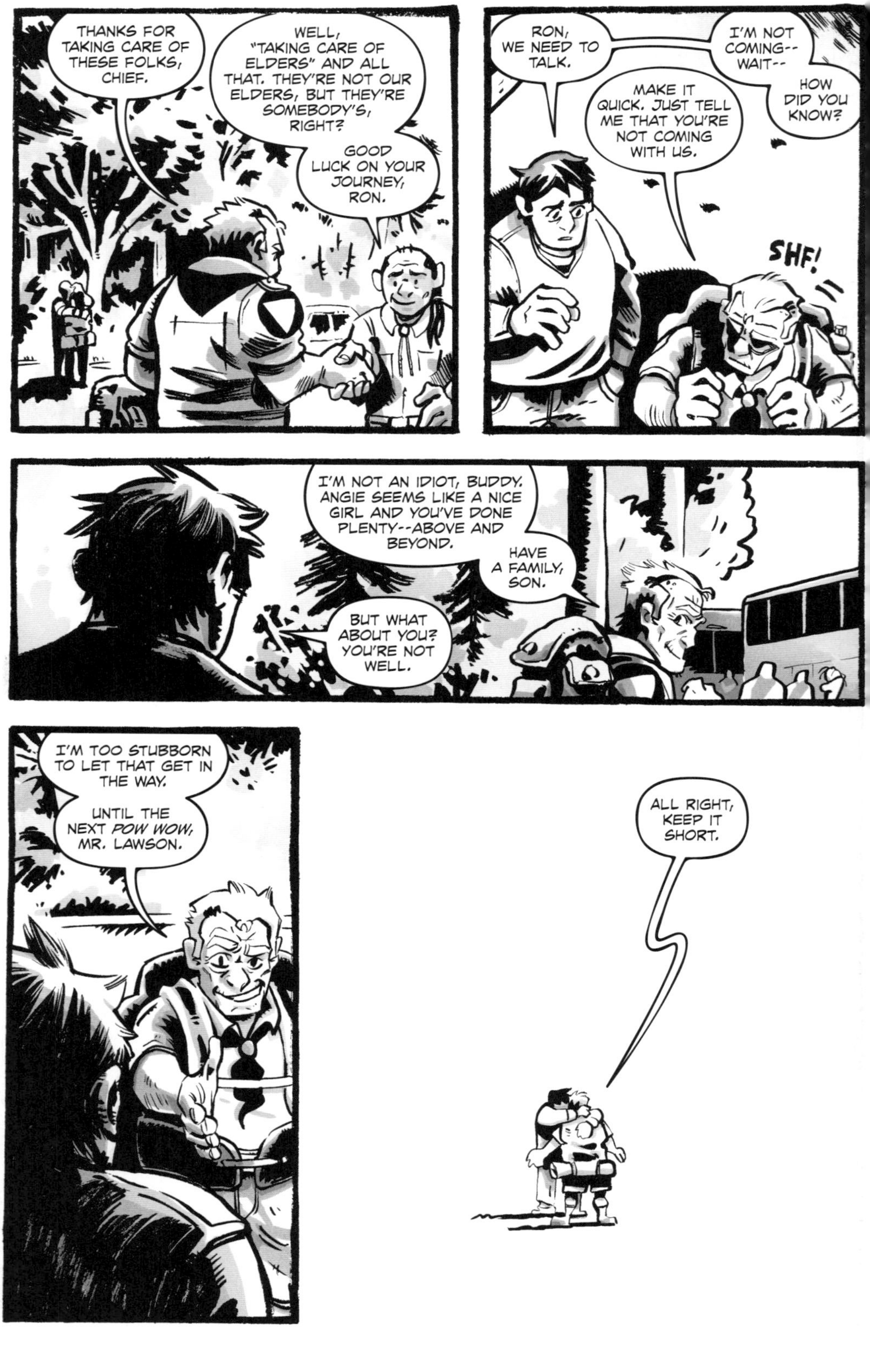

THANKS FOR TAKING CARE OF THESE FOLKS, CHIEF.
WELL, "TAKING CARE OF ELDERS" AND ALL THAT. THEY'RE NOT OUR ELDERS, BUT THEY'RE SOMEBODY'S, RIGHT?
GOOD LUCK ON YOUR JOURNEY, RON.
RON, WE NEED TO TALK.
I'M NOT COMING--
WAIT--
MAKE IT QUICK. JUST TELL ME THAT YOU'RE NOT COMING WITH US.
HOW DID YOU KNOW?
SHF!
I'M NOT AN IDIOT, BUDDY. ANGIE SEEMS LIKE A NICE GIRL AND YOU'VE DONE PLENTY--ABOVE AND BEYOND.
HAVE A FAMILY, SON.
BUT WHAT ABOUT YOU? YOU'RE NOT WELL.
I'M TOO STUBBORN TO LET THAT GET IN THE WAY.
UNTIL THE NEXT *POW WOW*, MR. LAWSON.
ALL RIGHT, KEEP IT SHORT.

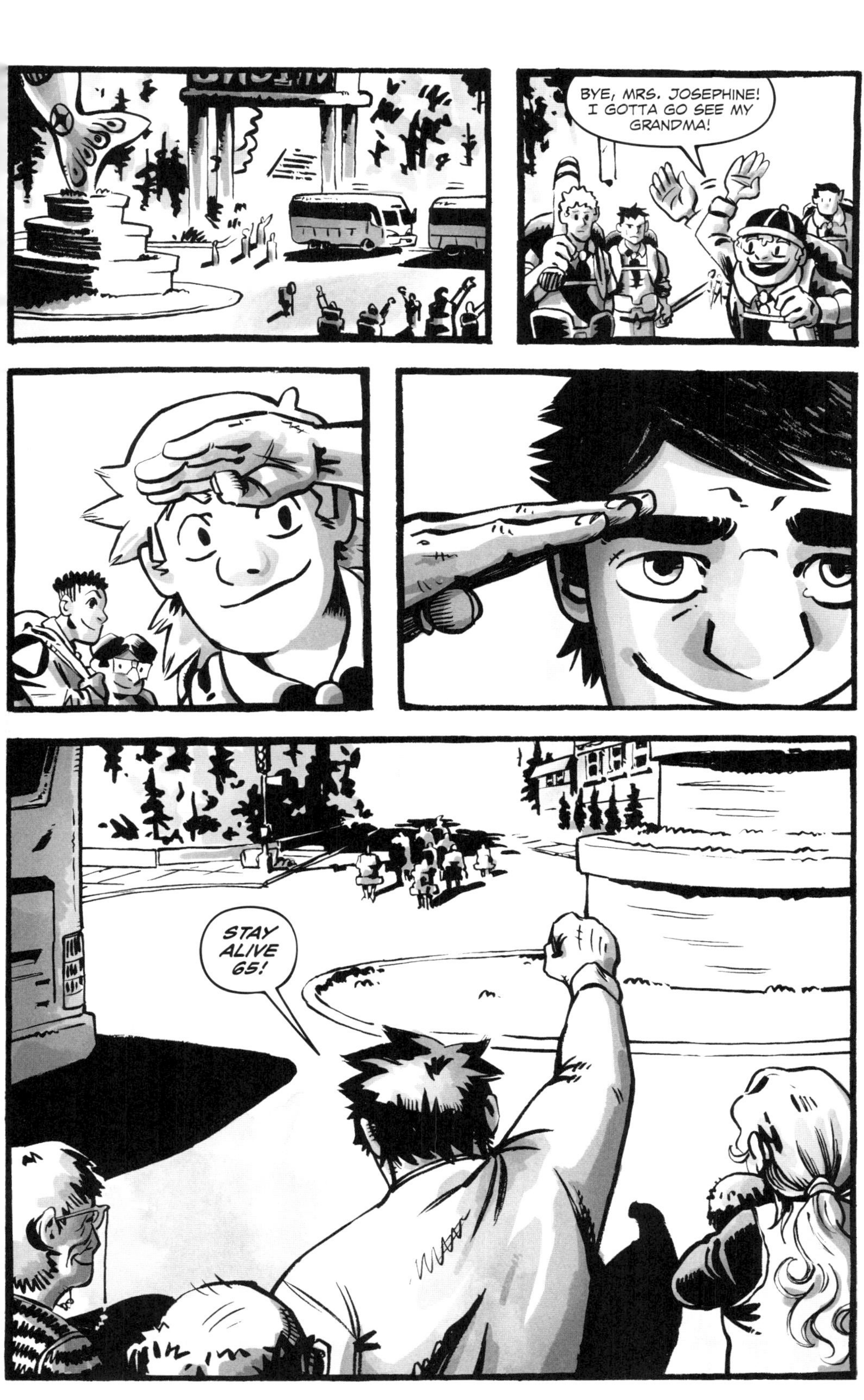
BYE, MRS. JOSEPHINE! I GOTTA GO SEE MY GRANDMA!
STAY ALIVE 65!

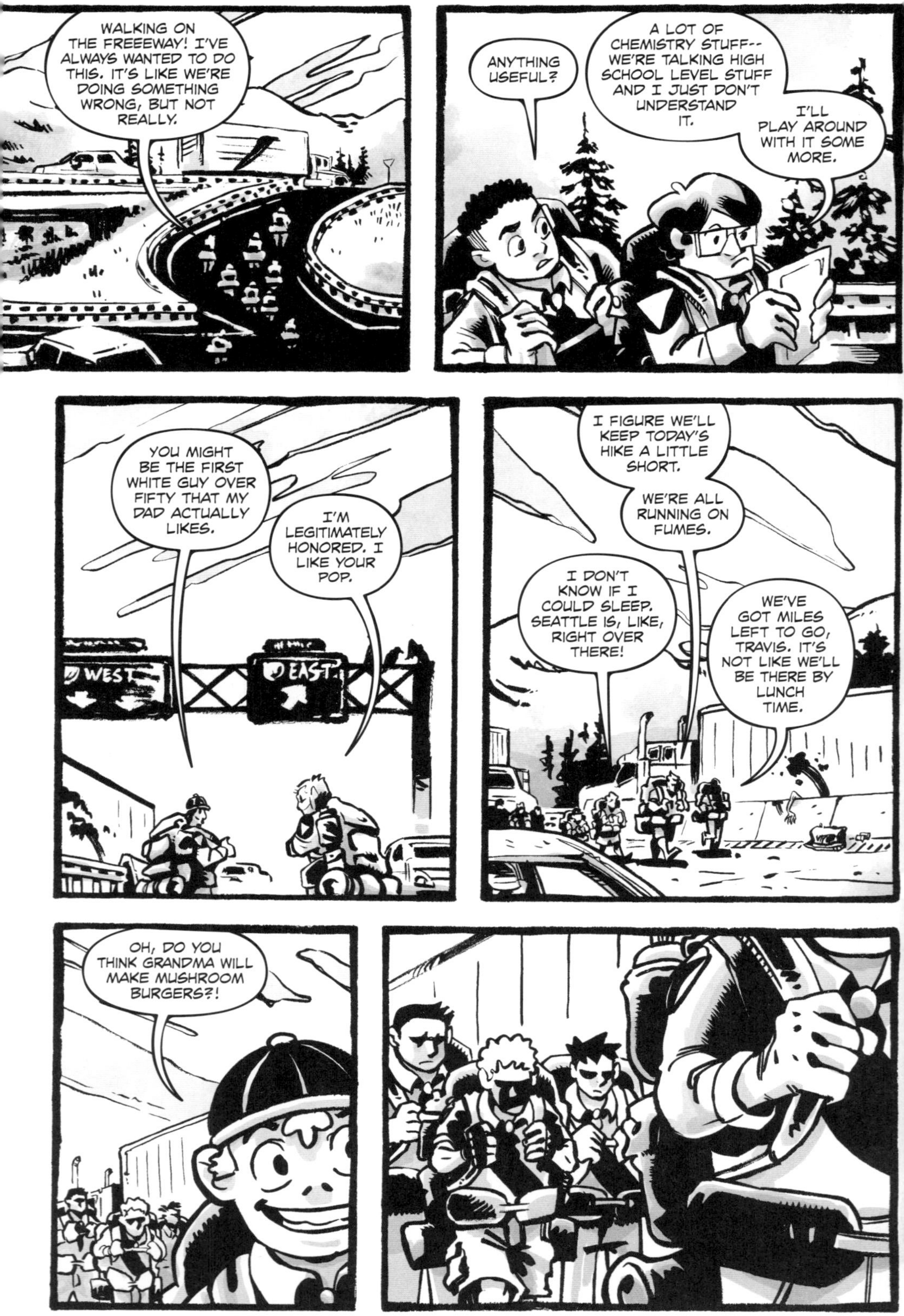
WALKING ON THE FREEEWAY! I'VE ALWAYS WANTED TO DO THIS. IT'S LIKE WE'RE DOING SOMETHING WRONG, BUT NOT REALLY.
ANYTHING USEFUL?
A LOT OF CHEMISTRY STUFF-- WE'RE TALKING HIGH SCHOOL LEVEL STUFF AND I JUST DON'T UNDERSTAND IT.
I'LL PLAY AROUND WITH IT SOME MORE.
YOU MIGHT BE THE FIRST WHITE GUY OVER FIFTY THAT MY DAD ACTUALLY LIKES.
I'M LEGITIMATELY HONORED. I LIKE YOUR POP.
WEST
EAST
I FIGURE WE'LL KEEP TODAY'S HIKE A LITTLE SHORT.
WE'RE ALL RUNNING ON FUMES.
I DON'T KNOW IF I COULD SLEEP. SEATTLE IS, LIKE, RIGHT OVER THERE!
WE'VE GOT MILES LEFT TO GO, TRAVIS. IT'S NOT LIKE WE'LL BE THERE BY LUNCH TIME.
OH, DO YOU THINK GRANDMA WILL MAKE MUSHROOM BURGERS?!

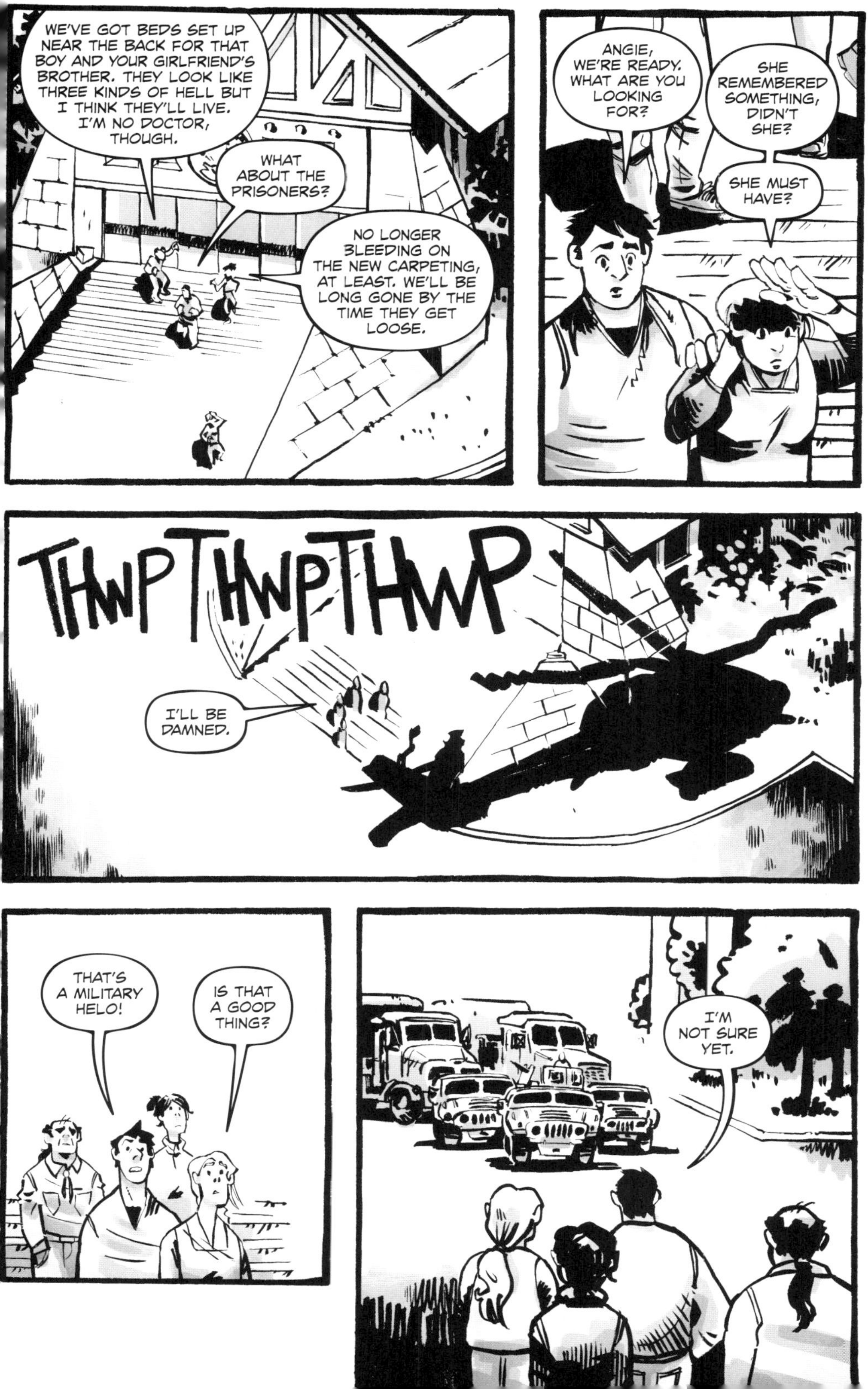
WE'VE GOT BEDS SET UP NEAR THE BACK FOR THAT BOY AND YOUR GIRLFRIEND'S BROTHER. THEY LOOK LIKE THREE KINDS OF HELL BUT I THINK THEY'LL LIVE. I'M NO DOCTOR, THOUGH.
WHAT ABOUT THE PRISONERS?
NO LONGER BLEEDING ON THE NEW CARPETING, AT LEAST. WE'LL BE LONG GONE BY THE TIME THEY GET LOOSE.
ANGIE, WE'RE READY. WHAT ARE YOU LOOKING FOR?
SHE REMEMBERED SOMETHING, DIDN'T SHE?
SHE MUST HAVE?
THWPTHWPTHWP
I'LL BE DAMNED.
THAT'S A MILITARY HELO!
IS THAT A GOOD THING?
I'M NOT SURE YET.

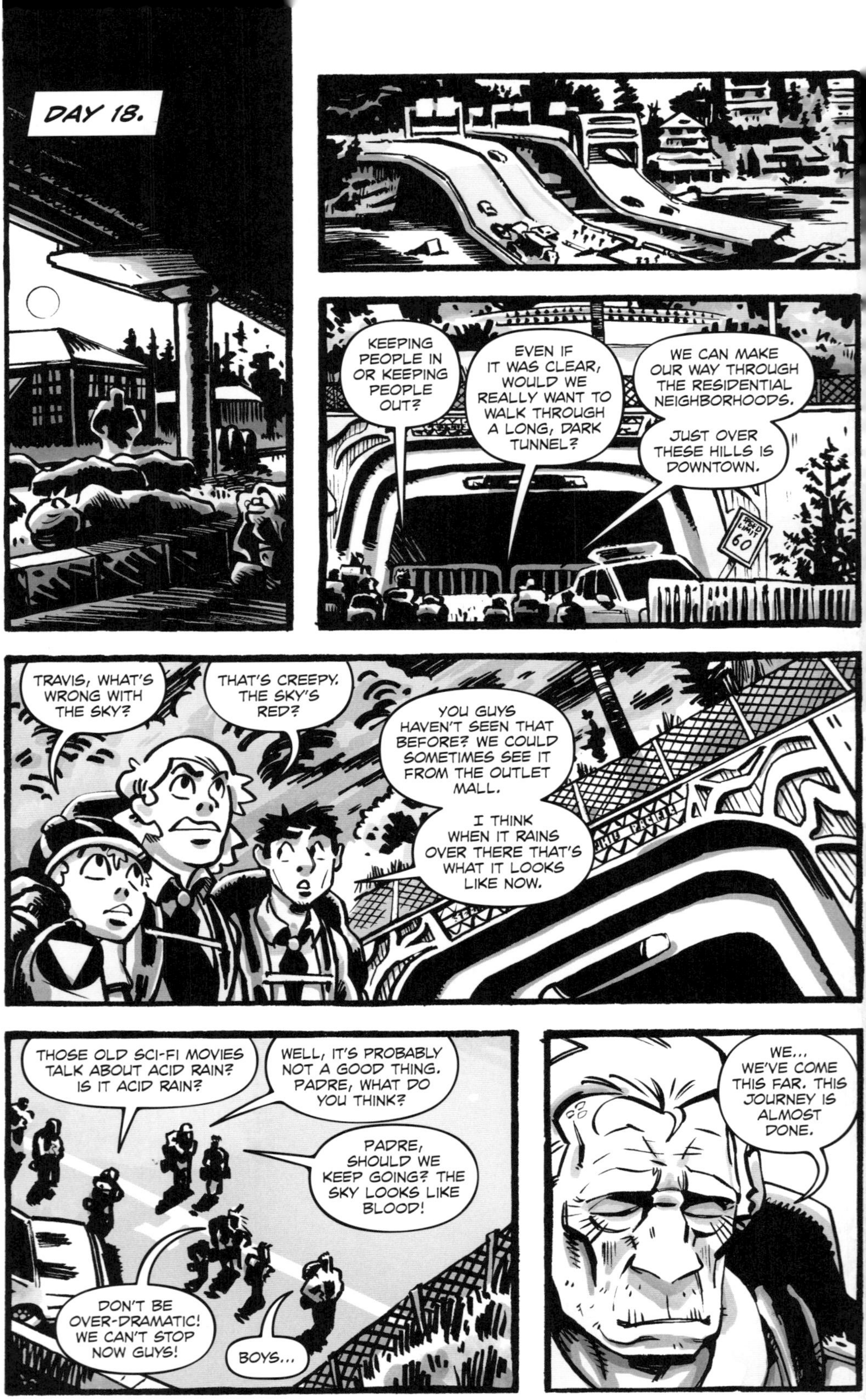
DAY 18.
KEEPING PEOPLE IN OR KEEPING PEOPLE OUT?
EVEN IF IT WAS CLEAR, WOULD WE REALLY WANT TO WALK THROUGH A LONG, DARK TUNNEL?
WE CAN MAKE OUR WAY THROUGH THE RESIDENTIAL NEIGHBORHOODS.
JUST OVER THESE HILLS IS DOWNTOWN.
SPEED LIMIT 60
TRAVIS, WHAT'S WRONG WITH THE SKY?
THAT'S CREEPY. THE SKY'S RED?
YOU GUYS HAVEN'T SEEN THAT BEFORE? WE COULD SOMETIMES SEE IT FROM THE OUTLET MALL.
I THINK WHEN IT RAINS OVER THERE THAT'S WHAT IT LOOKS LIKE NOW.
THOSE OLD SCI-FI MOVIES TALK ABOUT ACID RAIN? IS IT ACID RAIN?
WELL, IT'S PROBABLY NOT A GOOD THING. PADRE, WHAT DO YOU THINK?
PADRE, SHOULD WE KEEP GOING? THE SKY LOOKS LIKE BLOOD!
DON'T BE OVER-DRAMATIC! WE CAN'T STOP NOW GUYS!
BOYS...
WE... WE'VE COME THIS FAR. THIS JOURNEY IS ALMOST DONE.

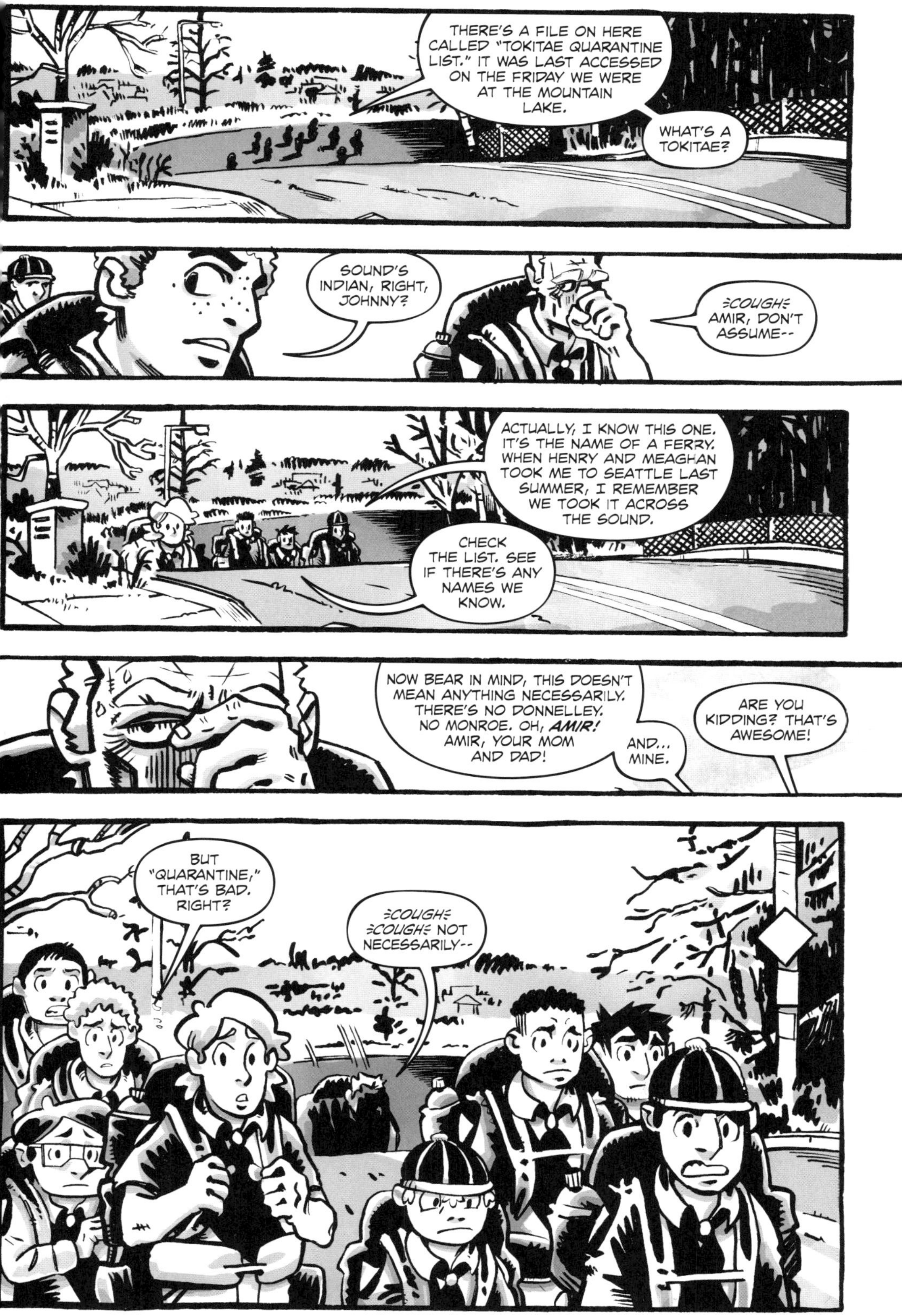

THERE'S A FILE ON HERE CALLED "TOKITAE QUARANTINE LIST." IT WAS LAST ACCESSED ON THE FRIDAY WE WERE AT THE MOUNTAIN LAKE.
WHAT'S A TOKITAE?
SOUND'S INDIAN, RIGHT, JOHNNY?
COUGH AMIR, DON'T ASSUME--
ACTUALLY, I KNOW THIS ONE. IT'S THE NAME OF A FERRY. WHEN HENRY AND MEAGHAN TOOK ME TO SEATTLE LAST SUMMER, I REMEMBER WE TOOK IT ACROSS THE SOUND.
CHECK THE LIST. SEE IF THERE'S ANY NAMES WE KNOW.
NOW BEAR IN MIND, THIS DOESN'T MEAN ANYTHING NECESSARILY. THERE'S NO DONNELLEY. NO MONROE. OH, ***AMIR!*** AMIR, YOUR MOM AND DAD!
AND... MINE.
ARE YOU KIDDING? THAT'S AWESOME!
BUT "QUARANTINE," THAT'S BAD. RIGHT?
COUGH *COUGH* NOT NECESSARILY--

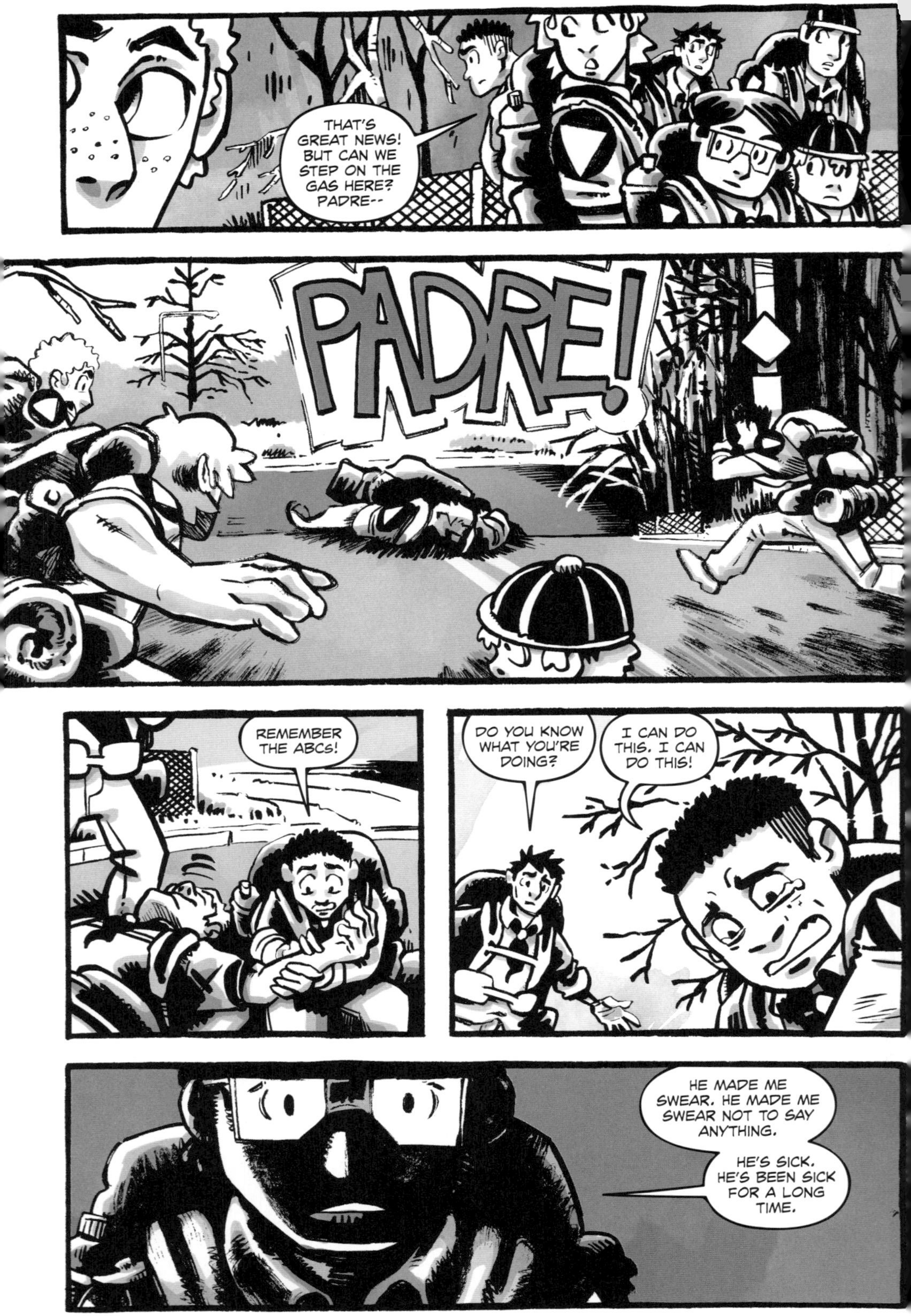
THAT'S GREAT NEWS! BUT CAN WE STEP ON THE GAS HERE? PADRE--
PADRE!
REMEMBER THE ABCs!
DO YOU KNOW WHAT YOU'RE DOING?
I CAN DO THIS. I CAN DO THIS!
HE MADE ME SWEAR. HE MADE ME SWEAR NOT TO SAY ANYTHING.
HE'S SICK. HE'S BEEN SICK FOR A LONG TIME.

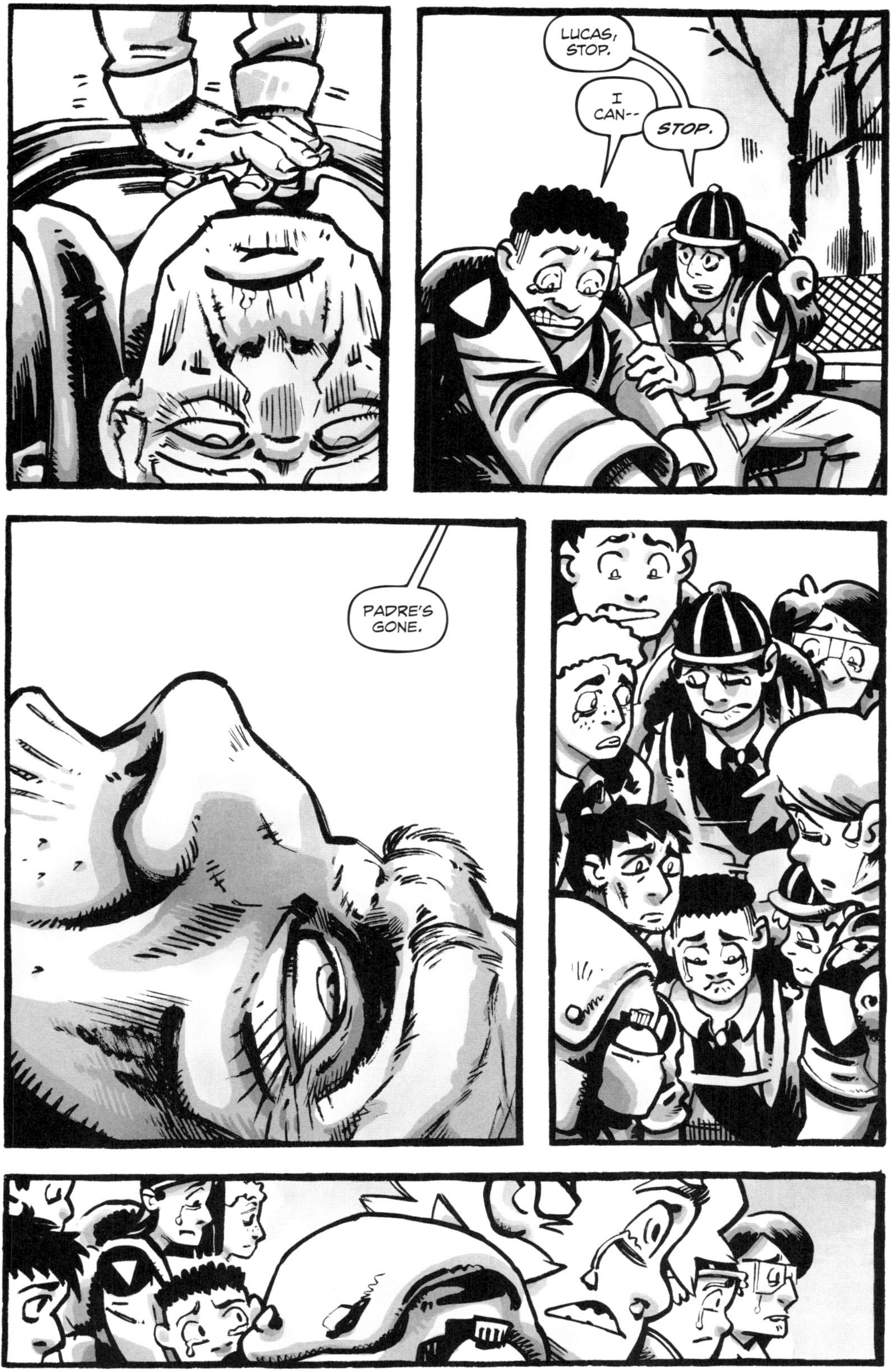
LUCAS, STOP.
I CAN--
STOP.
PADRE'S GONE.

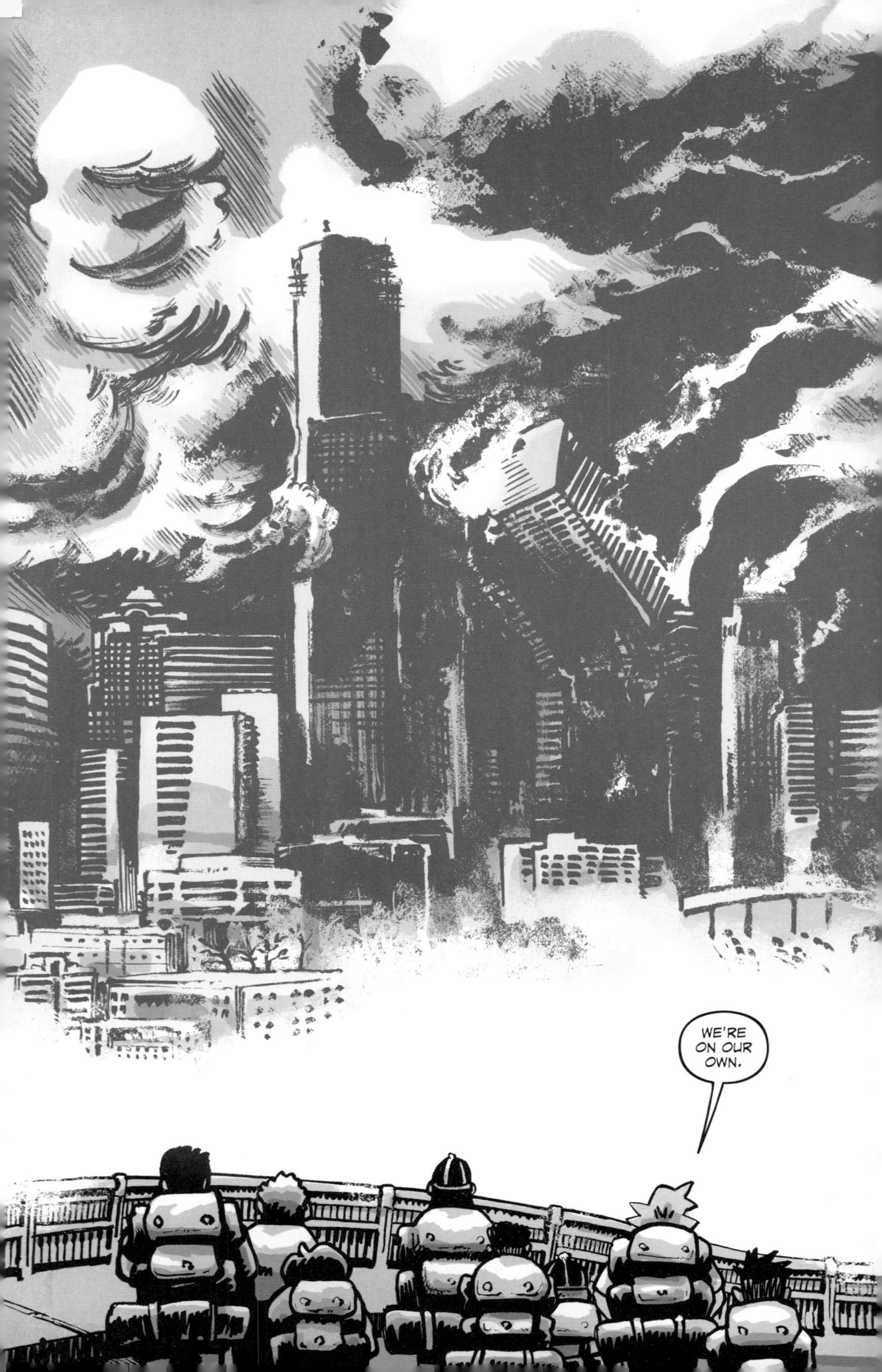
WE'RE ON OUR OWN.

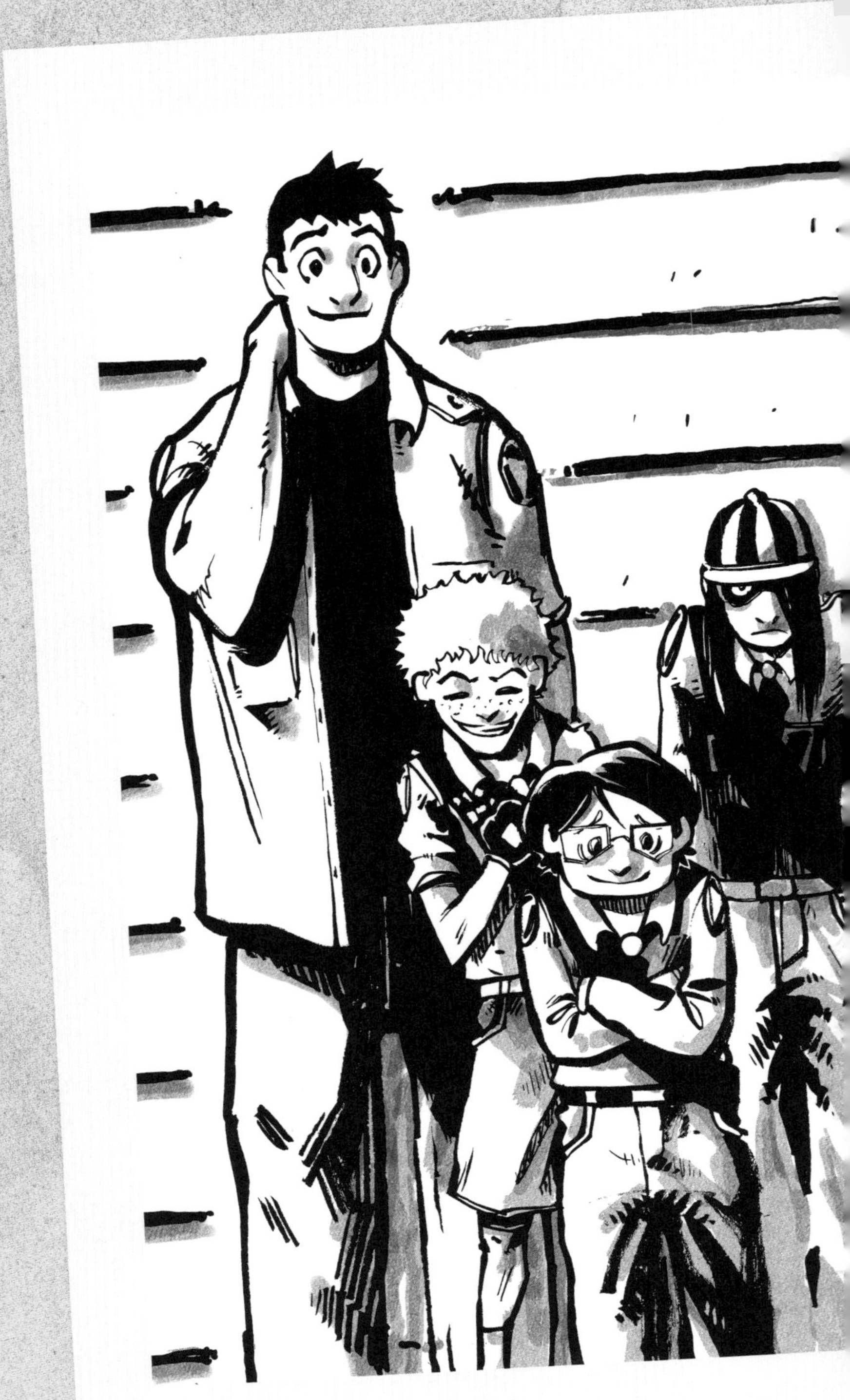

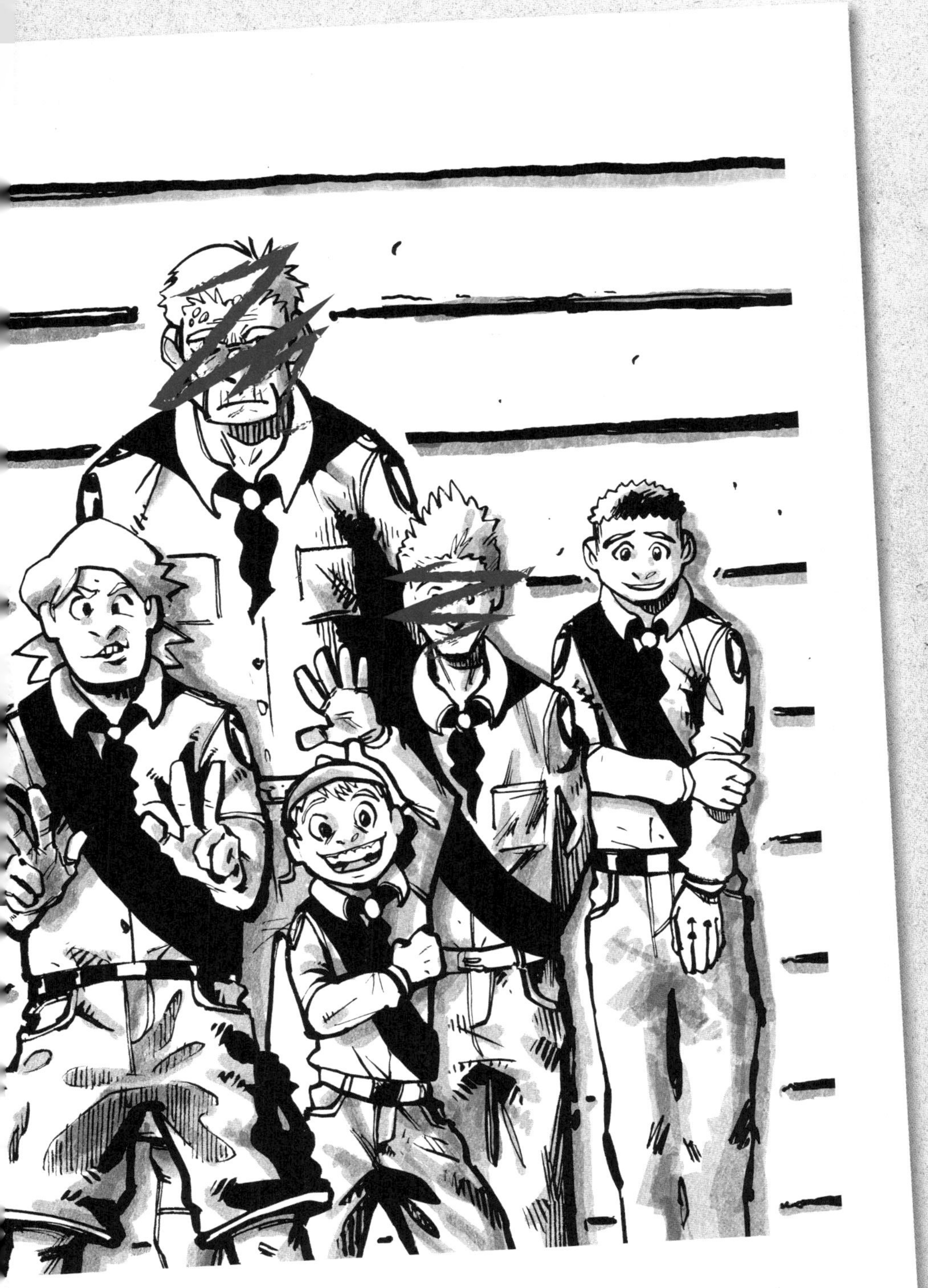

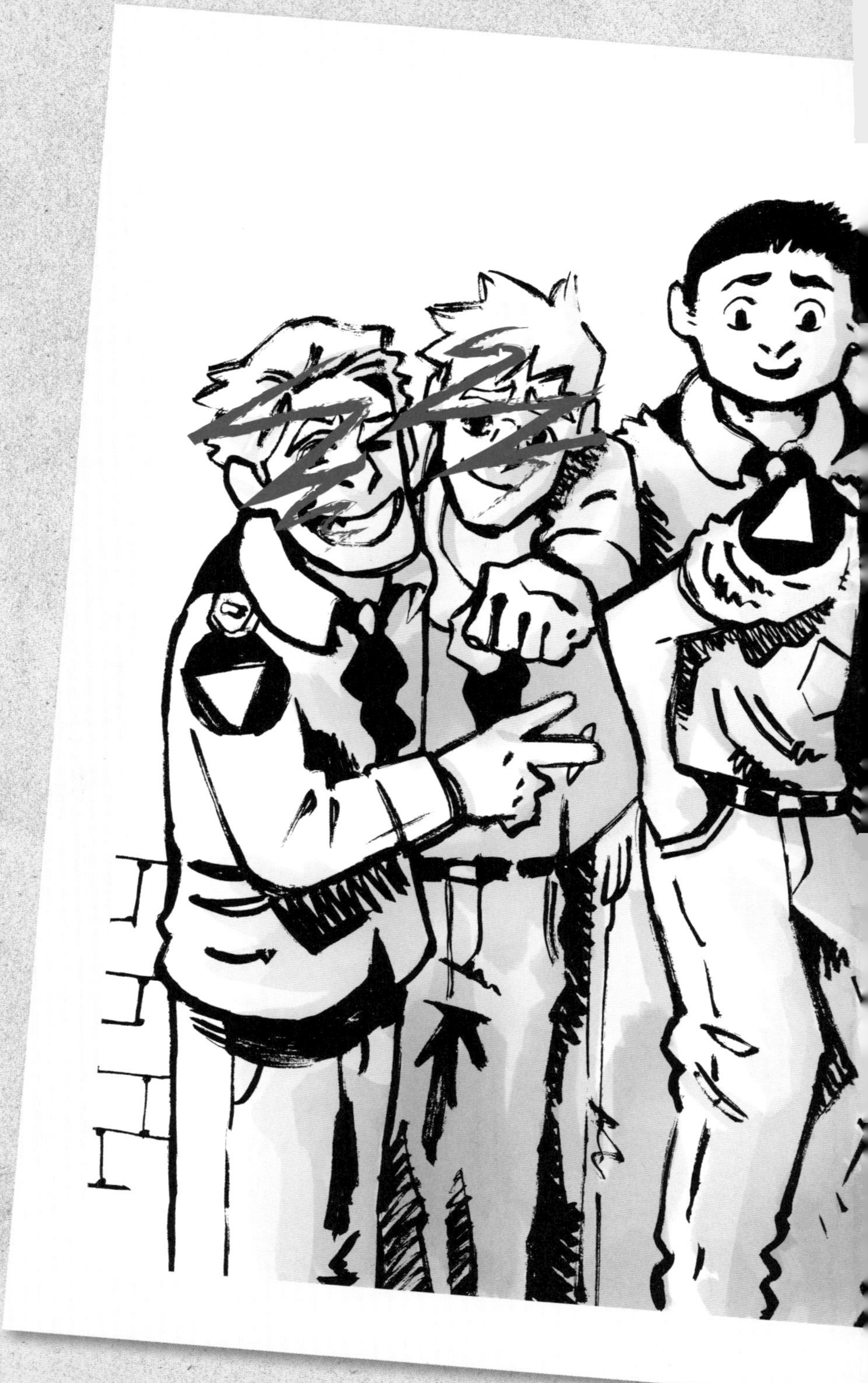

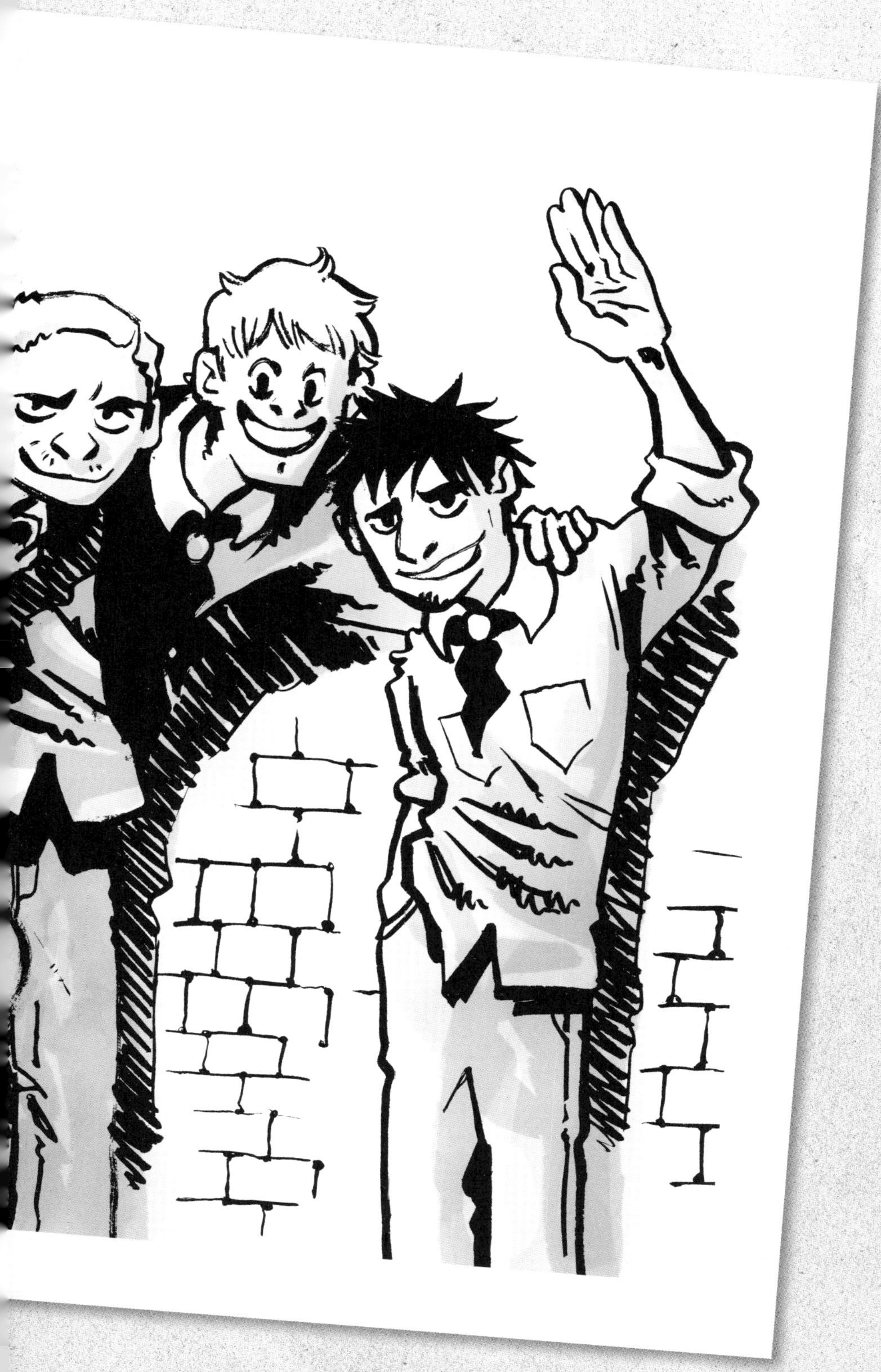

GREGORY K. SMITH

Greg grew up in a culturally diverse working class household. He was smitten with books at an early age when his assistant librarian mother brought him to work during summer breaks. Later, his father got him into Boy Scouts, where he achieved Eagle Scout Rank.

At some point, a good teacher or two told Greg he should write. So he took more classes and he wrote. He wrote a lot. He met Mike in one of those classes. They wrote more together. They found a cool dude named Zach and he drew the things. Now, the three of them make cool stuff with the AWESOME people at Oni Press!

Greg and his wife Anne live in the Pacific Northwest. They have two dogs and one cat. When not trying to turn their house into either "Pee-wee's Playhouse," "Double Dare Challenge," or "Mini Museum," they can be found at toy shows, comic shops, and thrift stores wherever they travel.

Follow Greg and his life adventures on Twitter and Instagram @ThatAmazingTwit or on Tumblr at tumblr.com/thatamazingtwit.

—

MICHAEL TANNER

Michael was born in Great Falls, Montana—a thriving metropolis that is actually smaller than the neighborhood of Los Angeles that he currently resides in. He has a BA in Theater and Television Production from the Evergreen State College, which is also where he met Greg Smith.

Michael developed a love for comics at a very early age and credits the medium with expanding his vocabulary and imagination. His first published comic work was in the Oni Press anthology *Jam! Tales from the World of Roller Derby.* He feels incredibly lucky to have been given the opportunity to work in a field that he loves.

Follow Mike [and his LA Derby Dolls roller derby Enforcer alter ego] @mikeisernie, check out his reviews of Los Angeles's best, worst, and weirdest diners at dinerwood.blogspot.com, or visit his website, bymichaeltanner.com

—

FOLLOW BOTH MIKE & GREG ON TWITTER @2AMAZINGWRITERS

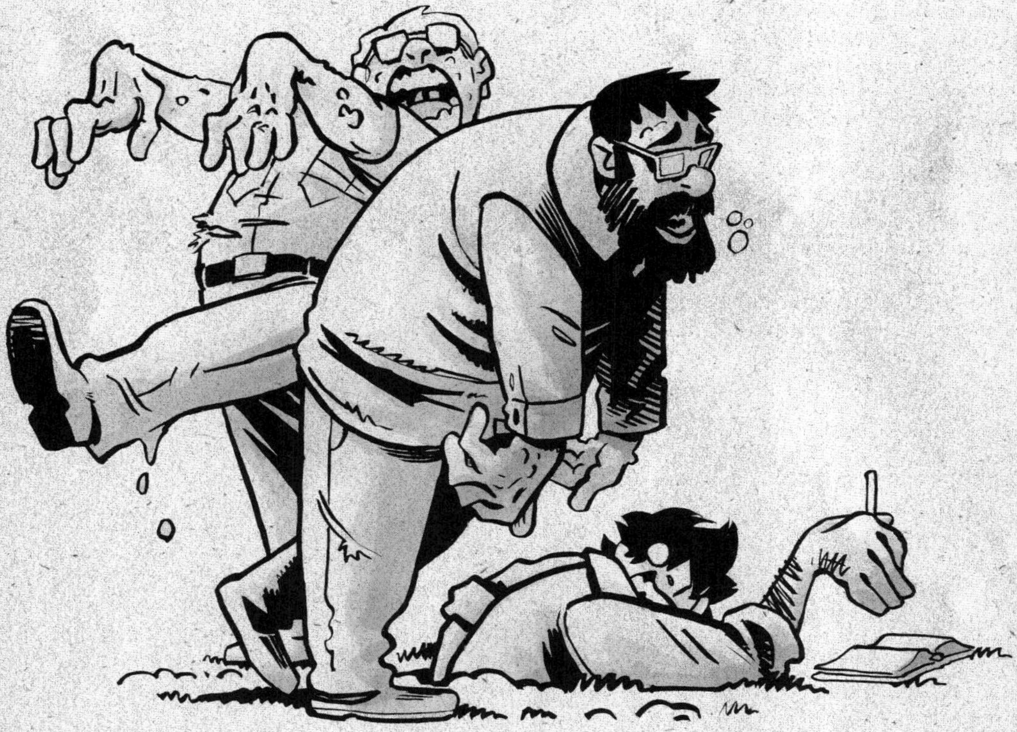

ZACH LEHNER

Most people start drawing when they're little. But drawing started Zach when DRAWING was little.

Drawing drew Zach and then Zach drew drawings, until he went to school for drawing, because drawings can't go to school.

When Zach left school he was drawing so much that somebody said, "Hey, you should draw this thing for us!" So he did, and now he is always drawing, and drawing is very proud.

You can see more of his work at www.zlehner.com or on Instagram @lehnerzach.

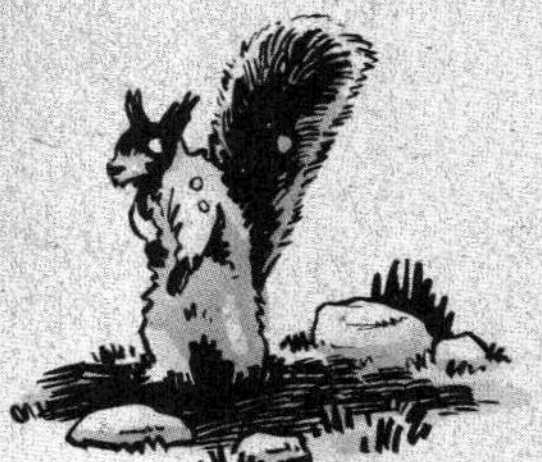

JUNIOR BRAVES

A BRAVE IS BRAVE

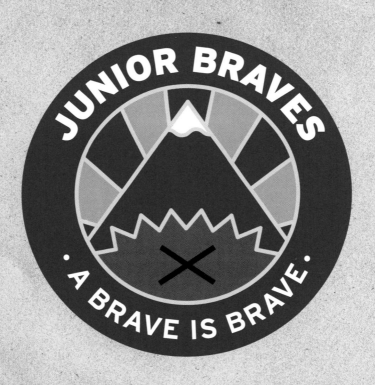

OUT OF THE WOODS

MORE BOOKS FROM ONI PRESS

SCOTT PILGRIM 1
SCOTT PILGRIM'S PRECIOUS LITTLE LIFE
BY BRYAN LEE O'MALLEY
COLOR EDITION

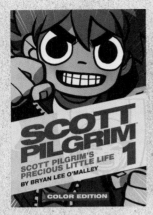

SCOTT PILGRIM, VOL. 1: PRECIOUS LITTLE LIFE
By Bryan Lee O'Malley
192 pages, Hardcover, Color
ISBN 978-1-62010-000-4

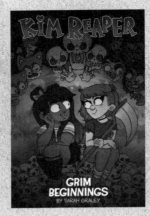

KIM REAPER
GRIM BEGINNINGS
BY SARAH GRALEY

KIM REAPER: GRIM BEGINNNINGS
By Sarah Graley
192 pages, Softcover, Color
ISBN: 978-1-62010-455-2

ONI PRESS
$10
Courtney
Volume One
Crumrin
The Night Things
Ted Naifeh

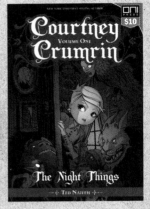

COURTNEY CRUMRIN, VOLUME 1: THE NIGHT THINGS
By Ted Naifeh and Warren Wucinich
136 pages, Softcover, Color
ISBN: 978-1-62010-419-4

RICK SPEARS
CHUCK BB
BLACK METAL
OMNIBVS

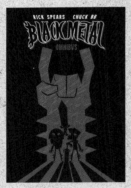

BLACK METAL: OMNIBVS
By Rick Spears and Chuck BB
472 pages, Softcover, B&W
ISBN: 978-1-62010-143-8

THE SIXTH GUN
CULLEN BUNN
BRIAN HURTT

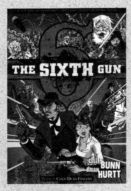

THE SIXTH GUN, VOLUME 1: COLD DEAD FINGERS, SQUARE ONE EDITION
By Cullen Bunn, Brian Hurtt, and Bill Crabtree
176 pages, Softcover, Color
ISBN 978-1-62010-420-0

bad machinery
The Case Of The Team Spirit
1
JOHN ALLISON

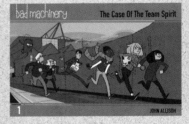

BAD MACHINERY, VOL. 1: THE CASE OF THE TEAM SPIRIT
By John Allison
136 pages, Softcover, Color
ISBN: 978-1-62010-387-6

ONI PRESS
www.onipress.com

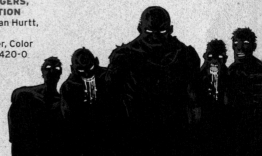

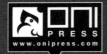

For more information on these and other fine Oni Press comic books and graphic novels visit www.onipress.com.
To find a comic specialty store in your area visit www.comicshops.us.